Other novels from Carl Mabbs-Zeno

Birchbark and Blackberry Thorn

Neige Noir

A Witness too Silent

A Pale Shade of Honor

No Hero Nor Heroine

Literary Guide to Bridge Construction

This is a work of fiction. All characters portrayed in this novel
are products of the author's imagination.

Mabbs-Zeno, Carl C.
    Ambition, in Final Draft
    Khotso Publishing, 2024
    ISBN 978-1-7375868-6-9
    1. Michigan parklands– Fiction. 2. Vietnam War
    draft – Fiction. 3. Summer of Love – Fiction.

AMBITION, IN FINAL DRAFT

Carl Mabbs-Zeno

Khotso Publishing, Peterborough NH

"When looking about to see what I could do for a living… I thought often and seriously of picking huckleberries; that surely I could do and its small profit might suffice – for my greatest skill has been to want but little…."[1]

"…nine bean rows and a hive for the honey bee."[2]

"I'm sick of not having the courage to be an absolute nobody."[3]

---

[1] Henry David Thoreau. *Walden, or Life in the Woods*, 1854.
[2] William Butler Yeats from the poem *The Lake Isle of Innisfree, 1888*.
[3] Franny speaking in "Franny and Zooey," by J.D. Salinger, published in *The New Yorker*, May 4, 1957

AMBITION, in Final Draft

1

1950 was the last year of the American baby boom, 29 births per thousand population. In 1951, the rate declined to 16 births per thousand, which was well below pre-war levels.[i] In 1950, the tensions of World War II continued to smolder, especially in Asia where the North Korean Army crossed the 38th parallel, igniting the Korean War and adding fuel to the Cold War. China took over Tibet. The Truman Administration was investigating federal employees for "communist tendencies" and the House Committee on Un-American Activities searched for communists among Americans. U.S. industry was rapidly retooling for the peacetime economy. The United States had escaped the destruction of its infrastructure and confidently dominated global affairs.

By 1967, the baby boomers were finishing high school and seeking their own place in society. They celebrated the Summer of Love. They avoided the starvation in Biafra, the Six-Day War in the Middle East, the civil wars in both Yemens, but not the Vietnam War where U.S. troop levels were approaching a half million.

AMBITION

At seventeen, Dieterich was a skinny, pale white, high school senior living in an outer New York suburb, who dressed without style (his mother played a large role in choosing his clothes), and who wore his light brown hair short and parted on the left, like his father but not as neat. He never tried hair oil even though his hair never stayed parted for long after his morning shower so it generally looked sloppy by the time he left the house, like the hair on most of the boys he knew. His skin suffered from excessive oiliness. That was his greatest weakness, he thought, and he was waiting to grow out of it so he could have a girlfriend. And he imagined someday he would get contact lenses and be rid of his out-of-style glasses. Through the rest of his life, however, he never got those contact lenses and he never decided there was such a thing as stylish glasses for men like him unless he got cool enough and smart enough to wear granny glasses like John Lennon. He never became that cool. He may have been regarded by the people he knew as smart enough to wear them without ridicule.

Dieterich grew without any effort, like most boys. That is, he became bigger every year throughout his teens. Like most of the boys he knew, his rate of growing was important because height and muscle mass were important. Dieterich tended to be a little ahead of his peers in height and unsatisfyingly low in muscles, although probably not actually behind most of the guys he knew. In theory, he could affect his musculature but not his height. In practice, he decided to wait to see if his body would grow more muscles when it stopped growing his bones.

His knowledge grew through his teenage years in about the same way. He knew more and more without any effort. He figured this was because he was smart. He listened in class and liked to read and sometimes read his school assignments, enough to get Bs. Math came easier to him than to most so he managed to get Bs from listening in class while skipping much of the homework. His teachers consistently told his parents during their annual interview that he was an underachiever and still a good kid. This message was passed on to him, giving him a silent pride in being more capable than his grades showed. This is how he interpreted the message: that he was better than his measured performance. At seventeen, he took the SAT exams and scored well. Then his mother signed him up for additional standardized tests, hoping his scores on those would get him into a good school. In 1967, standardized tests were a major factor in college admissions.

By 1968, the Tet offensive in Vietnam had lowered American confidence in military might, and the assassinations of Martin Luther King and Bobby Kennedy had damaged confidence in moral leadership. Young people were celebrating the power of psychedelic drugs, and the spirituality the Beatles had found in India and Carlos Castenada had discovered in Mexico.

At eighteen, Dieterich was relieved to learn his underachievement was not excessive.

"Deeter, this letter you got today is going to set you up for life. You'll have responsibility from here going forward to do some good for the world and you'll be able to do it. We are so excited for you. Lehigh! You know Lehigh's got as good an engineering program as anywhere in the world. You don't need to go into Mech E like I did, of course. Or join my fraternity or anything like that. Just do what fits you best and we'll see when you get out what kind of business you should take up. Feels great, doesn't it, to have college all figured out when you got your first application back? We can put this in the newspaper, right?"

Dieterich had not known what any particular form of engineering really meant. He had no thoughts yet about what it meant to go into business either. He had figured out that engineering was a skill and his career was supposed to begin with applying that skill in a large, successful company. Advancing from technical questions on company projects up the ranks of leadership, as his father had done, would require skills he could not imagine learning in college. Presumably they came of their own accord, like growing bones. It bothered him that his father suggested taking something other than mechanical engineering. It was the only kind of engineering he could visualize.

His father was grinning in a rare and unconscious way as he stuck out his hand for a congratulatory shake. Deeter was proud of his skill in handshakes, taught by his father years earlier: reach all the way in, firm grip, look in the eye, two shakes and release. His mother was now saying something complementary and unconvincing about Dieterich's talents. He could not focus on her words as his thoughts came too fast.

'No Mech E', he says, like he's giving me all this freedom. Well, I'm not going into Chem E or Nuke E. I don't know anything about them. Civil Engineering I can see and what I see is a second-rate, routine, uncreative rest of my life. Engineering is needed, I guess, no, really it is, but I don't need to do it. I just applied 'cause they thought I should. What about forestry? We talked about that too. Be in the woods. Know about the wilds. Live away from cities. Or wildlife management even if there are no big businesses to move up the ranks of.

He became conscious that his mother had stopped speaking. He looked into her face and smiled in answer to her presumed praise. "Yeah. Feels good. Takes off some pressure for sure. Hope I get a couple more acceptances. Could play with a few options, you know. But we got a good option here. Can't go wrong."

He did get an acceptance from his "safe" school and a rejection from his "reach" school. He had wished then he had applied to a school he could get in and wanted to get in. The obvious choice at a crucial moment in his young life, a moment he had watched approaching for years, was Lehigh over an embarrassing local college, for useful technical skills and the hope of spontaneous growth in leadership talent along with enlarged muscles and clearer skin.

By the summer of 1969, the number of U.S. troops in Vietnam had declined by ten percent from its peak of 543,000 in January as the Nixon Administration shifted its strategy to greater reliance on bombing. The United States and USSR opened talks on nuclear disarmament built on their having achieved strategic nuclear parity. The Cuyahoga River in Cleveland caught fire. The Gay Liberation Movement was launched in response to a police raid at The Stonewall bar in Greenwich Village.

At nineteen, Dieterich's bones had stopped growing, having given him just over six feet of height and a healthy square frame. He had hoped for an additional few inches but could not complain about what he got. His muscles had not grown substantially although his health was adequate to do all the usual things well enough; just not to do anything spectacular. His hair was grown out and hung without a part; it was long enough to fit his age but not long enough to be truly fashionable. He had adjusted to buying his own clothes, albeit with his parents' money, and tended toward bell-bottomed jeans and T-shirts in better repair than was common on campus. He had finished a year of engineering in an excellent university where he learned that the knowledge gained by casual reading practices and going to classes irregularly did not accumulate as quickly as the university required.

Thus, in the spring of 1969, he needed to find a different school to accept him and thereby provide a draft deferment. He could not blame the first school for kicking him out although his parents did. It was sad to see them struggling to accept his mediocracy. He had not learned at college what he had been clearly told would be required of him. He suspected he never should have gone to an excellent college in the first place and that he had been admitted only because his father had graduated from there. He would find an easier place and would take it more seriously. He would study something more interesting than engineering. He still felt smart and expected it to show through someday.

He sat on his thin, narrow dorm bed and wondered why things had gotten so far off track. There was the part about exerting so little on boring classes that had no use in any future he wanted for himself. How did he get into a position where those classes mattered so much? Some consequence from his behavior at school was fair, but the punishment felt disproportionately severe. He had done so many things right. Of the twelve principles in the Scout Law, he had rigorously obeyed two-thirds: loyal, helpful, friendly, courteous, kind, cheerful, thrifty and clean. He was not too bad on the other four, none of which implied being studious. He had not been tempted to abuse drugs, alcohol or women. He could not name any harm he had done to anyone in his life. He figured he might earn a place in heaven but not in Lehigh.

As the family was still passing around the string beans and mashed potatoes (actually powdered potatoes from a box) on the Thursday after Deeter came home from Lehigh, Deeter's father decided to talk about next steps. Deeter's younger brother and sister were silent for a change. They were more shocked than anyone that Deeter was out of school and facing the draft.

"It's all right Deeter. You'll be fine. You got a good head and a good work ethic. Just need some more time to adjust to the Lehigh level of pressure. More than you get in high school, right? That's how it is. Every level is harder. Let's learn from this. Take a year somewhere else. Pick up some of those general courses everyone's got to take. What language you taking?"

"French."

"Yeah, right. I took French too. Got to use it during the war. Glad to have it then. Funny, never used it again."

"Deeter, I'm looking into getting you in somewhere else." His mother was going to be part of the solution. "Lehigh will let you reapply after a year so we just need to get through that year. Most places won't accept an application while you are between years at Lehigh, but you can go to our community college."

"And that's enough to get a deferment?"

"Sure is. It's a good school of its type."

Back to his father's contributions. "I've served on its Finance Board. No problem with them. But you're going to have to buckle down, right?"

"I can do the work. I just never got focused. No excuses, but it'll be different."

"We just need to show Lehigh you're the kind of guy they asked for last year. Get some courses in. And here's the big difference. Do a good job this summer."

"Maybe. I'm better at doing a job than going to school." At this moment Dieterich was wondering how to get himself into someplace without an engineering program. That would be the best thing he could do over the summer.

Within a week, he had a job as a serviceman in a Detroit branch of his father's firm. He was surprised that his father had such reach. He was just a Vice President and there were at least three of them in the company. Even his father was not very clear on what a serviceman would do except that it was servicing hardness testers. Dieterich had never heard his father or anyone else mention hardness testers.

"It's an operation in another branch, one I don't manage. But it's an important one. We are the industry standard. The whole system of testing hardness of metals is based on our testers. Even other companies with hardness testers use our scale. Rockwell scale. Whatever's made of metal has hardness requirements. You'll be teaching me about them after this summer. Thing is, this will get you into an industrial experience. You may see some more than hiking in the woods and the things you did around here. Good experience and Lehigh will know it."

"Thanks a whole lot Dad. And Mother, too. It'll be all right." Deiter moved his focus toward the pork chop on his plate, starting with putting a dab of applesauce on it.

Got to admit, the Old Man came through. A deferment and a job. School is school. It should be easy enough to get me going again. It'll be good. Maybe real good, given the circumstances. The job looks bad. Summer in Detroit? In industry? It'll be a nightmare, one I probably deserve, I guess.

2

"Scratch an incompetent schoolteacher — or for that matter college professor — and half the time you find a first-class automobile mechanic or a goddam stonemason."[4]

Monday, June 16 Dieterich took a commuter train with his Dad on a misting Monday in June. His Dad negotiated a price with a cabbie for a ride across Brooklyn to JFK Airport and sent Dieterich off with a firm handshake. Dieterich's plane arrived in Wayne County Airport just after noon near the western edge of the eastern time zone, his first trip to Michigan, facing the challenge of getting to the new job before it closed down for the day at 5:00. The airport was in Romulus, Michigan, southwest of Detroit, and the job was in Ferndale, north of Detroit. He was operating on his pocket money now and doubted he could afford a cab. He found an information desk and studied the bus schedules. He took a shuttlebus to one of the downtown hotels near a city bus route that went through Ferndale. The closest stop it would make was six blocks from the office where his new boss would be expecting him and presumably would assign him a car and take care of a place to live for the summer. That was the plan. Dieterich was nervous about all the ways it might not work and he envisioned sleeping in a bus station with his luggage and then meeting his boss the next day if he did not get to Ferndale on time. He had the office phone number and the home number for his soon-to-be boss but he would not ask anyone to take any extraordinary arrangements in the event he could not get where he should be on time.

---

[4] Zooey speaking in "Franny and Zooey," by J.D. Salinger, published in *The New Yorker*, May 4, 1957.

It was great that his Dad had made arrangements and it was embarrassing to ask for any more special treatment.   While riding the shuttle bus, Dieterich reviewed the remaining part of the plan for the day. *Story of my life so far*, Dieterich thought. *Everything is fixed up for me by my Dad. If I just do what he has planned, it will all work out. I got a little independent at Lehigh and I can see I need to be careful about that. I'll be independent, want to be, need to be, absolutely can be; maybe not so fast though. Get through today and it will be easier. Whatever the hell this job is, I can do it.*

The shuttle bus was comfortable. The city bus was crowded so he ended up sitting on the aisle with his suitcase mostly blocking anyone behind him from getting by. No one seemed to mind or to notice him at all. He had to change to another bus at a stop that was no more than a sign on the curb. He waited thirty minutes for his second city bus to arrive. It was getting hot so Dieterich was sweating although some of the sweat might have been a response to the pressure he was feeling or to the fear of imminent failure. He thought of stripping down to his t-shirt and resolved instead to relax and ignore the stress. He had asked the driver to tell him when they reached 23rd street in Ferndale and the driver nodded to indicate he would but Dieterich was not sure the nod was enough. He wanted a clear statement, a smile to hint the driver was pleased to have Dieterich under his care, a signed contract would have been nice. Yet he simply found himself a seat and waited. He had no city map and no idea where he was. From the airport in Romulus until he saw a sign on a small restaurant announcing "Ferndale's Finest Food," the scenery had become more and more industrial. If he had passed through a part of Detroit, it was not a part with public buildings or parks or entertainment or housing like any he had ever entered in his life. Ferndale did not appear to have any ferns.

Dieterich found "his" car in the small lot behind the office building. It had to be his since the key the secretary gave him unlocked the door. His generic company car was a well-used Rambler American two-door sedan, possibly the most modest car he could imagine and yet he felt pride in it. He pushed the driver's seatback forward and shoved his suitcase onto the back seat. It was nearly like having his own car. He had never thought much about getting a car, figuring that was an issue for a day when he was out of college and had saved his wages for a year or two. He doubted his parents would be buying him a car someday. They would want him to earn it, which was fair enough. It never occurred to him to calculate how old he would be when he could afford one. For now, it was good to be driving a car his job had funded, not because he could not afford a car, but because it represented the company's confidence in his value. There was prestige in that. There would be prestige in saying it was a company car even though he knew the company had no basis for confidence in him. He would earn it. He was smart enough, in his imagination, to do whatever they were about to train him to do.

He sat inside for a couple minutes to look over the controls and review the map Mr. Elias had drawn to his apartment. The car was a standard and he had only driven his parents' cars which were three-speed, stick shifts. This car had buttons for forward, reverse, neutral, and overdrive. He had only a vague idea of what overdrive meant and decided to look it up in the manual that evening.

He drove across the lot to the street and tried out the right turn signal. It clicked, waited, clicked, waited until Dieterich checked for traffic and turned onto the quiet street heading north for Rochester Hills, a half hour commute, to rent a room in the house of someone from Mr. Elias' church. The map showed the route as a straight line and that is exactly what it was. The map was flat and so was the route. The "hills" of Rochester Hills served only to distinguish the name of the place from neighboring Rochester.

The house was a normal, single-family, mid-western building with gray siding in good repair on a street with residences that were not identical but could have been accurately described in the same words. A separate, one-car garage with a short, gravel driveway sat to its left. He parked on the street. A woman answered his knock and welcomed him vigorously, saying a few kind words about the Elias family along the way. She said he could use the kitchen and the refrigerator. His room was upstairs beside a room that was being rented by two young men for the summer. They usually came in late but he would meet them eventually. The rooms had been for her children before they grew up and moved away. She mentioned there was a small, inexpensive restaurant two blocks away if he wanted to eat out. And that was it. She said he should come downstairs and meet her husband when he got back after his Kiwanis meeting. She gave him a key to the house.

He sat on the bed after she left. He felt immensely satisfied with the arrangements.

In a half hour, he left to find the restaurant. He left his sport coat in his room because it was warm outside but kept his tie on for reasons not entirely clear to him. He was pretending, perhaps, not to be a student. For the summer, that identity would be put aside. He had a job in industry, in Detroit, with a car, and wore a tie and jacket when he worked.

Romero's Family Restaurant was perfect: a few tables, a few booths, one or two waitresses. Menus rather than a cafeteria with trays and food selections behind glass. The woman seated at the cash register called out to him, "Take any seat you like." Two of the booths were occupied, none of the tables.

"Hello." A tall, young waitress spoke before he noticed she had come to his table. "Are you expecting anyone for dinner tonight?"

"No, eating alone."

She gave him a menu and took away the extra set of flatware wrapped in a napkin. Dieterich had not looked her over conspicuously, but he could tell she would be pleasant company if any opportunity arose. Her waitress outfit did not give any basis for judging her personal style, although her hair was a little more finely coifed than was common among college girls in those days. His hair had been barbered to fit his parents' vision of what was proper for his job. With the tie, he might look a little formal for a place like this. He wished he could pass for a college graduate, but he did not look any older than he was. That was probably about her age, not less anyway.

She came back after he closed the menu and pushed it away. He ordered and could not think of anything to say with the right degree of friendliness without sounding like a pick-up attempt. *Things shouldn't be like that,* he thought. *And maybe they aren't entirely like that and I just haven't figured out how to talk to a girl without an innocent excuse. Next time I come for dinner, she will recognize me and might ask if I just moved here or if I am visiting someone. There can't be many reasons to show up at this place more than once.*

The roast beef was very good. Even the mashed potatoes with gravy seemed special and Dieterich knew he would be back. The waitress did not stand nearby and he did not notice her looking toward him but he did not look toward her often so she might have paid him some attention. In fact, when he finished eating he looked for her and quickly caught her eye. Like a sophisticated diner, he motioned writing out the check and she came right over.

"Would you like a desert? We have apple pie and you could get it a la mode."

The pie sounded pretty good to Dieterich although it sounded a little childish to make very much of dessert.

"No thank you." He did not say "thanks" or "not tonight," implying there would be another night. "Just the check please."

She stood in front of him while she wrote something on the check. Dieterich guessed she was adding it up although there was not much to add: one roast beef dinner and a glass of milk.

She placed the check in front of him. "You can pay up front." She nodded toward the woman at the cash register. "Have a nice evening."

Dieterich made a motion toward the cash register, pointing one finger from each hand without lifting his hands from the table. He thought it was an interesting reply, probably the only interesting thing he had done apart from showing up wearing a tie in the first place. He placed his palms on the table and looked up at her. "You too. That was a good dinner."

He noticed she had written on the check "Thanks, Cathy," and then drawn a smiley face. This was in the early days of drawn smiley faces so he could imagine, albeit with minimal conviction, that she was being friendly, perhaps recognizing they were the only two people in the place in their age range. He left a two-dollar tip on the table under the water glass.

Cathy had not, however, meant anything by the way she signed the check. She had been instructed by the owner to sign all the checks that way. Besides, she had scarcely noticed the slim young man wearing a tie and had not wondered anything at all about why he had happened into this place this night. The tie meant nothing to her unless it showed he was not a hippie which was not much to show since no hippies ever came into Romero's and very seldom turned up in Rochester Hills at all. She had once been asked out by a boy wearing a tie: Gabe Samuels. He had to wear the tie for his job as a bagger in the supermarket. She turned him down. There was nothing wrong with Gabe. He had been in a couple of her classes at school but she could not remember ever talking to him until the day he asked her if she wanted to see *The Graduate*. She might have gone with him if the movie he suggested had not been one with a sexy reputation. That would have been too much.

Cathy had gone on dates in high school, usually only one per boy. She liked going to dances more than the movies. A second date always felt like a step toward a commitment and she had never been asked on a date with a boy she wanted to be with for long. Now that she was out of school, she never saw any boys she knew and did not get any dates. She knew she needed to get a job in Detroit or near it, in a big company where she would meet good men at work. She was not looking for someone rich or high up in the company. Just a good man. Boys liked her. She was sure of that. A good man would like her if they got to know each other in some easy way.

For his first night in Michigan Dieterich was not surprised that things were working out. He had a job, the boss seemed pretty good, his co-workers were OK, he had a car and he had a room. None of the positives were a result of anything he had done but that was merely usual and he hardly noticed it.

<table><tr><td>Tuesday, June 17</td></tr></table>

Dieterich's second day of work, of getting paid a full-time, adult salary, started well enough. He did not get lost going into the city and he remembered the neighborhood of the office in sufficient detail to get him straight to the parking lot, arriving 20 minutes early. He waited in the car for ten minutes, careful to duck if anyone came near. Then he went inside and up the stairs to Mr. Elias' office.

"Dieterich, how was your room? The Tyler's were alright, weren't they? Good folks..."

"Everyone calls me Deeter. Thank you for setting me up with the Tylers. Everything was very good. Comfortable room. They offered to let me use the kitchen. A simple restaurant very near. Anyway, I'm ready to do some work now!"

"Let's go see if Rusty is in yet. He'll do your training. He's worked here a long time and knows all about the job."

Rusty had short, gray hair and a sparce, two-day beard. He wore wrinkled khaki pants and a t-shirt under a long denim apron. He was sharpening a chisel when they came into the workroom and scarcely looked up when Mr. Elias spoke to him to him. "Rusty, this is Dieterich; new hire. You show him how to service the hardness testers?"

"I'm called 'Deeter'."

Rusty lifted his head up halfway and rolled his eyes above the narrow reading glasses hanging on the end of his nose to take in Dieterich. He turned his attention back down to the chisel and muttered, "Okay. I'll get him ready."

"Right," Mr. Elias said to Rusty. "See you later or come see me if you have any questions," he said to Dieterich.

Dieterich stood silently for about half a minute while Rusty continued to hone the tool. Then Dieterich pulled a tall, metal stool over and sat on it. Thirty seconds later, Rusty handed him the chisel. "Think that's sharp?" he asked.

Dieterich tested it with a stroke of his thumb across the edge. He pulled up his sleeve and shaved off a few hairs. "Damn sharp, I'd say," he answered.

"Think you'd get it that sharp?"

"A chisel, yes. Just one angle on it and both sides sit flat on the whetstone. That mirror finish on both sides shows you've taken down to a fine stone. Knives, I'm not so good. Got to have a steady stroke. I'm too impatient to get it exactly right." He handed the chisel back.

"Your dad's one of the company execs?"

"Yep. Got me the job, obviously. I needed it. Got myself kicked out of school." Dieterich was shocked to hear himself say that. It was not usual for him to admit to any of his myriad weaknesses. This character in front of him was not a man easily fooled. He'd passed the chisel test and decided it was good to reassure Rusty that he did not expect to be treated like an executive's son. The man was an unlikely gossip. Dieterich saw he was about to test Rusty. He would see if that embarrassing news reached anyone else in Michigan.

"You deserve that?" Rusty asked, referring to being dismissed from college.

"Oh yeah, no doubt. Not that I did anything too bad. Really, just didn't take it seriously. Don't think I deserve to go to Vietnam for that." This answer was a little dishonest but he interpreted the question as another test from Rusty, still on the question of what class he belonged to. Dieterich was not very concerned about losing his student deferment and going to Vietnam. He would go to another college. He knew he was privileged and he knew he deserved to be kicked out. He would take credit for at least admitting as much. Still, at the moment he had no deferment to cover the fall semester, so his statement that being sent involuntarily to a war zone was a potential extreme consequence of the school decision to cease allowing him to take their classes.

"I was in the Marines right outta high school. Didn't have no combat in those days. Quit after five years. Good boys I was with. The Corps ain't for ever'body. 'Course I didn't have an executive for a daddy."

"I may end up in 'Nam anyway."

Rusty looked at Dieterich more closely and nodded as if to show the preliminaries were over. He started by explaining how a hardness tester worked and let Dieterich test the hardness of a few samples. Next Rusty took a toolbox out of a locker and gave it to Dieterich. "This box has everything you'll need. Always put everything back in the same place you found it."

It looked like a doctor's bag: black, shaped like a toy barn with a double handle holding the two sides of the roof together. Each side had small compartments for small tools and whatnots. Dieterich really liked it.

"Take out the cloth and spread it on the bench. There's just one rag inside but you'll keep more nearby. Always wipe your hands and your tools every time you use either one of 'em. Take out everything in the open space in the middle of the toolbox and put it on the rag. Line 'em up straight, ready to use. Half of what you do on the job when someone's looking at you is show. Make the company look good, like we know what we're doing, like it's important and precise, you know? We'll have you on your own in somebody's factory in a couple days and you gotta be the expert. We charge 75 bucks an hour for your time plus travel and parts. The parts are way over our cost and anybody can see that. Do something they can't do on their own and make 'em know they can't do it as good as you."

He watched Dieterich spread out the tools in the middle section. Then he showed how to take the hardness tester apart

A hardness tester is a simple machine, sensitive to abuse but not complicated. Nearly all the parts could be scattered onto a workbench in ten minutes by an experienced serviceman but some parts require specialized tools for removal so it is not an easy job for the usual workplace. After an hour, Rusty said Dieterich should just take the machine apart and reassemble it over and over until lunchtime. Each hour, on the hour, Rusty looked over Dieterich's shoulder to see how he was doing. Dieterich did not speak. Rusty would say one thing each time, such as: no reason to rush; wipe off the tools and the parts each time you move 'em; put everything on the cloth the same way every time. Dieterich said nothing at all.

At noon Rusty came over again. "When you get it all back together, eat some lunch. You bring anything with you?"

"No, I don't bring any. I don't need anything to eat. I'll just keep going with this awhile."

"That's not how to do it. You gotta eat somethin'. C'mere." They went to a window. "See the corner that way? Turn right, you'll see a sandwich shop off a way. Get back by one o'clock. Not a second later. Not mor'n maybe two, three minutes before. You gotta watch, yes? You got some money for a sandwich? Good. See you then."

In the afternoon, Dieterich was shown how to assess each of the parts of the machine for damage or wear and then Rusty talked about everything that could go wrong on a hardness tester. There were not many weak points on it but it was possible for an operator to damage a part, especially the diamond bit that was precisely shaped to sink into the test metal when the proper weight was applied, leaving a small hole that the machine measured to indicate the hardness of the metal. By five o'clock, Dieterich felt ready to identify any problem in a hardness tester. He was amazed to have a skill with some commercial value, 75 dollars an hour of value plus transportation and parts.

"Time to go. Never stay late. It makes the rest of us look like bums." Rusty was about to leave. He carried a rusty lunch box. Dieterich wondered if it had given Rusty his name because his hair showed no hint of red. "Look at your goddam hands, boy. Scrub 'em before you go; while you're on the clock, I mean. It's part of the job." He was gone by the time Dieterich finished washing.

He said "Good night" to the secretary as he passed her on his way out and she said he should see Mr. Elias before he goes.

"So Deeter, how was it? Ready to tear into the next hardness tester you see?"

"Rusty's real good. Makes it look simple, but he was warning me there's still a lot to go."

"Sure, he's a charmer. You have any plans for the weekend? No? Why don't you come over to our place for lunch on Saturday? We've got a pool. Bring some swimming trunks. You have any with you?"

"Yeah. That'd be good. Thanks. Uh, I've got some shorts I can use for swimming."

"I'll write out the directions. We live up near where you're staying. Probably only take fifteen minutes to get to our place. We can talk about what you can see around the state this summer. You'll be driving around

Michigan quite a bit. We'll try to get you close to the sights."

Dieterich had never heard of any tourist sights in Michigan unless he went all the way to the Upper Peninsula. Maybe even that was not something to be seen, just an oddity on the map. It would be nice, he thought, to visit Isle Royale, the wolf sanctuary beyond the Upper Peninsula, but he did not know if visitors were allowed or how to get to a remote island like that.

He drove fast on the way back to Rochester Hills, weaving through the commuter traffic like a regular on the route. The day had passed exceedingly well so far, and now he was on his way to see Cathy again. On his second dinner at her restaurant, he could speak up a little more and not seem too pushy. He played a few scenarios that might occur over dinner; nothing dramatic.

He did not see either of the Tylers when he arrived at their house. He went up to his room and waited for 6:30. He estimated that was the time he went for dinner on the previous night. On his way out, Mrs. Tyler saw him and asked how he enjoyed his new job. After he answered as politely as he could, including praise for Mr. Elias, she mentioned that he was welcome to come downstairs any time and watch television if he wanted to. He said he did not watch much television, which was true, and then mentioned that he would be doing some reading for courses he would be starting in the fall, which was not true. He was surprised at his lie. As he walked over to Romero's, he wondered if he made up the story about reading because he had been thinking about talking to Cathy and had allowed some exaggerations into those thoughts. If she were a college kid working for the summer, she might like to know he was a serious student, maybe an intellectual and if she were a high school kid she would not care what he said or did, and if she were a high school graduate not going to college and wishing she had a better job than waitress, she would find his boasting obnoxious. He hoped he would not have lied to her and wished he had not lied to Mrs. Tyler.

No one was sitting at the cash register when he entered Romero's. Two tables and one booth were occupied making this a busier evening. At one table sat two men wearing ties and white shirts with rolled up shirtsleeves. Dieterich had his sport coat on and wore his tie loosened, a roughly equivalent degree of formality. They were significantly older than Dieterich. He felt comfortable for being in their class.

The woman who previously sat at the cash register came out of the kitchen to take his order. After she left and he sat awkwardly waiting with no place to look, he considered asking if Cathy was working this evening. She might mention to Cathy that the young man in coat and tie had asked after her. It would have been too forward. So he had an uneventful dinner which proceeded quickly after his food arrived, averting any boredom. The waitress did not sign the check, thereby giving him a basis for hoping Cathy's little happy face was more than routine.

After dinner, Dieterich walked away from the Tyler's for the distance of a couple blocks to see what else was open in the town. A movie theater would have been excellent. The few retail places were closed: a drug store, a fabric shop and a hardware store. The pet shop appeared to have gone out of business recently. Lights were on at the fire station although he did not see anybody working there and a fire truck stood gleaming and silent behind each of the garage doors. He crossed the street and went home without seeing anything more. As he passed Romero's, he stared through the windows to see if Cathy had come in. He could not be sure whether she was there but he did not see her.

Entering the Tylers' front door, he recognized the gray flickers of a room lit by a television. He waved to the Tylers sitting behind their TV trays and walked quietly to the bottom of the stairs. The Tylers were both staring his way and spoke loudly to him, but their mouths were full of their dinner so he could not recognize any words, yet their sounds were brief and played a friendly note. He smiled to recognize their greeting and went up the stairs.

It was only a few steps from the top of the stairs to his door; a few seconds. He surveyed the room. His bed was made, just as he had left it in the morning. There was a dresser with nothing on top and a chair beside it. His briefcase stood on the floor next to the chair. He looked out the window and saw a light on in the house next door. That window was curtained so he saw nothing inside the house. Lacy curtains, yellowed by age, hung on the sides of his window. There was no point in pulling them shut.

Sitting on the bed, he struggled to devise an idea for something to do during the remaining hours before he could sleep. Push-ups were his first thought, to be followed by other exercises that required no equipment. He could exercise every night and get himself in shape by the end of summer. The idea fizzled out as soon as he stood up to remove his sport coat. A good idea came next: read a book. *I'm basically a smart guy. I've gotta start acting like it, not just be it. I should be reading something. And if I actually read in my room at night, I'll remove the stupid lie I told Mrs. Tyler.*

He took a pad of paper and a pencil from his briefcase to make some notes on what book or books he should buy. Nothing specifically useful for school made sense because he had no idea what classes he would be taking. *What do I like to read? Nothing from Lehigh for sure. I like books on the National Parks. They're mainly picture books, not what a smart guy reads over the summer. I like nature but not biology books. I liked history in high school a lot, not American history, not now with all the issues about patriotism during the war. The stuff published on cheap paper with drawings in the margin for guys my age by naïve guys like me about how to resist the draft or how to set up a commune or promote civil rights or what music is best or the latest music fads, the hippie stuff - that's not the reading I need. African history! It would be cool to be the one who knows something real about Africa. I'll get a book on that. Learn about their art and music and about colonialism!*

Someone knocked on his door. *Mister or Missus Tyler? I need their first names. It feels childish to be formal as a Brit in Victorian days.*

He jumped up and opened the door. Two men, young men but older than Dieterich, smiled at him. One held up a six-pack of Labatt beers, which Dieterich recognized as Canadian. Since he knew very little of beer culture, the best he could say to show he was a guy's guy was "Canadians are ya?"

They came in, sat on his bed and twisted the cap off a beer before handing it to Dieterich who did not like beer but knew enough to be appreciative on an evening that was about to become boring. Dieterich watched them take a swig and then realized he should be doing the same. While he was raising his bottle, they gave their names, Roland and Sam. Sam mentioned he was "Samson," not "Samuel." "Deeter," Dieterich replied as he saluted them with his bottle and took another drink. Now he was not behind in the sip count.

They had moved into the Tylers' other rented room a week before and had jobs in Detroit to carry them through the summer. Sam asked if Dieterich knew of any jobs they might get after they finished this one. For a moment Dieterich wondered how he could ask without saying anything about what work they did but Roland added in, "We can do construction. I do some welding. He likes to drive. Anything in a job site, you know. Well maybe you don't know, not around here. You just came, right?"

"Came from Pennsylvania this week and don't know anything but the road between here and Ferndale. Hardly even know what my own job is."

The two had met each other working in the oilfields of Alaska. Roland had been there more than a year and Sam had been there only a couple months. The pay was good, they reported, but they both hated the work and the place.

"You doing anything tomorrow night?" Roland asked. "There's a carnival settin' up by the river north on 150. Not too far. Ain't much around here. Maybe meet some girls up there."

Dieterich was swept up by their confident exuberance and their independence, living off the sweat of their labor, like figures in fiction and unlike anyone he had ever met in his age group.

"I've got nothing planned for the rest of the summer but working in the day and sitting in this room." Those were true words and not ones he was proud to utter although he knew they would not embarrass him before these two fellows. *Go to a carnival? The reason I've never been to a carnival is because I never wanted to go to one, not since I was in sixth or seventh grade and didn't know what was there and never went to one anyway. I don't want to spend money on silly games rigged against me with the potential at best to win a stuffed animal I would just give away to the first little kid I saw. And pick up a girl there? Was that a viable thing sometime in the past, say the 1930s? Why am I doing this? Do I want these guys for friends? I think they scare me little.*

Sam was talking and did not seem bothered that Dieterich had not been listening. Roland was holding an empty bottle, his second beer already.

"So you got a car, Deeter?" Sam might have noticed Dieterich was focused again.

"Belongs to the company. I'll be working jobs around the state."

"Yeah? What kinda wheels they give you?"

Should I make a joke of it, Dieterich wondered. *I haven't got the slang to do it.* "Rambler American."

"Whoa! That's a dog!" Sam was smiling and shaking his head in the negative.

"Sure it's a dog," Roland responded. "It's a car, ain't it? And didn't have to buy it neither. Probably in good shape 'cause the company takes care of it, right? Sam's got a Dodge Charger. Nice car; no dog that one. More like a hog the way it eats gas."

"That's a goddam quick hog you wish you had."

"Maybe I do but I'd take a company car with any name on the grill. What I'm wishing is we had a few more beers. That six is all we got. Let's ride that Dodge down to that place on Route 150. They sell beer. Get better than LaBatt."

"You coming, Deeter?"

"I gotta study the manual for work. Like I said, I don't really know how to do my job yet."

"No sweat. We'll leave the last one here for you. You can get the next round tomorrow."

3

<table>
<tr><td>Wednesday, June 18</td><td></td></tr>
</table>

Dieterich woke early since he had gone to bed early, not right after the two fellows from the other room went out but not very much later since two beers were enough to make him sleepy. He had not yet figured out how to get breakfast. Romero's did not open early and he did not know any other places. *I'll do some exploring this weekend*, he resolved, but that did not take care of today. He needed something to do on the weekend anyway. Lunch with his boss wouldn't take all day. *If he's got a pool, he's probably got some kids*. Dieterich did not mind that. He could get along with kids better than sitting half dressed beside his boss. *I'll check with Sam and whatshisname tonight to get a time to see the carnival, if they still want to do it.*

Dieterich walked past their door quietly so he would not wake them up. The light was on in the kitchen and Mrs. Tyler was standing in front of the stove.

"Good morning, Mr. Kahler. You're up early today."

"Good morning, Ma'am. Mr. Kahler is my Dad. I'm just Deeter."

"That's good, Deeter. You having breakfast now? Don't think you had anything yesterday morning. Roland and Sam already had some cereal and toast."

"They're out already? It's not even seven yet, is it?"

"Oh, they're always very early. Work hard, I think. I'm making Mr. T some oatmeal here. Wouldn't you like some? I just put it on. I can add some more to the pot."

Dieterich did not know where he would find some breakfast but he was not going to have it with the landlady. It was not part of their contract and he might be supposed to pay something for it if it became a regular thing, which it might, just to be polite. Having waved off her offer, he could not ask where to buy a breakfast. He did not even want to ask where he could buy groceries. He preferred to seem in full control of his living arrangements. As he hurried out of the house, he began to be pleased at the idea of buying groceries and having a supply of food in his room. It reminded him of the independence he felt when camping, having everything he needed in the pack on his back. How much easier it would be to have a car to do the carrying! He would not use the refrigerator except for a quart of milk for cereal. He knew he could figure it out, that is, being independent.

He stopped three times on the way into work, looking for the right sort of place to get a sandwich or similar thing for lunch. He got a bag of pretzels and two bags of potato chips in the first place, nothing in the second and more than he hoped to find in the third: two soft rolls, a package of baloney, mustard, a box of plastic flatware, a can of sardines, a large bottle of Coca Cola, and a small basket of apples. For breakfast, he bought a small carton of milk and some cereal. He could not find a bowl for the cereal and he doubted he could find another shop in the time left before work so he bought some cherry tomatoes in a plastic box he could use as a bowl. While munching his cereal contentedly, sitting in his car, he realized he should have looked for a small bottle or carton of orange juice to round out the meager fare with an additional traditional element. He drove to the parking area beside his workplace and waited until five minutes to 9:00.

Rusty was already seated at his workbench but he was reading the newspaper, not working.

"Good morning, Rusty. What have you got for me to learn today?"

Rusty looked at his watch before he looked at Dieterich.

"Hello, son. Well, not much to learn, I guess. You picked up everything I know yesterday. Let's see if Freddy knows any more'n me. You be with him today if he decides to show up." Rusty tapped on his watch which probably read nearly exactly 9:00. "He's been on the road last few days. Guess he can talk about that. I don't go out much anymore. Might be different now... Oh, here comes the bastard now. Freddy, what the fuck you sleepin' in on the very day you're meeting the Big Suit's son?"

"'Morning to you too, Rusty."

He dropped his briefcase on the bench and put out a hand to shake with Dieterich. "Welcome to Detroit. I'm Freddy Murtoza. Don't pay any attention to the old man over there."

Freddy was a big, soft man with short hair, a round face and an engaging smile. He was only a couple years older than Dieterich. He was dressed like Dieterich, cheap tie, white shirt and worn down, generic sport coat.

"He learned everything yesterday. Why don't you take him out on some rounds and let him do your work for you?" Rusty suggested without looking up from the bench where he was fitting a lens into a complex metal frame.

Freddy led Dieterich to a heavy metal table and pulled over a chair for Dieterich. He sat his briefcase on the table and then took a file out of a nearby cabinet. As he looked through various folders, he talked steadily without giving Dieterich a chance to reply. "How long you been in town? Couldn't be more than four days 'cause I was here on Monday. Wes wasn't real sure when you'd be getting here."

Freddy paused for less than a second while Dieterich remembered Mr. Elias had introduced himself as "Wesley Elias," so he was "Wes."

Freddy continued, "The old man says you're trained up already. Don't you or me believe that. I guess you go a couple places with me this afternoon and fix something. Let's look through what's waiting for us; just the nearby ones, Detroit or the places that might as well be Detroit."

He showed Dieterich the file on places scheduled for hardness tester repair or maintenance, and explained how to prioritize them: do a couple close together to save travel time, do the places with no back-up tester, do repairs before routine maintenance, etc. Dieterich wrote some notes although he expected to remember everything important in it. It seemed simple and obvious.

"You got a briefcase? Probably not. Why bring one to a new job? Nobody said you'd need one right? They're expensive but I got an old one. It'll be fine. You need to keep the tools separate from the papers when you go into the factory boss and give him the invoice. We're not cheap so we really got to show 'em we know what we're doing. Lemme show you how to write up the invoice. Hey, Old Man! He's just doing hardness testers, right?"

"Don't call me that just because I been around long enough to know more than you'll ever know. It's not from getting old, it's from paying attention. You were right beside me grinning and thinking about getting out early when Wes laid out the program for our junior executive here. Yes, he's only doing hardness testers. That's half the business anyway. Did you know he's only here for the summer? Did you know we got to turn in our invoices first thing when we get back from a trip instead of waiting 'til after lunch or something so you can play professor to the new fella?"

"Thank you for all the help, sir" Freddy called back with his smile intact. "Listen Deeter, you know we don't take any of this noise serious. We're good buddies, Rusty and me, and he knows I turned in my invoices before I came in here and that's why he said that just now to let me know he knew that's why I was a few seconds late walking in. The point is you only need to learn the hardness tester invoice. It's easy after you've done a few. Do 'em slow, the first few. They need to be absotively exactly right. You do receipts for motel and gas. That's no trouble. But doing the hardness tester itself is the easy part. The old man tell you that? It's even fun to be the expert, you know. The guys who operate the testers don't know how they work exactly. We have some specialized tools to get them apart so nobody but us can get in them. Besides, if they open them up, we don't certify them anymore and they need a certification on their testers to get contracts. And you know what's worse than the paperwork is finding the damn places where they're at. I'll give you my map of Detroit and all. I got another one in the car. It's OK to call up the places in a city you never been to and ask 'em where they are but then they hardly ever tell you clear how to get to 'em. Hey, Old Man! Our young exec is telling me you just did the easy part of his training. Now he's getting the important stuff." And then still speaking loudly enough to be heard across the room. "Don't worry about it. The old man knows I'm lying. I'm always lying to him."

Freddy talked constantly while Dieterich took apart a hardness tester in front of him and serviced it, meaning cleaning or oiling or checking for wear on each part, depending on what form of attention the part should receive. Freddy watched closely and just a few times pointed to something or shifted Dieterich's fingers on a tool.

As noon approached, Dieterich could feel Freddy's mood shift although it might have been in anticipation of eating or stopping work for an hour or finishing what he thought Dieterich should know before they go on an outside job in the afternoon. At five minutes to twelve o'clock, as read on Freddy's watch, Freddy said to pack up the toolbox so they could take it with them to lunch. He packed some papers into Dieterich's briefcase: blank invoices, of course, but also a parts catalog and a diagram of a hardness tester in case something needed explanation and some catalogs of other company products the customer might want. He even had some certification certificates in case any of the machines they serviced were reaching the end of their current certificate.

Dieterich made sure to pass near Rusty on the way out. "I'll try not to embarrass the company, Rusty."

"You'll be fine. There's another thing before you go." He took something small from a drawer below his work bench. "Just put this in your pocket. If you have to put in a screw or take one out, stare at something on the machine like it needs to be looked at and then turn the bolt onto the nut in your pocket so you're sure which way the thread goes. Yeah, I'm sure you already know but you'll be in a new place with people staring at you so you might as well be careful to get it right. Feel the bolt turn on the nut and twist that screwdriver like you been doing it everyday."

"Thanks. I'll do that. I see your point. See you Monday."

Freddy had a place in mind for lunch so Dieterich left behind the food he bought on his way in to the offices. It would be warm in the car but the baloney was still sealed in plastic so it had a chance of surviving. Of course he wanted to see if Cathy was at Romero's at dinnertime so the baloney would wait until Saturday. Maybe it would be breakfast. He had not eaten baloney for years and looked forward nostalgically to trying it again; a humble food, obviously, certainly acceptable when dining in private.

They went to three factories that afternoon. All were different and all fit a pattern: find the plant manager; smile confidently and shake hands firmly; meet the guy who works the tester and write down his name along with the start time (after introductions are over); wait for the manager to leave and then ask the machine user how it is working. Even if the worker has explained everything in front of the manager, ask again. Even at the first place, Freddy had Dieterich do everything on the machine: lay out the parts as they came off the machine and give each one its proper attention. In the second factory, they serviced three machines. Freddy did one and Dieterich two, one of which was under Freddy's close observation, thus, Freddy was not taking it easy.

They drove back to the offices to get Dieterich's car and Freddy suggested they go over to his place afterwards, have a beer in the backyard and grill some burgers. Dieterich was surprised to feel some relief that he would not go to Romero's for a solitary dinner and either see Cathy without passing a word between them beyond some of the ones on the menu or not seeing Cathy and worrying his local restaurant for the summer would offer nothing but overly familiar and solitary dinners. He should have been assertive and said he was busy for dinner tonight but let's do it soon. No, the lesson from his senses was not that he should skip dinner with Freddy but that he should, as soon as he saw Cathy again, be assertive with her (assuming he does see her again and that she is still as appealing as he imagines and that being assertive is not being obnoxious). Just feel her out to see if she might be available for a friendship one step higher than waitress-and-customer.

Dieterich drove behind Freddy to his place because he said giving directions would be too complicated. That worried Dieterich because sometime next week he would be navigating himself to jobsites and he was expecting someone to provide clear directions. He really hated the idea of calling customers to ask how to get to them. He had driven his parents' cars many times, of course, but now that he thought about it, he always went to places he already knew or someone in the car knew. The route seemed easy enough for thirty minutes, taking them outside the city and then down a gravel road for a couple miles to an unmarked dirt road next to a row of mailboxes. Dieterich sensed the neighborhood was comprised of cheap seasonal housing. Freddy did not seem like the type to have a summer cabin but he might be renting one or even just acting as caretaker. Then Dieterich saw the inconsistency in his idea. Summer cabins are used by owners in the summer. This would not be a ski lodge.

A sturdy sign in fancy lettering read "Woodbrook Mobile Home Reserve," which sounded like a place for endangered trailers. Freddy parked beside the fourth trailer on the left. On the only road in the Reserve, trailers were comfortably set up in a staggered arrangement, one on the left then one on the right, about a hundred feet apart. Freddy waved to the space beside his car as the place for Dieterich to park. Dieterich struggled to think up something positive to say about Freddy's place without being patronizing or assuming why he had such an arrangement.

The trailers were not the sad variety he had seen in movies and on country roads in the South, composed of small rusty boxes waiting for a natural disaster: flood or hurricane or forest fire. Most of the ones he could see here had a well-tended lawn with some sculptural element, such as a gazing ball on a pedestal, garden gnome, birdbath, or trellis arch. Freddy had a low, white fence made of durable, weatherproof plastic across the road side of his plot. From its gate, a brick walkway led to the brick patio along the side of the trailer with the door. There was a handmade roof over the door, a homey touch.

"Welcome to my mansion," Freddy said without embarrassment, maybe even pride despite the irony of his words. "I've got AC so we ought to sit inside until the shadow covers the patio. Then I'll get out the grill."

"Sure. I can see you put the patio on the shady side."

"Yeah. I don't use the grill in winter so I don't ever need the sun on it."

Freddy held the door while Dieterich went up the steps and handed out his planned compliment. "You really got a quiet place out here, just like you don't even work in the city. Are we going to hear the crickets tonight; see some stars?"

"Of course it's cheaper than anything in town or close to town. I could afford bigger but I gotta save up. I'll have a wife and family someday."

"You have a specific wife in mind?"

There were two chairs and a couch/bed in the living room/kitchen. Dieterich sat in the one closer to the kitchen in case Freddy was going to do some dinner preparation.

"You could say I know a potential wife or two or three but only one of them knows she's on the list. I still got time, you know."

"You and me, we're too young to be feeling any pressure. It's just that you don't want to let the right one get away while you're saving up for to do things exactly right."

"Pressure? I don't feel pressure. Not much. Not any more than a flea on a dog. That's a big dog, I mean. And it's on an elephant and the elephant's got both front feet on my head and both back feet on my balls. Yeah, I got a specific girl in mind. She's the right one. She's not begging to get married but I see her waiting for me to be ready. Well, I'm way ready personally. It's just that I need to get higher up in the company or maybe another company. I don't want her living in a tin can like I do even if I'm in the tin can with her." They sat silently for a few seconds. Deeter felt Freddy wanted to say something more. "I don't usually tell people about that. I like to be positive, you know, not scared."

"I hear you, Freddy. I haven't calculated it out for me. I can see you need to have things ready when she makes the move. You can't wait for everything to be perfect though. We're in a big company. It may have more potential for you to move up."

"See, what you're doing is great for you; summer job; make enough to save some for when you're back in school. Me? Where I am is no way right for me but it's a step. The money's going to be in sales. I'm getting around to companies all over the state. They're getting to know me and I know them. When I'm the sales rep, I'll have a whole line from our company: hardness testers obviously, optical comparators, Mettler balance, dual column tensile strength tester, elastometer. 'A city like this tests and retests if it wants to stay in business', I'll say when I'm the sales rep. We don't have one now, not one who works out of our office, not one in the state. It's Wes' idea for me to do it. I was working on him to find me something better and damned if he didn't do it. Guess he's still selling the idea up the line. I don't mean your Dad got anything to do with it, just saying it's what I'm looking at down the road. Not too far down the road either. Maybe by spring. I'm studying all the testing products. That's where you come in. If you take some of the load off hardness testers this summer, they're our biggest line, I'll get to work on all the other stuff. I'm already experienced on the optical comparator and that the most complicated thing we got."

Freddy suddenly remembered why he had a beer in each hand so he gave one to Dieterich before he sat down on the couch, lying back with his arms spread, his workday over, his time to relax.

"You ever been in a mobile home before? You know it's not actually mobile right? It's got wheels, but it ain't goin' nowhere."

"I've been in two. The first time was on the way to Florida when I was still in junior high. We stayed one night. The motel was not full but they had a place like this ready for families. There were five of us. We loved it. Not as big as this one, but full-sized, all the rooms. You must have three bedrooms in this one."

"Just two. One more than I really need, I guess. Use the spare for storage."

"Two is what we had at the motel. I was on the couch like you're sitting on. My brother and sister were in one and my parents in the other. After that, us kids said we should always look for mobile homes when we drive to Florida, but my Dad wasn't too excited by it. Maybe it was expensive by the night."

"What was the other one?"

"The other mobile home, you mean?" Dieterich felt awkward saying "mobile home" every time instead of "trailer" which is the term he would have used if the owner were not his audience. It was even more awkward to talk about his second time in a mobile home since that was a lie. He had only been in the one on the way to Florida. Why lie about it? He had wanted to make it sound normal to be in a trailer. Adding a second time was not enough to make it normal but he did not think through the lie before telling it.

"That was in Florida a couple years later. We went down to Miami every couple years to see my grandparents. My grandfather had good friends who lived in a mobile home down on the Keys. Smaller than this one and not in such good shape but it was just two old folks, living simply. We visited them a few times, just me and my grandfather. I went along on those half-day trips because everyone thought I should hear their stories about the old days in south Florida. Everyone was right; it was great fun to hear them reminisce with my grandfather. The area changed a whole lot in one lifetime. I probably learned more about getting old from those visits than from anything else in my life so far. It didn't sound too bad either, not if you still have your friends like they did."

What a fine lie he told! It did not serve its purpose well, but it gave more truth than he expected to be telling and it moved the conversation away from embarrassing class distinctions. It was all true but for the bit about anyone living in a trailer.

While they were grilling their burgers a few of Freddy's neighbors stopped by to talk. No one stayed long enough to sit even though Freddy had unfolded a couple extra lawn chairs and offered each of them a beer or Coke. Everyone did take a beer. Freddy and Dieterich were standing beside the grill so all the chairs were empty.

The first person was a retired schoolteacher. She seemed friendly and intelligent, inspiring Dieterich to focus on the question of why she was living in a trailer at this stage of life. *Teachers ought to be paid enough to live in a better place*, he thought. And following this thought, he worried what career he would have that would lead to retirement in a house; a cottage would be enough, especially if it were in a nice, non-urban setting. He was free to wander mentally because the teacher and Freddy kept up an active conversation on recent events in the life of her two sons, both living in California now. Dieterich decided his cottage would not be in Michigan, at least not in any part of Michigan he had seen so far, and not in a place like the Woodbrook Mobile Home Reserve; with terrain too flat, trees too small and, obviously, too many trailers instead of modest, handcrafted cottages.

As the teacher was leaving a young couple appeared. They said they came for the beer but that was a joke. They were Freddy's contemporaries but not his peers. While Freddy was culturally old-school, like a vision Dieterich's parents might have of a suitable co-worker for his summer, this couple was right out of The Whole Earth Catalog: long hair, loose cotton clothes, sandals, a suspicion of marijuana on their breaths. They reported in passionate detail to Freddy on how their garden was doing, especially how it was saving money and improving their nutrition, all from a plot 10 by 15 feet beside their trailer. Dieterich doubted the veracity of their agricultural economics although the economics of living at Woodbrook made sense for them. He felt sorry for the aesthetics of their housing arrangement. They seemed to occupy a social niche that would demand more in their immediate environment, and he also wondered if their trailer might be hand-painted in paisley and moonbeams. Of course, he did not reveal his stereotypical prejudices in conversation and hardly said anything at all. The personable and loquacious Freddy filled in any gaps in the discussion with genuine interest in whatever topic they raised.

The gist of the discussion was the visitors trying to talk Freddy into trying some of their garden's vegetables and he was refusing, partly to keep their agricultural economics balanced, and partly because vegetables were not a priority for him, even if they were more nutritious than usual.

When the burgers were done, Freddy offered to give them the first ones off the grill. This was enough to run them off politely although Freddy laughed quietly as soon as they were out of sight and commented to Dieterich that he knew they would not accept a hamburger of uncertain origins. Dieterich could now speak with enthusiasm. He was hungry and ready to load his bun with the condiments Freddy had prepared. He saw four large burgers on the grill, so he planned two combinations of lettuce, sliced tomato, chopped onions and two types of pickle relish. Mustard was for hot dogs and ketchup was only a poor man's tomato slice. Freddy had some corn on the cob on the grill. The few burnt kernels promised a savory charcoal taste to top off the beautiful balance of tastes, scents and textures Dieterich was anticipating.

Another neighbor came around the corner of Freddy's home. "Hey Fred, my man! What's for dinner?"

"Tony! Where you been hiding? Takes a grilled burger to get you outside these days." He slapped Tony on the back. Shaking hands was not a popular greeting in Woodbrook. "Grab a beer. Fix yourself a burger. Meet my friend from work, Deeter. He's from back East."

Tony smiled and waved at Deeter. "Enjoy. Me, I've got dinner all set tonight. The band's got a gig at a private party over in Southfield with dinner for us included. Should be some fancy stuff on little plates and I'm thinking it will be very tasty too. I just wanted to say hey, Freddy. It's not me hiding out in my trailer. You been on the road again, right? I'm watching your place; make sure nobody's messin' around, you know."

"Well, thanks, I guess. There's nothing in here worth anyone messin' around."

"Don't doubt you, my man. Gotta get goin'. Nice to meet you, Mr. Deeter."

Dieterich had just taken his first bite of his stuffed burger bun and could only grunt and wave as Tony left.

Woodbrook was closer to Rochester Hills than Dieterich realized. At eight o'clock he was opening the Tylers' front door. They were watching television and interrupted their concentration on the screen to greet him. He said his hellos and quickly went upstairs. He flopped on the bed as soon as he was inside his room, stared at the ceiling and began replaying his dinner with Freddy. It was more interesting than he would have guessed. Freddy had more of a plan for the future than Dieterich ever had. Why, he wondered, did his own future feel more secure than Freddy's? He knew at a conscious level that people of his background did not always end up living at the standards of their parents.

A knock on the door caused Dieterich to say "hello" even before he realized how surprising it was at this hour. Roland tumbled in with Sam on his heels, both smiling as if they were ready for trouble of a good kind.

"You're back and we're ready. You want to take off that white shirt before we take off? The girls at a carnival ain't likely looking for junior executives to give 'em a good time."

"The carnival? You still going then?"

"What the hell else there's to do in this nowhere place?"

"Come on. Rochester Hills's got to be a boomtown compared with an oil rig on the arctic circle."

"You just got here but I bet you know there's nothing here more than a bed to sleep on."

"Yeah, hang on a minute. I got a shirt in here. Maybe some jeans too."

Dieterich went over to the closet while the two guys stood quietly. He thought of saying he would go over to their room when he was ready but shrugged off the intrusion. He changed his pants and shirt while they lingered silently and, as far as Dieterich could tell, disinterestedly.

Sam had his Charger parked in front of the Tylers' house. They crowded three across with Dieterich next to the window. Sam drove a block away and then put his foot to the floor, burning his tires and pressing Dieterich to the back of the seat in a way he had never felt before although he recognized it from cheesy TV shows. The rest of the way, just two or three miles, they sped but did not slide around any corners or run a stop sign. Sam and Roland did not speak nor did Dieterich. It was not clear if the speeding was showing off to Dieterich or merely the usual way Sam drove his pony.

Dieterich did not mind hanging out a little with these two guys though he had nothing at all in common with them. He suspected he liked being nearby to prove to himself he was not inclined to be like them in any way. Already he had reassured himself he did not want a Dodge Charger. A Rambler American was almost a joke for a young person like himself but it was also respectable as a step toward adulthood, not projecting emergence from teen years as his goal.

"You should know," Dieterich spoke as if he were the experienced one of the group, "down here in the lower forty-eight, girls at carnivals think a good time is winning a stuffed bunny. I know it but if you've got faith, go ahead and see what you can dig up. I'm just here for the lights and the noise and I never liked cotton candy. So, let's see the lights!"

"Oh, there'll be girls. If they like some spice once in a while out here in the sticks this is the only place to be, right Roland?"

"Sam's damn good at rooting out some pussy if there any around. You'll send some my way, won't you, buddy, not too young, right?" Roland answered as if there were a serious discussion underway. And then he showed he was not as irresponsible as the act they were performing and probably performed most of the time. "If we get separated, meet back at the car at ten. Right?"

The three of them wandered down the mid-way, presumably displaying their youthful vigor and availability in the way they strode and their confident, friendly glare at anyone who happened to raise an eye toward them. For his part, Dieterich strode as normally as he could, overtly rejecting any notion of being on the prowl. He kept a step behind Sam and Roland so they would not feel he was hurting their aura, although there was a sense in a quiet part of his imagination in which a lonely young woman would notice his modesty and would give him an opening to start a conversation.

Before long two high school-aged girls did look back at Sam and Roland which was enough for them to stop and lean against a metal fence to take out cigarettes and nod back casually. The girls were too young to be interesting to Dieterich and should have been too young to interest anyone older than him. They wore lipstick which reminded him of his mother. Their attire was probably suburban-Michigan-chic but looked juvenile to Dieterich whose tastes had already adapted to the look of the counterculture even though he lacked the courage to embrace it in his own stylings. They stopped their stroll, talking between themselves and giggling. Dieterich slapped Roland on the shoulder and said he was going to try the nearby booth with a game based on an empty Coke bottle. Roland said, "Yeah, sure," with the understanding that there were only two girls on offer so Dieterich was just getting out of the way while he and Sam made their play.

The game was simply to use a forked stick to lift the neck of the bottle until the bottle was standing up. The carney in the booth demonstrated. He lifted the bottle three times out of four tries. On the fourth, the bottle tumbled over backwards. Then he went through his act again, talking quickly, using the same words and yet delivering them with passion. The game was simple. Dieterich could not see any opportunity for cheating although he knew there was something difficult in it. Presumably the carney had practiced the trick but there was not much to do but keep a steady hand as the bottle neared the vertical. "One dollar to play gets you two tries and pays you back five if you get the bottle up or take your choice of a toy." None of the toys looked worth a dollar. Dieterich watched the carney lift the bottle four more times to see if he was twisting the forked stick or turning it to spin the bottle slightly or any other subtle movement. He saw nothing but what the carney showed openly; no fan to blow the bottle over, no tilt to the table, no oil on the surface. He would watch to be sure the carney did not bump or kick the table. He looked over his shoulder to be sure Sam and Roland had not left. They were still talking up those girls. He put his dollar down.

Of course, the bottle fell over on both his tries although it almost stood up. The carney walked around well away from them and cheered him on. There was one older man watching silently. He nodded appreciatively to Dieterich. One buck was not much. He could afford to lose that. If he went once again and lost, he would only be out two bucks. If he won on the second dollar, he would be up three. He decided to go again, but he wanted to see the carney do it again first. Rather than ask for another demonstration, he said he probably had enough of it but he stayed there. The older man called his wife over and explained the game to her. The carney showed her how it worked. Dieterich decided to leave if the man did the trick. He could be in on the game, but the wife said she did not like any of the toys so they walked away. Dieterich put down another dollar. He tried to lift the bottle to vertical more confidently, thinking that might make him steadier. The carney had been quick and casual in his moves. The effect of his revised strategy was for the bottle to fall more quickly both times on this dollar.

Four boys came to the booth and watched the carney demonstrate. Dieterich imagined how many times this skinny, greasy-haired guy had stood up the bottle and figured it might be a real skill albeit useless anywhere but here. Dieterich also figured he was good with his hands, better than most, and a little practice might be enough.

Roland was reaching out to one of the girls, trying gently to take her hand while she pulled back and slapped his arm and laughed. Sam was talking softly to the other girl nearby but not close enough to Roland to be overheard.

The boys made a deal with the carney. For one payment of two dollars, each of them could try twice but then they would get a bonus try for whichever one of them had gotten closer. The payout would be ten dollars. Dieterich thought this was a creative approach to get a bonus shot and was surprised the carney accepted it. The second boy got the bottle to wobble for a second before falling. He took the bonus shot and their two dollars stayed in the carney's pocket. They ran off as if they were embarrassed to have lost a dollar each at a carnival.

"You gave the boys five tries for two dollars and said if any of them gets it upright, you'd pay ten. Can I get that deal?"

"No man. I could see they were just boys and were too busy playing with each other to concentrate. You'd be better at it. Let's say for two dollars you get five tries, that's a bonus try, and the payout is still five. That would leave you ahead since you only gave me two dollars so far."

Five more tries to get the bottle to stand once and he would be a winner. Dieterich looked over to Roland and Sam who were still playing the girls for something more than giggles. It would feel good to say he won at the carnival while they wasted their time. He put down two dollars. The bottle fell five more times. The carney offered sympathy.

Dieterich spoke to him before he left. "Guess I learned something I should have already known. Thanks for the lesson."

"Hey, it's all fair. People win a few times every night. I hardly make anything on it."

"It's alright. I'm not complaining. I appreciated playing the game."

He thought he might try out one of the rides. He had loved the rides at the county fair, the ones that scared him a little. This was before he heard of a ride actually crashing and before he noticed how flimsy their construction was. He did not like rational fear, just the kind that comes from the primitive portion of his brain. He would assess the quality of a ride before buying a ticket.

He waved his finger in a circle over his head to indicate to Sam, who was looking toward him, that he was walking about. Sam held up his hand in a stop signal. Then he said something to the girl and put his arm around her while they came over to Dieterich. "We'll go with you and see what they got here." Then Sam whispered to Dieterich. "Ain't going nowhere with this broad."

"Hey. I'm Deeter." Neither she nor Sam gave the girl's name.

Sam looked over the toys in each of the game booths to see if the girl wanted something. She settled on a stuffed giraffe in a booth where Sam was to throw a softball to knock over a stack of three heavy-looking "milk bottles." He did not win, which obviously did not surprise the newly sophisticated Dieterich although both Sam and the girl were surprised. At least Sam did not try to defend himself with claims the game was rigged or just deceptive. Dieterich thought his easy acceptance came from a history of failing. It was simply normal. Sam was smart enough to dismiss the prize as not worth any further investment.

The three of them toured the rides, all lit up like Christmas, spinning and rocking and playing music like life would center on festival if you let it. Most were pretty tame, designed to attract children although most of the children had a parent sitting beside them, telling them how fine it is to be swooping about in a teacup or riding a boat on a track though six inches of water.

"Check it out!" Sam pointed to the Ferris wheel where Roland and his girl were clambering into a carriage. The girl pecked him on the cheek when the safety bar was lowered onto their laps. Roland had managed to pay, guide his girl into their seat and then climb into his seat without relinquishing his grasp on her.

"Keep watching," Sam advised.

Roland waited until the Ferris wheel moved forward to let in the next riders before maneuvering into a full embrace and smooch.

"Nice! You and me should go for a ride," Sam suggested to his girl.

"I don't think so," she answered in a way that clearly meant "no chance of that."

When Sam put his arm around her to steer her away from the Ferris wheel in a direction generally away from the lights, she leaned away from him. "It's been nice taking to you but we gotta get home soon so I'm just gonna wait here for Dotty to finish up whatever she's doing up there."

"Oh, don't worry about her none. You can't get in much trouble on a Ferris wheel."

"Uh-huh," was all she answered.

"You want some popcorn or something," Sam was trying to be nice.

"No, I'm just waiting to leave. You go ahead."

Sam made a face to Dieterich, a face trying to communicate the girl had no cause to be pushing him off, he wasn't smooching her girlfriend and he hadn't taken any liberties with her and anyway, he doesn't need to hang out with a kid like her.

"Yeah, good idea Sam. I didn't have any dessert with dinner. Popcorn sounds about right. I couldn't take something sweet and sticky on a night like this." Dieterich then nodded in a way to communicate the two of them should go get popcorn since it might be good to do something and this girl was not worth troubling over any more.

"Sure?" Sam asked her. "Anything? No strings attached? How 'bout a beer."

The girl turned toward the Ferris wheel and held onto the railing around the ride as if Sam might try to drag her off. Sam took a few steps toward the smell of popcorn before twisting to look back over his shoulder but he did not stop and did not look long.

"Ah, that's how it goes sometimes. Don't see anything hot so you spend your time with some kid who isn't ready to grow up some. What I do to her to get her so proud, like she's got a bod I can't live without?"

"You don't want my advice, Sam. What do I know? Well, one thing I know, that girl was no great loss. It's hard to see in the lights around here, blinkering, colored up, moving, all the time, but what I see is she's not much to look at and I doubt she'd be much to feel up."

"Yeah. It just seems that's what was available tonight."

"Sometimes you gotta soak in the colors and the noise and cheap food smells and screams of kids on the rides and the cute little families and the goddam carnie cheats and the mud in the midway and the time passing away without climax, and just save the pursuit of girls for nights when there's girls worth chasing."

"Yeah, well, I guess that's right. But you know that tease up there with Rollie ain't no prize either."

"Yeah, I'm sure you're right about that, and I bet he knows it better than you and me anyway."

Roland did not say much about his ride around the Ferris wheel, his silence confirming Dieterich's guess about what had been achieved in the high and moderately private. His silence was conspicuous so he broke it with an insincere suggestion that the evening had been successful.

"Maybe I'll see you here next Saturday, right?"

"Sure thing, Honey. I'd like that. Let's say seven o'clock. Give us a little more time," and the two girls hurried off, skipping on their feet while tipping their heads toward each other to whisper whatever the other had missed. Dieterich assumed the carnival would have moved on by the following weekend but he said nothing more about it. He also assumed Roland and Sam and the two girls knew there was no date for Saturday.

The drive back to Rochester Hills kept below the speed limit. The conversation centered on the construction job Sam and Roland would be working next week. They did not mention any trade skills in their work, just time and effort. Dieterich did not ask what they did. It sounded like raw work, perhaps hauling materials like lumber or sheet rock or pipe or shingles, driving a flatbed truck or possibly a fork truck, or shoveling out the details in a foundation. Whatever it turned out to be, it would be hot and sweaty.

4

Thursday, June 19 On Thursday morning, Dieterich awoke feeling surprisingly resolute. In the shower, he began to organize his summer life. Firstly, he was not going to hang out with Sam and Roland. Secondly, he would start to take showers at night instead of in the morning. Morning had been good at college because he tended to stay up late. Ironically, he was a "morning person," was most clear-headed in the morning, such as while having this thought. It was a waste of his best energy to shower in the morning rather than getting out of the house and into whatever the day held for him. Thirdly, he needed to make a list of forests and trails to visit during the summer; maybe some beaches on the Great Lakes too. Fourthly, he had no time to begin that list because he was as clean as he was going to get and needed to dry off.

He waited in his car until five minutes before eight o'clock and then went inside his building, meeting Rusty's standard of arriving neither early nor late. From the car to a position in front of Rusty for the day's instructions took a little over three minutes. Rusty apparently always arrived early, earlier by more than two or three minutes; Dieterich did not know how much exactly and did not consider it any of his concern. This day, Rusty had a bin of slightly rusty metal parts for Dieterich to clean; sand paper for heavy rust, fine steel wool for light rust. Bright steel should shine, dark steel should be smooth to the touch. Then everything should be wiped with an oily rag. Dieterich did not know what he was being paid but he suspected and hoped he was making more than the cleaning job earned per hour. *Maybe,* he silently speculated, *Rusty is testing me to see how I take it. Argue it is boring, do a sloppy job, apply myself as if I believe it matters, fake it until lunchtime. If it's a game, I'm in. If it's not, I'm in too. What else am I doing? If I'm not earning something for the company, that's on you, Rusty. Look at that: "Rusty." I'll think of some kind of rude joke about this job and his name.*

"Morning Deeter!" Freddy called warmly when he came into the shop from the backroom. He had come early too, but Dieterich planned to keep to Rusty's instruction. "Rusty, check out my push awl. It's got a bend to it."

Rusty took the tool from Freddy. He held the 4 by 3/16 inch shaft close to his eye for a moment and then rolled it along the edge of the table so the handle hung off the table and he could feel the size of the bend.

"Sure is. What'd you do? Try to pry open a can of paint with it?"

"I woulda but I didn't have a can of paint. Think it can be fixed? It's pretty stiff. I was afraid of making it worse if I put too much push on it."

"Just take the one outta Deeter's kit. He won't need it today. Let's see if he can straighten it out."

Dieterich pointed to his toolbox on a shelf.

"Thanks. Going over to Royal Oak today. Going to need a push awl. You ever notice these things, Deeter, how nice they're made? Look too fancy for such a simple thing, shiny metal, shapely little handle that fits in your hand just right? The shaft is supposed to be, used to be, straight as a light beam. Notice here on the tip how it's flat but has rounded edges so it can't scratch you if it slips off the pin its pushing? You can't buy one of these. They were invented and crafted within this company specially for our toolkits. And the artist/engineer, none other than our own Rusty!"

"Frankly, Freddy, I have noticed that tool was well made and fits perfectly in the odd use we have in taking apart a hardness tester."

"Deeter," Rusty responded testily, "I hoped you weren't as full of shit as Freddy."

"Maybe I am and maybe I'm not, but I am dead serious about noticing the awl."

"Oh yeah, Deeter," Freddy answered. "I almost forgot. I got something for you. I don't remember where I got it. It's been lying in a drawer for I don't know how long." From his jacket pocket he took out a map and placed it on the table before he went over to Dieterich's toolbox and removed the push awl. Dieterich called out his thanks for the map and the dinner last night as Freddy was returning to the back room to finish packing for the day's work in Royal Oak. He did not mention that the company car came with a state map in the glove compartment however, he noticed later that the map was really about the state's parklands and marked all city, state and national lands on one side and gave a few facts about the larger parks on the other side.

<table><tr><td>Saturday, June 21</td></tr></table>

Saturday broke foggy and cool. Dieterich reached down to his shoes beside the bed and dug his watch out of one of them. It read 8:oo, a half hour later than he had been getting up. This scared him, not for this day but for the next workday, for Monday. He would need to get an alarm clock soon. He reached over to the tablet on the floor beside the bed and wrote himself a reminder to buy a clock and then added buying a book or some magazines for after dinner during the week. Lying in bed and wondering what other notes he needed, he remembered the stuff he bought for Friday lunch. It was still in a paper bag in the back seat of his car. He added a notation to throw away the baloney and bread rolls. Then he started a list of food items, including fresh baloney and milk to keep in the refrigerator downstairs. It was only the start of a shopping list but he felt better organized to have it in writing.

After a shower, he trimmed his toenails. He could think of nothing else to make himself more presentable at the swimming pool. There was not enough time to become more tanned and muscular. It would not matter if he looked as mature and athletic as he wished to be, as he had wished to become by the time he was eighteen, as he knew now, he would never be except that he would have to become more mature eventually, probably not soon and very likely not the movie star variety of it. He still had hopes to develop a heavy beard. It was just a visit to his kind and proper boss who was probably constantly conscious that this callow youth was the son of one of the company's top executives. The thought was a minor relief, albeit an embarrassing one, to shelter in his father's social rank. It was even more embarrassing that he was not even sure of his father's job title. A couple years ago, his father became Vice President, that much was certain, but then it turned out the company had lots of Vice Presidents. He had overheard his parents at dinner talking about Executive Vice President. It was unclear if his dad was about to move up or was just thinking about it. His dad was ambitious and was probably thinking about it from the day he joined the firm so that conversation must have been about some progress toward a promotion. Dieterich wondered if he would have been told of the promotion. He did not hear much about his father's work.

Wes Elias was a good man but not as easy to talk to as Freddy. Maybe Freddy would be at lunch too. Maybe not and maybe no one but himself would go in the pool. Most people who had swimming pools, as far as Dieterich knew, also had children so maybe he would be in the pool with a few kids. That would not make him seem more mature. *What the hell*, he voiced aloud to himself and then silently thought *I like playing around in a pool. I like diving from a board or from the side. I like swimming underwater, seeing how far I can go. There's no need to worry about being judged – I'm not getting graded on how well I do lunch with the boss. I'll be unpretentious, like always. Wes will like that. Most people do. That's my best card: embrace my insecurities!*

He dressed with his cutoff, denim shorts under his jeans. The combination felt a little tight but would not show on his slim frame and would simplify his going swimming, if he actually did go swimming. If it was just Mr. and Mrs. Elias and himself, it would be odd to swim with them. Would they suggest a game of water volleyball or some other favorite pool game? They might suggest he go swimming on his own. He might do that to avoid having to talk very much to two people he knew so little, two adults facing a disgraced student. They probably did not know of his disgrace or maybe it had been mentioned as a justification for giving him the job. Was he a sad, charity case in addition to a son-of-the-executive case?

He took out fresh underwear for after the pool. He would hang his damp bath towel over the passenger-side seatback in the car to dry out before going over to the Elias'. He figured that would be all he needed to take along. Unless, he suddenly realized, he should take something to add to the lunch. *Whoa*, he thought proudly, *that would be a classy move.* It was a good moment followed immediately by insecurity. What could he take with him? He should have asked when he was invited whether he could take something. Flowers for the house or for Mrs. Elias would be awkward, as if he were going to a prom in the 1950s. A six-pack of beer would be a cool move, assuming they drank beer. Fortunately, he was not cool enough to consider that option seriously. He did not like beer himself and he had not forced himself to drink it at school even though he was old enough to drink legally in Pennsylvania. He did not feel old enough to change his tastes. They had changed automatically in some ways, not including adult foods and drinks. *Slow to mature*, he confessed to himself for the thousandth time in the past month. At least he had that one good, adult idea about taking flowers and had enjoyed it for two or three seconds. When he was in a different situation, the idea might return more easily now that it had emerged once already. In a different situation, it could be good enough to implement.

By the time he was leaving the house to do his shopping, the fog had mostly burned off to reveal a thin overcast above him and the possibility of a bright, hot day to come; good for swimming. It was early for shopping although he thought supermarkets should open very early on weekends. He had not heard anyone awake in the house although that did not mean they were late. It was more likely that one or both of his housemates or the Tylers had already gone out to start a weekend full of activities.

He had no idea where to buy groceries and a book and a clock, so he walked in the direction of Romero's to see if anything nearby was open. He might get a suggestion from a clerk or a customer or a pedestrian. At the firehouse, he might find someone on duty, bored by a morning of inaction, his equipment already clean and shiny, his passion for public service awaiting a task. Dieterich's boyish looks, normally his curse, would serve well to put strangers at ease in a small town on a Saturday morning.

It had not occurred to him that Romero's Family Restaurant would be open for breakfast. He knew it did not serve breakfast on weekdays but there it was with an inviting sign in the window so he went inside without hesitation as if this were his set destination. The woman at the cash register said "sit anywhere you like" as if the room offered a range of unique locations for patrons to assess, although, to be fair, there were subtle differences between tables and booths and their proximity to the kitchen door and the window facing the street. Cathy was wiping off a table and said "I'll be right with you."

Dieterich replied "Thank you, Cathy," and saw no sign she heard him. He had overplayed his hand. He could not call her by name again until he was leaving or it would seem like he was trying to impress her that he knew it, which he was, although he did not want to be obvious about it.   He left the menu on the table and considered how he would handle Cathy's return. If he ordered right away, she might leave before he asked about shopping. If he asked about shopping first, it might appear that talking to her was his reason for coming in. It would have been his reason if he had thought she would be there. He settled on asking about shopping first because he could then end that part of the discussion in a businesslike way by ordering, proving he was not trying to talk her up.

Soon the conversation proceeded much as he planned.   Cathy was friendly and smart and self-confident. Dieterich did not look closely at her but close enough to decide she was very attractive. Her waitress smock was not stylish and Dieterich cared little about style. It revealed enough to imagine a firm, slim female figure underneath but not an overly sexy, intimidating frame beyond the reach of an ordinary fellow between his freshman and sophomore year of college. Physically, Cathy could pass for a high school senior, but her poise assured him she was old enough to be approachable.

"I need to buy a few groceries. Is there a store near here?" His simple question startled him with its clarity, as if he were entirely comfortable talking with her. She gave him clear, simple instructions in return.

"The nearest supermarket's not the best one. It's good enough for a short stay in ol' Rochester Hills. About two miles north on Livermore. On the right. Doubt you could miss it. You can walk from here. Go out the door and turn right."

"Guess I could walk four miles round trip. I'm not too busy today. Want me to pick up anything for the restaurant?"

She ignored his joke, and he did not blush only because she had teased him a tiny bit with her own question. "Anything else you need to know?"

"OK, here's a harder question. Is there a bookstore nearby?" He noticed and liked the little pattern he had started of prefacing each question with a statement. It sounded more conversational and less like an interrogation than going straight to the question.

"How near does it have to be?"

He should not have asked for a bookstore. He had not noticed it might sound like he was trying to appear intellectual. "I guess I didn't mean 'near', I meant 'easy for me to find'. It's just I didn't bring much with me for my summer job and thought I could read a book or a magazine after dinner sometimes."

"Yeah, there's not much to do around here; a movie theater over in Rochester, just one screen. And a carnival set up over on Route 150 by the river. I don't know of any bookstore. Maybe you could look in the Yellow Pages; probably end up going into Detroit. Is that where your job is?”

Dieterich worried he was keeping her at his table too long. No new customers had come in but maybe she ought to be wiping the tables or something. “Yeah, almost Detroit. It’s in Ferndale. Pretty sure there’s no bookstore near that place. I’ll check the Yellow Pages. Good idea. Thanks.”   She nodded and waited for him a couple seconds to say something more.

“Have you seen the menu?” She probably knew he had not even opened it. The room was too small for any unknown movements.

A sassy reply began to emerge in Dieterich’s mind (“seen it, haven’t read it” or “no, I’m waiting for the movie version” or maybe something that was not stupid) but he knew in the four seconds he allowed himself before answering he could not pull off anything appropriately humorous and casual so he decided it would be clever enough to skip the literal question and go straight to “two eggs, scrambled, small orange juice, coffee and wheat toast. Do you have sausage links?”

“Links or patties.”

“Good, the links please, just two of them.”

“I’ll bring the coffee right away.”

He did not actually want the coffee and preferred white toast but his actual preferences were too unsophisticated to reveal them to a waitress whom he could not stop himself from trying to impress. It seemed easier to him to impress Cathy than the girls he met at Lehigh. The college girls in an engineering program were likely smart and disciplined. If he also judged one of them as especially attractive in appearance, that only tallied another relative deficiency in himself. Cathy certainly looked good – he could be very sure about that even in her dreary outfit. It stretched over her breasts and hips but drew in where her apron was tied around her waist. Her hair was too coifed, styled like a girl from a small mid-western town, out of date by Eastern college standards. She might sense this and regard him as the sophisticate in the room although that would be unreasonable since he showed no contemporary flash. What did he have to offer a charming young lady of respectable but unknown background? *Maybe she would like my personality. I have friends who seem to appreciate me. Maybe it would turn out we have some shared interests. Is there any chance she likes birdwatching or fishing or watching football?*

When the bill came, it was again signed "Cathy" and embellished with a smiley face. Dieterich felt he had not lost face in the encounter although he would have to do much better than break even next time. At the very least, he should look her in the eye. If he could hold the look for few seconds while saying something, he could get a better look at her face, and then he could remember her more clearly in his dreams.

He found the grocery store and agreed there was little chance of a bookstore nearby. He nearly bought some cheese for the lunch party, planning to use the price to decide which variety was best. He could say with nonchalance that it was a type his father favored. Obviously, a youth like himself would have no idea of quality in cheese. Yet that would be a deceitful act for the shallowest of reasons. Besides, it might sound like suggesting his father's taste was something Wes should follow. Dieterich could find no gourmet section in the store to provide another gift idea so he shrugged and accepted he would go without pretending to be more mature than he was.

For the most part, Dieterich was relaxed as his AMC Rambler entered the long, straight, gravel driveway to the Elias house. It ran a hundred yards through a flat, barren field, covered with sparse, unmown weeds. The house was excessively symmetrical, as a child architect might have imagined it. The front was flat except for a shallow porch, no more than ten feet wide, in front of the front door, with a flat roof that served as the floor of a narrow balcony for the second floor. On each side of the porch and on each side of the balcony were three identical windows. On the left of the house, attached to it, was a tall picket fence which Dieterich correctly figured surrounded the pool. A shorter picket fence of the same width was attached on the right of the house. Dieterich guessed that was a place for the family dog or dogs to run outside, but it turned out to be a vegetable garden.

The door opened before Dieterich could ring the bell. A short, middle-aged women with a brilliant smile came bursting out. She wore a white, terrycloth robe over, Dieter presumed correctly, a bathing suit.

"You must be Deeter! I'm Wanda!"

"If you know who I am, this must be the right day to come," Dieterich answered. It was a compromise between ridiculing her vapid observation and saying something as empty as her greeting, yet he liked her already. *She's enthusiastic and she looks pretty good in a motherly way. Wes, I believe you've got a good women here.*

"You've got a towel, I see." Wanda further observed. "Do you have some swimming trunks rolled inside?"

"More or less. I'm wearing my shorts underneath. Best I can do for swimming."

"Good, good, good. Everybody's out at the pool. C'mon this way."

The "everybody" Wanda mentioned meant Mr. Elias, whom he was trying to remember to call "Wes," and two girls, possibly Dieterich's age, possibly a year younger. Wes had been lying on a plastic chaise longue and he jumped up as soon as he heard Wanda call out, "Deeter's here. Exactly on time like you said." The two girls looked up for an instant, more a reaction to the sound of Wanda's announcement than any interest in the new arrival.

Dieterich was surprised to have a reputation for being exactly on time. He did try to be punctual. Was that good or was it petty or was it being uptight? Males his age in this era were not supposed to be uptight. A boss would likely think punctuality was good. Two girls in bathing suits (a two-piece and a one-piece) would likely count it against him if they were cool girls. Were they cool? It did not matter. He was visiting his boss. It was impractical to deal with him and simultaneously maneuver through the perilous task of getting to know a new girl or choosing between two girls dressed in revealing togs; and more difficult if he were stripped down to his shorts too. Was Freddy coming to the party? Would he bring his girl?

Wes rushed over to shake Dieterich's hand. Wes wore only his swimming trunks and sandals. He was tan, as a man with his own pool ought to be. His thin torso and slight paunch were comforting to Dieterich although he envied the blond chest hair.

"Girls, if you're not going to get in the pool, come over and meet Deeter. He's dying to meet you, right Deeter?"

The girl in the one-piece looked over her shoulder and called out "Hi Deeter," and slid into the water. The one in the two-piece stood up and waved before she turned around and dove in.

"The one who spoke is my daughter Elise. The one who waved is her friend... I can't remember her name; something beginning with an R or an M. Sorry they're so shy. I don't think either one of them has done much dating."

Dieterich lifted both hands in a gesture he hoped communicated "It's all OK. That's the way some girls are." He had neither shouted nor waved a greeting so he could not criticize their poor social grace.

Wes suggested going in the pool until they were tired and then start cooking the burgers and dogs. Dieterich readily agreed to whatever Wes suggested and he admitted he was especially looking forward to burgers and dogs since that was the principal fare at all the outdoor events with his family and yet he did not make a move toward changing into his swimming shorts. He thought it would be more adult to talk first. He had not spent more than fifteen minutes total with Wes so far. He also wondered if anyone else was coming. And he did not want to be playing in the water alone while the two girls sat on the side and watched him. Already they had left the water and were drying off. Dieterich kept his eyes toward Wes and asked a few questions about the house and the town. He was preparing to ask what had brought him here to live when he stole a glance at the girls and caught his breath. He was not sure he had seen what he thought he saw and pretended to be relaxed, breathing normally and listening to Wes who was saying something about a hospital in the last place they lived. Dieterich heard the word hospital and knew his eyes had not been fooled. One of those girls was missing most of one leg. It must have been the one who had not stood up to wave before diving in. Which girl was that, Wes's daughter or the friend?

It's a withered leg. His mind formulated the thought rather than just wondered at the surprise of it. *Here I am thinking about how sexy these girls might be and suddenly I feel like a jerk for thinking about that. They are just people, and some people are female and close to me in age and don't especially want anything to do with me because they have other things in life than worrying about some skinny guy who works for Wes. And what the hell is Wes talking about? Was that a question for me?*

"You know, Wes, my head is in that pool already. I loved lake swimming at camp and swimming in a hotel pool when we drove to Florida and fighting the waves in the ocean but the only water I've been in since going to school last fall was from the shower or the sink. Let me get to know my boss a little better after I've revived some of the tomfoolery of my all too recent childhood. Look, I've got my shorts on already. You look dressed for it. Coming in?"

"Of course!" Wes called out "Wanda, do all that later." She was putting lunch things on a wooden picnic table. Beat me in the pool if you can!" Wes dropped off his sandals and ran to his daughter and pushed her over the edge into the water, then he jumped over her with a cannonball splash. Wanda was running toward the pool, so Dieterich held back to let her in first. Then he did a flip into the deep end, not a beautiful dive, but his best trick and a reliable one. He came up and looked over the pool. He could swim the length on one side without needing to steer around anyone, so he did that, getting to the shallow end, and then breast-stroked slowly back to the deep end and looked at what the others were doing.

The girlfriend was standing up, talking to the daughter. Dieterich could not remember the daughter's name and he doubted he had been told the friend's. It did not matter because he was fulfilled by looking at her. Somehow, he did not feel as if he were staring while doing his slow breaststroke. *Alright, she's a looker! Got to be my age at least. Not much older though. I could enjoy being around her. But that's not going to happen here. I need to include the daughter, maybe favor the daughter if there's any conversation at all with the girls.*

Dieterich reached the deep end and hung on the side and looked around. The beautiful friend bent down to say something to Elise (the daughter), and Elise grabbed her by the wrist and pulled her into the pool. They shrieked back and forth, possibly saying something. Dieterich was not sure if the beautiful one was feigning offense and then he saw her ducking Elise so it seems they were even. He laid back and kicked as hard as he could as if he were trying to push the end of the pool away. It felt good to splash. Suddenly Elise popped up beside him. She had approached underwater. He stopped kicking and looked into her face. The wet mop of her dark hair draped down to her shoulder. She was smiling and breathing hard. And her face was as beautiful as any he had ever looked into other than on a movie screen.

"What was I told your name was, Deeker, Decker, Depher? Stop me if I get it."

"Probably Wes said I am Deeter. My name's Dieterich but no one calls me that."

"Welcome to the Elias pool, Deeter."

"Thanks. Hey I'm sorry. I don't even have a guess at your name."

"Elise."

Alright here is where I do something right and not ask for the other girl's name; don't even mention her. "Is that your real name, Elise Elias?"

"Yep. See if you can say it five times without a mistake."

"Elise Elias. Sounds like I'm trying to decline a Latin noun. Let me guess your middle name. Wait while I think. I don't actually know any Latin. Is it Elaine? Elise Elaine Elias?"

"Could be. That's better than what Wes and Wanda came up with. Thanks for the suggestion." She ducked her head and swam underwater back across the pool to her parents. Dieterich imagined she was requesting a new middle name from them.

He took a full breath, pointed himself under the water toward the length of the pool and pushed off to see if he could get all the way to the other end without coming up for air. Then he backstroked the length the other way. He nearly ran into Wanda and definitely splashed the girlfriend, so he flipped over and went the last few yards with a breaststroke. The girlfriend was hanging onto the side and he apologized for splashing her. She cupped her hand and pushed a wave into his face. As he washed it off, she said, "Sorry. Were you saying something?" He started to say something, not sure what, when she expertly splashed him again. *I can win this*, he thought. *I've been in more and tougher water fights than her. But then this is different. Winning isn't piling more water on her and making her turn away to breathe. Not sure what I'm trying to do and really not sure what she is doing. I can't play with her and leave out Elise but it would be first rate fun, assuming she is playing and not actually mad at me. And I can't float a while to figure it all out.*

"You, win. You win." He lifted himself out of the pool and bowed in defeat. After a single second, he spotted Elise in the middle of the pool watching, then leapt high over the girlfriend and hit the water in a well-practiced form, holding one leg and leaning back so he created a double splash. He swam two strokes over to Elise.

"Can't you control your friend? She won't leave enough water in the pool for the rest of us."

Wes looked down on them and seemed to be laughing as he climbed up the ladder to leave the water. Elise said, "No one can control Miriam." She held onto the side of the pool and kicked water at Dieterich. He splashed back halfheartedly. He suspected Elise was pushing as much water as she could with one functional leg. Miriam came from behind and yelled something unintelligible as she attacked. It sounded conspiratorial so Dieterich assumed it was directed at Elise. This was a moment with high potential. He could in all fairness have grabbed one of the girls. He would not have dunked whomever he grabbed, just exerted control. It would have been too personal to hold her face-to-face so he would grab both arms and hold her from the side or from the back. What if he did a cross-chest lifesaving hold and carried Miriam down to the shallow end? He did a surface dive, his prettiest move, and swam under Elise, staying under water to the shallow end. He stood up and ran as if in terror up the wide cement stairs and out of the pool. He took up his towel, covering himself as he dried off, pleased that he did not have to display his skinny chest to the two lovely girls. Leave them to accept a little longer the illusion he was worth chasing.

"What was that all about?" Wes was smiling broadly. Dieterich thought he must be enjoying the sight of his daughter playing with a young, innocent man.

"Who knows the whys and wiles of the female? Those girls just turned violent all of a sudden. I guess they wanted the pool to themselves."

"They might let you back in if you behave."

"You know what, Wes? I think it would feel great to let the sun dry the drip outta my hair. I feel a hot day on the way."

Wes and Dieterich sat on aluminum-frame lawn chairs with webbing made of plastic strips that clung to their bare legs and talked about the trips Dieterich had taken in or around Detroit to service the company's customers. Wes was very pleased to hear Dieterich accepted moving to different cities every day or even more often. And he admired how easily Dieterich had learned to find the factories tucked away in industrial zones and then to get along with the men on the shop floor. Although he knew the company's products were not very complicated, he was surprised Dieterich had never yet failed to satisfy a customer.

Dieterich did not care about complimentary words from his boss. This was only a summer job. With complete sincerity, he pointed out the excellent guidance he received from Rusty and Freddy, mentioning specific tips they had given him that had already been useful on the job. For example, Rusty has noticed Dieterich hesitate before turning a screw and advised him to always have a nut and bolt for practicing the feel in his hand so he would never need to think about it again. Dieterich was already embarrassed to have taken a job his father got him rather than earning the job, thus, he would never consider working again for this company and had no use for a recommendation from Wes. Yet it was important to Dieterich to respect the work Wes and the company did. Michigan was a huge industrial complex that represented a major part of the practical economy, the environment for engineers, the "real world," as his father called it.

Dieterich had positioned himself so he could see the pool without facing it directly. He turned slightly from time to time when he heard a loud sound, a splash, a shriek, a yell. Those glances were too quick to see much but they were clear enough to keep an image of the two girls. Once he turned his eyes and saw Miriam posing on the edge, as if waiting for him to look, she held his gaze and dove ever so gracefully into the water. He did not turn back for several minutes. And then got up without a glance toward the pool, put on his T-shirt, and walked away to help Wanda set the table. He savored the image of the beauty performing for him but he would not acknowledge that pleasure to the world outside his head.

During lunch, Dieterich talked with Wanda about her job as a secretary for the School District Superintendent. Dieterich was making calculations in his head about how the combined salaries of Wes and Wanda might compare with his father's and whether that explained how they could afford a house nearly as nice as his family's. He also figured in the relative cost of raising his family's three kids versus the one girl here along with the cost of whatever excessive medical bills might have accompanied her handicap. All these estimations led to no conclusions but they occupied his mind while the Eliases prattled on about the tourism attractions of Michigan and the many achievements of Elise during high school. The only excursion in Michigan that appealed to Dieterich would have been a camping trip on Isle Royale but Wes confirmed that would be nearly impossible to arrange. Elise and Miriam mostly talked to each other. Miriam was going away with her family over the Fourth of July week to someplace in Ohio, probably visiting relatives. Elise seemed disappointed as if she had no other friends to go with her to the fireworks.

Strawberry shortcake for dessert! Of course, Dieterich had room for that. It was the apt cap to a lunch of mid-American cliches. He felt square for enjoying the day as he had. There was no harm in adding one more chestnut to the event. Wes suggested a game of horseshoes after lunch but Dieterich begged off. He tried to make an excuse about something else he planned to do but really had nothing to claim.

"You don't play horseshoes in Connecticut, I suppose. And not at college either, son? Time for another dip then?" Wes almost sounded like he wanted male company amidst the women.

Does he wish sometimes he had a son, a healthy one in a good college? I wonder if he will ever know what a poor son or son-in-law I would make. "Your household doesn't stick to the no swimming for an hour after eating? I agree with relaxing that rule, but I'm dry now so it'll be comfortable driving back like this." *That was a weak thing to say. Change the subject...* "But I have a question for you. I was looking for a bookstore to get something to read in the evenings. Is there one near the office? I might go there after work on Monday. Tuesday I'm off to Lansing. Freddy got me seeing four places up there. He did not figure I could get them all done in a day including travel. I'll phone on Wednesday morning to see if he has more assignments for me in the area." Dieterich hoped it did not sound like he was boasting about doing the job alone already. He had not meant to boast but he did mean to impress Wes so that was about the same thing.

"Freddy said you were ready. He thinks you're about as smart a guy as he ever met."

"No, he doesn't. He knows very well he and Rusty only trained me on the hardness tester and that's the easiest machine in the company. Freddy is just a generous guy. He said that to make sure I can take the trip. He knows it will make me more useful if I do the hardness tester repairs and certifications. It frees him up to handle the trickier things."

"Alright, let's not fight about it. We can agree Freddy's a nice fellow."

Wes said he did not know of a bookstore but he would ask around and find something for him on Monday. They shook hands. Dieterich thanked Wanda for arranging the lunch, especially the dessert, of course. He told Miriam she had been too vicious in the pool for his taste but that he appreciated meeting her. Then he turned to Elise and looked into her eyes and without having planned to do it, asked if she would show him the way to the Fourth of July fireworks. She turned her eyes toward her father and returned them to Dieterich a second later.

"Yes, Deeter. If the weather is good. I'll find out what time they're supposed to start. We haven't gone in a couple years."

"Me neither. It'll be fun. Bye everybody! Thanks for everything!"

5

"I know where there's black squirrels, Daddy," Nick said. "All right," said his father. "Let's go there."[5]

Sunday, June 22

The closest woodlands on Freddy's map appeared to be in Wenzel State Recreation Area, 900 acres with trails. He was not looking for the Rocky Mountains, just a day under the trees; see some birds, eat lunch by a pond if he was lucky. It was on 27 Mile Road, a typical Michigan address. He studied the road map from his glove compartment to see the pattern: east-west road numbers increase as you go north within a county, sometimes every mile, sometimes every half mile. It was like living on a cartesian plane. It was like New York City planning extended into the countryside. It was not like nature.

Few cars were in the lot when he arrived, but it was a large lot on a beautiful, sunny day so he expected to be sharing the trails most of the day. Without binoculars, he was not going to see many birds close enough to identify anyway. He felt ill prepared in every way, having only bread, cheese and a couple bottles of Coke in a grocery bag. This was fine. Some days are meant for spontaneity, although a less crowded place might be better suited for those days. He decided to walk away from the lot quickly, keeping ahead of the masses as they worked their way into the woods. That was a good idea that did not quite pan out. In his spontaneous mode, he

---

[5] Ernest Hemingway. "The Doctor and the Doctor's Wife," *In Our Time*, Bonnie & Liveright publisher, 1925.

had no trail map to show when he was approaching another parking lot. "Recreational areas" were meant to be accessible, and Wenzel had several entry points.

It had good forest trails, flat and wide, and undemanding of attention or effort. He could just wander and look for plants that were familiar or interesting or unfamiliar or otherwise attractive. Without a camera, or even paper and pencil to make a list of finds, he was free to roam aimlessly.

One lake, the largest he found at the park, floated a few quiet boats with fishermen. He had admired fishing as a hobby but never invested much effort in it and never eaten fish he had caught on a camping trip although he had tried fishing a few times. He needed someone to show him how it is done. A book might help but he did not like the idea of learning a wilderness skill by book. As the day warmed into summer heat, he preferred to keep to the small ponds where no one else was likely to be. He played his usual game of imagining he was far from the nearest road, living off the land except for the lunch tied onto his belt.

Some of the ponds were encircled by a trail and were marked by a sign giving them a name. These features conflicted with the premise of his game. After going most of the way around four or five ponds, he went up a hill and climbed the largest tree to find what direction showed the least effect of man. West looked good. He looked to the sun and to his watch so he could keep a constant direction and left the trails for the tiny wilderness ahead. Soon a power line crossed his path, an unwelcome intrusion, although it gave him a clear view in two directions. He saw no trails crossing under the wires and gained confidence that once he passed to the other side, he might be alone for a while.

He ate his lunch beside a pond twenty minutes farther on his westward line. He had not felt tired although he had walked steadily for nearly four hours. He settled on a gravelly part of the shoreline and leaned back comfortably on a log. He enjoyed the lower view of the lake from this position, and he enjoyed his own stillness, listening to the small lapping waves and the rare breezes and the sound of redwing blackbirds over in the reeds. In his imagination he slept for an hour in the shade but he was not sleepy and was soon bored with the scene he had aspired to enter. His shade had moved away from the log behind him so he was dripping with sweat even while keeping still. The small stones under him began to press too hard on his buttocks, begging him to shift his position every few minutes.

He imagined a different scene for himself alone in the wilds. He stripped off his clothes and waded into the pond. The bottom was silty mud which squeezed between his toes and around his feet as deep as his ankles. The water felt cold, but he knew that was only the contrast to his sunny spot on land. It deepened quickly and he could swim with a full, natural stroke. He rolled on his back to inspect the shore behind and be sure he would easily find his way to his clothes. Then he swam hard for the opposite shore. A few cattails grew there, not as many as on the north side of the pond where the redwings were calling out their property claims. He did not swim among the reeds but turned to the south, paddling along the edge as if he were in a canoe looking for bitterns and rails and snapping turtles. His foot touched the muddy bottom when he kicked so he moved away from the shore. He soon felt he had conquered the pond and looked for the place where he had come in. He did not recognize it but he knew it was toward the north end and he cruised in a mixture of crawl, side-stroke and dog paddle until he saw it. When he stood on the gravel shore, he was cold again which was fine with him because he knew he would be hot soon. He wiped off the water with his hands as much as he could and then skipped stones for a few minutes until he was dry enough to dress.

He knew he was only twenty minutes west of the power line and was likely to stumble on a trail soon after that. There would be signs pointing the way to the parking lots. He would be in his car well before dark. He hoped he got back too soon to feel much thirst. Two Cokes were not enough liquid for a day in the sun.

| Monday, June 23 |

On Monday morning, Dieterich was certain he had arrived at work exactly on time. The receptionist was not at her desk, which did not bother him. Her hours were none of his business. It did bother him that neither Rusty nor Freddy was in the shop to give instructions. He did not want to be sitting stupidly on a stool when Wes or one of them came in. He decided to take apart one of the hardness testers he had used in his training. First, he laid out his tools on a rag in the formal way Rusty had recommended. He hoped to get enough parts out of the machine to be clear he had shown initiative and started right away on something. He had only removed the cowling before he heard Rusty, standing at the door of Wes' office. Although Rusty was speaking loudly, Dieterich could not understand his words. He recognized Wes laughing at them before the door closed. Rusty came in the shop and nodded at Dieterich as he walked by to get his lab coat from its hook. Then he was ready to speak.

"Good morning, Deeter. Feelin' good enough to go out with me to one of the Ford operations today?"

"Sure. Are we leaving right..."

"What the hell you doing to that poor ol' boy? Don't you know how many times that machine's had his guts spilled out on the table already? He's never going to read hardness any better than he did when you came in this morning. Put his clothes back on and let him have some peace and dignity in his old age. It's more than I'm likely to be gettin'."

Rusty had Dieterich drive them. He said it was so he could see if Dieterich could drive properly but he made no comments on the driving. The big car manufacturers did not have factories all around Detroit, like Dieterich expected. The Ford operation was in a large building but seemed to occupy only a tiny section on the second floor. They entered from a metal staircase on the building exterior, so Dieterich never saw what else was in there. He did not see the Ford logo or name on a sign or on the paperwork they had signed at the end of the day. Rusty said they were in a testing lab for the Mustang division but Dieterich never saw the word "Mustang" all day either. The only person in a lab coat was Rusty. They were recertifying each tester in a row of ten.

Dieterich did not how the testers were being used but Rusty subtly played the professor all day, eventually giving out enough hints that Dieterich understood that when parts were delivered from contracted manufacturers, they might be sent to the laboratory and tested against the order specifications. Sometimes every part was tested in various ways in addition to hardness.

Other times a sample was tested. Either way, many parts were likely to come in at once so having a bank of hardness testers was efficient for them to get the parts out to the assembly plant quickly.

After they returned to their own building, Rusty went over the invoice to be sure Dieterich understood what was needed even though they had gone over the invoice form several times before and the forms were essentially self-explanatory anyway.

Wes asked Dieterich to stop in his office before going home.

"I did my homework," he told Dieterich. "If you want to get a magazine or stationery or something like that, you can go to the drugstore in Richmond Hills. It's pretty good on those things. There's a decent bookstore at the shopping center on 11 Mile Road in Royal Oak. Maybe that one has best sellers and gift books, according to Wanda... you remember her name, my wife."

"Of course, Wanda. She's the one with the smiles and the parsley sprinkled on the potato salad."

"Yes. Or there should be a good bookstore at Wayne State University. That's probably the biggest one in Detroit. Uh, it's right downtown... a Black school mostly, I gather. Oakland University's up near you in Rochester. The school's pretty big, a state school. Here, I got the addresses written down.

A good bookstore is unlike a good grocery store. The grocery store has everything you want in the quality you want at a good price. The bookstore leads you to ideas you never had and some items better than you could imagine and offers some books at a price below what you thought fair. The bookstore Wes recommended to

Dieterich was large but not a very good one. He entered with the general idea of getting something entertaining for his evenings and, possibly, something to build momentum for at least one of his classes next year. Calculus came to mind. He'd gotten a D, indicating he had not learned the subject well but he had thought he understood it when it was presented in class. Still, he had to admit he could not do the problems on the test. Maybe, he wondered, he lacked something engineers need to solve concrete problems, like the ones on his tests, but he had a grasp of the theory. He could talk about calculus much better than one would expect from a D student. He knew the history of calculus and what sorts of uses it had and what symbols were used to write out problems to be solved. So he looked for a calculus book that might have problems to solve and show how to solve them. He was proud to ask the store clerk to point out where the math books were shelved.

There were four books with "Calculus" on the cover in a large font. He leafed through the one that seemed least academic. It had a bit on history in the opening chapter. Dieterich dismissed that part as too elementary for him. He recognized the graphs and Greek letters in the following chapters although by the time he was at the midpoint of the book, he knew it was dealing with issues he had not even been assigned to learn yet. He looked in all four books to see if they had an appendix of problems with their solutions. None of the books was organized in that way but three of the four had problems at the end of each chapter with some explanation of how to answer them. Dieterich realized he felt bad about failing at school even though he rarely thought about it consciously.

Whatta jerk. I coulda done the damn calculus. I'll need it for something later, for getting a degree if not for an actual job. I am the kinda guy that knows things like calculus. I just assumed it would pop into my brain. Isn't that about the way I learn everything? It usually worked in high school. Get outta high school, boy. I gotta do the homework now. College isn't as much fun as everyone said it would be. It's the first step to getting on my own. Be somebody. I'm not going to make it, get a great wife, do an important job, take trips to strange places - not on the basis of my good looks or my fastball, or my charisma. I need to be smart.

He needed to be smart but that meant doing well at what he was doing this summer, not what he failed to do last winter. With his record, showing D in calculus, he would need to take the whole class again. He had a head start from the theory he had picked up on the first time through the class. With better resolve than he had last year, he would be all right. Today he would look for something entertaining, not a comic book, not soft-core porn, not fancy literature.

Dieter's thoughts on calculus were self-deprecating as they needed to be but they were not exactly fair to the truth. The truth is that he was already over-confident in his first term when he took Calculus I. He had scored above average for Lehigh students on his math SAT and expected to enjoy calculus. He had a good head for math, according to that test. He sat near the front of the lecture hall during calculus classes and did initially enjoy the professor. She spoke very clearly and logically. The symbols she introduced were not hard to remember. He did not mind reading the assigned chapters in the calculus book, although he might have taken advantage of his interest in the subject to show off a little by reading it in the dorm lounge where the book title might be noticed. By mid-November he was imagining graduating as an engineer to take advantage of this talent and interest. While taking the mid-term exam before Thanksgiving break, he felt betrayed. She did not ask him to explain the principles she had taught and he had learned. She did not use graphs to illustrate concepts. The test was straightforward numerical problems, like the ones in arithmetic in elementary school, only harder because they could not be worked out on fingers and toes.

He knew the theory, he thought, the rest should be simple. But engineers do not care about why the second derivative of displacement can represent acceleration. They just replace the Greek designations with numbers and get a result, a thoughtless, mechanical exercise prone to small errors precisely because it was not founded on deep understanding. Engineers were satisfied by being close enough. He, Dieterich, might fit better as a theoretical mathematician. He made errors on his exam not from poor understanding but because he had not rehearsed the placing of information into the formulae and tended to confuse which of the measurements was relevant to the problem at hand. That was the stuff of homework, not listening in class and reading the book.

He managed a C on the mid-term and stopped reading the book at all. It was hard work to do the homework based on the lectures. He started to see the game that engineers play instead of fundamental mathematical comprehension, and he did not enjoy that game or feel its relevance to the non-engineering career that lay in his future. He had a C- on the final and a C- for the term.

His professor in Calculus II was not as easy to understand in class. He hardly spoke to the students, constantly facing the blackboard and speaking to it instead. No one raised a hand to ask a question since the hand would not have been seen. A few times someone shouted a question and sometimes even then it was ignored. Dieterich altered his goals. He only wanted to get a C and get out of the engineering program without damaging his academic record. Although he had never aspired to engineering, it had been a career he could visualize and without that idea, the wide world of options was overwhelming. Every other career he could imagine was childish or impossible. The long run did not trouble him greatly. He had talent enough to find a niche. First, he had to finish the term and get into a more appropriate college. A C in calculus would not be good on his record but it should not be a severe barrier to a career that does not require it, like most things people do.

His midterm grade was a slightly encouraging C-. All he needed was a C on the final to get a C overall and then be done with calculus for life, although he could forever say he had taken and passed it at Lehigh, a school known for engineering. If he had applied himself toward raising his grade he might have gotten that C or, possibly, better. He saw no reason to waste energy on getting better. He had other classes not likely to return him any glory. The final was on the last morning before summer break. Since it was his last exam, he had not crammed for it yet. His only preparation was to attend the last class, a week earlier, and take careful notes during the summary for the term. He also scheduled taking a nap before dinner so he would be able to stay up late, possibly all night, to focus on calculus one last time.

He now knew the theory and application of derivatives from first term, even better than his passing grade implied. He needed the same facility for integration. It was used for different problems but was built on the same background. With the guidance from that last lecture, he compiled a list of the kinds of problems possible on the test. There would be no surprises like he experienced in the first term; he understood the limited concerns of engineering calculus. Then he went through the book and wrote out the formulas that would be used.

It was only ten p.m. and he had the basic knowledge on the page in front of him. He knew what all the symbols meant although, obviously, this was not arithmetic, and the calculus operations are not as obvious. Still, having the formulas was a major step. After all, he only needed a C. He had filled two pages with his formula collection and began to visualize the smallest piece of paper that would hold them, using both sides, of course. He could write them on two pages small enough to hold hidden in one hand. Equipped with a precis of the term, he might do better than a C. He reasoned: even if he had been going to all the classes and taking good notes and working the homework, he would not necessarily have absorbed all the formulas.

What is fair in taking a test? Does it matter if the test is only to facilitate moving onto a more appropriate course of study? It was not like the test a doctor takes before treating patients, or even like one an engineer takes before designing a bridge. No one would ever care how much calculus he knew back in May of 1969.

The clock-radio on the small pine table the dorm had provided as a desk showed nearly eleven p.m., a little past his usual bedtime. He was not tired. He could study for a few hours and still fit in some sleep. The exam was at eight am, unfortunately early. He set his alarm for six thirty and checked it carefully to be sure he had done it right. He compared the time with his watch. They matched. It was time to finish his studying. He looked through the formulas and flushed cold when he did not recognize some of them. He placed a name or some few guiding words next to each formula, even the ones he knew, to remind him of their use. It was a good document. He rewrote it completely on three full pages so the formulas were shown clearly and as he wrote he imagined the use for the one he was writing. Then he wrote them out again on three pages, again, not merely arranging Greek letters and calculus symbols, but thinking of their application.

At four a.m., he counted how many pages he had written. He had 76 pages. Then he threw them all in the wastebasket and started writing three more pages without looking at a previous draft. He threw these away as soon as he finished them until he estimated he had filled one hundred pages. He took the last three pages and compared them to the first three. They were identical and he was nearly ready for the exam. He laid on the bed and took a power nap of ninety minutes, then took a shower and put on fresh clothes. There was time for a light breakfast in the dining hall. Only six other students were there so early on the last day of exams. He did not recognize anyone.

The test had five questions and two hours to complete them. The time was not a problem because

Dieterich left three of them blank, having no idea how to proceed. He thought he did a good job on one of them and he thought he had the right formula on another one although he could not simplify the formula into a form that answered the question. He struggled with his three blank responses and considered writing out some formulas in case the professor would recognize something appropriate to the question and assign partial credit. Or maybe he would simply have sympathy for someone who clearly had learned something. In the end, he did not write any formulas as guesses and hung his hopes on the grading curve. The prof would not flunk everyone nor would everyone get most of these problems. He was right to expect a curve and the prospect of partial credit. Very few did get all five problems right. Getting four right or three with additional partial credit was worth a B. Two right without partial credit on the others was given a D. He did get partial credit on one problem but the curve was not nearly steep enough to pass him.

He could have met with the professor in the next term to see exactly how he did but there was no point in doing so. The professor was generous enough to grant him a D for the course, given his passing the midterm.

His grade in Philosophy, which he had abandoned early in the term and where he hoped the professor had forgotten he existed, combined with his grade in English where his term paper had been too short, too late and too stupid for professorial sympathy, and his grade in Biology II, a subject that did not touch on anything large enough to be seen with the naked eye, left no room for debate about returning in the fall. He was advised by the Dean's office to take off a year and demonstrate some maturity by holding a good job in the interim.

The Dean had not taken account of Deiterich's draft eligibility. Taking a year off was not actually possible. He would be back in school in the fall somewhere, looking for some easy credits and better study habits. His mother would take care of the paperwork to apply and his dad would pay whatever it took. They, mother and dad, would collaborate in selecting the school. Dieterich was to work in a solid job in Michigan and then go to the school they gave him.

Dieterich knew he would never read a calculus book to pass the time in the evening in his room, even if it might do him some good. George Schaller was an author he recognized favorably although he could not name a book by him. The shop carried *The Deer and the Tiger* which had come out recently. It was about wildlife ecology in India as told though the relationship of tigers and their primary prey. This was a book to respect, not a field guide, but an analysis. The summary on the book flap spoke of the importance of ecology. Dieterich knew the term although it had never come up in any class and he doubted he knew anyone who could define it. This was a field he could embrace. He paged through the book envying the author for his knowledge and experience but mostly for his finding a way to do something so exciting. India was not the right place to begin. Maybe there was a textbook on ecology. It might be a grown-up's version of the Nature Merit Badge handbook. That would be a good start.

The clerk said he carried no textbooks but had a section on nature. Dieterich always looked through the nature section of bookstores but he never bought books that were not required for a class. He had a different mindset now: maybe he wanted to learn something, maybe he wanted to figure out what he should be doing instead of engineering.

He fingered a paperback copy of Aldo Leopold's *Sand County Almanac*. It was not what he was seeking, not an answer to either quest: getting ahead in school or figuring out who he was yet it was hard to put down. He read a few passages and they said things he would like to have said. It spoke of familiar, wild places with deep appreciation. It was not a recent book, but it seemed completely relevant. And then he saw his goal for the summer. He would take a step toward being an ecologist but not the way a course at a school would do it; he would write an almanac - take notes on the natural world as he observed it, not research but appreciation. *Sand County Almanac* would provide a model. Sand County was in Wisconsin; he was in Michigan, separated by the lake. He bought a blank journal to be the draft of his almanac.

6

Friday, July 4

All day on the Fourth, Dieterich was thinking of meeting Elise to see the fireworks. He could identify dozens or a hundred stresses in their date. His unconscious mind would conjure a risk, a danger, a trap, a responsibility he would face that evening and he would immediately put it aside with his conscious mind. Why had he not asked out Elise's friend? That would have been a leap toward maturity: a girl that sexy and smart and just the right age. Impossible! That would have been an embarrassment, one that may have gotten back to Wes, and he might see it as an insult to his daughter. In avoiding that embarrassment, he made a date he did not want with Elise and it looked embarrassingly as if he did it to impress his boss with gallantry.

The fireworks were a good idea; he should have used it to invite Cathy, the waitress, assuming he could find a way to do that without looking a fool. What was done was done and now he had to finish what had begun.

He might buy a six-pack except that he did not like beer. The thing was too casual to make a fuss with preparations. You can't take flowers to see the fireworks. It was fundamentally easy. Just show up on time at the Elias' house. Be friendly. She would know the way to the lake. Watch the fireworks. Tell her about seeing fireworks back home one year. Remember to ask her some things, like when she watched fireworks in the past. The process of getting through the day was much like the way he handled his challenges at school. When class was coming up in a half hour and he was not prepared, he would wander off toward the library where he would be doing something educational, if not exactly what he ought to be doing and then, along the way to the library, he would turn off the path and head over to the stream to see how high it was that day, and somehow the obvious guilt due him would fade behind the scene his eyes beheld where he placed all his attention and one more missed class seemed unimportant. He could learn whatever was in that class by reading later. There were many ways to learn and he preferred the ones that came later to the ones available in the present moment.

"Now go down that dirt road on the left," Elise directed. Lake's down below. We can park anywhere on the grass."

Picking up Elise had been very smooth. He jumped out of the car to knock on the front door, expecting to say something to Wes and smile more than usual when he first saw Elise, but she came outside before he was halfway to the door and she went straight to the car. He managed to open the door for her but did not hold out a hand to help her get in. It might have seemed patronizing. She needed no help.

The drive to the fairgrounds by the lake took twenty minutes. Elise did most of the talking while Dieterich pretended to need to focus on driving, asking her questions whenever he could think of something appropriate. She had lived in Ypsilanti until high school. Two years of that time she lived in a hospital, dealing with whatever condition led to her withered leg. She liked living here; was active in her church's youth group; sang in the high school choir. She had graduated from high school a year ago but stayed on for a post-graduate year. She had fairly good grades, acceptable SAT scores but had not taken the most challenging courses so the University of Michigan admission office suggested she prove herself with Calculus I and Journalism and Chemistry II. He did not engage her in discussing calculus theory.

"Where should we park?" Dieterich felt it was a bad question. He should suggest a place, not ask her to be in charge now that she had already guided them here. And asking where they should "park" might sound a little like he was thinking of making-out, which he was not.

They settled far enough away from the lake to have a view over the cars to come. He turned off the engine. The Rambler American sedan had a bench seat so it would have been possible to snuggle up at some point. Her weak leg was on the right, away from him. He looked her way with his full smile, but she was not looking back his way. *She is a pretty girl. Got to admit that. Way better looking than me. Except for... Not to my taste though. Kinda short. Not very womanly, whatever that means.*

"Does the radio work in this hot rod?"

"It'll play the stations. Can't promise it's got good tunes on it."

"What's good for you?"

"The short answer'd be Motown. Since that's where we are, it ought to be on the air?"

"Motown? We're in Rochester Hills. That's farther away from Motown than wherever you came from, what is it, New York City?"

"I'm from the outer suburbs of the City - in Connecticut. I've only been to the City a few times, mostly to see the Museum of Natural History with my mother. But we do get radio stations from New York. Cousin Brucie – you ever hear of him?" Elise looked at him blankly. "Murray the K? Wolfman Jack?"

"I don't know, maybe. Big city DJs? You live near the center."

"You're the one next to Motown. I hear New York radio but I'm not that much into popular anything. My folks are old-fashioned, square you know, and I'm the same. Don't really want to be. Just don't know how to get out of it."

"You're going to college. That's where it's happening."

"Not Lehigh. We're trying to be engineers, not rock stars."

"But you said 'Motown'. Was that just showing off?"

"No, that's real. Marvin Gaye: *Heard It Through the Grapevine*, Smoky Robinson, The Temps..."

"What's the best of theirs."

"Best? I couldn't pick one but I'll say *I Wish It Would Rain*. What do you like?"

"I can't believe you didn't say The Beatles. Every album so different, every song a hit, A side and B side."

"Okay, did you think *Sergeant Pepper* was better than *Revolver*?"

"They don't have to compete with themselves. Who could have guessed something like *Sergeant Pepper* was coming?"

"I liked *Eleanor Rigby*. That was unique."

"But you're saying you're not into the Beatles?"

"Right. Gotta respect the range, like you said. And gotta respect the quality of performance."

"You like them wearing suits, like Gary Puckett?"

"I'd change the station if he came on."

"What albums do you have at home?"

"Nothing. We don't have a record player. I don't think I ever hear the radio play at home either."

"I play singles in my room. My folks play Andre Kostelanetz in the living room."

"I'd like to hear some of your collection someday."

"That could happen."

"I pledged a fraternity at Lehigh. We have a ritual kind of hazing. Ate some stupid food, raced around the frat house naked in the dark. One thing was we had to sit blindfolded in a room for one hour while Leslie Gore singles were playing at top volume."

"And that was your torture?"

"That was damn stupid, all of it. I didn't quit, of course, but I knew it was stupid."

"What do you want to do with yourself, I mean, in life?" Elise abruptly shifted the topic and the seriousness of the conversation. Dieterich wondered if this was the second of her prepared questions to take them up to the fireworks. If so, he did not mind. He did not answer immediately. He had no idea what to say, but it was effective to delay as if he were framing some insight.

"You're right, I think. That is a question befitting the setting: a guy and a girl on their first date, waiting for the fireworks."

"It's not my first date."

"I'm sure you knew my meaning. You and me. Getting to know a little more."

"So this is a date? And you think I want to know more about you?"

"Maybe not more about me, but that's how your question must appear to anyone listening in. The car windows are open... No, it could be you just want to hear what someone our age is thinking about the rest of his life. It's a good question anyway you might have been motivated to frame it. I too have been on a date – dates - before but none of them got as far as a question like that. One got into the poem *The Groundhog*. The groundhog in the poem is dead and rotting. I did not know the poem then and did not handle the conversation well but I read the poem later and still admire that girl a year later. I never saw her again though."

"You want to study the question and admire me a year from now?"

"No, I'd like to take a try at an answer. ...It's getting darker. We ought to get out of the car."

"They won't be starting real soon."

"I like this big field, it's open space around and above, being part of the place and the event and the crowd. Let's sit on the hood."

"I look better sitting here."

"I don't look good at any angle but I don't think about that."

He reached into the back seat and picked up the blanket he had brought from his bed. When he was outside the car he felt the car hood to be sure it was not warm and then spread the blanket on it.

"Like that," he said, pointing to a car thirty feet behind them where a couple sat on the front of their car, leaning their backs against the windshield.

"I can't get up there."

"You were pretty agile in the pool. I'll give you a boost."

Dieterich scooped her up, one arm behind her back and one behind her thighs, and placed her on the hood. Then he slid her and the blanket up to the windshield. She was not heavy but it seemed to be a powerful gesture.

Before he fully settled himself on the car hood, not very near her, Dieterich began his answer. "The true answer is I don't know what I want in life, not specifically... not what it should be either or what it is likely to be. Do you have a vision of your future?"

"I do. I have some clear ideas of what I want. Not sure what I'll get. But you're in college, tell me what you are trying to learn. And then I'll ask you why you are learning that."

"Oh man! You're so far off already about me. I might as well tell you about it a little. Me? I'm not trying to learn anything at school. And since that's true, I can boast I am pretty damn good at not learning anything."

"And are you rebelling against the war or your parents or capitalism or what?"

"It is kind of you to suggest I have a rational reason behind me. No, I am not rebelling against anything. That would be too cool for me. I'm not sure why I am so lazy. I tend to do what my parents want. My teachers think I am respectful. I don't go to demonstrations although there aren't many to go to at Lehigh anyway."

"So maybe being rich makes you lazy."

"Probably a factor. I sure don't feel rich. We don't have a pool at home like you, or anything else that looks rich - what I would call rich. This crappy car you're sitting on belongs to the company, not me. But yeah, I never needed money yet, not to eat or get clothes or pay tuition. Maybe I would try harder if I felt hunger. I doubt it though."

"I don't believe this story. You making fun of me. You got into a damn good school. My Dad says you're smart and reliable and hardworking. You sound like an English prof when you talk. What are you going to be?"

"I sound like an uncreative white boy from the suburbs. Would I sound more credible if you knew I was kicked out of school? After this summer I hope to be in a school so desperate for applicants that it will take me despite my grades last year. Hey, let's get to a rosier topic, say, like what do want to do in life."

"All that's real? You gotta stop now if it's a joke. I'm not laughing and I will be a bitch of a problem if you're making fun of me. I know I'm not much of a date but I won't take any humiliation."

"I am smart enough to know a joke that bad before I tell it and I would not disrespect you or anyone else. I'm inexplicably lazy, maybe spoiled rotten, but not rude or cruel. Truth is, I like you plenty and offer you more honesty for your question than I've ever given anyone."

She was sitting upright and staring at him. She turned away and laid back on the windshield.

He asked "Could you show me the example of someone in better control of her future than myself?"

"No, not me, not yet. But what do you like to do?"

"Funny thing is, I am a happy person. That doesn't make sense with my failure at school and how school figures into everything at my age. No way would I want to be dependent on my parents forever even if that is all I've done so far. I've worked; worked every summer in high school. I was not lazy mowing lawns or working construction or any of my jobs. Not lazy working for your dad either. I figure I'll get some kind of job when I finish college. ...Still pretty sure, real sure, I will get through college eventually. I won't have a particular profession, like law or medicine or chemistry. I won't do sales either. Not fixing cars, not teaching, not politics, not farming, not... not anything I can think of. There's got to be a lot more options. Say, like what your dad does. I don't really know what that is just like I don't know much about what my dad does. They probably did not come out of college ready to make a profit for some company."

"I was asking what you like to do, maybe outside work."

"OK, let's start there. I like walking in the woods. I mean, I really like it. Not just forests, of course, any natural place. It's more than a pastime. I am connected to the wilds like I am a part of them more than here. This part of the world, where most people live and work and do all the important things, is the shadow. Time here is borrowed from the real world. It's where there are few people and infinite mystery. I love the way everything exists together, not like heaven where harmony reigns but where life can flourish amid all these connections and competition and somehow for no rational reason it is so amazingly beautiful. Maybe I should be a park ranger but probably not anything that requires me to know much detail, like a biologist. This question has me feeling pretty damn worthless.

"So what? I'm pretty damn worthless. We all are, aren't we?

"Yeah, probably so. But I don't want to be worthless. I have some advantages. I'm not as dumb as my grades imply. I just got to get over this laziness thing. Somehow, I got to see how to live my life responsibly like I do the job for your dad's company."

"Yeah, your dad's a big shot, right? He must put some pressure on you."

"I guess he's pretty big. He sure wants me to be something important and he imagines important means managing a company. He does not pressure me except by having expectations for me. You know, I want to make him proud but more than that I need to be myself. I really like him. He's really ambitious. Competitive too. I'm easy and I like my friends to be easy. I play sports for fun, not to win. Fun is sometimes doing a good play, making a hit, being smooth and seeing my friends do those things. I don't enjoy putting down the guys I'm playing with. My Dad does not get that way of thinking. He always wants more. There's no such thing as success in his world, only striving. He'd not describe it that way."

"So doesn't he want success for you?"

"Sure. He wants it a lot. Way more than I do. But I think he's right in a way. At my age, it is important to succeed: do well in school, learn how the world works. Later I could get relaxed; later, after I have a good job and a reputation and I know how to do something useful. My best skill before this summer was how to mow the grass in a suburban lawn. I am actually good at that. Now this summer I know how to fix hardness testers."

"Yeah, that's more than I can do. You like doing it?"

"I am surprised. I do like it. I like going around the state like I know how to get something done. No one needs to supervise me. This guy I work with, Freddy, has a life built on this. But he's expanding the things he can repair and he's looking into sales. I can visualize doing his job better than I could think of doing my father's job. Mostly I know he goes into an office and works with papers.

Dieterich thought of Freddy. *He likes his work and knows how to do it well. Still, he wants more money and sees a way to get it. He has a girlfriend and a trailer to get himself started. He's got a good, practical plan. I believe he will be just fine in life. Am I a snob,* Deeter wondered, *to think Freddy's future is so completely unacceptable for me, to insist there must be more to life than Freddy would ever experience and that I should, and can, get it? Except for an inexplicable and obvious character flaw, things will pull together for me. I just know it. I'll get out of my skinny teenage stage. A really great girl will see my potential. I know it has to be.*

"There's more cars coming in." Elise sounded loud, maybe from the quiet of the past few moments, maybe because she thought he was falling asleep. "Most folks are spreading out beside the lake. Want to go down there?"

"Well, I know we've got to get off this car. I'm getting stiff from this halfway sitting."

Dieterich rolled himself off the hood and almost fell because it was higher than he expected, and his feet did not touch the grass until his weight had left the blanket. But he took one awkward step forward and caught himself. When he looked back to see if he had embarrassed himself, he saw Elise sliding herself and the blanket forward, about to drop off the front of the car. In three quicks steps, he was in the spot to catch Elise as she fell. She giggled as if she had challenged him intentionally and he had won. She hopped on one foot while he steadied her. He held her hand after she was balanced and then let her limp in her clumsy but secure way around to the passenger-side door.

Dieterich was stunned. The feel of her in his arms for a second and the pressure of her falling against his chest had been electric. It had been entirely innocent on his part but he felt otherwise, not guilty, yet thrilled suddenly by a body he had not wanted to experience, too much a stranger, accidental, so the excitation seemed to be legitimate, perhaps even deserved. He wondered if she had felt it and if she might have even arranged it. Would a girl of her age and attractiveness, with a handicap like hers, have thought about hooking a boy like him by falling into him? Would she have done this before? Or was this brief incident nothing but a minor accident overblown by his naivete?

"So," Dieterich asked while he was stowing away the blanket, "have you been here every year?" She did not reply. "I mean, the last few years, like a family outing kind of thing?" He settled in behind the steering wheel.

"We came a couple times. When the weather was right. They put it off sometimes a day or two until the sky's pretty clear or the clouds are high up at least. We

never went if the fireworks weren't on the Fourth. Last
year I just skipped them. Artie was ten last year and he
really wanted to go. I guess I'd seen them enough to skip
a year."

"Who's Artie?"

"Oh yeah, sorry. He's my cousin. We always went
with his family."

"Well, I've only been, oh, three or four times ever.
And not in a while. We live in a funny kind of town, just
residents and schools, no jobs, no community activities.
My Dad commutes into the city, New York. Takes the
train like somebody in an old movie. You know the book
Man in a Gray Flannel Suit? People do stuff with
churches, yes, and the synagogue. With the schools too,
of course. But the town government? I never heard of it
doing anything but paving the streets."

"You go to public school? The town government
probably runs them?"

"Oh yeah, sure. I do go to public school. I used to,
I mean. Lehigh's a private school. Anyway, I don't think
the town has fireworks. I've got a younger brother, like
you, and a younger sister. I don't think they've ever seen
fireworks. Too bad. It's really a big thing the first few
times, don't you think? You hear about celebrating like
that and you think you'll do it all your life, once a year.
Love your country's history and its values while you're at
it. Like you said, it just isn't that exciting when you know
what it is. There's no surprise. All the flashes and bangs
become familiar and they're still exciting in a way. Not a
memory of past wars, righteous wars, the country's
freedom from, from Britain, I guess. But it's not about
Britain. We aren't mad at them anymore. They're our
best friends unless you count Canada separately.
FREEDOM FROM OPPRESSION! So I don't pay a whole
lot of attention to the news and never went to a

demonstration but I do know we've got a war going on now and it is not clear to me why but I don't see it's got anything to do with American freedom from oppression."

Elise giggled some more. "Do you know what you are even talking about?"

"No, no I don't. Not at this moment and hardly ever. I did when I was saying I love the wilds. I am going to see all the national parks during my lifetime. Before I am thirty, if things work out right. I'll celebrate this country for saving those places. Let the fireworks stand for that: the color, the excitement, the surprise, the brilliance of nature preserved from human industry!"

"Good to hear now you have a reason to be here."

They sat quietly looking at the cars parking in jagged rows, filling the spaces nearby. A tinny loudspeaker began playing music, instrumental versions from the "American songbook."

"Elise, it is pretty nice to be talking frankly. It's not so common for me. But believe me when I explain, I was really looking forward to being here with you, to this minute right now. The fireworks and the holiday are OK for making an occasion. How else could I make a date with you? I don't know you well enough for a date, just the two of us. I'm used to knowing girls from class and church and, maybe, parties or something. I liked going out with you, knowing you better."

"How's it going?"

"Damn glad to be here with you, that's how it is with me." He wondered if she would offer her assessment of their date so far but he did not want to ask.

"I like your thing about making this a celebration of the national parks. I never thought of that. I never could have thought of that. Very smart."

"Really? Was that smart? I have good reason to wonder if anything smart is likely to come out of me.

Wait! Did I say that? I meant to just be thinking. You are doing something strange to me, girl, with this frank talk. Boundaries are fading. I have too many hang-ups. I know I should be working on that, so thank you. It's good to be with you."

Elise reached across herself with her right hand to punch him in the chest. He grabbed her hand and placed it gently in her lap and then took her left hand and held onto it.

"Let's keep the violence in the sky above," he suggested, and she answered "Peace" while holding up two fingers. They both looked out the windshield and waited as if they knew the show was about to begin. He still held her hand. She stroked his hand with one finger as if she were giving a massage. Neither spoke for some time, 30 seconds, a minute, two minutes; neither knew how long. Both were focused on the hands between them, wondering what they meant and why they seemed to matter so much. Finally, they heard a rush of hissing sounds and knew the opening round of rockets was rising. The rockets lit up the clouds high above them with unnatural colors followed by the delayed booms of their explosions. The crowd cheered after the booms, as if waiting confirmation that what they were seeing was real.

Dieterich suggested they go back to the hood of the car and Elise said she was comfortable just as they were. Dieterich regarded that positively although it seemed to mean they should not squeeze together and advance beyond their hand contact. There could be another day for them. This date need not set more records for his anemic love life.

"I forgot there was a crowd out there. It felt like we were alone among the cars, the machines, we the last of our species," Dieterich mused.

"Yes, I felt that too. For sure, they're out there. As far as I can tell, they're always out there. And it does not matter if they are. Every car is another planet, lightyears between them."

After a silence inside and out of the car while a new flight of rockets was being prepared, Dieterich spoke up again. "Reportedly I said something smart once. May I say something stupid now?"

"Go for it."

"Planets are very rarely separated by lightyears."

"You're right. That's pretty stupid for this moment."

"It was especially stupid since the thing you were saying about each car being its own planet and how those people out there don't matter, not to us right now - that was an especially smart thing to think up."

An explosion stopped the conversation and then several louder ones came fast but spaced evenly.

"Sorry. Did you say something?" Dieterich asked.

"Yes, I said 'thank you'. You know, because you called my little metaphor something smart."

"It was poetic, I think. At least it was an original metaphor in a conversational flow. That's a rare thing to do when you're sitting in a car. I don't know much about poetry. Too bad. My mother appreciates it immensely."

They watched a rocket climb and heard it still hissing when it exploded into a gigantic dandelion of light. The sound of the explosion came as the dandelion was drifting downward.

"Guess I was thinking about stars and planets 'cuz the sky up there's dripping with sparks."

A battalion of rockets went up together, trailing sparks that then disappeared.

"What was that all about?" Dieterich asked but the was no chance for a reply because higher up each rocket blew up again to release a shower of spiraling sparklers. They popped out of existence as they neared the earth.

The fireworks did not last very long and they were not as impressive as the displays Dieterich remembered from the July the family spent in Florida. Of course, they were better than the show he had watched from his bedroom window two years ago. It was on the horizon and he could barely hear any of the explosions.

After a quiet minute or more, the biggest display came up, obviously the final one. Cars all over the park honked their horns awhile and then began maneuvering out. Dieterich wondered why there were these displays. He'd been told they were to celebrate American independence. He thought they emerged from the War of 1812 rather than the American revolution, like the national anthem, a commemoration of the siege of Baltimore. So that did not exactly add up. He could not remember learning any more about why there was a war in 1812. Were fireworks on the Fourth celebrating war itself, and the fact that America had won all its wars? Except it was still an open question for Vietnam, of course. And didn't Korea end in a truce, a stalemate, not a win?

"So Elise, does all that light and noise make you think of America's glorious wars? I'm not making fun of patriotism. I'm asking for real what you think."

"I should think about that; should have an answer for you. The movement is not much in Rochester Hills but I know there's people our age who are protesting things. The war, obviously, but lots more than that. You know, we're getting too old to believe the stories they told us in elementary school. George Washington chopped down a cherry tree."

"He threw a silver dollar across the Potomac," Dieterich added.

"The war in 1861 was over state's rights."

"Good one. I heard it was the War of Northern Aggression," Dieterich noted.

"The Battleship Maine was blown up by Spain in Havana Harbor."

"I heard of that somewhere, but I forgot it. Spanish-American War, right? Teddy and the Rough Riders? That's all I know of it. Minor war."

"Vietnam attacked us in the Gulf of Tonkin, practically another Pearl Harbor."

"Did they? Is that why we're over there? I thought we were fighting Communism. Or are we fighting for Capitalism?"

"You better figure it out, Brother. 'Democracy' is the word we use. It could turn out to be why you get a free ride to Asia."

"Democracy? Are we fighting for that? How come I can't vote but I get a draft card?"

"I don't have a draft card either: too young like you, wrong sex, too crippled anyway." There was a heavy silence. Dieterich knew he should say something, but he could not find anything to say. He was thinking: *she has the worse deal by far.* He would not trade places with her. Even being so good-looking was nothing to mention.

Elise was not waiting for a reply. She had her own thoughts, and they were not in the realm of self-pity. "I don't need to be draftable to hate the war."

"God, Elise, I wish I knew enough to know for sure this war is not for some good reason. I should have paid more attention to it. It's easy to listen to the President and my parents and teachers. Even the minister in my church says it is necessary."

"Aren't you scared of going?"

"I've thought about that. We talk about it in the dorm, you know. No, I'm not scared. The jungle doesn't scare me. I'd like to see it. Even if I go, I probably wouldn't get hit. Most guys come back and move on with their lives. It not like being Vietnamese and your whole life you're in it."

"Almost all the cars are gone. Guess we ought to get going too."

"Not yet. One more thing." He was emboldened by still having her hand in his and feeling her rubbing his wrist with her thumb, a friendly thing without heavy sexual implication. "Let's arrange another date."

"I was really surprised when you asked me to come here. I was not thinking you noticed me at all, just your boss's daughter."

"Are you surprised now that I'm trying to ask you out again? I'm pretty surprised about it. I don't have one-on-one dates, just parties and a couple dances and the dances are really tough to get through."

"Good, 'cuz I don't dance. Maybe a movie. Have you seen *The Good, The Bad and the Ugly*?"

"I haven't seen it or hardly any movies. I'll look in the paper to see what's playing."

"Don't look too hard. We're going away on vacation starting tomorrow. When you get back, I'll call you. I don't have a telephone where I'm staying."

"Really? That should be nice for you."

"OK." When Dieterich started the engine, he had to withdraw his hand. He delayed before shifting into drive, turned to face her and kissed her, not intimately, not long, but on the lips and ending with the broadest smile he could remember ever forming on his face.

7

Dieterich woke early on Thursday, forty minutes before the alarm on his cheap, new, wind-up clock was set to ring. It was too exciting to sleep any longer. He would be on his own for a few days as much as if he were doing a hundred miles unaccompanied on the Appalachian Trail, carrying all he would need with him. The car was easier than boots and a backpack but the responsibility to accomplish something more than survive the time and distance was thrilling. He did not understand why he had not felt this way when he went to college, but he was certain this was different. He would not be confused this summer about when to have a good time – the parameters of the job were clear. What he did not comprehend was how he had seen college as all about himself; learning was to benefit himself while parties and football games and such were to entertain himself. That is how it was always presented to him, and he felt free to make his own judgement about which to do when. Any harm from a wrong choice accrued only to himself. In a job, he was to benefit the employer and/or the customer. He was paid for that, not being charged for it. Entirely different. His logic was highly flawed and that is part of why he was not satisfied by it. Emotionally, it was accurate enough.

First stop after breakfast would be a factory in Lansing. He knew the name and address which conveyed no hint of what they made. Every place he had gone with Freddy had been near Detroit and had some connection to the auto industry. He might be curious to see what they did in Lansing but it was not a good idea to ask about it.

Act as if you know something. You don't need to prove you've never been there or anywhere like it before. You're charging them seventy-five bucks an hour plus travel expenses (prorated among all the stops on this trip).

Dieterich had worked the previous summer in Rocky Mountain National Park and felt good he had saved two hundred dollars for nearly three months of work. He was no more than a shopkeeper with a beautiful backyard that summer, plenty good for his station in life he had thought. His station was rapidly changing.

Freddy said it would take an hour and a half to reach Lansing, probably less because Rochester Hills was closer than Freddy's trailer park. He had an appointment with the plant manager at 9:00.

Rusty had said: Don't be early and don't be late, and then be patient... The customer is assumed to be busier than we are... Three appointments a day is not busy... Minimum charge for time is one hour. If you can fix the problem in five minutes, give them an hour. Take the machine apart and clean everything. Inspect some parts with the loupe if you need to... The manager won't know what you're doing as long as you are moving quickly and systematically. The operator might watch and probably knows how everything works inside the machine anyway, but he won't care how long you take... Don't waste time and don't leave short of an hour. Give them 80 minutes and charge them for 60... The contract says we round off to the nearest half hour, but the rounding always goes in their favor... Once they've bought our machines, they're stuck with us but we don't take advantage of that in labor cost or effort. When we're in front of them, we give them a good deal... The company sticks it to them when they charge for parts which they only get from us. They understand. Nothing personal about that. Most of our customers are making parts for someone else.

Dieterich left early and skipped breakfast. He was in front of his first address by 8:15 so he drove around some more to find a place to eat. The café had a waitress older and, obviously, not as cute as Cathy. It would have been nicer if Cathy were there, but that thought was disloyal to Elise. How could he be disloyal? They were not a couple and were not going to be one, not in the scant time remaining in summer. After early September, they would not cross paths again in life.

He was back at the factory twenty minutes before his appointment. He waited five minutes in the car, looking at the cover of *Sand County Almanac*, afraid to start reading in case he lost track of the time. He checked his hair in the rearview mirror and felt his tie to be sure it was tight, then took his tool case with him to the main door. The street number was right but the sign on the door said "Mantelli Rotors," not "Mercury Auto Parts" like on his invoice. He felt his cheeks flush, and his mind flashed back to the moment he read the first question on his Calculus II exam. He was on time in the wrong place. He looked at the address on the invoice, which matched the street and number on the door. He went inside to ask if ownership had changed. He faced a small room with a smooth concrete floor and cinder block walls. The room was interesting, with a very high ceiling and a metal staircase like an indoor fire escape. The only furniture was a desk with three chairs, one behind and two in front. A receptionist sat behind the desk and a huge picture of a new Mercury car hung on the wall behind her. The two windowless metal doors were ajar but not open enough to see behind them.

With false confidence, he asked the receptionist if this was the right place to meet Ivar Krakow, and she said it was and added "Are you Mr. Kahler? Yes? I'll tell him you're here."

Dieterich watched the two doors until he heard Ivar Krakow clanking down the metal staircase. He wore a crisp white shirt, open at the collar with a loose tie and rolled-up sleeves, which Dieterich recognized as the uniform of an engineer. Dieterich squeezed as hard as he could when shaking the plant manager's hand before they stormed through one of the doors and down a short corridor to the working space for Mantelli Rotors. He understood why there was such a high ceiling in the reception room: the factory floor had cranes overhead. There was no assembly line, but he should have known that because this place apparently made, or did something, only with rotors, whatever those were; something round in at least one plane he supposed. It was noisy although not so much as to need ear protection. It might be loud enough over years of exposure to do some harm. There was a nice odor of machinery.

"We've got three of your Wilsons in this shop and one in the lab."

Dieterich had never heard the hardness testers called "Wilsons." It was easy to say – the name of his company – but they made other testing machines, so the name only works where only one kind is being used.

"And this is Sergei over here. He's the foreman of this area and he'll get you whatever you need. Sergei. Dieterich. He's gonna tune up the Wilsons for us, then you'll take him over to the lab."

Dieterich tightened the grip in his handshake as much as he could and managed to hold on long enough to be felt. Sergei had a looser grip but a hand too meaty for Dieterich to reach around completely.

Sergei looked serious and barely answered the plant manager's remarks. The handshake proved he understood what was expected of him. After the manager left, Sergei kept his eyes on Dieterich and pointed with his nose toward a nearby door with a glass window. Dieterich assumed the lab was behind that door and shook his head slightly as if they had completed a secret communication. Sergei began to talk so softly Dieterich wondered if he was only talking to himself. What was audible was not decipherable although his meaning was made clear enough through hand gestures. Dieterich was shown a place to spread out his tools and place the parts as the machines were disassembled, cleaned and inspected. Dieterich did not assume his English was understood so he accompanied himself with gestures to show he understood all he needed to know and got to work.

He looked over the first machine for any sign of damage, particularly in the alignment of the diamond tip. Then he tested the machine's performance by measuring hardness on some test blocks from his kit and noted the scores in his trip report form. The rest of the procedure came naturally. The parts had to be taken out in a specific order and each part had its own personality requiring a more or less unique, personal response from Dieterich. Everything was repeated on the other machines; no surprises, no challenges, nothing broken to add onto the cost. He signed and stamped the certification sheet for each machine. He was finished in two hours with the first three, which was a little faster than Rusty would have liked. Rusty was an advocate of moving deliberately to emphasize how complicated the tasks were, as if there was a subtle adjustment in the process for each machine.

When he finished with the machine in the lab and had his toolbox packed, he looked around for Sergei. He thought he should not be wandering around the factory unaccompanied but that is what he did in looking for Sergei. He could hear his father talking in his ear, proudly explaining what the heavy, noisy machines were doing, tasks beyond the ability of any man working with the hand tools that were the limit of Dieterich's experience until this summer. He was impressed and fascinated. He could see this was productive labor. If he had a class in using one of these, he would have felt the purpose in the training and would have excelled.

He watched a man drilling holes in a thick, shiny metal disk. He did not measure, just placed the disk against a form, a jig, and then stepped on a pedal. The drill bit descended at a pace consistent with its capacity to cut the hole while spirals of metal waste curled out of the hole onto the floor. He, that is, his machine drilled two sizes of holes, four of one and eight of the other, squealing with accomplishment despite the small jet of oil or water or something onto the bit. Water, Dieterich decided, was the coolant. Then the disk went into a bin on wheels, a specialized cart. He wanted to ask if he did the same type of disk all day and if he did other kinds of tasks that added some variety to his work. Perhaps he filled the cart with drilled disks and then took them to another machine for whatever else is needed to make a rotor. Is that disk a rotor or part of a rotor? Do they make anything other than rotors here? It would be a safety hazard to engage the worker with questions.

Sergei approached and Dieterich waved to show he had been looking for him, not staring at a simple task a professional like himself should find familiar.

"Ready you see Ivar now?"

"Just one thing first, Sergei. What the hell is a rotor?"

Sergei did not smile or frown, but he looked squarely at Dieterich. He said, "car brake" and held one hand forward as if to shake hands. Before Dieterich could reach out, Sergei added "rotor." He made a fist with his other hand and said "brake pad." Then he quickly rotated the front of his fist on the palm of his other hand, soon slowing the rotation and completed his explanation with "car stop." He pointed to his palm, the rotor, and added "Rockwell 80," implying that is the grade of hardness required on the rotor surface. Dieterich had to smile while he held up one thumb to indicate his comprehension and Sergei nodded supportively.

Two more factories with eight more hardness testers introduced Dieterich to chrome plating bumpers (toxic atmosphere) and to warehousing a diversity of metal connectors (bolts, sheet metal screws, rivets, etc.). Everyone was busy, everyone was courteous, and everyone seemed relaxed and content with whatever he was doing; no apparent stress, competitiveness, discomfort, boredom, rush or other industrial problems he expected to see in the fringes of the automotive industry. It was too small a sample to reach any conclusions about industrial work, but it was enough to warn him to distrust any preconceptions he had. It also encouraged confidence that the summer would pass pleasantly.

8

Friday, July 11

Problems turned up on Friday. Firstly, his hotel insisted he had reservations for the weekend, and he needed to pay for his room even if he did not use it. Apparently, Wes's secretary had made the reservation because she heard he was not returning to Rochester Hills until Monday afternoon. Wes had authorized his staying at the hotel all weekend, but Dieterich had never intended to use the hotel on Saturday and Sunday; never said he would use that overly generous offer from Wes. It smelled of pandering to a boss's son. He would be camping somewhere those nights. To further assert his independence, he checked out on Friday morning. He would camp out that night too. The hotel clerk gave in. There was not much he could do about it and he was not the hotel owner so did not care much anyway. That was a job Dieterich would hate to take: hotel clerk. He could imagine all kinds of unpleasant issues and difficult personalities involved in the business. All that struggle over the hotel room nearly made him late for his first appointment. He had only a cup of coffee for breakfast. He did not need to eat in the morning, but he enjoyed it when not pressed for time.

His first assignment was Magna, Inc. where chassis structures were created. That sounded like a solid heavy industrial component where more marvelous technologies would be on display. Certainly, raw metal was converted into valuable and recognizable form in their operation. Dieterich had a very hard time getting the second hardness tester apart. One bad screw can defeat the entire process. He began to sweat by 10 am after spending thirty minutes on one screw but felt very positive when it finally succumbed to his persistence, and yet he did not want to charge for more than the necessary time any more than he wanted to charge for less time than he actually spent. Someone needed to be a loser of this wasted time and it was hard to find a way to put the onus on himself without falsifying the paperwork. So he picked up the pace of his work and focused hard on remembering each step and each movement within each step. When he left Magma, he did not feel like looking around for self-education.

Then at Bosch, after lunch, where he quickly learned he might see brake pads, rotors and power brake assemblies compatible with the rotors and associated products at Mantelli, he felt pressure to get out early and find a place to stay for the night. *You have the rest of the summer for an inside look at the American auto industry. Don't feel you have to see everything there is to see,* Dieterich counseled himself. *That's impossible. You will see plenty. You won't change your personality and join the UAW or embrace an engineering career no matter what you see here. Worry about today first and tonight after that and the rest of your life tomorrow at the soonest.*

The problem with the second hardness tester at Bosch was not caused by his rushing to get out early. It showed up before he did anything to the machine. It was the first time the initial testing flashed a serious warning. When he used the machine to check the hardness of his known sample, it not only erred, it made different errors each time he ran the test. Rusty had mentioned this possibility and said it could only be fixed by returning the machine to his workshop. But he also said something about what could cause this and Dieterich had forgotten that part. It had not seemed worth learning since Rusty would be doing the repair. *Need to pay attention in class, not judge what parts of class to learn. If you knew that, you'd be the professor.*

He looked at the diamond tip through his loupe and saw no chip or imperfection. He examined the base of the diamond for anything unusual - maybe a dead fly was stuck on the bottom. And he reinserted the diamond assembly and felt it for any wobble, but it was perfectly firm. All these felt like possible causes and he felt proud for thinking of them but none of them explained the problem in this instance. If he called Rusty or Freddy, he would probably be told to just take the machine into Ferndale. He already knew that would be their answer so there was no reason to call. He stared at the machine until he could no longer see it because he was searching his memory for the comments from Rusty.

"Been having trouble with this one lately?" he asked the operator who had been assigned to help as needed.

"We don't use that one anymore. Guess we'd like to have it fixed."

Dieterich wondered if the defect had been mentioned to the plant manager. The work request only called for routine maintenance. He hated to give up on it and take it back to Ferndale. He would look like the junior repair man he actually was. He tried again to recall the day Rusty talked about this. One word came to mind and seemed relevant: leverage. One word was enough to start a new chain of logic. The harness tester worked by placing a known force on a diamond tip such that it sank into the material being tested. When the force was removed, the depth of the mark indicated the hardness of the material. Leverage came into play because the machine used a lever to generate different levels of force using just one weight, thereby simplifying the machinery. He tore into the mechanism to look at the lever, a piece he normally scarcely inspected. It was just a simple, shiny stiff rod with several insertion grooves for the fulcrum. It looked fine. He placed it on the table and it rolled slightly. It was not straight. The machine could not bend it so he was never told to look for that. But an operator may have taken the machine apart and accidentally or intentionally bent it.

Dieterich had helped his dad build and repair things around the house. He had not enjoyed this but accepted it was only fair to do a share of the work. Helping on Saturday morning was more interesting than emptying the trash or mowing the lawn. Sometimes he even learned something useful. For example, he knew well enough how to turn a screw even when the wood was green or the thread was damaged or the slot was buggered. He had learned a little about electricity and could use a table saw without fear. But some tasks were mere drudgery, like sweeping the sawdust and filling wallboard seams and straightening nails. His dad saved nails and screws and other hardware whenever he took something apart. Then, when there was nothing important for Dieterich to be doing on a Saturday, he might be asked to dump out the nail bin and straighten the ones that were strong enough to save. He had done that to nails of various sizes with various degrees of initial bend. The Bosch worktable under the hardness testers was flat and solid. For an instant he thought of hammering the lever rod on the tabletop and quickly saw that would have been dangerous. He might have damaged the table. It would have been inappropriate to even disrespect the table by banging on it.

"You got a heavy hammer I can use a minute, bigger than this toy they put in my toolbox?" he asked the operator. *This could be the guy who broke the machine. He's going to be happy if I get it fixed.*

Dieterich put the rod on the concrete floor and hit it half-heartedly one time and then looked at the rod to see if he had made a mark. It might not work properly if it was straight but had a flattened area. He saw no mark from the hammer. He tried again with a firm stroke and looked for damage. Then he reasoned that the worst case would be for the machine to go back to Ferndale for repair so he could go ahead and take the risk of ruining the rod when he tried to straighten it. He rolled the rod to feel for the bend and then hit the highest part hard with the hammer, just as he had done for hours with rusty nails. Then he rolled it again and hit it again until the rod would roll across the floor steady and straight. He rolled it on the tabletop to confirm it was true and then did the rest of the maintenance process. The final tests came out perfect. He would not tell the plant manager about this, of course. Nor the operator who might not be the one who bent the rod.   Nor Rusty who would have said the machine should have been sent to his shop. He might tell Freddy but he knew he should not because it would only be boasting. All in all, he felt good about the job at Bosch and forgot he was missing the chance to see power brake assemblies being assembled.

As he was experimenting with the lever, he remembered the push awl Freddy had bent and traded for the one in Dieterich's box. It had worked acceptably but felt stiff when it was pushing the pin into its channel. He took it out and rolled it on the edge of the table. A few taps with the heavy hammer on the high part of the arc had it rolling true. He thought he would not mention it to anyone and he hoped someday Rusty would ask if he was using Freddy's damaged awl.

Despite the euphoria of crushing a problem that should have been beyond his means, as soon as he turned the key in the Rambler's door, he was overcome with the sensation of arriving at an exam unprepared. He had no place for the night. The days are long in July but the parking lot was already in the shadow of the surrounding buildings.

When his family drove along U.S. Route 1 to Florida in the summers after Dieterich's fifth and sixth grade, they began to look for a motel around dinner time, checking for neon signs that said "TV," "pool," "air conditioning," and "vacancy." Motels advertising "radio," or "Magic Fingers," were considered tacky. If the motel sign said "bar" or "lounge," they would drive on. When they first saw the neon "no" lit in front of "vacancy," the family's standards suddenly dropped, and they would take the next respectable place for the night.

Now, five years later, Dieterich had no additional experience in selecting a motel room. His first idea was to go to a phone booth and look in the Yellow Pages but he had no basis for knowing which ones were appropriate. He did not need a pool, but he valued cheap and safe and easy to find. His experience from watching TV suggested hotels were downtown and motels were outside the most urbanized area. He preferred a motel. He drove back to the motel where had been staying and looked for another in the area. He saw one on his way. It looked acceptable, as good as the one from last night except for the "no vacancy" sign. His selection standards dropped. Approaching his hotel, he slowed down to see how respectable or not it appeared. When he first went there, he had not bothered to judge it. Now, it looked fine. He noted it had no pool which was probably usual on the urban fringe in Michigan. The "vacancy" light was on without the "no" light. He was not going back there. He drove around some more. Route 1 on the East coast was a magnet for motels. There was no counterpart around Lansing, at least none that he could find quickly.

He found a steak house and decided he could postpone making a housing decision. It was similar to deciding he could play cards tonight and study for the exam later except that he could skip the motel without damage to his grades. In the back of his mind, he conjured the temporary solution of driving out of town after a steak dinner with baked potato, finding a dark place and setting up a tent out of sight of the car. He could put a note on the windshield saying the car broke down and he would be back in the morning with a tow truck.

He ordered a medium-rare ribeye with baked potato and salad. He was not sure exactly what a ribeye was so he had selected it on the basis of price. He looked around the room. It was busy: couples composed of men in working men clothes along with wives or girlfriends, and some families of three, or four or five. He liked the vibe, Friday night dinner out with the kind of guys he had seen on the shop floor. He took off his tie... no one to impress here and no one who would be impressed by a tie. He had a Coke in a tall glass with crushed ice and a straw, just what he wanted, although he was a little jealous for the beer he saw on many tables. That would have been the adult option. He had tried beer a few times, mostly the low alcohol beer served to 18-year-olds in Estes Park, Colorado, and decided he did not like it but could take it when socially demanded. His parents drank cocktails sometimes and wine sometimes. He never drank either because it felt like pretending he was them. He would try beer again someday. For now, he removed the straw since it seemed childish.

He should have studied Freddy's brochure before arranging the Lansing trip so he could go camping over the weekend. At least he was noticing the value of studying. Eventually he might actually do some before he took a test.

The map in the brochure was going to be very good for Dieterich's purposes. It located all the state lands in Michigan. He looked for the largest ones first. As expected, they were all north of the place where Michigan's thumb separated from the palm or they were on the Upper Peninsula. If he could get a few days off, maybe at the end of the summer, he would go up there; look for wolves.

His dinner arrived. It looked delicious but he was in no hurry, so he savored a single slice of the steak before buttering his steaming potato and turning to the salad which he consumed slowly, perusing the map between bites and half thinking of the steak that waited.

Rose Lake Wildlife Area was near Lansing on the northeast. It was too close to the city and too small for camping, but he might park there tonight and sleep in the car. Burchfield Park to the southwest had a river but was probably too small for camping incognito. He looked farther from Lansing and noticed Sleepy Hollow State Park 20 minutes north of Lansing. The real Sleepy Hollow, of course, was on the Hudson River, in Westchester County, New York, near his home in Greenwich, Connecticut. The copycat one would have no colonial era history or literary fame yet its Ovid Lake and Little Maple River were more what he sought for his weekend. It closed at ten o'clock each evening. No camping, not officially anyway. If it closed before dark, there would be no one to care if he was sleeping quietly within its 2,600 acres.

The salad was finished. He cut another piece of steak. Oh, was it tasty! He was young and had a date with a fine girl coming up and would be free for two days and did not feel much like living inside the persona he had worn thus far in life. He felt one with the people in the restaurant. They all knew how to get a really good meal on Friday night. He mashed the white of his potato with his fork, then salted it lightly and peppered it heavily. During the potato, he looked over the brochure for what to explore on Sunday. He could not go very far and still get to the ZF plant by 8:30 on Monday morning. He could take a risk if the reward was good enough.   The Shiawassee State Wildlife Area south of Saginaw was nearly 10,000 acres. The brochure did not say much about what was there but that was what exploration would reveal.   It, too, was closed at night; a small challenge with so much open land.

On his way out of the restaurant, Dieterich stopped in the gift shop, mainly because he was curious to see what trinkets would be sold in a Michigan steak house. Even after a month in the state, he could not think of any distinctive regional character other than the car industry and the rural places above the thumb and the wilder places above the mitten. The theme in the shop was Michigan State University sports, as he should have anticipated: caps, sweatshirts, mugs and such.   He considered buying a six-pack of one of the local beers, but he was not sure of the drinking age in Michigan and was not about to ask. Surprisingly a box of Bull Durham tobacco and rolling papers was on sale. That would serve if he were to adopt a young cowboy personality. He had smoked a few cigarettes experimentally, only inhaling a few times since inhaling was obviously stupid. It did feel pretty interesting to go through the motions of smoking, not enough to take up the habit as if he believed he was a World War II fighter pilot or Sam Spade. Altogether, his experience amounted to less than a single pack which was all he expected to ever smoke - but rolling his own? People still did that?

There was plenty of time left in the day although the dusk was nearly faded to black. He went east to where he assumed East Lansing would be and, thus, Michigan State. There he hoped to find a small shop open where he could buy something for breakfast and lunch. He found a loaf of bread, a block of cheese, a can of Vienna sausages and a two-quart jug of orange juice (or orange drink - he did not look very closely). One steak dinner on a weekend was plenty for a roaming free spirit. On his way to the cash register, he spotted a large, plastic tote decorated with the image of a Spartan soldier. Better to carry the mascot of Michigan State than Clutch, the Mountain Hawk, mascot of Lehigh. The tote could serve as his pack if he went for a long walk over the weekend.

He drove north for twenty minutes until he came to a T. He went west less than a mile and took a road north again. In Michigan the cardinal directions were all one needed to know. The hazy mental map in his head showed he should be approaching Sleepy Hollow. That small park near Lansing was not his destination for the night and seeing Sleepy Hollow was only his plan for Saturday. If he saw an indication he was near it, he would start looking for a place to park for the night. Two more times he came to a T and each time he went left and soon turned north again. By tending west, he assumed Sleepy Hollow would be to his east.

He drove with the window open to feel the breeze. He was not driving very fast, why should he; the night was long. The air became cooler yet he left the window open and shivered a little from time to time. He passed few houses and no towns. It was not wilderness but the area was quiet and natural. Finally, he came to a wider road with some directional signs: St. Johns to the west, Ovid to the east. Lake Ovid was in Sleepy Hollow Park, so he went east on the lookout for a place, maybe just a wide place in the road, to park for the night. He passed through Ovid a little before nine o'clock. If it had more than one street, he did not see it. He saw one store with its sign lit but it was not open. A few houses had lights glowing from inside where Michiganders were watching *Gunsmoke* or *The Man from Uncle*. Past town, he noticed crickets singing their steady song. He doubted the improvised camping opportunities were going to dramatically improve soon and he liked being near Ovid so he could find Sleepy Hollow in the morning. The road was steadily invariant but for a scattering of driveways and gravel roads that were probably driveways. No more than one car passed him in a minute. A pond appeared on the left, his north, and he slowed down to look more closely. There was a pull-over just past the pond, a place for poor folks and sporting boys to park while they angle for bass or catfish. He drove onto the gravel, and maneuvered carefully to get as far from the road as possible without placing his tires in mud that might trap him.

He shut off the headlights, turned the engine key and relaxed. There was no need to discover a more private place. And he knew as he had known all along, he would not sleep in the woods tonight. It would be fine to sleep in the car for the night. He got out of the car, closing the door quietly without locking it. His quiet was to respect the remoteness of the place. He planned to walk around a little and would not allow himself to picture a thief lurking nearby to steal his orange juice.

I can't walk in the woods or the field over there in this darkness. He remembered walking at night in wild country and knew it was dangerous; vulnerable to tripping or sloshing into mud or scratching on briars or (and he hated to recall this) going straight into a tree trunk. He had learned to be very slow in the dark and did not feel like walking defensively before settling into bed. So he went on the road. He had seen a few cars on this road, fewer as the time passed. He took the direction away from Ovid since he had already seen what lay between here and there. He looked to his watch to give himself fifteen minutes before turning back. He might be tired enough then to sleep. He could not read his watch in the dark. He already knew the moon was not out but he looked up to see if there was light from a city on the horizon. No clouds reflected light from civilization and the air was too dry to give a hazy glow. The environment provided only starlight. He rubbed his eyes to clear them of possible mucus, held his wrist over the road where the starlight would be unobstructed and leaned close to read the time. It seemed to be 9:35, a plausible hour. He stopped at 9:50 but did not return. He had seen nothing on his walk although his eyes had adjusted enough to keep him on the side of the road. It was not good to end a walk without getting somewhere. When he was on an overnight hike, he usually had a goal for the day. When he did not have one or had to give up on reaching it, he would continue until he found something memorable. He was not ready to sleep in what was likely an uncomfortable bed.

He stretched to relieve the building tension; spinning one arm, then the other, then both. He turned his head as far as he could in every direction to loosen his neck. That felt good so he knew he had been tense. He bent over to touch his toes and then grabbed his calves to pull his head against his knees. He heard a soft sound at his feet. A dragon fly landing? A moth? A snake? He dragged his fingers across the pavement in front of him, ready to pull back his hand instantly if he felt something. It was the package of Bull Durham that had fallen from his shirt pocket. When he put it back in his pocket, he fingered around to be sure he still had the papers and matches in there. He would not light a match and ruin his night vision.

A car appeared far ahead. He stepped off the road and faced away to preserve his vision and then closed his eyes as it went. When he opened his eyes again, he could not see the roadside, blinded for the next five minutes or more.

Rolling a cigarette for the first time was likely greatly hampered by doing it blindly but he did not need a perfect job. He had seen marijuana rolled and knew it was easiest to make a thin joint, especially on the ends. He licked the edge of the paper and pressed it to the cylinder, feeling more like a cowboy than a hippy but when he twisted the ends to keep the tobacco inside, he felt like a hippy in training. He cradled the match in his palm and lit the cigarette. That felt like a World War II scene in Paris. He drew on the cigarette gently, held some in his mouth in search of a taste in it, and puffed it into the night having never let it in his lungs. He studied the moment, finding nothing objectively pleasurable to account for the popularity of smoking, yet he had to acknowledge something attractive in the process, especially the rolling stage. He looked forward to tossing the butt and stamping out the coal when he was finished. He was play-acting and he knew it so he found it ironic to be enjoying it without any audience. He wondered if he should be embarrassed at himself and wondered how one can be embarrassed with no observer. It was more perplexing than that foolish question about a falling tree making noise or not in an empty forest.

Now he could walk back to the car. Smoked two more cigs along the way, refining his technique from the stage of withdrawing the pack from his pocket to casually dropping the butt and carefully, in his actual personality, smearing the ash to ensure it was out. Each time he lit a new cigarette, he checked his watch in the dark so he would not miss the car and end up in Ovid.

No one had gotten into the car, as far as Dieterich could tell. When he opened the car door and the inside light came on, he looked over the seat at his scattered jacket and food and suitcase. It was surprising how familiar the location of everything was. Just to be completely certain and secure, he opened the suitcase. Everything looked good. Despite his apparent private location, he decided to sleep in jeans and tee shirt. He moved over to the passenger side and tipped the seat back. It might be comfortable enough for a full night's sleep. He was tired now, ready to recover the energy to undertake an exploration of Sleepy Hollow in the morning.

Tap, tap, tap, tap... Dieterich heard a sound which he assumed came from nearby but was not urgent enough to give up his sleep. TAP, TAP, TAP... The sound came faster and louder but what bothered Dieterich most was that it was on the other side of the car now. He cringed reflexively and opened his eyes to a world full of light brighter than day. The tapping stopped and he heard the sound of the door handle being rattled. The light came from a flashlight. Someone wanted in the car. He held his hand in front of his eyes to block the painful light and the flashlight moved. He looked at the window above the door and saw a policeman in uniform shining the light on himself.

Dieterich rolled down the window and began to prepare his story. He had not done anything wrong unless he was trespassing or vagrant or something harmless like that. He could say he was on his way somewhere and started to nod off so he took a side road to find a place to sleep, etc, etc.

"Good morning, Sir. How are you feeling?"

"Feeling, yeah. Sorry. I was really sound asleep there. Sure, I'm fine. No drinking involved. I never drink. Don't like the taste of it or the feel of it, you know."

"Step out of the car, please."

So he is not just checking on my welfare. Maybe there is some local ordinance. In the worst case, I have all day to straighten this out; all weekend even.

"Face the car. Place your hands on the roof. What's your name, please?

"Dieterich Kahler"

"Got a driver's license?"

"Sure it's in the glove compartment."

"I'll get it out...

"You from Connecticut then?" What you doing out here?"

"I'm working this summer for Wilson Instrument in Ferndale. I go around the state servicing and certifying our company's hardness testers and factories and laboratories. That's my toolbox on the floor in back."

"You been smoking that weed you got on the back seat?"

"Weed? Never tried it. What about the backseat? Oh, I see... Please take a closer look at that bag on the seat. You heard of Bull Durham?"

Following a few seconds of police investigation, the encounter took on a much friendlier tone.

"That's a new one on me. Sorry I got so excited. We get pretty imaginative at this time of the morning."

"Can't say you did anything wrong." Dieterich could be generous now. "From what you could see through the window, weed is a much more likely explanation of the little bag and packet of cigarette papers."

"How come you roll your own? How's that better?"

"I doubt there is anything better about it. I don't know. Maybe it's better 'cause it's harder to chain smoke. This is the first and last time for me. I don't even smoke squares[6], except for trying it two, three times just to see why it's cool."

"So it just jumped into your head to roll a few?"

"Yeah, that's about right. I saw it for sale last night after a nice dinner in a steak house. They had a little souvenir shop. I can't say why they sell it; maybe just waiting for me to come by one night. You want to try one? Make sure it's just tobacco."

"Let's talk about why you're sleeping out here."

"I worked Thursday and Friday in Lansing and go back to Lansing on Monday at a few more plants. I was going to hike around Sleepy Hollow State Park tomorrow, or today, I guess. My company would have paid for a motel but the reservation fell though for tonight. I was in Lansing for Thursday night. Sleepy Hollow Park closes at night so I just parked out of the way, much as I could. Am I trespassing or something?" Alice's Restaurant[7] was not a steak house but it came to mind. He did not remember the ballad exactly, but he thought Arlo might have been charged with trespassing along with littering. He would look into that later so he could tell the story of this night someday, not stealing anything from Arlo but drawing some parallels, like starting his story with a restaurant thing.

He was robbed of becoming a cult hero in this particular way by the cop who abandoned all threatening

---

[6] A term used in prison for a commercially made cigarette. It was used in film noir scenes.

[7] This satirical song by Arlo Guthrie tells the story of a young man arrested for littering, and how authorities thereby overreached their public duty, a parallel to the Vietnam War draft.

behavior, explaining he would leave a message for the next shift to tell them to leave Dieterich alone, just a young man sleeping harmlessly, which is what Arlo would have wanted, assuming he did not know his arrest would make him famous. Dieterich realized that his own event had been simplified because he did not look like a hippy (or a black or a gypsy or an Indian or a migrant worker or a wino and so on), not to judge this particular policeman, who had behaved perfectly, but, well, he had always been judged good by persons of authority despite his being as self-involved and... his mind searched for a better word than "lazy" but could not find one without effort and he did not want to exert himself.

"You got a place lined up for breakfast in the morning?" the policeman asked.

"Thought I'd see if they have something at that place in Ovid."

"No, don't bother with that. They don't have anything. I'm thinking you'll be making an early start and they don't open before eight anyway. Run over to Owosso. It'll be worth it. Not too far. You're on Route 21 now. Go east. First town. First thing in town on the left is El Potrero Mexican Restaurant. They open early and fix a good breakfast."

"Wow! Glad you stopped by, officer. I'll do that."

9

Saturday, July 12 When he woke in the daylight, he got out of the car and stretched out the kinks of a night on a car seat, drank half a quart of orange juice, peed in the woods, and took the officer's culinary advice which led to his surprising himself by thoroughly enjoying his first ever Mexican meal. He was the only customer when he arrived. The waiter helped him make a selection, taking him into the kitchen to see what they offered. He picked tetelas first because they were essentially bread, likely to safely ensure him of some nutrition. He turned down covering them in refried beans or other condiments he could not identify. He chose huevos rancheros because he recognized the fried egg on top and took all the toppings the waiter recommended, not sure if he was being so daring to impress himself or the waiter. He washed up in the El Potrero rest room, and felt fresh for adventure when he got back to his table with his breakfast already set out for him.

The signs at Sleepy Hollow directed him to a parking lot by a small headquarters. He studied the map posted by the entrance to see where he could hide his car at night and walk safely to a hidden place to camp. Inside the building, that daring adventure was quickly aborted when he saw the park offered campsites. Then he saw a sign announcing the spaces were already reserved for this night so he reverted to the hidden site idea. Like sour grapes, the sites did not look appealing anymore. He explained to a man in a khaki uniform bearing a Sleepy Hollow Park patch that Dieterich envied him for having, that he did not go camping with a trailer and did not want a tent in a wide parking space near families sitting in lawn chairs. He said this in words respectful of the park patrons. The man seemed to have a job equivalent to what Dieterich had in the far more impressive Rocky Mountains National Park except that Dieterich had not worn a patch looking this official. Dieterich had worked for a concessionaire and this fellow probably worked for the State of Michigan.

Dieterich was told they had rustic sites, too and these could only be reserved on the day of use, pointing out it was early enough that most of these were still open. For the very low rate of ten dollars, Dieterich was given a block of wood with a site number (his receipt) and a map of the park. The ranger circled his site on the map.

"Think it's a good site?" Dieterich asked more to say something friendly and unbusinesslike than to get his opinion.

"Depends. It's on the lakeside of the access road. That's good for sure. I'd say it's got mosquitos at night. You got netting in your tent?"

What tenting Dieterich had brought from the Army-Navy store in Detroit consisted of a half-man mosquito net for the part of him outside the blanket and a sheet of heavy plastic for an informal tent. Now he wished he had bought a backpack but at the same time he was glad he had not paid good money for cheap versions of equipment he already had back home. It added to that sense of independence so essential to the pleasure of the wilds that he had minimal equipment. His blanket, borrowed without permission from the Tylers, was enough for the overnight chill. His food supplies, "tent," mosquito net, and matches were rolled into the blanket which was tied into a horseshoe shape with his belt linking the ends. He carried it over one shoulder and then the other for the mile walk from his car to his reserved site.

He made a cursory inspection of his site and hoped no one would occupy it since he would leave it looking empty but for his bedroll hanging in a tree. He was not going to put up his plastic tarp. It would not be stolen but could be removed as garbage left behind. He had slept outside with no more protection than this and knew how to tie it up effectively for shelter, assuming the wind was not excessive. He made a plan to go down the west shore of the lake and resupply himself with water at the boat launch which he hoped had good water available. Then he could either continue around the lake, a good plan of about 12 miles for the day, or, if the lake seemed too developed, he could take a trail farther west, going back north to his site. He saw the possibility of going beyond the park boundary on the northward run if that was the wildest route.

Before he started his hike through the park, he made the first entries in his almanac:

> July 12, 1969
> Sleepy Hollow State Park, Michigan
> Clear skies, (warm days recently, expect same today).
> ADD A THERMOMETER TO HIKING PACK
> Paid $10 for rustic site 17, located 10 yards east of Lake Ovid
> Sounds of blue jays and chickadees
> Short, branching pine trees with short, pointed needles in bundles of two along lakeside.
> Scattered ferns and thorny bushes underfoot.

AMBITION

He was no Aldo Leopold but he was certain Leopold's first entries were not memorable literature. The most important thing was to start and he had done that. The next most important thing was to keep at it. He would see if he could do that part too. He promised himself to write every day at least through his time in Michigan. Once he was back in school, it would be best to put it aside during the week.

Going south on a horse trail, he did not see the lake for the first thirty minutes which did not bother him since he saw no people (or horses) either. He traversed a forest of slender pines, sometimes tall but never more than six or eight inches in diameter. Without his binoculars or his Peterson guide, he could not birdwatch effectively but he, nonetheless, hoped to see a certain warbler, the Kirkland's, one of the rarest birds resident in North America and limited to Michigan's jack pines. He did not know what field marks distinguished the Kirkland warbler or a jack pine, but he knew the warbler was not extraordinary looking and the jack pines grew in poor soil so it was just barely possible he might make the best avian sighting of his life here this day. He sketched the needle bundle and pinecone of the trees around himself into his journal. He had no artistic talent, but he could produce a credible record of these details.

When the lake came back into view, Dieterich was very pleased to find a short footbridge to an island in the lake. *Blessed are the State and National Park Services*, he prayed. The completely wild lands were ideal in Dieterich's value system, but when he came across a rustic bridge or a spring with a pipe to show the water was potable or a trail to a vista, he was happy for that much from civilization. The bridge had a railing on one side on which Dieterich rested his elbows and listened to the familiar sound of redwings and watched them flying around in the reeds on both ends of the bridge.

Of course, the island attracted hikers. Although they were not numerous when he arrived, the trail around the island perimeter was well worn and he passed a group every five minutes or so, too often to preserve the sense of being "away." The island shoreline was not as beautiful as a rocky isle on the Maine coast or an empty sandy beach on Nantucket, but it would do for a favorable mention in his journal. It would not serve, however, as a sanctuary for meditating into his journal, not even if he went into the middle of the island where he would be spared the sight of other hikers but not the knowledge of their proximity. In twenty minutes, he went around, appreciating the long views of the lake and ready to continue among the, possibly, jack pines ashore.

In the next half hour he passed a dozen riders, usually in small groups, obviously going to the island and possibly on toward his camp. Seeing so many encouraged him in his presumption of finding water when he reached the road and, indeed, there was a tap there for watering horses, riders and fishermen. He drank some more of his orange juice and filled the plastic container with water on top of the remaining juice for the next part of his hike.

A sexy woman, in ponytail and riding breeches and boots, sat on the pier apart from the fishermen and looked off to the east, generally at a smaller island than the one Dieterich has circled. He imagined himself sitting between her and the fishermen, closer to the fishermen, writing in his journal about the people who populated the edge of the wild parts of parks, open to the possibility that she might be so bored by waiting for her party to arrive and the unchanging image of the low, green isle in Lake Ovid that she would ask what he was writing. He acted out his fantasy by looking east to see what she saw. He saw a lone merganser floating near a raft of what he supposed were mallards. Mallard was his guess because he was used to their being common in Connecticut. He could easily identify a mallard, even when black duck were nearby to confuse the casual observer, but he had no binoculars and the ducks were not very close. The merganser was easy to name with its characteristic bill. He thought of it as having a nail through the tip which may be something he read in a book or maybe something he pictured himself. And the bird clearly did not have the raised crest of a hooded merganser so it must be the common merganser. He would call it the American merganser when he asked the woman if that is what she had noticed out there, halfway to the small island.

Why do I make up such an absurd scenario? If it miraculously proceeded as I foresaw, the story would end as I foresaw, in nothingness. I am already stuck on a real girl for the first time in my life and have no idea, not even an absurd one, of how relations could progress with her. I can hardly believe I have almost made a second date with her while everything about her is impractical. She lives in Michigan and I am in Connecticut or some college I will be embarrassed to mention to her... Stop thinking to forever and have a nice date in the present. That is plenty for one summer.

Dieterich ended his reverie without opening his journal to make any notes and marched to the west toward his one certain love, the unknown land away from the people of the park.

The trail tended north, roughly parallel to the lakeshore. It was flat, like the whole mitten of the state. Again, he was hiking alone, not "alone with his thoughts," just alone, not lonely either, just alone. He could have thought of Elise and how it was to have a good, adult conversation with a beautiful girl and then kiss her and have a date coming up when she gets back, or he could have replayed fixing the hardness tester with the broken rod which he could casually mention to somebody back at the office and the whole office would come to see him as adept beyond his training, or he could have given in to the problems of last term at school and what he would face next term but giving into such temptations for his mind would not be living in the hot, green jack pine forest where he walked free of responsibilities, independent, young and capable of meeting whatever would come up in this unplanned afternoon.

He wore a watch and nearly consulted it although he did not make any part of the motion of lifting his wrist into view. Precision was not useful when the time did not matter. His stomach was not complaining, yet it seemed time for lunch so he began to look for a place to settle down. It was his policy to take lunch or make camp in places with some special quality. Moving water or a long vista were ideal. A blooming bush or a boulder or an ancient tree could serve well. Today nothing like these had appeared or was likely to turn up. Being farther from the lake, all he saw was scrubby pines and unfamiliar bushes bordering a substantial, meandering path. The map showed another trail farther west and running north-south like the lakeshore and the path he was on. He had no compass to direct himself west so he raised his wrist to see his watch, pointed the hour hand in the direction of the sun and knew north was the direction halfway between the sun and the twelve of his watch.

He was disappointed to find the new trail before he felt the need to check his direction again. It was only ten minutes from the last trail. The new one was less worn and therefore a better fit for his mood. It did not offer any hope of imminent escape from the pines, but it was good enough to stop for lunch. He walked on a few minutes more to find a fallen tree for a bench and found one off the trail far enough that he might not be noticed if an unobservant hiker went by. A few slices of bread and a few chunks of cheese washed down by very thin orangeade would not sound like much to a gourmand. Dieterich appreciated it more in the manner of a starving man though his hunger was no more than the habit of stopping every six waking hours to consume something. For the moment, life was simple, lacking nothing, easily accomplished.

Some voices could be heard, apparently farther north on the trail. They came from children shrieking about something, probably not anything relating to the scenery, more likely about each other. Their parents or whatever adult accompanied them did not care or had given up worrying about destroying the ambience for a quarter mile in every direction. He slid off his log to see if he could keep out of their sight as they passed. The voices became louder. A mature voice shouted something that Dieterich hoped would draw the children into their setting, but the squeals continued as if the children had recently discovered a new way to make these unintelligible sounds. And soon he noticed the sounds were receding. They had passed like ghosts without physical form. They had passed while walking the other path, the one ten minutes east unless the paths came even closer together at this point.

I'll go farther west, out of the park, he decided, so he consulted the sun and his watch and went west again.

No unfriendly fence marked the park boundary, just a large red dot on every tree along a line exactly north-south. Nearly all boundaries in Michigan, like the roads, ran in the cardinal directions of the compass. He continued west. The terrain was constant. He began to look for a tree larger than the others. The canopy, too thin to earn that name, was fairly constant until he saw a tree to the southwest that looked tall. When he approached the tree, he examined it for climbing handholds. Shinnying up a pine tree is messy on one's trousers and on the tree. He thought he might reach the lowest branch by launching himself against the trunk and pushing upward with his feet. It took three tries. He climbed as high as the tree would permit, it swayed enough with his weight that he worried it could break and he listened for a cracking sound, although none came. He saw far enough to suspect there was an open area a half mile and a little north of west from his perch. That was something other than jack pine. As he started to climb down, he noticed a linear aspect in the distance to north. He lifted himself as far as he could balancing to keep the terminal stem erect. It must be the Little Maple River that feeds the lake. Thus, he knew his plan for the afternoon: see the open area, be it agricultural or logging remnant or whatever, then find the river and follow it to the lake.

The field was too irregular to have a recent agricultural origin and soon revealed itself to have been created by fire. Trees less than five years old, Dieterich guessed, grew on the field edges. He found a huge blackberry patch on the perimeter. It was past its most productive season but there were enough berries to spend a while plucking and eating them, not saving any for later or for some imaginary pie he might bake over a campfire that night with a crust made from the kneaded dough in his bread. The seeds stuck in his teeth so he carved himself a toothpick and worked his teeth clear as he moved on. A pair of deer, a doe and a fawn past the age of wearing spots, stared at him from across the field. The open area did not offer much grass for them. Course stems and thin, thorny thickets filled most of the space bare of trees. He recognized a few plants like steeplebush (not really a bush) in its homely, post-bloom stage. Some tickweed blooms remained, lending their orange color in a few places, and competing with a white raft of daisies along the best southern exposure. Sumac was growing under the line of larger trees as deep as the light penetrated.

After a check of his watch for north, he struck out for the river. He was alone here beyond the park and its paths, but his wilderness was small. The river arrived too soon. He knew from his map he was less than a mile from the lake and his campsite was only a mile or so from where the river entered Ovid. The Little Maple was littler than Dieterich expected. It ought to provide at least enough water to offset evaporation from the lake although there could be other sources of input. Some lakes had no visible input because they came from springs within their own depths.

He had time to hike another trail. His map showed a dense network of them all around the lake. He went to the northern boundary and then to the east and south along that boundary until he was satisfied he had seen the quietest lands in the area, of which none was very quiet. After his summer in the Rockies and the summer before that in the Adirondacks, his wilderness aspirations for Michigan were scaled greatly downward. He resolved to enjoy where he was, having essentially put himself here. He refilled his water jug at the camp headquarters and went the last mile back to his campsite, being sure to arrive in plenty of time to set up his plastic tarp, assuming no one had taken it or his blanket or his hank of rope.

His gear was no more sophisticated than a ten-year old boy might have packed from home to run off to the circus so it was likely to be safe from anyone old enough to be exploring the park on his or her own. He had just a little worry about it but he wondered more seriously how other people set up an expensive tent and left it for the day. He would not even do that when he camped on the Appalachian Trail even though he always camped far enough from the trail to be unseen by other hikers.

He cleared away the twigs and pinecones on an area between two trees and spread out the plastic sheet. Then he staked two corners, seven feet apart, by tying a loop of rope around a pinecone folded into the sheet. About three feet from that edge, he staked a point on the edge, using a pinecone again to attach the rope loop without cutting the plastic and then another on the opposite edge. He lifted the unstaked plastic over a rope tied four feet high between a pair of trees. It was held to that height by a rough pole made of a branch with a fork to fit. The end of the sheet was stretched over the first edge he had laid out. That was his shelter, triangular in cross section. If the wind did not blow in the direction through his tunnel, he would keep dry in a rain. He tied his undersized mosquito net onto the rope in the ridge of the shelter and staked the corner near his head.

He thought of building a fire just for the quiet company of it. Quietness had come to mind because he could hear the voices of a group nearer than he wanted, possibly setting up their tents. The park required any fire to be within the concrete hearth at each site. He did not need it for his evening meal, and he guessed it would be hard to find fuel in a place as heavily camped as this and, further, there would be no hardwood fuel within a mile. Setting up had taken longer than he expected. Dinner was due but he feared it would be getting dark soon which would end his time to write some notes on the day and then read from the *Sand County Almanac.* Camping for the first time in the Midwest, some words from Leopold would be just right. He would eat his dinner while he was reading. It might not be too dark to read until eight o'clock, he guessed.

His notes were brief, again relating only bare facts, seldom graced with any sentence structure. Insights, if any were to come, would build out of fuller experience and reflection. He found enough facts to report for the day before the light was gone. He took a leisurely dinner of Vienna sausages, bread and water. He did not intend to report every meal in his journal, especially not ones as humble as this, but he decided he had a comment on the topic to share with his future self. He liked Vienna sausages and had liked them since he discovered them when he was in ninth grade. He first bought them when he was shopping for campout food. They did not need refrigeration or cooking, and came in a tin can with a lid that could be removed by pulling on a tab. Sardines were similarly convenient although they required a key (attached to the can) to be opened.

He was ready now to learn the wisdom from Aldo Leopold. He examined the book. He had a paperback version with a simple cover, obviously not a technical book. An engineer would not have picked it up from the table in a bookstore. Inside were sketches of natural scenes and close-ups of animals and plants. The sketches were not artistic, but skilled in showing something realistically, if mere lines can do that. He had always wished he could represent what he saw but his meager efforts to draw always appeared childish. He looked for Leopold's name or initials on the sketches, and was relieved to see they had been done by someone else, presumably a professional artist. It was too dark to read so he stored the book in his Michigan State bag.

The sounds of other campers were not bothering Dieterich. He could not make out their words. They were companions in the park, respecting the place by spending the night in their own, low impact shelter. He heard them no more nor less than he heard the breeze in the trees. It was so until the music began. It was loud enough to recognize as *Hair*. He knew it as music of his generation but it sounded more structured than the characters in the story it was telling. It was show tunes, a genre he did not like. It always felt like a high school band selection or like the sleezy posters on the wall of a train station. It was not loud but it was clear so he was distracted from his thoughts. They played the whole album. Then the music shifted to *Piece o' My Heart*, by Janis Joplin and he wanted to hear it better. He scooted out of his tube of a tent, put his feet into his sneakers and jogged over to the sound.

Two girls and two guys, Dieterich's age or a little older, were dancing around a boom box. They were in full hippy regalia which was lent credibility by the wear on the hems of their bell bottoms and the hair length on both guys. The girls' hair was as unstructured as the culture they apparently represented. As he watched them from the edge of the light from their fire, he nodded to the beat, communicating his appreciation if they were to look his way. One of the girls saw him and stared in a friendly way, then, without looking away, tapped the guy next to her and pointed. He waved at Dieterich to come closer. Dieterich had sympathies for the culture but he could not claim to be part of it. He did not know enough of it and what he knew he understood as a caricature, the representation offered to his parents. He had no connection to the real thing.

Enjoying the freedom of anonymity, he extended his arms and rolled his hands and turned slowly in a circle as he imagined a traditional Eastern European might dance. He would not attempt to dance in the recognized fashions from high school and movies: the frug, the locomotion, the mashed potato, the swim or, especially, not the twist. He rolled his head to relax his upper body. His dance felt good to him and he did not care what they thought.

Janis wailed another song and then the cassette clumsily switched to *Cry Like a Baby* by the Box Tops. The hippies all waved him forward but he stayed on the edge and rocked himself to the beat. It is a short song made for the radio and the last song on the cassette. Dieterich waved goodbye and started back to his site. The encounter had been a pleasure and would be entered into his journal which was not following Aldo's lead very closely. He heard the four dancers rushing toward him. It would have been rude to run off so he stopped.

"Thank you, thank you for the tunes. Thanks for letting me dance with you. I'm headed back to bed now," he weakly protested their invitation yet allowed the four of them to grasp his arms and pull him close to their fire.

"Come on, man. You pick out a cassette. Take a toke with us. What you doin' out here alone?" asked one of the guys.

The other asked at the same time, "You from around here? Know the city? And I'm Micky."

"City? What city? Doesn't matter, I don't know any city in this state or any neighboring state. And I'm Deeter." Dieterich worried that he was setting himself up to be a victim, telling them how alone he was. And then he remembered he had nothing they would want, apart from a few dollars in his pocket. He would tell them he had no car, just hitchhiked here.

The girls gave their names as "Sunny" and Cloudy." Although it was nice to be near friendly females, they were not especially attractive, nothing to complain about but very ordinary looking inside their shell of hip youthfulness. The first guy had gone back to the tent. It was a round tent with a single peak in the center, like a miniature circus tent. There would be shelter for the four but no extra room inside. The guy came out quickly with three joints and a pack of matches. Everybody sat on the ground cross-legged except Dieterich who did not find that comfortable. He laid back, supported on one elbow.

The hippies had hitched from California and were going to Woodstock, a place that Dieterich did not recognize. He did not ask where it was or why they were headed there because they peppered him with questions. It seemed they had been in their own company so long they hungered for new conversation. Dieterich did not give them much detail on himself. He felt his most interesting contribution to a group like this, which he presumed to be open to his frustrated aspiration, was to speak of Aldo Leopold. He said he had started on a journal in the general imitation of *Sand Country Almanac*. It would need his own voice, he told them, and it would have to be completely rewritten if he ever found something to say. He doubted he had the skills to say anything well but he would not be deterred by insecurity. For now, it was a start in a direction not prescribed by parents or school. They listened sincerely.

"Drive on, Deeter!"

"Tres cool!"

"Deeter's grooving!"

Cloudy had no admiring comment but she handed him the joint, already half its starting length. Dieterich passed it to Sunny sitting on the other side of him and asked Micky for his story. It was a necessary courtesy to direct attention to someone else and he was curious about how these four managed to live.

Micky explained he was in his second year at a California junior college and worrying about getting into a four-year school with a deferment for the next two years when he got his draft notice.

"Major, major bummer there. My dad is not into the resistance thing, but he's a doctor, just a podiatrist, not big time or anything, and anyway he knows doctors and he hooked me up with one who dug real deep and found me a medical out. Blessed be my dad for real! So I'm pretty down with doing more school but I got no rush. So I went to Sandy and... Sandy, you never gave Deeter your name, did ya? Deeter, Sandy; Sandy, Deeter... Sandy dropped out last year. Quit the world, right Sandy?"

"Right on, Brother! Couldn't hack it, couldn't take any of it: the goddam war, the uptight teachers, the pigs in Chicago, assassination (Bobby and Martin, you know). I mean I could not take any more of it. This is my youth, my time! ...the best years I'm going to get? I was going out of my head, so I was getting into some heavy shit that only made my head worse. Well, I don't have a daddy, doctor or anything else, and I can see no place to go, so here, just quit the thing. Ain't got no name, no numbers, no school, no bank account no more." He waved his hands in circles in front of his face, like a magician. "Deep, deep underground, man."

"Heavy," Dieterich answered more softly than he intended.

The group was quiet. Dieterich thought his own situation did not seem as bad as these two except that it was actually nearly the same situation. It just looked worse when viewed from the outside.

Micky broke the silence. "Heavy times we are in, my friends. I got to make the point that it ain't as bad as that little summary. We found Sunny and Cloudy and nothing is bad when they're around. Right Sandy?"

"Right on. Right on in spades."

"We're makin' it along. Right now, we're crossing 'Merica," Micky added optimistically.

"We're livin' free, you know," Cloudy explained. "Not free like no money, but like doing what we feel like. No one makin' us do anything. Especially not makin' our men go off somewhere to kill or get killed in the name of the military-industrial complex."

"Goin' to Woodstock," Sunny explained although Dieterich had no idea what she meant.

After a minute or so of quiet, Dieterich got up to tend the fire.

"I see the motive. I got some of it myself. Don't think I've got the guts to drop out. Not sure about that. Pretty sure I'm not smart enough to make it work. But I don't need much. I could live cheap for sure. Maybe the big thing is I don't have a sun or a cloud to carry me."

"You can have one too. We're not special," Cloudy averred sadly.

"Don't ever say that, Baby. You gotta know it ain't true," Sandy exclaimed in an angry tone.

"Baby, you know it is tr..."

"OK, not special like a movie star or something famous. But goddam, what a human being! You love mankind and you're smarter than me or Mick by a hundred times. You'll make your mark once you get goin'."

Cloudy was the cuter one of the girls although Dieterich was not too sure because of the low lighting. Micky moved closer to her and rested a wrist on her shoulder, stroking the back of her head lightly.

"This girl graduated with honors. I don't remember what the Latin name is for the honors but I know she got the grades," Micky added softly, speaking to her more than to the group.

Cloudy defended her worthlessness. "Mick, none of us here gives a shit about grades. It's not even what you know. It's what you do."

"It starts with if you got the heart, m'dear," Sandy rejoined. "And then there's if you got the talent to matter. You got these. Just be patient and take care of your friends until Woodstock and then we all figure what comes next."

"Hard to know where to go after this. What you get in a year of trying to use your worthless degree, Sunny Girl?"

"You callin' my fine degree in French history without any honors attached worthless? I coulda used it to get this fire started if I had it with me. That would have been worth something. Besides, I got a job working at Belks with it and proved I had the versatility to work in housewares or in women's clothing. 'Course I'm not sexy enough for the perfume counter."

"Wrong!" Sandy shouted. "Ask a man. Ask Deeter."

"You wanna lie to me, Deeter?" Sunny asked.

"I met you all in the dusky light when you were sexy indeed and the more I hear you, the sexier you're getting. It's not my way to make a big thing of it and I'm not going down that road much more tonight."

"I quit that department store gig 'cause they made me wear their clothes if I was gonna sell 'em. Even wanted me to cut my hair and curl it or something, like Doris Day."

"Thank you, Sunny, for staying who you are. You'll get something better but don't ask me how to use French history," Dieterich added because he thought he had not been supportive enough.

"I'll tell you what I know from French history. I know America's friends, the French, exploited the

Vietnamese like all the colonial powers do and when Uncle Vo[8] kicked them out, 1954, America decided to take over. Times changed and the whole World War had got in the way of keeping up colonies so America don't want to grow rubber trees in Southeast Asia but it sure wants to run the place and to hell with democracy over there."

The group accepted the quiet. No one knew which persons were contemplating Sunny's situation or her sudden obscure reference to the war or which wanted to move to a more innocent frame of mind.

Dieterich had heard of Uncle Ho Chi Minh and he had heard of Uncle Sam but not Uncle Vo. He was not going to ask her if she said the name wrong or he just heard it wrong. Furthermore, he was certain 1954 was a long time before America was involved over there. Yet she clearly knew more about the war than he did, even if her tongue slipped on a very short word and a date from before he went to school. He did not follow the war news or its history. What he heard was always complicated by the bias of the sources and their constant reference to political perspectives rather than to facts. He thought to ask what America wanted if it did not want what the French had considered valuable. He had never heard America wanted colonies or domination of the far reaches of the planet.

He knelt over the fire and arranged the last of the wood from the pile, building up a bright flame. Then he stood up.

"I don't see any moon tonight. It's black as a coal mine back in the trees and dawn comes early in July so I'm back to bed. You feeling some raindrops? Really good to meet you. Keep on truckin' y'all!"

---

[8] Vo Nguyen Giap was the Viet Minh General at the Battle of Dien Bien Phu in 1954.

He moved so confidently; he was out of sight before his new friends could intervene. They had already entered the mellow part of the evening and only felt like objecting to his departure while in a seated or prone position. He had not been especially interesting but more than one of them had hoped he would bring something to drink before the night ended. After all, they were on a very tight budget and he had a job.

In the ten minutes it took for Dieterich to get back to his site in the dark, stumbling against branches when he lost the path and once walking toward what felt northward to locate the access road, he realized he was tired and ready for sleep. The rain was too light to be a problem, but it would have become uncomfortable to stay very long lying exposed on the ground by the fire.

No rain had penetrated inside his tent. The drops were so small and few, he scarcely heard them on his roof. Under his blanket, in the confined volume of his shelter, he felt cozy and far removed from the reality outside. He imagined the hippies wandering around the woods, searching for him with better or worse purpose, seeing his crude sanctuary and thinking it was just someone's bedsheet hung out for children to play under. They would not know it was a technology he had used before to save weight on overnights, and how it was fully functional for one person. His next thought, as far as he could tell, came to him in the daylight. He looked at his watch and realized there was less light than usual for eight in the morning. He had slept well.

10

Sunday, July 13 Overnight his surroundings had shifted from a sparsely populated heaven among friendly strangers into a damp, muddy Hades from which everyone would likely depart within an hour. The rain pounded loudly and steadily on his thin roof. He might have been wakened by the sound of thunder; he was not sure.

When he sat up, his head pressed against the mosquito net. The part that had been staked out beyond his head was wet. He untied it from the rope on top and rolled it into a bundle. He examined his blanket which was still dry. His only breakfast fare was the water in his jug. He drank most of it and felt satisfied for the present. People survived for days without food. Breaking camp in this rain was not an inviting idea and not a necessary one either although he did need to urinate very soon. He had slept in his underwear, so he stripped that off to keep it dry. He had only one clean set left in the suitcase in his car. Yesterday's would have to do for today. Then he wriggled naked out of the foot of the tent. First, he looked in the direction of his friends from last night. He could not see their tent nor could he see anyone else's site. He was not sure whether he could see other tents yesterday. Maybe, he thought, everyone has left already or maybe the rain is hiding them. He peed and he inspected the area around his tent. The water was running off the plastic and forming a rivulet on each side, flowing smoothly past the foot end. It looked safe enough for now. He crawled back inside, dried himself with his towel and dressed in yesterday's clammy clothes. He packed everything except his blanket into his bag. The blanket was folded as a cushion to use while reading or napping (he had slept seven hours and was capable of more).

Maybe the rain will die down and I can strike the tent without making too much of a mess. Don't think I'll be exploring any of the smaller parks around here today. I'll just read for now.

Aldo (Dieterich thinks of the author on a first-name basis) reports in his July entry that the Sand County clerk's records show he owns 120 acres, but Aldo says "...at daybreak I am the sole owner of all the acres I can walk over." Dieterich wished he had his poncho. He would have hiked over Sleepy Hollow as if he were its sole owner, fearing no encounter with any human since none would be fool enough to tread the trails on a day like this. He is not completely certain about his own assertion that none would be as foolish as himself or he might have taken his hike wearing only his sneakers. It was warm enough to be comfortable like that.

"Like other great landowners, I have tenants," Aldo asserts. "They are negligent about rents but punctilious about tenures." His "tenants" are the birds and other animals living on the land and he records the schedule of their appearance in territorial birdsong and unroosting and making their rounds for groceries. Aldo begins his account with the sound of a field sparrow at 3:35 in the morning. Dieterich feels several levels of jealousy: that Aldo rises so early to experience the land fully, that he can tell what bird is making each sound, and that he can write his experience with simultaneous emotion and humor and science.

By noon Dieterich had read over half of Aldo's book and written five pages of thoughts that came from the reading. These notes are more extensive than any he took for a required book in his year of college. And now he is ready to deal with the rain. It shows no sign of ending and the flat bed on which he has been reading has become unbearable for his stiff joints and damp hide.

I'll pack my underwear now and do without until I get back to the car. I need to be properly dressed when I'm working. They're paying me to do things right.

Rainwater had formed a small stream from the base of the tree holding up his tent rope and into the corner of his plastic tube. It ran all the way to the foot of the tent. The blanket was wet although Dieterich had not realized how wet. It was warm where he lay on it and the general damp of the air and his clothes seemed merely inevitable. Abandoning his jeans and shirt to the rain would not be much change. Packing up inside the tent took no more than five minutes. He expected it would take another five minutes to roll up the tent with the rope and stakes inside and then ten minutes to reach the car. He felt again for the car keys in his pocket, and crawled out of the tent into the rain.

The messy bundle of the tent under his arm did not project the image of a skilled backpacker except, he imagined, a good backpacker cares more about getting the job done than looking good at it. He was breaking camp in fifteen minutes. That takes skill.

He began walking back to the car with quick steps. Halfway there, he slowed down. His clothes were saturated, his pants were splattered in mud as high as his knees. He saw no reason to rush. Nor did he see why he should waste the solitude now available.

He put the tent and whatever he had rolled into it in the trunk of the Rambler and the plastic tote in the back seat. There would be a trail along the near shore of the lake, probably a wide one, with no one using it. He went south and looked over the lake from various viewpoints to see the waters rolling from raindrops. He went south a mile and another mile. The rain slowed and he thought he could see the island with the bridge to the opposite shore. Nearer, he guessed he was seeing the island the woman had been watching intently at the fishermen's dock. He had not quite gone entirely around the lake, just far enough to feel its size, which was small. He could easily go entirely around it in a day. Of course, he did not linger for such a meaningless achievement. He had much to do in preparing to get back to work in East Lansing by 8:00 in the morning, looking like a respectable representative of Wilson Instrument.

He had seen enough of Sleepy Hollow to know there would be a path running more or less parallel to the one he had just traversed but he was not in the mood for exploring a couple more miles indistinguishable from the rest in this park except for having no lake view. He thought going backward on the trail he already took would give him as many new sights to see, yet that was only an excuse for declaring Sleepy Hollow had been conquered and he was taking the known route back to get on with other business. After a mile, the rain stopped and started and stopped entirely. The lake was so smooth it was hard to accept how rough and noisy it had been on his first pass. When he neared the park headquarters, he could see the corner of the lake where he had camped and where he had danced and met some interesting hippies, older and even more lost than himself. He wondered where they were now. Had they hitched a ride toward Woodstock, or sat in the miserable rain at the park entrance, or diverted to some other adventure? He envied their apparent courage but not the excessive freedom they had found.

While he looked to visualize his evening by their fire, and when the pleasant odors of petrichor conflicted with his imagined scent of a campfire, he knew it was time to return to reality, dry himself off, get into last Friday's clothes, clean up at a gas station and see what's for lunch at El Potrero.

While waiting for the lunch special #2 (chalupita, corn taco and rice) to be served, Dieterich studied his map. Rose Lake Wildlife Area looked interesting for a short afternoon's diversion. He might find an unofficial place to park or camp for the night. If he rose early on Monday morning, which his alarm clock would ensure, he could easily get into Lansing in time for his first appointment.

Rose Lake was bordered with swamp or marsh for much of its perimeter with only one stretch of trail running along the lake shore. It was, as the name implied, more for wildlife than the variety of human entertainments in Sleepy Hollow. What he appreciated most was the diversity of hardwood trees in its forest, clearly an area with more productive soil. He did not wait for evening to enter impressions in his book, and most of his entries were accompanied by sketches. Not surprisingly, a couple hours of drawing did not improve his skill perceptively. He thought he would try redrawing them when he had time for it, developing some techniques. He would look closely at the sketches in *Sand County Almanac* for ideas on technique. Here, in the field, he would gather information on what is interesting to see, mostly small things that a casual visitor would not notice. Someday, he imagined, in a library with various field guides, he might go through his sketches and identify some of the plants he had represented, so he was careful to be accurate. He tried a few scenic views too. In these he avoided concern over details, conveying the overall impression being the essence of the task. The time passed quickly without his noticing until the sun dipped below the trees across the lake. Although he was only a mile from his car, he suddenly worried he was late to make preparations for the night. On his walk back to the car, he focused on the path ahead, missing whatever there was to see off the trail. He could leave his car on the trailhead where he had entered the park and put a note on the windshield saying he had lost his key and would be back with his wife's key between 8:30 and 9:00 in the morning. He would first find some dinner somewhere, not Mexican this time, and set up camp in the dark.

It was a bad plan. He argued with himself over it, pointing out the virtues of self-reliance and low cost, compared to the problems of illegality and discomfort. The winning point was his wish to sit in a lit space to work on his notebook. The ease of getting to work clean and on time was also a factor in his deciding to face the risk of finding no room at the inn, a risk he accepted because Sunday night ought to be a slow night for motels.

He returned to the place where he had slept on Thursday, his first night on this trip. He had cancelled his reservations on Friday morning despite their objections but he did not mind asking again for a room. The clerk did not seem to recognize him or he may simply not have cared that Dieterich had come back. They had rooms and did not turn away or harass customers. The clerk even gave directions to Shoney's Big Boy where Dieterich put everything he wanted for dinner into a bag to be eaten in his room while he filled in the text of the day's entries.

With the ease of a motel supporting him, he did not worry about getting to the job in the morning. Thus, he stayed up late, that is, past his ability to write usefully. He shifted over to improving his sketching. He used the stationery the motel provided, three letter-sized sheets, to copy the effects used in *Sand County Almanac*. None of his sketches looked good, neither in his notebook nor on the hotel stationery, but in both places, he could look quickly and know it was the work of a naturalist, albeit poorly skilled. And he was proud of that much.

<table><tr><td>Monday, July 14</td></tr></table> The Hyundai Mobis manager who met Dieterich on Monday morning (at five minutes before the appointed time) was the least friendly person Dieterich had met in Michigan. He acted as if Dieterich had been to his plant before, or should have been there, and should know what his company needed done but he did condescend to show him the first of his hardness testers and even made a few comments on them individually, proving he knew his own shop in detail. Before he left to do more important work, he challenged Dieterich to ask him a question, implying by his manner that there should not be any questions and there would be no chance to ask any other questions until the work was completed. Suddenly Dieterich recognized him – he was Rusty MacIntyre in a younger form: capable, proud and confident. Dieterich suspected he was also as generous as Rusty although he would not show it unless it was needed. Or perhaps he was exactly what he projected: arrogant and unsympathetic. Either way, Dieterich was not intimidated. He had nothing to lose here.

"Thank you for the heads-up on the history and performance of these three machines." Dieterich placed a hand on one of the hardness testers affectionately. "The invoice says you've got six more in the plant. If that's the right number, nine altogether, I can take some guidance from the operators here to reach the others or you can send me to someone else. I won't be wandering around the plant on my own."

"Damn right you won't. This ain't no place for a young kid. One of the boys working the pressers will show you where the others are. You got your own schedule, but the plant closes at six. Be out by then. Before you go, you tell me if you need to come back."

"Will do," said Dieterich with a smile and he stuck out his hand for a handshake. *Call me a kid if you like. I know I'm young and don't know much of what's going on in this place, but I know my part and you got to respect that if you're working with companies like ours. You asked for me, remember.*

Dieterich did a little math in his mind as he laid out his tools on a clean rag. *Nine machines in nine hours, leaving some time to get started and to get out of the building. I can do a check-up and maintenance in thirty if all goes ideally. Rusty requires me to spend thirty minutes for lunch whether I eat or not. Might get it all done. Don't cut any corners. Tomorrow is only scheduled for five machines and they're not far away.*

None of the nine hardness testers at the Mobis plant were new and none of them were broken or unduly worn. Since the machines were spread among four locations around a large factory, Dieterich decided to credit the strict discipline of the manager with running a good operation.

At 5:30 p.m., he was at the reception desk. He had no message for the manager saying he would be back but he wanted a signature on his invoice. It was not clear if the manager expected that. He asked the receptionist if he was in. She called another office and asked if Dieterich could go in.

He was greeted by a question asked loudly as soon as he entered the room: "Anything wrong with them?"

"All's well." Dieterich walked up to the desk and opened his briefcase. "The certifications of proper performance are with each machine. Here is the full report on each of 'em." He was thinking *They are very simple machines and simple reports.* "This document can serve as certification if needed. And I need a signature on my invoice." He put the invoice with three carbon copies beside the certification report.

"So you're done now? You got them all?"

"Right."

The manager scrawled his signature on each of the carbons without reading any of the papers. He pushed the papers aside and looked down at what he had been doing when Dieterich came in. Dieterich picked up the invoices and detached a carbon for the manager. One handshake per day seemed all he would get from this man so he thanked him for the work and went out for dinner at the steakhouse.

11

 When Dieterich pulled the Rambler into the small parking lot behind the Ferndale office on Tuesday morning, he saw it as if it were his first day, but through the eyes of a permanent employee watching for the arrival of the temporary summer hire, so new he did not know what job he would be doing, where he would live, who he would work for, or if he would eat a meal that night. The actual person he was now, that is, six weeks later, saw an undeserved confidence in his former self. Confidence was far better justified now that he had completed all the living arrangements, trained for the job and actually done some of the job. What's more, he accomplished something he had not even imagined would be on the list for the summer: kissed a girl and been kissed back. Appreciating that confidence was better justified now than it had been a month earlier was itself good, not great, since it was merely confidence in his summer, an isolated period where anyone his age should be feeling good. It was depressing to look beyond the summer. Better to do well and enjoy his talent for managing a simple job.

And this focus on the immediate task served well in the next moments as he backed his car into the only available space. He held his right arm on the back of the passenger seat, using it to help twist his body to see directly behind and he checked several times in the side mirror. The space was narrow, without painted lines on the gravel. He did not hit the wall with his bumper, but he got as close as he could and then squeezed out the half open door and went behind the car to see how close he had come. Two inches was closer than he anticipated. He was sure the brick wall would have not been marked by a tap from his car yet it was satisfying to be so close, as if he had preternatural skill to sense the distance so precisely. "Just luck again" was a thought that did not imply belief in luck, that he would be lucky the next time he needed to be. No, his thought implied he had not been skilled and he ought not to trust himself to repeat the performance.

A month was too little time for the building entrance to have changed although it seemed shabbier now. The door seemed friendlier on that first day because it bore the street number he needed and the name of the company where he was due. Now it bore the familiar name of the benign company that kept him busy eight hours a day, five days a week, a firm entirely lacking in prestige and deserving of a windowless door of dented steel construction and scratched paint, whose hinges squealed painfully every time it opened.

The receptionist gave a coy smile and silly wave when he looked her way. "Welcome back, Deeter! We were taking bets on whether you would show up for work again. I put a buck on yes, he'll be in. So, not too bad in Lansing?"

"Have you ever been to Lansing? The neighborhood where I was working has no palaces or gardens. Lot of jobs there though. Good jobs, I'd guess. The people I met were really nice to me. Didn't make me feel like a teenager in a summer job. You know, I think the company has a good reputation. Wonder why."

"You have to ask Mr. Elias about that I guess. Of course he's on vacation this week. Careful you don't screw up everything before he gets back."

"I'll ask him about Lansing when he gets back. I'll have time to screw up some other city by then. They said Freddy had been to a couple of the Lansing places six months ago. Bet that's what they were thinking, I'm the new Freddy. I hope they aren't feeling any worse about the company when Freddy goes back next time." *So Elise will be away for the rest of the week, dammit.* "Can you give me Wes' home number? I'd like to get his thoughts on something as soon as possible."

Rusty came out of the workshop because he recognized Dieterich's voice. "You say Freddy screwed up Lansing or was that you yourself doing the screwing? I'm the boss around here today so come on into my office and tell me how much damage you did."

By "office" Rusty meant his workbench where he sat while finishing a hard-boiled egg and Dieterich looked over his shoulder to make his oral report.

Rusty leafed through the invoices and brief trip notes. "What's this about the machine might of got wet. What's that mean? You washed it or something?"

"Not me. I'm just guessing it was wet. It had a rusty screw. I didn't say anything to the plant manager about it but I think the whole reason they asked for a maintenance visit, which was a little ahead of schedule, is that one of the machines, they've got four of 'em in a row there..."

"I know the set up. Been there a few times myself."

"Sure, okay. I think the operators asked for the maintenance trip like it was routine and didn't tell their supervisor, or not the plant manager anyway, that one of them wasn't reading right, didn't match the reading on the other ones, you know?"

"So, you're thinking the one got wet?"

"Yeah. I had a hard time getting that set screw out, the one on the bushing 'round the main sensor shaft? It's a bad angle to lean into the screw but I saw right away the middle of the crosshead was buggered. I reached it with a bigger driver, but it wouldn't budge. That was good 'cause it meant I was getting solid contact with the driver.

I gripped it hard and tapped the driver with the ballpeen as I turned and it finally came out."

"You had a replacement screw?"

"Of course I did. You put it in the kit just like every other damn thing that might come up in the field. Put some of that sewing machine oil in the hole and taped it up to hold the oil while I cleaned the rest of it. Turned the set screw tight and loose a few times. It seems good enough now."

Rusty made an indeterminate sound that did not need any reply.

"Do you think soaking it in oil helped any?" asked Dieterich.

"Doubt it. Seems like it didn't do no harm either. Did ya talk to the operators about the water thing?"

"There was one guy watching me close. I didn't ask him anything, just said it seemed to have got some rust in there and that was pretty unusual."

Rusty asked no more questions until he looked over the travel receipts. "Just the gas and a couple meals here. Missing half the hotels. I hoped you saved 'em."

Dieterich explained he had slept in the car or in the woods. Didn't eat three meals every day. Rusty was pretty upset about that. He could not believe Dieterich actually preferred travelling like that. He suspected something odd, like having a girlfriend in the Lansing area or that Dieterich was too shy to get a hotel room or, worst of all, he was trying to save the company the cost of a room. Dieterich was untroubled by Rusty's objections until Rusty added that it was a bad precedent. Dieterich realized he could not explain himself to Rusty. It had been fun when he did it but now it seemed odd to himself too. He changed the conversation over to the invoices he had prepared. They were entirely routine, properly charged, including prorating the travel expenses, fully signed by the plant managers or shop foremen and by Dieterich. Rusty checked Dieterich's toolbox. He said he wanted to be sure any used parts or oil or rags were replaced but he was actually looking for signs of how the whole kit was maintained: were all the tools there, clean and in their place. Dieterich had enjoyed being meticulous about the tools. They were perfect for working on hardness testers. The specialized ones that fit the deep hole to release a hidden rod and the skinny oiling bottle that fit the machine like a hummingbird bill fits a trumpet flower were more important than the training from Rusty in enabling him to do what the factory workers would have found difficult. He knew Rusty would be looking for anything out of place and he knew if Rusty found nothing wrong, he would not mention it. If Rusty found nothing to correct, he would know Dieterich knew this was an inspection. Having the toolbox just right would have been sufficient reward for doing what he should do.

"We'll keep you busy 'round here this week. Get you upstate on Monday again. I saved a few old machines to keep you busy this afternoon. Rebuilding. We get 'em back real cheap. Sell 'em ten or fifteen percent cheaper than new but they gotta work perfect, and they'll have a full lifetime. Good for us; good for them. I'll show what parts to switch out. And we got the cowlings repainted already so they'll be beautiful."

Freddy came in. He said "Excuse me" to Rusty and went to Dieterich to shake his hand. He turned back toward Rusty. "Whadda ya think, Rusty. Is he ready to run on his own yet?"

Rusty said Dieterich had given his report and shown no reason to be fired. Then he suggested Freddy see if he could dig deeper to look for anything left off the report. His sarcasm was meant to suggest they sit somewhere else in the workroom and talk about the Lansing trip.

Freddy was excited to hear some details. He knew the factories in Lansing and the people Dieterich met there. He also knew there was unlikely to be anything difficult to handle on the machines as long as Dieterich did not run into trouble with the people. He wanted to tell some stories of difficult people he had met on trips like Dieterich's but he knew learning to handle personalities required experience, not lectures.

As they talked, Freddy set up a workstation for Dieterich and their talk drifted from describing time in the field to what goes into an overhaul of a hardness tester. Under their table sat a row of used hardness testers. They replaced all the pieces that were prone to wear, regardless of whether the wear was visible. The refurbished machines would be sold at a discount that still guaranteed ample profit.

At lunch, Freddy asked what Dieterich had done on the weekend. Dieterich's answers were short because he had not done much worth talking about. It made him wonder if his journal was worth writing or maybe it was simply more likely to interest a different kind of person. Suddenly he felt guilty for not showing any curiosity in what Freddy had been doing.

"Maybe I shouldn't be telling you this. I haven't said anything to anyone else. But, you see, my favorite girl... I make sound like I've got lots of them. I know some nice women but you always have a favorite, right?"

"Makes sense to be but I've never been in a position to wonder about that."

"Right. So, my favorite girl? I didn't want to think of her that way in case I lost her and then someone else would be my favorite?"

"Sounds like the safe way to think."

"Her name's 'Natasha', her parents are Polish, people call her 'Tasha', well, we had a really good date and then she came over to the trailer. Well, Tasha and me did some thinking about building onto the place. It just shows how we fit together so good. We agreed on a bunch of details, like where we could attach a living room, and, I shoulda said this first, we decided to move the angle of the trailer so the new part would have the view of the lake. The best thing about my site, the lake."

"Sure is. Also, it's quiet out there and you like your neighbors, and you got those shade trees, but the lake's the best."

"You can tell I keep saying 'we can do this' or 'we can do that' so we were talking like more than a dating couple. I didn't propose to her. I would have remembered that. And she didn't propose to me but that would have been okay. Easier than coming up with the words myself. I'm going to get her a ring and get down on one knee and everything to make it official but now I'm pretty sure she's going to say 'yes'."

Dieterich hid his inability to say something wise by rushing over to Freddy and patting him on the back. Then, when Freddy stood up, they hugged.

"You found the right woman! That's got to be one of the hardest things in life and it moves you to the best place. No need to compromise for Fred! He's getting the best girl!"

"Yeah. It feels great. It's not official, but she even suggested we have you over for lunch on Sunday if you can make it. It would be a little better than burgers or maybe we could have burgers with some nice salad she'd make. I don't know what they eat in Poland exactly."

Dieterich felt good for Freddy. He was surprised that Freddy had been shy about proposing. Even a guy with a big personality can be troubled when it comes to asking a question this important. This led directly to how a guy without a big personality, like himself, could get a good partner for living a life. Freddy had simplified some complications by living cheaply, skipping college and taking an entry-level job. He had a future in sales where his broad, sincere smile would move him ahead. Dieterich did not have it all figured out but he had progressed against the absolute hardest part. He had his first girlfriend. It was a relief to know that part had finally started and he sensed he would be better with girls from now on.

Roland was sitting at the kitchen table, chatting with Mrs. Tyler, a plate of brownies between them. Dieterich was there to put his milk in the refrigerator. Milk was the only thing he left in the kitchen. It was for his breakfast cereal.

"Deeter, my man! You been away, right? Getting a vacation already?"

"Nobody goes to Lansing for vacation, not the part of it where I was working."

"Alright. I never been there and now I know I shouldn't go anyway. You agree Mrs. T? That's no place to be?"

"Lansing is a wonderful city! It's big, of course. Like all our big cities, I guess. It's got lots of Black people. Not as much as Detroit. Michigan State's right up there. You probably know more about that school than I do Deeter."

"Well, I didn't see the school, just some factories. They seemed productive, more productive than anything I ever saw in Connecticut. That's probably unfair. Bridgeport must have some factories but I never saw any of them from inside."

"Wes Elias' company reaches all over the state, doesn't it Deeter?"

"Sure does."

"Hey Deeter, they having robberies up there too?"

"Robberies? I suppose it's the same as anywhere. I don't know."

"You heard about them around here, right? Same two guys hit some place every couple days. They did a service station in Rochester Hills over the weekend."

"We don't have much crime here so that's a terribly big story for us." Mrs. Tyler shook her head sadly, picked up another brownie, and then pushed the plate toward Dieterich.

Dieterich hoped Cathy was waitressing tonight. It was in and out of the back of his mind all day. When it was out, his subconscious was missing Elise. He had not focused on either girl until he started walking to dinner. He knew his time in Michigan was passing quickly so he surely had no time for two girlfriends. One kiss did not make a girlfriend. Maybe it did, but not a major affair. And they would be having a second date. Pretty good. So why flirt around with Cathy? Well, because she was so damn good looking. It would not go anywhere. She was over his level and she smiled at him like any waitress does; part of doing a good job; maybe helps with the tips.

As he came within sight of the restaurant, he thought he might call that beautiful girl he met at the Elias' pool. As long as he was dreaming of going out with girls over his level, she would have been good. That idea was so stupid, it stopped his speculations altogether and he resolved not to care if Cathy was on duty or not.

It seemed only fair when he stepped inside Romero's that Cathy was not there. More than fair, it was good, for thus he could forgo the game of catching her eye and dwell instead on his only realistic, feminine partner prospect, Elise. He missed her now that he could drop the distraction of Cathy. Conversation had flowed so easily with Elise. They had kissed most comfortably, just as a kiss should occur. She would be interested in hearing about his weekend trip. He would enjoy telling her about it, reliving his independence and self-reliance. And he would enjoy hearing about her vacation no matter where she went or what she did. His would be the grander tale but hers would be a view to a girl's private life. She would tell him her thoughts and might even mention wishing she had been with him. They would also have to conduct the business of planning their next date. The spaghetti western! She even suggested a movie that he was sure to like, not some surfer film or teen romance for suburban ingénues.

"You came back! I thought we lost you."

Ooh, Cathy was so fine. When he turned his head to face her, she was not smiling unless that was a smile expressed in her eyes. She was wearing eye shadow. He had never noticed it before on her, maybe because he had not looked her in the eyes for more than an instant.

"Suddenly, it's awfully nice to be back," he answered. It was a good answer but uncalculated, merely honest, almost like a thought instead of a come-on.

He picked up the menu and looked it over. "Haven't tried this yet." He was not sure what entrée lay under his finger, but he was sure he was pointing to the dinner section. "I was in Lansing. For work. Hashed around some woods over the weekend. Camped out kinda rustic. Don't have any equipment with me over the summer."

"You went camping in Lansing?"

Her question could not have been serious.

"The most nature I saw in the city was the weeds growing out of the cracks in the sidewalk. Don't knock it, they've got some big weeds and lots of cracks."

"Yeah, okay. Glad you had a good time, sir. I worked both days. Made some overtime so I guess that was good for me."

His surprise dinner was fish. Without the menu, he could not say what kind of fish. The fries were not perfect, but he was not paying attention to his food. He was enjoying telling all about his weekend to either Cathy or Elise. As he formed words in his mind, he shifted his audience. The story fit best with Elise, but the unusual exchange with Cathy, who was there in the restaurant with him, kept bringing her into the imagined conversation. He did not care who was in the fantasy, the weekend had been a huge success, something to remember despite its humble scale compared to the spectacular views during his summer in Colorado. Why did he feel so proud of it? He wanted to study this question. He ought to try explaining it to Elise if he could find any explanation. Maybe he was a solitary man. Maybe he would be a good hermit. Maybe he would like a career in a Rocky Mountain fire tower. That would not require an engineering degree.

"How about some dessert tonight?"

Dieterich nodded while he searched for a reply. Go with the truth, respectfully, was his guidance to self.

"You have a good idea there, Cathy. I like pie as much as anyone can. Wish you mentioned it earlier. I can't stuff anymore in my skinny stomach tonight."

"So you've got to get home now?"

"Not exactly home. I live in Connecticut. Sorta. Since I went to college, I don't live anywhere for long."

"Yeah, I know. You live at the Tylers. They're in my church."

"Really! So is my boss. In that church, I mean."

"She leaned forward as she put the bill on the table."

"But do you need to get back right now?"

"Well, no, not..."

"I'm sorry. I'm not trying anything funny. It's just with those robberies around, I don't feel safe walking home. I live close. Maybe you could just walk a couple blocks with me."

"Sure. No problem. I heard about that. Some place in Rochester Hills yesterday, wasn't it? So what time do you finish up?"

"Nine o'clock, usually. Sometimes it's a little longer to finish cleaning up everything."

"It's OK. Don't rush. I'll be outside."

"Just the walk home you know. Nothing else."

"Yeah, just a short, safe walk. Not a big deal."

Dieterich paid the woman at the cash register and made no further sign toward Cathy, not a glance. No matter her intentions, she probably did not want to be seen soliciting a customer.

It was not yet eight o'clock. He could be back in his room in ten minutes, read for half an hour, and be back at the restaurant ten minutes before nine in case she left earlier than usual. That left twenty minutes of walking time and thirty minutes of reading time to guess what this was all about. No, not guess, it was not a solvable mystery. He could devise some possible rationales for Cathy's sudden attention and then devise proper responses for them.

First of all and obviously, his planning began, *no matter what she is thinking, this is not going to culminate in a sex scene, not tonight, let's say. Second, is there any chance she is actually scared of the robbers? I don't know much about them, maybe she has read about them or heard more than me, but I thought they were moving around the state and robbing stores so it would be outside their pattern to molest a girl just walking at night near the same place as the last robbery. But girls have been scared for less dangerous scenarios and they have been right to be careful. Maybe she is what she said she is. Still, I've got to think a girl that attractive knows that asking a stranger - almost a stranger - she knows where I live - if she knows that she probably talked to the Tylers and they would say I'm a nice, safe guy — but what girl with a face so sweet and long legs swishing around her waitress outfit wouldn't know a guy in my place might be a worse problem than some very unlikely robbers? Could be she's not that smart. Could be, and this is more likely, she can take care of herself pretty well with someone like me but not so much with the robbers in the news.*

Dieterich lay on his bed with his book and did not read an entire page during his allotted thirty minutes. He lost track of the game of planning how to respond to whatever came up on their walk and instead constructed scenarios that ended in sexual scenes either this night or soon.

He washed his face with cold water and went downstairs quietly but Mr. Tyler looked away from the television and asked, "You going out again tonight?"

I wonder if he cooked up this walk-me-home idea with Cathy after church on Sunday. "Yeah, just a little. I have some thinking that needs to get done. So just walking around the neighborhood."

Mr. Tyler laughed and apologized for sounding as if he were checking on Dieterich.

At nine fifteen, he started to worry he had misunderstood the arrangement. He thought he had said he would meet her outside, but she might be waiting inside for him. Maybe he should have waited at a back door because that's the way she normally left the building. He did not care very much if he had misunderstood. It would have been unfortunate but the whole idea of walking her home did not make much sense to him.

When she stepped outside, she looked around and saw him quickly. He was on the edge of the light coming from the inside of the restaurant and before he could wave to her, the light went off and she could not see him. She skipped along the sidewalk like a ten-year-old as he came toward her and their eyes adjusted to the darkness so they could see each other.

"C'mon this way," she said and grasped his arm which he quickly bent the way his mother had taught him for escorting a lady. It bothered him that he was not escorting her from the street side as his mother had advised was appropriate to protect the lady from horses and mud.

"Thanks so much for doing this. It's probably completely safe just like it always is. Just you have to think a little more with the news talking about crime even around here."

"Well, Cathy, to be completely honest, I feel honored to be asked."

"An honor is it? I never felt scared around here before and now I still don't. What's your name? You never said?"

"I'm called 'Deeter'."

"That your real name?"

"My real name is Dieterich. Named after my grandfather. No one calls me that except my mother when she's mad at me about something."

"Yeah, that happen much?"

"Not lately. Been at school and then doing this summer job."

"Where d'ya go?"

"Lehigh."

"Where's that?"

"Pennsylvania. It's known for engineering which is what I'm taking but I need to change to something else. I'm not the engineering type, like my dad." He wanted to ask her something to show interest What came to his mind as the natural thing was an awkward cliché: what's your major. He was afraid she had no college aspirations and would feel embarrassed.

"I'm going to Central Michigan this fall. I took off a year to make some money. So then I go for a year and I'll need to take off more time to pay for the next year."

"Uh huh. What do you want to study?"

"Probably nothing they have to offer. I'd like to study the world. Get out of Rochester Hills and not be in Detroit either. That where you work: Detroit?"

"Worse. Ferndale."

"Okay, I live here." They had walked just over two blocks. She dropped her hand from his arm and pointed across the street to a two-story apartment building behind a lawn no more than ten feet deep.

"It's a nice night, Cathy. And very nice to meet you."

"We could go around the block," she suggested.

They reached the first corner without speaking again. There was no longer any gallant pretense that he was protecting her return home – this was a try-out for a date. She directed him across the street, a sign that they were going more than around a block.

"You know what I want to do? Not now, next month? I haven't told anyone but I've been thinking of it. You know that music festival in New York, rock music, upstate?"

"No. You thinkin' you want to go to it?" Dieterich was wondering if she was asking him to take her, if that is why she asked to see him. Or maybe she just wanted him to buy her ticket.

"I'm thinking I want to grow my hair long and straight and wear a thin braid on one side and go around in worn-out jeans and meet kids who've been to Kathmandu and listen to Otis Redding live. Would that be wild?"

"Is that you or do you just want to try it on.?"

"Definitely want to see if I can be like that. Not really doing it now. I live with my mother. She'd be happy if I kept living with her and moved up someday a few years on from waitress to cashier. She'd be happy if I never needed to buy any more clothes but would not put up with it if I was wearing anything that looked too worn. She'd say we can't look poor but we're pretty near there."

Dieterich could see a shadow of himself in her position. His was the brighter identity, far brighter prospects, but similar in his parents' wanting for him what they had for themselves. He worried about disappointing them by being anything else and yet it was only in the minor matters of clothes and speech and course selection that he was fulfilling their expectations.

"I should grow some hair. I don't want a job where I gotta wear a tie."

"You wear a tie now."

"It's just for the summer. It's who my folks think I have to be, I mean, not this job but a job where you got to wear a tie. They would say I have been lucky and can have a respectable profession. That's how they say people like us are not better than plumbers and taxi drivers and factory workers. Our jobs and our pay and our houses are better, not us. So they would say, I think. Maybe I shouldn't say that. They don't talk about our class of people, probably don't think about it much. It just is."

"Oh shit! So you're rich. Forget it. You can grow your hair but you can't drop out and find another place to be."

He sure did not feel rich but he knew he could not argue with her about that. No one gave him a car when he turned sixteen. He'd never been on a fancy vacation. His parents were aware of not spoiling him or his sister. If he said his family was not rich, just "well off," he would prove himself an idiot.

"Don't give up me completely, please. I'm not sure you're wrong. I am a fuck-up. Doing bad in school for the very good reason that I've been too lazy to be a student. But I'm not too lazy to work. I'm good at this job I have. It's easy, but I work."

"Bad schoolwork? Well, that's something. Will Daddy pay for you to go somewhere else?"

"Oh yeah. And I'll take it, I guess. And be a better student at a worse school." They walked quietly, still going away from her apartment. "Damn, Cathy, this is embarrassing. When I was just a quiet young guy in a tie and decent table manners, you could imagine I was somebody worth meeting. I could have told otherwise. I got some good qualities, I think. Hard to see, hard to be sure."

"Not so confident with girls either, I'd say."

"You'd be right about that although it doesn't bother me. I figure I'll love a woman and be married someday. I can be a good person. Helpful, handy at things, not greedy." *Not nearly enough for you. Not in your class,* he thought, but he knew she would not understand those words as he intended them.

"I admit you dropped a few points with that bad student story. Didn't flunk out completely yet, right? So you don't want to wear a tie. What do you want to do?"

"Getting that question a lot lately and don't have a good answer... I didn't expect to or especially wish to ever go walking in the night with you but here we are and this should have been on my list of what I wanted to do."

"Not what I was asking."

"I know it wasn't but it's true and I know it when I don't know the answer to your real question. Be fair. Tell me what you want to do in the years after you get back from the concert in New York."

"Wait a minute. You weren't hoping to go out with me? Never noticed me at the restaurant? Just went there for the food?"

Dieterich was sure she knew he had been aware of her and had an eye on her although he was too polite or shy or modest to look longingly in her direction. He was not ready to declare her the woman of his dreams if that was why she was pushing this discussion.

"I've already lost points down to near failing. Before I drop any farther, let me hear your idea for tomorrow and beyond."

"Guess I'm not as irresistible as I thought I was in that waitress skirt."

"I was not resisting. You made a positive impression in which I took appropriate pleasure. Now if you had more relaxed hair and a loose blouse and tight jeans and no business function to perform, it would have been hard to act blasé."

"What's blasé?"

"Blasé? Not sure exactly. Disinterested, I guess. Doesn't matter. You're just torturing me to embarrass me for being insecure with a firecracker like Cathy the waitress. Come on. What's your idea for your future?"

"Who knows at this age? I'm 19 and I know I'm not going to big-time college. I'll get married but I got to find a boy first and I'm not doing so good on that. Don't want to have kids and everything too soon; no hurry, you know. Not into trippin', or maybe I could be. Wish I could sing. I'd like to be in a band; live that life a few years. We're too young to settle into a life before we know what's possible. I don't want to be my mother. I love her for sure but that's not the same thing."

She grabbed his arm and steered him across the street and turned back toward her house.

"I'm getting cold now. My mother will be expecting me."

"Here take my jacket."

"Oh my god! You really are a good boy, aren't you! No, I'm not that cold. I'll just hold your arm."

They walked silently for a block. Dieterich liked the contact yet he felt uncomfortable because the conversation had stopped. It was his moment to act. "Think there's a concert we could go to around here, coming up? I mean probably in Detroit."

"There must be. I can look in the paper. I never went to one except in my high school. I saw posters in town for Simon and Garfunkel."

"Tell me tomorrow at dinner what's your fancy."

"My what?"

12

<table>
<tr><td>Wednesday, July 16</td></tr>
</table>

Again and again while at work on Wednesday, Dieterich felt himself losing focus. And every time he noticed it, he took a deep breath as a signal to himself to be serious again. Flunking out of school had taught him something. His future could no longer be assumed to run at or near the level of his father's. The opportunities that had always been available when needed would not keep coming. He could not picture himself on skid row but it had become hard to picture where he was headed. Wherever, he was not going to flunk out of this job. He could do it and do it well and for the summer that was absolutely necessary. As for having two girls, that was secondary, utterly amazing, but secondary because he would have no girls if he did not grow up and take responsibility. Going to class had not been the most enjoyable way to spend time but a few hours of it would have kept his future alive. After work, he would think about the amazing dilemma of having two girls. As soon as he thought that phrase "two girls," he started to think in a dozen directions but before he chose one, he took another deep breath and focused on the machine in front of him.

He tried not to watch the clock as the end of the day slowly approached. He knew quitting time would arrive eventually and free him to explore the issues he had been actively ignoring. In mid-afternoon, Freddy even said Dieterich should take it easy. He was too intense and might get tired of working there. Freddy suggested they should step outside for a break. He told Rusty they would be back in ten minutes. He needed to check what had Dieterich so revved up. Dieterich appreciated Freddy's concern but he could not explain his anxiety even if he tried, and he did not want to say anything about having a date with Elise. Freddy would know of that eventually, but not in the context of his acting stressed or what Freddy thought he was seeing.

Dieterich bought a Coke for himself and one for Freddy from the vending machine. They lingered outside on the shady side of the parking lot while Dieterich explained how excited he was by the chance to work on his own, to have the trust of the company behind him and how he was not going to let them down.

On the way home after work, Dieterich drove more slowly than usual because his mind was trying to organize thoughts on Elise and Cathy. He kept returning to the idea that he did not need to choose between them now. People dated, they saw each other, and they sometimes kissed and did other intimate things without any understanding that they were committed for life. There were several stages to pass through and he ought to expect to do it with more than the first two girls he dated seriously at least one time.

By the time he was back in his room, he had convinced himself he was not facing a dilemma. He was going to dinner and hoped to see Cathy. If he did, he hoped she would be friendly again. If she was, he would suggest he would like to walk her home. If she agreed, he would talk about going to a concert together. That was this stage. He need not plan any further right now. The proof that he had convinced himself of this was that he then read the rest of *Sand County Almanac* before dinner and was not distracted about seeing Cathy. The proof that he was not entirely free of worry was that he first checked his watch at 6:45 p.m. This was the exact time he should wash up for his short walk to Romero's.

The restaurant offered two tables beside the windows facing the street, four booths along one side wall and six tables in the middle of the room. Dieterich did not adopt a favorite location but he avoided the booths and the window tables so they could be used by others, "guests" rather than a regular like himself. He did not prefer the table closest to the cashier because he felt he would be more easily watched there. As usual, the room was not full and he had a choice of four tables that fit his selection rules. He sat with his back to the cashier, not to be rude to her, he did not imagine she would notice or care where he sat, but to avoid paying attention to her if he was having a conversation with Cathy.

"Hello, Deeter. Welcome back."

Oddly, Dieterich had to turn around to see Cathy. "Oh my god!" he uttered quietly but loudly enough for her to hear. It was not a phrase he normally used, probably never used before, but it was the only thing he could think of quickly. Anything else would require thought.

She moved around to face him. She was smiling beyond control but that is not what held Dieterich's attention. She had cut her hair very short.

"Don't say anything now. Meet me after work. OK?" She stopped smiling and returned to her waitress face, but Dieterich remembered the smile had been there.

Dieterich did not say anything. He just stared until he winked and smiled as big as he could. "Oh, I will be there. 9:00? Pick out something for my dinner, please? I'm gobsmacked here."

She had never heard of "gobsmacked" and figured he made it up on the spot which sounded pretty clever to her. She wrote "cheesesteak sub, baked potato, slaw, iced tea" on her pad, tore off the page and took it to the kitchen without saying anything more.

Having invested so much energy in worrying about his moral responsibility vis a vis his two feminine prospects, he decided to compromise on the themes in his almanac by writing out the questions and answers he had covered since leaving the office. He used the clock to limit the entry for the day although it was among the longest entries so far because he wrote more easily than usual.

At 8:45 he left the house for the five-minute walk to Romero's. He thought of rolling a cigarette and immediately wondered how he could have been so stupid. It would have been a petty, hipster move to do it in front of her, which he would not have done, but worse, he would have had the smell of smoke on him. Even if she did not mind that, it would have branded him a smoker which he was not and he did not want to be classified as one. *Why then,* he wondered, *had he carried the Bull Durham along and why had he thought of smoking one?*

Cathy came out before 9:15 and apologized for being late. She had been even later last time he walked her home, but he liked the apology and took it as sincere. He was tempted to ask if she was still afraid of the robbers; he sensed she would not like to be teased. The false excuse for asking him to walk with her was the second-best thing that happened to him in Michigan.

"OK, let's go," she said as she approached Dieterich who was standing outside the light from the restaurant. She walked quickly as if she were in a hurry and did not care if he were near enough to converse, as if he were there to protect her from some unlikely bandits. When he neared her, she walked faster and still said nothing. He followed to the end of the block where she turned. He stopped at the corner and watched her continue away.

She said I should meet her and then she said OK, let's go, he reminded himself.

Then she stopped, not very far away yet and looked back at him.

"That's good," she said. "But come along now. They can't see us anymore."

When he reached her, she took his hand and explained the cooks and the cashier were whispering loudly in a way to annoy her about that guy in the tie has a little crush on her like they were teenyboppers. And about how he just wanted to get his hands on her since she was just a waitress and probably didn't know her way around city boys like him.

"We didn't do a goddam thing in front of them or anywhere else. My boss, the owner's wife, the goddam cashier, tells me to be nice to the customers, friendly, not too friendly, so what's her problem if I said a sentence to you?"

Dieterich could not think of what to say. He wanted to tell her how beautiful she was. He put his arm around her and pulled her close to his side.

"And she said you were laughing when I stepped away, laughing at m-my h-haircut." As she spoke her voice broke and she began to sob. Dieterich stopped, and stood in front of her with one hand on each of her shoulders.

He looked into her face although he could not see her clearly in the dark. It took two or three seconds to find some words. He spoke softly.

"Cathy, I cannot imagine why they would be so cruel. I don't know them and they don't know me. They have no way to know what I was thinking and if they did, it would have been outrageously unkind to mock you like that. I know what I was thinking and I am thinking it still – that you were never more beautiful than you were tonight. The short hair... I can't describe your effect... I think you suddenly look more modern, like a model for eye shadow maybe... how young women wished they looked. I think you were stepping away from Rochester Hills with this look."

"Oh Deeter, you know it, what I was doing. I wanted to be up to the times. These are exciting times to be our age but not by waitressing at Romero's. I cut it to so I could have long, straight hair. First, I got rid of the perm. And my mother can't send me to the salon to get it back. She says I look like a little boy, a pretty little boy."

"No, there is nothing of a boy in what I am seeing. She is used to seeing her little daughter. Growing up is hard for her to appreciate. You look like a woman, Cathy, a stylish, intelligent, sexy woman."

She reached her arms around his neck and pulled his head down to kiss him hard and long on the lips. When she pulled back a few inches to breathe, he leaned forward for a quick touch on her lips and then stood up straight with his hands running through her hair. He kissed the top of her head.

"C'mer. Let me show you something," she said as she ran across the street and up the block. He chased her until she stopped by a tall fence. She shoved him into the fence to a corner that was dark and protected from the street. They kissed again.

"I'm sorry, Deeter, for being such a baby about their stupid talk. I feel better now."

"Me too. I feel way better."

"Do you think we could go to that concert, the one with Simon and Garfunkel?"

"Of course. I've been looking forward to talking about it again."

"I looked into it. They're doing the *Bookends* album. I think it's good for me. It's about going through stages in life, you know, like books on a shelf. And I feel like it's time to get into a new stage."

"I do too. And I'm guaranteed to be starting a new stage after this summer." He did not explain exactly what he meant by that. "Do you know when they are coming? Should I get some tickets?"

"They'll be in the Olympia Arena for two nights in the first week of August."

"I'll tell my office I need to be here then."

"Do you know the Olympia, the Old Red Barn where the Detroit Red Wings play?"

"No. They do concerts there too?"

"The Beatles been there twice already, and Elvis too."

"Well, you don't get any bigger shows than that. Guess I can figure out the tickets."

"No, Honey. I'll get the tickets and then you pay me for them. Can we do that?"

"That would be perfect, Dear." It was not a perfect arrangement. The tickets might be more than he wanted to pay. Or, more ominously, she might ask for more than they actually cost. He was hooked hard now and he knew he was going to give her whatever she asked for. And then he retracted that thought. There were limits to what he would give her. He was not thinking only of money here. She was a finer woman than he ever expected to have for his very own and it was destabilizing to feel her interest in him. And it was frightening to consider what would happen when she found more of his weaknesses.

"Thank you so much, Deeter." Cathy leaned into him, pressing herself against his chest. He embraced her and moved his hands across her back while he imagined he was feeling her breasts against his chest. She held her kiss only a few seconds and said she was terribly tired now by the stress and the relief he had brought. Then she skipped away toward home with one look back and a wave when she was a half block away. He was still watching her.

Thursday, July 17 Dieterich spent the next day refurbishing hardness testers. He ate lunch with Rusty and Freddy at Rusty's workbench while Rusty talked about what Freddy would be doing if he focused on sales: about using maintenance appointments to look for expanding operations that might be constrained by a shortage of testing equipment and setting aside time to visit new factories with foundry operations and going to conferences of plant managers and finding other ways to put the company forward. He even talked about working in other states with additional salesmen once he established himself. Freddy asked few questions but he was obviously especially curious about how much time the company would allow him on sales efforts and what commissions he was likely to receive. Rusty was vague when assessing the earning potential of going into sales but his estimates were clearly much higher than Freddy would ever make on his current hourly job. Always Rusty emphasized the importance of knowing well both the products he was selling and the needs of potential customers. "Build a reputation for the long run, not just to make the immediate sale," he repeated in various applications spoken in his own expletive-laden patois. Freddy was attentive and excited to hear the lessons although Dieterich doubted Freddy could retain all the ideas without taking notes.

That night, Cathy was not working at Romero's. Dieterich could not remember which was her usual day off and he worried that she had quit out of embarrassment over some thoughtless teasing. Or she may have confronted her boss, the cashier and owner's wife, and been fired for getting out of control. Or she might have quit because her radical hairstyle was the opening round in her rebellion against the outdated mediocrity of Rochester Hills. She might have been sick. She might have gone away for some reason with her mother. Or it might have been her normal day off, a fact he should have known. He did not ask about her or act as if he noticed she was missing. He smiled at her replacement and said a sentence or two on a subject he immediately forgot.

| Friday, July 18 |

On Friday evening, Cathy was on duty as usual if her short hair could now be called "usual." When she came to his table, he looked into her face without showing any expression. When she looked back, he rolled his eyes up to her hair and smiled hard. He pointed to something on the menu, a soup and salad, and said, "I'll meet you around the corner after nine." She answered "very good, sir," completing their conversation until they met later.

Around the corner, a little past nine o'clock, Dieterich met Cathy who was in a good mood.

"Were you here last night?" she asked, walking beside him. "Did you miss me?"

"Yes, I was here, that is, I was back there at the restaurant. And I missed you."

"I sometimes have Saturday off and I'm always off on Sunday and then maybe one more day but I don't know what's the one more day much in advance. They think I don't do anything in the evening so I'm always available. Probably my mother told them that. She got me the job."

"And what did you do yesterday?"

"Went into Detroit. Went to the Olympia and bought some concert tickets! Pretty good seats too. I'm sorry, I got good seats and they were kinda expensive. Don't worry, I'll pay my half."

"You got them? Right on, right on! What's expensive mean?"

"Sixty dollars. I picked the seats before I realized how much they were. I couldn't believe them. But that's what they are. I mean sixty dollars each. And it's gonna be twelve dollars to park. I'll get half of that, too."

Dieterich looked up and down the street. Then he leaned over and kissed her quickly on the lips. "What a sweet deal I got. The deal was you get the tickets and I pay for 'em. You did the work. All the way into town just to get them. I'm glad you got good seats. We're gonna have a good time."

"Did you know they'd be so expensive? You been to a lot of big concerts?"

"I've been to the Fairfield Symphony, maybe four or five times. And I've been to some school band concerts and one dance and the prom. The prom was the only one that was expensive, not as expensive as this and nowhere near as exciting."

Saturday, July 19 On Saturday, Dieterich consulted Freddy's map and went hiking in Mayberry State Park. It was not very far west of Rochester Hills. At 950 acres, it was more than adequate for a day trip, providing ample ecological fuel for his journal. Also, more than adequate was the fast-food chain restaurant where he had a fried chicken dinner.

13

On Sunday, Dieterich got up at his usual time because he wanted his body to keep on schedule. He was vying with his alarm clock, trying to wake up within five minutes before it rang. When he went downstairs to get his milk from the refrigerator, he met the Tylers leaving for church. (They did not mind that he never went with them.) He said Wes and his family might be back from vacation and asked the Tylers to say hello for him if they ran into them.

He was, of course, hoping such a welcome-back message from him might reach Elise. Despite the more numerous and protracted kisses he had shared with Cathy, he remained very interested in Elise. While slowly chewing his way through a large bowl of Rice Krispies alone at the kitchen table, he remembered the frisson of leaning close to Elise's face and seeing her receptivity. She was a completely different person from Cathy but kissing her was identically marvelous to kissing the other. This was surprising. He could not decide if it was frustrating that an automatic preference was unclear, or was intrigued to await for nature to assert itself. *Whatever you do*, he advised himself facetiously, *don't meet any more girls in Michigan.*

Back in his room, he whiled away the morning sketching various details. The corner where two walls and the ceiling met was simple. He did all four corners of the room from his perspective while leaning against the head of the bed. He shaded the three planes appropriately. This was encouraging, almost an artful collection. He would get a sketchpad somewhere and try some more sketches in the woods. Freddy's invitation to lunch was for one o'clock, so Dieterich sketched a few more things in the room until eleven o'clock: the corner where the floor met two walls complicated by the nearby closet door, a close view of the corner of the window showing only one pane with the curtain pushed aside to

simplify it, and his sneakers lying as he had left them on the floor. The sneakers were poorly drawn, a challenge he could repeat another day when he had more time to see if he could do better. A few attempts of the same subject might make an interesting page in his sketchbook.

On the way to Freddy's, he stopped at the grocery store to buy some flowers. He had asked Freddy what he could take to lunch and Freddy insisted his girlfriend (he had said her name was Natasha which Dieterich frequently reminded himself so he would greet her properly) was in charge of the arrangements and would have everything. Dieterich would make it clear the flowers were for her in recognition of her efforts for the lunch, not for his buddy from work.

When Dieterich arrived at Freddy's trailer, very nearly exactly on time, he did not see anyone outside nor did he see the grill or lawn furniture where they had been on his previous visit. He searched his memory for evidence that this was the right time and place. He recalled several times they had confirmed the arrangements although it had always been verbal and might have reflected the prejudice of his original understanding. "See you Sunday" might mean another Sunday. "See you Sunday" might be a mishearing of "See you Saturday." One o'clock had always seemed late to meet for lunch. Maybe it was eleven o'clock or maybe it was six o'clock for dinner. Checking what was stored in his memory brought back the incident when he was in sixth grade and went to his music teacher's house for his trombone lesson and Mr. Burt met him at the door and asked why his mother was driving away, just as she always did when she dropped him off. Dieterich had not remembered that this was the week when he was to play his recital. And he had not known at all that he was the only student at the recital, a special opportunity for Mr. Burt to show off his star pupil to a small group of music teachers. Mrs. Burt, who would be playing his piano accompaniment, took him into the bedroom to try on one of Mr. Burt's oversized white shirts and ties to replace the tee-shirt on Dieterich. Dieterich hoped he played well that evening to make up for having no parents with him but he had no recollection at all of the performance fourteen years ago. All he could do now was knock on the door and see what comes next.

Sounds of two people rushing to the door preceded the knob turning. In those brief moments, Dieterich shifted from worrying whether this was the right day to guessing what Natasha would be like. Freddy was a very fine fellow, but not what society usually regarded as a good catch. He was not even better looking than Dieterich himself since he was soft in the paunch and round in the face with a hairline too high for a man his age. Dieterich also thought for a single instant that women would think of his prospects as an earner were much higher than Freddy's and then he remembered that, even if women thought this, the image was false, that he was the one who had flunked out of college and had no idea of how to earn a living, while Freddy was being groomed for promotion.

Freddy opened the door and was immediately pushed aside by an attractive young woman, too attractive for good ol' Freddy, maybe Freddy's sister. "Deeter!" she shouted and stepped into the door to throw her arms around him, pulling him inside the trailer. Dieterich could not remember if Freddy had told him his sister's name. He certainly had no idea of it. He smiled as hard as he could and held onto the woman, who might be a sister rather than the woman who was supposed to be there. He held onto her arms and said more loudly than normal for him, "What a great greeting! Let me go out and knock again so I can get another one."

Freddy was looking very happy. He took the flowers and asked "Are these for me or Tasha?"

"I just handed them to you for you to put them in a jug for Tasha."

"I told her you would be right on time. We were just cutting up some tomatoes in case you want some on your sandwich. Everything's ready. The table and chairs are set up by the lake. We'll go down there, kick back, have a beer. If it's getting hot we can take a swim. Eat whenever you want. Row out on the lake. I got my neighbor's boat for the day."

"It's all good. Tasha, I heard you had some ideas for fixing up the place, adding on or something?"

She took Dieterich by the hand and explained their plans for expanding. Freddy followed behind and did not interrupt her presentation. Dieterich decided

Tasha was a little pudgy for someone her age and therefore likely to cross the line into heavy in a few years. He also knew how superficial he was for thinking this. Having a woman this bright-eyed and personable by his side someday was as much as he could wish.

That evening, Dieterich had no interest in dinner. The sandwiches and salads and desserts at Freddy's were enough for the rest of the day. He was tired from rowing in the sun but he expected to long remember the pleasure in pulling the oars to full speed across the pond without a break, and then sitting in the stern with one oar, wiggling it to slowly return along the shady shoreline, looking into the reeds and bushes while Freddy and Natasha chatted quietly. It could have been his future self he was transporting, if his future worked out very well. Of course, he did not see himself with Natasha but he was not sure if he was seeing Elise or Cathy leaning into that man's shoulder.

He arrived back at the Tylers about six. He would write in his journal, read for a couple hours and go to bed early. Cathy never worked on Sunday night so she would not miss him at the restaurant. After he finished writing, he settled on the bed to read and Roland knocked at his door. Dieterich called for him to come in. Sam followed closely.

"You coming down, man?" Roland asked. "Mrs. T says we should watch the TV with them."

Dieterich was pretty sure he had a standing invitation to watch TV with the Tylers and he assumed Roland and Sam did as well. Maybe the Tylers had not mentioned it to them before. "No thanks. I'm beat. Maybe another time."

"Suit yourself. Later," concluded Roland. Sam waved and grunted something intended to be cordial.

Ten minutes later, Mrs. Tyler knocked. "Come, Dear. You have to come downstairs. They will be landing soon."

Dieterich's mother had always regarded television as a low form of entertainment. After he had grown out of Saturday morning cartoons, watching TV was limited to evenings on non-school nights. He had not wanted to see any more television, partly because only two channels came in clearly at his house and partly because no one he knew ever mentioned seeing anything on television apart for a fad one year for Soupy Sales. There was extraordinary television coverage in the aftermath of the Kennedy assassination, but he knew of nothing similar before or since.

The Tyler's had raised three children in this house, but their living room was small. Sam and Roland were there before Dieterich so they were on the couch and Dieterich sat on the floor, as if he were just a kid. It took only a few moments to realize why he had been invited to watch and who was doing what landing. He had forgotten, or never known, what day it would occur. He had missed the landing of the lunar module but the announcer spoke of the next step as the most important, when an astronaut left the module. Soon Dieterich would realize the announcer would always label whatever step was next as the most important one, getting back in the module, lifting off from the moon, docking with the main ship, etc.

It took six and a half hours to progress from landing the module to opening the door for Neil Armstrong. During the latter part of this time while the television broadcast live, there was almost no news from inside the capsule. The television replayed highlights from the launch and the three-day flight and the orbiting of the moon and the landing, mostly as described verbally. There was not a lot to see once they left earth although some cartoon drawings illustrated the main ideas. Much of the drama was lost on Dieterich because he had faith in the ability of NASA. He was not very impressed that the rockets worked and the calculations to reach the moon were correct and the landing was completed as planned. Were the scientists and engineers and others involved not competent? This was their job. If they could not do it safely, they would not send men on the mission. The television announcers acted as if every accomplishment was worth astonishment. He did not notice how his confidence contrasted with the insecurity others felt, but later this moment returned to him as a lost opportunity for insight. He had not watched history closely enough to see how messy it is. High school textbooks summarize what happened in certain past times without saying anything at all about what could have happened if one additional nail had fallen off a horseshoe leading to losing the battle and the war and the civilization. The moon landing was unprecedented in obvious ways and yet felt routine from the viewpoint of a boy of Dieterich's experience and easy acceptance of what he absorbed from his surroundings.

After an hour of sitting on the floor to watch a small screen across the room, Dieterich was as well informed as if he had been paying attention to the meager news sources he had followed at home, and he was impatient to see the module door open. He was tiring of the repetition in the commentary with nothing new happening when just before ten o'clock, the promise was kept, the module door opened and Armstrong worked his way down the ladder.

"A small step for a man, one giant leap for mankind." Armstrong hopped onto the soft lunar surface. There was applause in the NASA control room but no one stirred in the Tylers' living room.

Nah, I don't like that mini-speech. Dieterich was disappointed in the big moment. He easily forgave the scratchy, black-and-white imagery, but the build-up had him expecting an emotional connection he did not feel. *It was obviously prepared by someone back at NASA headquarters or, maybe, the White House. It does not come from the astronaut's heart. Oh, I guess it's all right. He's not unlike a football player who does not speak his own truth at the end of a game, sticking to the platitudes he has been taught by the PR office. And it is kinda humble to point out that hop onto the lunar surface is not his personal achievement so much as the product of a huge cooperative effort by scientists and engineers.* No one mentioned the taxpayers' contributions to the effort.

As the moonwalk progressed there was no greater moment. Setting up a camera to show the astronauts cavorting and setting up a flag with a stick so it would hang as if in the wind brought out how much of the effort was public entertainment and braggadocio as opposed to science. And that led to wondering what science should be doing on the moon. Spokespersons for NASA did not hide from the comparison. They spoke of the inspiration this exploration provides for Americans generally and young Americans more specifically.

I do not feel inspired by all this, Dieterich answered silently. *I am entertained, but not by enough to justify all the effort that went into this. Isn't there much more important science research needed for problems on earth? Medicine, more efficient machines, understanding the environment, hunger...Sure, it's a big deal, and very cool. I like knowing about the moon geology and the nature of stars and stuff. Personally I, more than most people, love exploration and would love to go into the upper Amazon or the lower Grand Canyon or cross the Zambezi at Victoria Falls. I don't care about being first. And another thing... so what if the Russians got to space first and America got to the moon first?*

When Sputnik was announced on television twelve years earlier, Dieterich listened to his parents express fears about Russia but he did not see why. Sending a basketball-sized probe with long spikes around the world did not compare with the things he feared in those days, like nuclear war. For the duration of his life, he did not understand the importance most people attached to the symbols of international competition. On the night of watching the lunar landing, he noticed no mention of beating Russia to the moon and gave the idea no thought, but it was touted in most accounts he read or heard after that night. It had been a triumph over the entire world the astronauts had seen through the tiny windows of their capsule and photographed over their heads like a giant moon although, as far as Dieterich could tell, only one country other than America wanted to place footprints in the powdery surface up there and he was not even sure they were trying. Kennedy had famously said we wanted to do it not because it was easy but because it was hard. Dieterich saw that as excessive bluster. Puffery, he had been taught by sources he could not specify, probably Sunday school or Boy Scouts or his parents, was short of evil but no better than bad manners.

He went to bed late while Neil Armstrong and Buzz Aldrin were still collecting rocks and dust to bring back to earth for science. He did not bother to worry whether they would have any trouble getting off the moon, into the return vehicle and completing their perilous journey. He would not call them fools for the risks they accepted for they knew far better than he what odds they were facing. Neither did he call them heroes for he could not see the point of it all.

When Roland and Sam came upstairs to their beds more than an hour later, Dieterich did not hear them. Sometime on Monday and again on Tuesday, he heard the astronauts were on the way back without serious incident, but he was in no conversations about the event for the rest of the summer.

14

Monday, July 21

On Monday, Dieterich and Freddy were scheduled to travel together to several places in Detroit. Dieterich was the hardness tester guy and Freddy covered issues on other Wilson Instrument equipment. Freddy could not fix everything that came up on the more complex equipment, but he would always speak confidently of the company's ability to fix any issue back at the plant, meaning Rusty could fix anything.

First, Freddy checked Dieterich's toolbox and Rusty checked Freddy's. Then the three of them went over the paperwork for all the places they might visit, depending on how long each job required. If Freddy finished at a place before Dieterich, he would help on the hardness testers. If Dieterich finished before Freddy, he would observe Freddy's work to learn from him although Dieterich could not envision ever expanding his responsibility beyond the hardness testers.

Before they left for their first appointment, Wes asked Dieterich to meet in his office.

"Seems like things went well while I was away. You kept an eye on those two, didya?"

"Everything seemed good from the viewpoint here on the bottom rung. Those two are great to work for. They insist on doing things the right way, never a rush."

"That's right. It's a good team. Probably need to hire some more though. Look I asked you in so you can call Elise. She's waiting for the call. Probably been waiting all week to get back. You can use my phone here. I'll step out."

"Wow, thanks. I was gonna call her as soon I had a chance, like at lunch. This is better. Thanks. She's at home now? Do you have the number?"

He's an awfully good man but that still felt awkward. Good to get it over. Wonder what he said to Rusty and Freddy. Probably nothing. Doesn't matter. Got to get my head back to Elise. It's a good place to be but not when I'm at work...

"Hi Elise," he said too casually.

"Deeter!" she answered with verve. "Thank you so much for calling. I know you can't talk long at work. Good thing I have connections with your boss, huh?"

"I hadn't quite worked out when I could reach you. Good thing you are more clever than me."

"Are you in his office? Is he standing there?"

"I'm in his office but he stepped out. Very courteous as always."

I missed you, Deeter. You don't have to say you missed me. It doesn't mean anything specific anyway. If you say it now, it sounds like you had to. But I did miss you. I thought we might be starting something."

"I wanted to talk to you. I had some things to share. Freddy's about the only one I know and he's really great... you know him, right?"

"Freddy? Yeah, I know who he is."

"Well, there's lots of things are quite good to talk over with him or about him. But I did meet his girlfriend and spent Saturday at his place on the lake. Beautiful day. I'll tell you later. You have a good vacation?"

"Oh sure. I'll tell you everything but you don't have time now. Can we get together soon?"

"Can I call you tonight around six? We're going to go to a movie, right. Not tonight, but we can figure that out."

"Six o'clock. You'll call here, right?"

"Mmmm, we'll talk at six without my boss standing at the door waiting for me to finish."

"Thanks, Deeter, Dear."

The call had not lasted long enough to suggest they were a couple lusting for time together. In fact, they had not even made a date, which Dieterich could mention if anyone asked. He went back to the workroom where Wes was talking to Rusty and Freddy. None of them looked up when Dieterich came in. Ten minutes later Dieterich and Freddy were out the door.

Dieterich figured it would be an easy day with Freddy doing the driving and deciding where to go and when to quit. Besides, it would be good to talk with him. It would take about twenty minutes to reach their first appointment. Dieterich decided to keep the conversation on Freddy.

"That's a great set-up you have on the lake. I don't remember many days as relaxing as yesterday. You guys had everything laid out. I just ate my share, soaked up some sun, rocked in those little lake waves and got to chat with one really sweet woman. I don't think you said exactly... you're engaged, right?"

"Yeah, I guess I gotta admit that. I mean, yeah, obviously we're getting married. We do all this planning on how it'll be when we're together. It's just we don't talk about a ring or a ceremony or stuff like that. There's not much to say about it. Her folks live in Iowa with her brothers and they're not real close... Don't talk regular or ever write... Probably want a wedding out there someday... My folks live upstate here. They like Natasha a whole lot. We've been up to visit a couple times. My big sister's in New York. She don't keep in touch except for Christmas cards. So we'll do something but we'd rather talk about fixin' up our place. She'll move in after she finishes nursing school and gets a job."

"She'll make a good nurse. She'll be careful with the medical part and she'll make the patients comfortable. Give them confidence, too. So, when does she finish school?

_ (Freddy replies)

"You already got some pretty specific plans for fixing up your place. Are you going to start on building the addition and other things soon or do you have to wait? Maybe you want her to have a job first or you want your promotion or something like that?

_ (Freddy replies)

Freddy, I gotta ask. You guys want kids soon too?

_ (Freddy replies)

I hope you don't mind all my questions. You're quite a few steps ahead of me and I like seeing what may be store if I can somehow find a woman and a job and a place like that."

Freddy did not mind all the questions because he had answers to most of them. They were not ideal answers from Dieterich's viewpoint, but they were not bad answers either.

Through the rest of the morning, they worked in separate parts of the factory. When they met for lunch, Freddy asked if any of the machines had been a problem for Dieterich. Dieterich did not answer the question. The deafening silence about his morning isolation in Wes' office needed to be broken.

"Freddy, you know Elise, Wes' daughter?"

"I know he has a daughter. I never met her."

"Wes had me in his office this morning so I could call her. I've met her a couple times. We're going to a movie maybe later this week."

"Yeah? Maybe?"

"We didn't pick a day yet. Depends on what she wants to see."

"And then what? She's a nice girl, right?"

"She's too nice to be with me, but she doesn't know it yet. She's really good lookin' and easy to talk to. I'd say smart, too, except for not figuring me out too fast."

"C'mon. Everybody thinks that when they meet the right one."

"I just thought I should mention it. It might have seemed funny when Wes left me in his office."

"A little odd. Wasn't any of my business."

"Anyway, this is a pretty good sandwich. The bread's warm. I bet they baked it here."

"Stop with the 'she's too good for you'. You'd be a good catch."

"Oh yeah? Did you know I got kicked out of school? And not for getting drunk or something like that. I flunked out 'cause I didn't try hard enough. If you had a smart, beautiful daughter, you'd want her to find someone better. I'd be OK to see a movie with if it's a good movie."

"But you're just here for the summer, right? What'll you do in the fall?"

"Trying to get into another school, an easier one with low admission standards."

"Or you could stay here and work your way up. See this beautiful girl some more. You could move up in the firm."

"I can't work in this firm. You know my dad is an executive here? It wouldn't work. But I can see taking a job like this. I've been thinking about it now that I've seen some of it. Maybe I could do it if there was a job like this with some other company. Could be this summer experience would help."

"Wes knows lots of firms all over Michigan. He can get something for sure."

"I don't know. Think I belong in a job in the woods."

"Really? Like your summer in Colorado?"

"Not that job. This one is way better. But a place like that."

"And Ellen doesn't know all this?"

"Elise. No, we've talked but I haven't seen that much of her to be confessing this much. I'll leave in the fall and go to some easy school and work harder than I did last year and she'll forget about me and she'll be a really good memory that pushes me to screw up less so I can have a real girlfriend like you have in Natasha." Dieterich took a bite of his sub. Freddy was masticating his thoughtfully. "You want my pickle?"

Freddy had a phone number in his wallet where one could call and hear what movies were playing in the area. There were separate numbers for downtown Detroit and the northern suburbs. Dieterich called the number from the phone booth at the gas station in Rochester Hills. He had to go through the listings five times to get the times and locations onto his tablet. After hearing the blurbs promoting the films on the first pass, he only looked for showings of *The Graduate* (not good if he was going to a Simon and Garfunkel concert with Cathy someday and also might raise more questions about sex than he was ready to address); *The Good, the Bad, and the Ugly* (not really a date movie); *Butch Cassidy and the Sundance Kid* (also a western but OK for dates); *Bob and Carol and Ted and Alice* (probably too adult for him) and *Easy Rider* (not sure what is was but the drug culture was not relevant to their discussions).

It was five past six when he was ready to phone Elise. She picked up after the first ring and answered saying "Deeter?"

"Hello Elise. Good to hear you a second time today!" He felt he was being awkward but he doubted he could have scripted a good opening line. She knew something about all the available movies and was very pleased that he had figured out where the ones he thought best were playing. They settled on *Butch Cassidy* which Dieterich also realized would give him a chance to say something about Colorado, not about what he did but about the appeal of the place. He could be enthusiastic on that topic. This was the longest phone conversation he had ever had. He worried that Wes would be conscious of the time and think it signaled some level of commitment Dieterich was not intending. It was only their second date! He ended the call apologizing for being overly businesslike.

"I want to hear about your vacation and everything... just not on the phone while I'm standing in a gas station. The movie's at eight o'clock. I'll pick you up at seven o'clock. Thursday feels a long way off, Elise. See you then."

"It's all right Baby. We'll have more time later. See you Thursday." He sure liked being called "Baby" by a beautiful woman. He hung up the phone and scooped his remaining coins into his pocket and opened the phone booth door. He stood there for a minute or two, listening to the passing traffic, looking at the telephone as if he could see himself still talking. He did not recognize the figure. He had never done such a thing before. Arranged a date with a girl like her, who called him "Baby" and was excited to be doing something with him. For all the strangeness of the moment, he also knew this is what he should be doing at his age and there was no reason it had taken so long to achieve it. Just as clear was that this moment and the ones to follow from this path were not predetermined and he would have to watch his steps so he did not trip up.

He had just enough time before he should enter Romero's to get to his room and wash up.

In mid-May a year ago, Rochester High held its graduation in the gymnasium because it had more room than the school cafeteria. The senior class officers organized their friends and the art teacher to dress up the event although they could not afford to buy anything more costly than rolls of crepe paper and poster board. The shop teacher found enough unused materials to build a grand gateway outside the door and a tunnel of paper flowers inside the room. Everyone agreed the seniors had transformed the place beautifully. Cathy had not worked on the decorations because she was not part of that clique though she respected the kids who had done it. To her, the graduation ceremony was exciting. To her mother, of course, it was boring but for the thirty seconds when her daughter's name was read and she was handed her diploma.

After the ceremony, Cathy's mother hosted a party for family. Cathy would have invited some of her friends, but her best friends were going to some party just for new graduates. Her brother could not be there because he was in Panama, serving in the U.S. Air Force by doing something useful with personnel records. Her father lived in Kentucky and sent his congratulations and a check for $100. Her father's younger brother, Patrick, and sister, Anna, still lived nearby and they came. Her mother's parents and siblings were there, and a total of seven cousins brought youth to the affair, all together making this the biggest family gathering she had experienced. No one tapped a fork on a glass to quiet the rooms for speeches; no signs of congratulations hung over the doorways; no one grilled meaty treats over charcoal on the patio, because there was no patio or much of a backyard to hang out in. Nothing marked Cathy's achievement as the purpose of the gathering, yet everyone made a point of saying something supportive to her. Cathy did greatly appreciate that her mother had made the effort and that her family was recognizing her.

By nine o'clock, all the guests had left. Cathy's mother was pleased with the affair and with herself for pulling it off. She was also a little drunk.

"Cathy, dear, we can clean this up tomorrow. I don't have to be at work in the morning and your shift won't start until four. Let's have a little ice cream, sitting here on the couch. We should talk some."

The invitation seemed innocent enough. Cathy served the ice cream and tucked her legs under herself on the couch.

"Thanks for all this, Mama. It was nice to mark the end of my high school years. I got a few more signatures today in my yearbook. You wanna see it?"

"Not right now. I need to talk about some practical things." She hesitated before continuing slowly, seriously, soberly. "I'm sorry your dad couldn't make it today. He really wanted to. But the other thing is, well, you turned eighteen back in March and, well, he doesn't need to pay child support any more. I mean, you know, you're not a child. Congratulations on that, I guess."

"Yes, I guess I knew that would be ending. I thought maybe he'd wait until I got to school in the fall. He's still going to pay for board, isn't he?"

"I don't think so. He always said he didn't have to and, you know, he's got a new family going and Sally already has two young kids so she doesn't have a job or anything."

"Shit."

"Yeah." The only sound in the room for the next minute came from the click and scrape of their spoons cleaning up the last of the ice cream."

"I can get a morning job for over the summer. If I had a car, I could live here and commute to school."

"You don't have a car, dear, and one's not coming from a summer job. It's not so bad, though. Don't be discouraged. Just wait a year. EMU will wait a year won't they?"

"Yeah, I think so." The ice cream was finished. A sharp listener would detect only the sound of two women breathing.

"Did you talk to your Uncle Patrick tonight?"

"Sure. He's always nice. And he gave me a necklace with my birthstone on it."

"That's good, good. Yes, he is always nice. You know he always liked you. Did you ever notice he was a lot better at business than your dad? He has a wonderful big house."

"I never saw his house."

"You did when you were little. He never made too much fuss over you but he always liked you and now, well, with you growing up, he might want to get your attention."

"My attention? What for? What is he, thirty-five, forty? Is he twice my age?"

"He's never been married. He worked too hard."

"What are you saying, Mama? What does my uncle have to do with me? You want me to chase after him?"

"Of course not, Cathy. You should only do what you want to do about men. I'm just passing on the fact that he is interested in you and I happen to know, and know for certain, he would be happy, very happy, to marry you. And I know it is a fact that he can afford to take care of you."

"Does he want to pay my board at college or just have me to play with at home?"

"Don't be mean, Cathy. He's a serious man, a good man. There's nothing wrong with him liking you. But you never have any boyfriends so he's not in the way of anything you're already thinking about."

"Yeah, he's not in the way and I'm not thinking about him either. Hey, I'm surprised Daddy is dropping the ball. I've thought about it. You're right. I have to wait a year, work hard and get some money together. I'll do it. I can earn enough for a car over the summer, some kind of car."

"If we don't get any more child support, we got to cut our expenses from where they already are."

"I see that. It sucks but I'm not sure how bad that is if I work a second job. Lemme find another job and then we can calculate it out. Forget this Uncle Patrick thing! I don't want to hear about him again. I don't want to see him either. You can take his goddam necklace back or I can flush it down the toilet!"

The conversation went on for a few more minutes but nothing further was offered or given by either Cathy or her mother. In the morning, the two of them were tense. Cathy's mother was fully sober and not sure what had been agreed between them. Cathy spoke as if there had not even been the post-party conversation.

In just two days, Cathy found a second job slightly over thirty minutes away by foot. The supermarket offered very flexible hours. If she could give them confidence in her while restocking the shelves, she could move up and make decent pay as a cashier. She could work eight to three at the supermarket and then four to nine at Romero's. She could still have two days off or set up a couple easier days... at least for the summer. And in the fall, she would reconsider her options for a more permanent work schedule.

Dieterich would be late for dinner if he did not rush back out of the house. He stripped to his shorts in the bathroom and bathed while standing beside the sink with a washcloth. *How can I be late at a restaurant where I have no reservation? I need to clean up. I feel sticky. I'll be later than usual, but not late. Late enough someone might notice a break in my pattern but not late.* His logic was sound although there remained a small chance that Romero's would be full when he arrived.

He owned five shirts he could wear with a tie. This was so he could do laundry on weekends and be set for the week. His Monday shirt was damp from the warm day he had spent in it and wrinkled from his wearing it under one of his sport coats (he owned two) whenever he had to meet a customer. He had not worn the coat during the drive back to Richmond Hills and he had kept the windows open while driving to feel the breeze, yet he was still damp. He hated to put on Tuesday's shirt for dinner on Monday but he reasoned it would dry out overnight and he could iron it again in the morning. He skipped wearing the jacket for the evening since he would be wearing a crisp shirt. He would wear the tie loosely knotted, casual but still coming more or less directly from work as usual. He did not feel guilty about hiding his relationship with Elise. He had not reached the point with either girl where it was sinful to omit something neither had ever asked about.

He had tried to devise a good greeting for Cathy, not too sassy or personal or contrived; something within his personality but smart and kind; something reflecting his appreciation of her bold new hairstyle without making her self-conscious, something to show he was not focused on her breasts or her legs but recognizing her attractiveness. He knew what his opening should convey but he could not devise one meeting any of the criteria he set for it.

"Hi Cathy! Hope you had a good weekend. Two days off must be good."

"And I hope you can walk me home."

"Yes, dear, around the corner. And please let me have the roast beef dinner with a glass of milk."

"Very good, sir."

When they met "around the corner" Dieterich was ready to gently press his lips on her face or anyplace else. He was aware he had no such thought about Elise at this moment. They did not touch, just started walking together. She led him quickly and quietly past her street and then turned along a parallel street. She stopped beside a tall hedge across the street from an empty lot, a private place to stand.

"Do you know where we are now?" she asked.

"Not really, but I know why we are here."

"Good enough. That's what I meant."

He took both her hands in his. "Damn, Cathy, I like your haircut. Now you've had it a few days, you own it. You are the updated version of a very fine girl I met a couple weeks ago."

"Yeah, okay. If you say so. Listen, I have some big news. It seems big to me anyhow." She took a breath without continuing and Dieterich knew he should ask for her details."

"Solid! Lemme hear about it!"

"I got money for school! I got into EMU last year but I couldn't afford it. Now I qualified for a government loan. With some tuition help I already had, financial aid, not a scholarship exactly, I can start in the winter semester. I'll be in debt for the next hundred years but that's tomorrow. Back to school! And I'll work until January like I am now and should be able to get a car and commute from home to save on expenses."

Cathy was getting excited by saying all this aloud. She had not told anyone since she opened the notice she received in the mail on Saturday. She was not aware she had started to hop up and down, small hops, mostly pumping her legs quickly enough to lift her an inch or two at a time.

"Fantastic! That's the best news I've heard in a year!" It was the best he had felt about any news since he read his admission into what was then his first choice for college two Januarys ago. "You're going to EMU? How far away is that?"

"It's in Ypsilanti. I don't know, under an hour, I think. Eastern Michigan U. It's a pretty good school. Four years. It's got everything, anything you want to study."

"You know what you want to study? Please don't say engineering."

"Don't worry. I wasn't going to say that. Not how to be a waitress either. I don't really know what to take. In high school I didn't think about college much. I hardly know anyone who went to college except for a couple friends who finished high school last year. Guess I'll find out."

Dieterich was surprised to notice he was embracing Cathy. He kissed her forehead and held her tight while he responded. "You're ahead of me now. I don't know where I'm going next year."

She was surprised and leaned back, not to reject his intimacy but to focus on her question. "Did you run out of money?"

"No. I'm just changing schools. I don't want to be an engineer. Don't worry about that. Let's celebrate your future for the next four years." He pulled her close and swung her around in a circle. Without a jacket on, he could easily feel her body pressed against him and the softness of her breasts on his chest.

Dieterich was relieved that Cathy took little note of his admission. It was her party and appropriate that her news was the only news of importance. Still, he was glad to have mentioned it. If he needed to say more about it some other time, it would not appear to be a secret he had kept from her. For now, he remained a privileged person, possibly (probably) relatively rich. The secret so far was in his immature behavior over the past few years which he hoped to change before she needed to know about it. He knew what was wrong with himself and that was why he could fix himself.

When the spinning dance died down and Cathy was still breathing heavily from the exertion, she switched over to the other good news she was bursting to tell: that she had received in the mail their tickets for the *Bookends* concert coming up August 6. And since he had dismissed her question about paying his expenses at college, she was now confident he could pay for the concert tickets, too. She hated to ask for money, but she had written out everything: the time to pick her up, the date, and the cost. It was a few lines written on a full sheet of notebook paper folded into quarters, an object that suddenly felt ill prepared. She should have used letter stationery although there was none in her house. She might have found an envelope in the house and put the paper in it. She should have cut the paper into a size befitting the small message or, at least, cut off the holes for fitting into a binder. It was a high school sort of note, not even a senior in high school level presentation. And it should not have been folded so many times as if she were nervous to have it and was hiding it from herself or afraid to give it to him.

Dieterich was very pleased to have the paper. He wanted to go on a regular date with Cathy and saw so many complications in the way, yet suddenly he learned she had prepared everything. And it was more than a regular date, his first concert with a nationally known, popular music artist. A hundred twenty dollars plus parking was steep but he had it. If he had that much less for school, it would make no difference, his parents would ensure he had what he needed. It was almost as if they were paying for his date, which would not be fair, especially as they had not agreed to it, but it was done now. They might have agreed to pay if he had asked although he had never asked for entertainment money. He did not spend much on entertainment, did not buy records or concert tickets or, well, he could not think of any entertainment costs he had ever incurred, but if he had, he would have paid them out of the money he earned from summer jobs, like the one he was doing this summer, and that was the source of the dollars he was about to spend. He could see he was making a circular argument reflecting an unimportant moral slippage.

Dieterich put the paper in his wallet while reflecting on who was paying for the tickets. Following those thoughts, he was surprised to notice Cathy was working her fingers inside his shirt and pulling it up so she could feel the skin on his back and chest. He flexed to prove he could be firm even if he had no bulky muscles. He was embarrassed that he had no chest hair for her to discover but she seemed happy enough. He relaxed and enjoyed her attention. Soon he realized he ought to be showing his appreciation. He massaged her back and she pressed against him. His hands drifted lower, touching below the waist briefly and that was too much for him to do without being someone he did not recognize as himself. It was only fair, he reasoned, to do as she was doing so he pulled at her blouse and touched her back. He pushed his fingers against her flesh and dragged them from her waist to her shoulders. She moaned faintly. He had skipped over her bra strap one finger at a time and noticed how narrow it was. He touched one finger from each hand into the back of her armpits, exploring blindly, randomly. She kissed him on his neck. He wondered if she would leave a mark. He would not mind a bite but he had heard of raising a strawberry mark by sucking and that felt obscene rather than passionate. Suddenly she withdrew her hands and tucked his shirt back in.

"Oh boy, Deeter. Here we are on a public street with possible robbers wandering around. Better get me home."

Deeter laughed and held her hand until they turned onto her street where he adjusted to just walking beside her. When they stopped at her house, she suggested they go swimming at Lexington Beach on Saturday afternoon.

"I can be out of work by noon. It won't take an hour to get there."

"I thought you had Saturdays off?"

"I do. Off from Romero's. I do Saturday at my other job, but I can get out early."

Damn, why does she have to work two jobs on top of everything else. I don't deserve this woman. How dare I hang around with her for the opportunity to suckle her breasts? Swim? See her in a bathing suit and at the same time show her my skinny self? That would be the end of it right there.

"We're at your place now and can't stand around too long without making a show. Let me see where the company is sending me this week and we'll talk about the weekend tomorrow."

15

"...hoping he will measure up to his father, knowing how it is so that all boys grow up and pull away from home to unmake the world in the guise of making it, nature decrees it is so."[ii]

Tuesday, July 22

Dieterich had left Freddy's map in the car, so he made sure to get back to the car early to see if Lexington Beach was indicated. It was marked as a state park and was on Lake Huron, not very far away. Cathy had a reasonable idea here. He planned to ask Freddy about the beach at lunch. They would be working together all day, right from the start, but he wanted to stick to a courteous greeting at first and then just talk on work-related topics. The job was not much to Dieterich, but it was to Freddy and, therefore, had to be respected. However, this focus was threatened within minutes of his arrival as Wes called him into the office. *Don't be a call from Elise*, Dieterich thought, although there was no reason to assume Wes had a phone call for him.

"You're right on time this morning, just like every day," Wes said while they walked together to the office. "There's a call for you. From your father. I need to talk to the men in the shop. Come on out when you're ready."

Dieterich was about to apologize for using his phone again and suddenly stopped as he was forming Wes' name. He covered his error in a cough, followed my muttering. "All right. Thanks." Elise had called on Wes' phone so it might seem a criticism of her or of Wes if he said such a call was inappropriate.

"Hello Dad. You caught me just before going out to a foundry at one of the Bosch operations in Detroit."

"Yep. Wes said you'd be coming in about now. Glad I caught you. Listen, you need to call your mother more. At least once a week."

"Yeah, I'll be careful to do that. There's not that much to say but I'll check in with her."

"It's OK. I'm calling right now about the applications for the fall. You got in two schools, and you could go to either of them. Some of the better schools seemed interested but they said they'd like to wait a year whenever someone is dismissed. Give a chance to get settled in and adjusted, you understand? The two that are ready to take you don't have all that much to offer. Might be a waste of time. So I talked with admissions at Lehigh. They still want you, Deeter. They know you can do the work, just like they know you weren't a screw-up with drugs or protests and things like that. You're a good young man, maybe just a little younger than what was needed last year. Lehigh pretty much promised to take you back, maybe give you some special direction on course choices and professors and things, if you go in the service first. They like what you're doing this summer and Wes is real pleased with you so you'll get a good recommendation from him. There's a possible plan, a start of a plan. What do you think?"

"I don't know. What do you want me to say? You already know I screwed up at Lehigh. I didn't harm anyone but myself and, I guess, you and Mother. Doesn't seem like going into the Army is the best thing to do next."

"You lost most of the good opportunities..."

"Wait, I know that very well. Seems like I ought to be able to work at a job, just a regular job, to prove to you and some decent school and to myself that I am worth the investment of some more education..."

"What are you calling a 'regular job' when you don't..."

"Let me finish. I have worked beside you around the house. I can do that. I pay attention to what I'm doing. I'm careful. I have some simple skills like..."

"No one saying you aren't a good worker especially..."

"I know you're not saying that. It's just that what makes sense at my age with what I can do and how I screwed up that I ought to work at something that doesn't take a college degree, like what I'm doing right now. It makes sense, damn it, but it's not possible in this world. Not in this country anyway."

"You want to blame the country for your problem? What country would you rather be in?"

"Maybe.   Depends if the war makes sense somehow. I don't know about that. I don't know who or what to blame other than myself. I can be sure there is nothing to blame in my parents. Don't mistake that for sarcasm, I mean that much for sure. But I don't think I can do what makes sense to me, just work 40 hours a week at something useful until I can go back to school."

"If you didn't have to face the draft... Say you got a medical, then you'd want to work a year or two and prove yourself to whomever?"

"It's not a creative idea to do what seems normal."

"So seeing some of American industry wasn't so bad? You learn a little of how it can be better than camping out or joining a commune? You want to make a difference? Make something people need."

"I don't see a medical deferment. I doubt I could make a case for conscientious objector. I don't know enough about the whole thing to defend that. Can't say I'm all that scared about the Army, so I'm not going to hide from it, go underground somehow or run off to Canada. I heard Jeff White did that. Went to Canada.

Maybe he objected based on principles. He was a good guy; wouldn't run off from fear... Dad, you still there?"

"Yeah, I'm listening."

"I get how it's a bad idea to go to a crummy school. I could go to a lesser school, of course, but the worst schools are just another way to dodge the draft. And they probably get kids who don't have the experience to know how crummy they are. I get what you said about the schools that would take me could be worth going to just for a deferment. Let me think about it a couple days. Let it sink in. See if I want to see more of Canada or something. I'll call you. Not from Wes' office. I don't want to do personal stuff here. Wes is good about it. He's a real fine guy. The others are too, but still, you know..."

"Alright. You call when you're ready. I'm sorry we couldn't find something better. You know the Army can be a real growing experience. You go to OCS[9], get some real leadership background. I've seen you with the boys your age. They listen to you...You can call me at home after 6:30 most nights. Or call at the office. You have that number?"

"I'll call you at home. Give my love to Mother."

Now Dieterich had something he had to deal with in his main life, outside of Michigan. He would call home that very evening so he would not have this decision hanging over him. He already knew what he would say. He simply did not want to say it. He would pretend to debate some options (he had options) until he got to the gas station with the phone booth. He would not call collect. He would be polite and brief. He knew what he would say on the call, but a call so important needed to be thought through anyway. He would do that after work. It

---

[9] Officer Candidate School

was embarrassing enough to be using Wes' phone, he could not let himself be distracted from his job.

He could imagine living in a trailer next to a pond for a couple years, working honorably, having a girlfriend, camping out in all seasons on weekends, writing in his journal. First, he would have to fail his medical evaluation. He had already proven himself adept at failing exams. He could be lucky and have some defect that did not matter for anything other than getting out of the draft. Or he could earn a medical deferment, gain a hundred fifty pounds before the physical and keep the weight for (what had he heard?), for three years. More likely, he might be able to cut off a toe or a finger. He had heard losing a toe might get a deferment, but maybe that was only for a big toe. He could disguise it as an accident more plausible than shooting himself in the foot. He worried his parents would not be fooled. An act of protest against the Vietnam War could be done with honor, but cutting off a toe would be hard to link to a protest motive.

They would disagree with an act of protest but they would be devastated by an act of fear. He would realize when he was taking the exit off Interstate 75 onto local route 59 toward Rochester Hills, that fear had no claim on him. His parents might know that too. He had never feared anything. It was a central weakness. He had been successful enough in school and his first seventeen years to suffer no calamity, never giving more effort than he felt like making. He wondered if this is what it means to be spoiled and then decided it is. Like a six-year-old brat, he was spoiled. Perhaps it was not even his fault any more than it is of the brat, but that argument does not make him a worthwhile human being. The security of his upbringing had not prepared him to worry about failing in college. Now that he had failed and faced greater consequences than he had imagined could lie in his future, he would soon no longer be spoiled by good fortune and the care of his parents and the advantages of his class. These thoughts would occupy his drive home. For immediate purposes, his brain put aside the pressure of agreeing to the option he would take of his own free will.

"Sorry, Wes. Something came up that needed a decision. I'll try to get my calls after work."

"No problem at all. I needed to get with the fellas anyway. You can call from here whenever you need to."

Dieterich waited for Wes to continue with whatever talk he was having during the phone call, but Wes said he was just wrapping up and retreated to his office.

Rusty spoke up next. "As a matter of fact, Mr. Deeter, we thought you could work for me today, maybe more. The boss wants the shop here shifted around better, expanded into the storeroom, move the stock into some new space he got for us from the muffler factory next door. Looks like they're goin' outta business. Don't mind moving outta hardness tester repair for the rest of the week, do ya?"

The work was interesting to Dieterich, involving mostly collecting surplus industrial furniture from Rusty's friends in other companies so the new space would be efficient. Dieterich could sense how much fun Rusty was having designing the space and contacting his buddies on the phone. Dieterich was aware he was being trusted to act properly by the standards of Rusty's circle of friends, the reliable men who knew every component of the machines that built the cars that drove the economy.

His drive home went fast because he was speeding more than usual. He looked at the speedometer and saw it holding at eighty, so he backed off some. It was easy to drive fast. Being faster than the commuter traffic let him weave around the slow cars as if he were in control of them. He did not ask if joining the Army was making him misbehave. He was thinking the thoughts of how he had no realistic alternative to the Army and how his parents would be pleased that he was not going to compound his problems by fighting the draft.

His mother answered the phone. She was almost angry that he was calling from a phone booth. It made him seem to her like a little boy who does not know how to do things properly and since he was out of college with no way to get back in soon, his incompetence was more distressing. Dieterich listened to her for a while and then interrupted to politely shift over to his reason for calling. Dieterich's father came on the extension phone. He was more focused. In times of stress, he stuck to what was relevant which was hardly ever affixing blame on anyone.

Once the irrelevant issue of how an intelligent person like Dieterich could get himself into such a fix was set aside, Dieterich briefly summarized his decision, not theirs, to contact his draft board immediately after the lottery to schedule a physical and to get an estimate on when he would be called up for induction. His Dad was relieved to hear no silly ideas about how to proceed and his mother was comforted that Dieterich had spoken firmly and reasonably as an adult ought to speak on such important matters. They passed around promises of love to each other. He had to put in more coins after the first three minutes and finished less than a minute later so no additional coins were needed. Calling from a pay phone had helped make the call short.

Dieterich pulled off his tie and hung up his jacket. He pushed the hangers to one side just to measure how much space he was taking. His clothes filled a quarter of the rod. The Tyler child who had grown up in this room would have had winter clothes and probably some clothes he or she had outgrown. More casual clothes too, he supposed, altogether filling the space. He wrote a summary blurb about his call home, his almanac having evolved into a journal and then passed into a diary. On the weekend, he vowed to revive the journal of natural sightings.

The weekend needed an answer. Would he go to the beach with Cathy just two days after going to a concert with Elise? Could he stand confidently before Cathy with his body fully exposed? He thought he could fake confidence, but he could not fake it and at the same time enjoy being next to her in whatever she might wear for the beach. And he might face questions about the future which would further erode any chance of projecting self-respect. Things had moved too fast. He was on the verge of intimacy with two girls and neither one of them understood what they were getting and neither of them would want what he had to offer them. It would be so easy to just drop them both, easier than choosing one when neither deserved to be dropped by such as himself. It was time for dinner now.

With neither tie nor jacket, he went over to Romero's. He assumed Cathy would not care if he was in his junior executive outfit and if she did care, they were no match. He was not an emerging executive, that image was unintentional fakery. If the other staff noticed his adjusted standard of attire, they could not read much into it. He was a regular now and ought to look different from day to day. As things seemed to be going, they would know he was linked to Cathy, and she would have to cope with whatever teasing that generated.

"Hi Cathy. Nice to see you again. Very nice."

Cathy did not look up from her ordering pad. She did not stand close enough to seem to be visiting him on a personal mission, but by standing away, he could see all of her which both of them knew was exactly what he wanted to do at that moment. She answered in a soft, throaty whisper, "Hello Honey. Is there anything I can give you tonight?"

They met after nine o'clock "around the corner." Dieterich knew he was going to accept going to the beach on Saturday. He only had to survive seeing two girls for a month or two before he would be free of everything for two years. If he had learned anything since high school, he knew two years was enough time for a complete change in everything.

They were quiet until they reached the privacy of the tall bushes on 123rd street, a block west of Cathy's street.

"Are you going to be out of the area for the weekend or going to the beach with me?"

"They have me going up to Grand Rapids for an early start on Monday. I'll probably drive out there on Sunday and spend the night... pretty far."

"So we're still on."

"We are still very much on... unless we're getting rain. Have you heard a weather report?"

"It's a little early to say but it looks good so far."

"If the weather looks bad, give me call at the Tylers'. Just leave a message if I'm not there when you call. I already wrote their number for you."

"Can I tell them we have a date?"

"Of course. Say anything you like. What could be better than having a date with this fantastic woman?" *But*, he continued inside himself, *it would be nice, Honey, if you did not say anything the Tylers might mention to Wes at church about how nice it is for me to be dating the beautiful waitress from Romero's. I mean, they don't seem gossipy, but they could just bring it up to say how socially successful their employee has been this summer. And I hope Wes or his wife does not run into the Tylers at church and say something about how their tenant is dating their daughter. And yet I refuse to advise you to be secretive. After you spend a day exposed to my narrow, pasty white chest, I may be down to one beautiful girl anyway.*

"So listen, I'm having dinner with someone from work tomorrow and then I have to stay around my room on Friday night to get a call from my parents so I'll just see you on Saturday." *Liar!* he acknowledged to himself, pleased at least to be honest internally. He even thought it was not a real bad couple of lies. It would have been worse to say he had to work on the weekend, morally equivalent, but nearer the truth somehow. The only way to be completely honest would be to pick one of the two beauties and drop the other. He was strong enough to lie but too weak to choose.

"Bummer. How will you feed yourself if I don't bring it to you?"

"I'll have big lunches. I still have the skills to buy lunch on my own. Okay, I know your house. Should I come by at, let's say nine or ten o'clock? I can meet your mother and try to convince her I am a good risk."

"Yes, no. I mean ten is too early. Let's leave at eleven. We can have lunch together since you know how to do that. There's plenty of time for the beach. I can stay out as long as I want. She doesn't care when I get home. She goes to bed and doesn't really know when I get home. You don't have to meet her. You could... come in for just a minute... If you wanted..."

Helping Rusty adapt to the new space was rewarding work. He made no decisions, just followed whatever Rusty said and Rusty, in his gruff way, appreciated how he helped: quickly, quietly, properly. He was never asked to do anything he could not do: move something (without breaking anything), take apart something (without losing anything), assemble something (always in obvious ways), inventory the contents of some shelves, count the pieces, push it closer; whatever simple thing was needed in the moment.

By Wednesday it was beginning to feel normal to do the odd jobs, the menial work, for the renovation of the workplace. Obviously, it was not a permanent demotion, simply a case of filling a temporary need in a company where he was a temporary employee. Dieterich did not mind if it was a form of demotion. He was working no less, just working with an iota less prestige and a full measure reduction in responsibility.

That evening, he drove fast again. Eighty no longer felt unsafe. It even felt pleasurable to go by everyone. He was careful, aways checking his mirrors before switching lanes. At his speed he felt no concern for anyone catching up. He did not tailgate. There were no close calls. He was being responsible if not exactly legal. *Responsible is better*, he told himself without conviction. He needed the speed to get ready for dinner and to communicate to Cathy. That was part of his responsibility.

Dieterich parked the car in his usual place past the Tylers a half block and around the corner on a dead-end street. He took out his briefcase and was thinking about dinner when a Camero pulled up to the curb in front of him. Two guys popped out excitedly and ran over to him. They reminded him of Sam and Roland.

One spoke to the other in a fashion meant to reach Dieterich as well. "Unbelievable! Dude in a tie and a suit drivin' a Nash Rambler with his pedal to the metal all the way from Motor City to Nowhere Hills." He turned to

Dieterich with a broad smile. "You lost us two, three times but got yourself hung up in the traffic. Pushin' ninety some! Then cooled down all the way when you got off the interstate..."

The other fellow asked "What you got under the lid anyway? You pay someone to doctor up the engine or do it yourself?"

"Yeah, maybe I was speeding some. The car's nothing special. It's the opposite of special. I don't know about the engine, but it barely makes the speed limit if I use cheap gas."

"So listen, man, we can hook you up, make some money. You drive, we handle the bets. You don't put in any money. We give you a good cut. You won't have much acceleration in that pig but you can drive. We seen it! And it'll be pussy and pie to get bets against a dude like you in a car like that. Do a ten-mile stretch at night. No cops ever out on the interstate after midnight."

"Not for me. No way. I was just in a rush tonight and I still gotta get to it. So thanks but no thanks."

"Come on with us a few minutes. We'll buy you a beer..."

Dieterich was walking away, looking over his shoulder every couple steps. He waved and then kept his eyes forward up to the corner, looked quickly as he turned away from the Tylers and walked faster. He heard a squeal of tires and turned around. They were burning rubber in the opposite direction. *Wonder if I should have put them in touch with Sam and his Charger.*

16

Thursday, July 24

As the workday was ending on Thursday, Wes came out of his office to look at the progress. Rusty had some questions for him and they talked quietly over the floorplans and pointed at various things while Dieterich packed a crate with out-of-date parts to be recycled outside the building. Then Wes came over to Dieterich and talked a little about the project in a friendly way, that is, without saying anything that mattered. Dieterich waited for him to mention the date with Elise but it did not come up.

Once again, Dieterich targeted the speedometer at eighty on the way home. There would be no time to eat before his date but he wanted to take a shower and iron his Monday or Tuesday shirt because he would wear his Friday shirt for the date and there was no time for doing the laundry before the weekend.

He left to pick up Elise at 6:33. It would take about two minutes to walk to his car and fifteen minutes to get to her house, but he had only been there once and worried he might not remember the way exactly. He drove by her driveway twelve minutes early and waited out of view from the house. He turned into the driveway at 7:03, not sure why he felt a minute early was worse than five minutes late. Elise was sitting on the porch as he came down the driveway. She walked out to meet him and opened the door to get in. Dieterich turned off the engine and came around the front of the car.

"Let's just say good night to your folks. I know them and they know me and everything, but they might think it would be proper so I ought to do it."

"No, we don't have to do that. Let's just go."

"Well, my mother would think it necessary. She might even ask, if she ever met your mother. Please, please, do this for my mother and the rest of the night will be for you."

Elise was going to say something funny about his being too close to mama or too scared of her, but she could not think of a clever way to say it and then the moment passed. She was actually thinking he might be too square if he thought the conventions of dating should be dictated by the norms of his mother. She said nothing, took his hand and went up the porch steps with him. He planned to walk on the side with her withered leg to support her, but she held out the other hand and then supported herself with the railing.

Dieterich sensed her hesitation and her acceptance of his indecision, guessing he was trying to be helpful and respecting she wanted no help. As they went up the steps, he was thinking of whispering something personal before they reached the door: how beautiful she was, how he was looking forward to the evening, how he had missed her... The right words did not come fast enough so he just had a short, friendly exchange with Elise's mother and father standing in the door, completing the ritual and then departing properly.

Elise guided them to a small city park where they could sit on a bench for twenty minutes and then walk a couple blocks to the movie theater. They did not sit close enough to touch. The familiarity they felt at the fireworks was remembered but not revived immediately. Dieterich asked her about her vacation with her family.

"We have the same vacation every summer. It was more exciting when I was smaller. Now I'm older and everything at the lake feels smaller. My parents are pretty cool as parents go, but there's nothing new about going out in a rowboat with them. They're not playmates at the arcade. Smashing into people in a bumper car is for kids too young to drive a real car... Miriam was there for a few days. You remember her, the girl at the pool when you came over for a swim?"

"Yeah."

"She's a good friend. Wherever we went in town the boys would hang around. She doesn't pay any attention to them but they're on her like flies on fresh cowpies. I don't want their attention but it's funny to be with her and all eyes turned her way."

"Not mine. That's just cheap thrills."

"Oh, I love Janis Joplin![10] Did you get that album?"

"Gotta love that one for sure. I never bought any album so, no, I never got that one. I know what it looks like though. Art by R. Crumb. I never bought an underground comic either."

"But you know Fritz the Cat, don't you?"

"I know what he looks like and I know he's disreputable. Not so sure about the exploits of the Keep on Truckin' guy. Is he someone I could introduce to my mother?"

"Yeah, I don't know what he does either. Just grooves along, I guess."

"Hey, you want some popcorn? Maybe we should start truckin' over."

After the movie...

Elise began the movie review. "That was good. The heroes are villains, and they die in the end and we're

____

[10] "Cheap Thrills" was the name of the second and final album by Janis Joplin with the Holding Company. It was the number-one album in America for eight weeks in 1968.

all fine with that 'cause they were such good-lookin', fun guys."

"It discourages me from taking up a life of crime. I'm nowhere near cute enough for it. I'd be killed off in the gang's first job.

But you know what I liked about it? They went to South America. Movie cowboys are always escaping to Mexico, but Bolivia is interesting. I wonder if that was one of the facts they kept in the movie. I'd like to see Bolivia. And that's even though I don't know a single thing to see or do there."

"I'd like to go to Bolivia too."

They were approaching the car.

"Sorry, Elise. I don't know this town or pretty much any town in this state. You know somewhere we can go to talk?"

"Somewhere to talk about what?"

"Pretty sure something'll come up. If we were in a movie, we'd go to a bar. I don't think that's our style. Maybe a place where we can get a snack, a dessert like a piece of pie or ice cream?" She did not answer. "Or just a place to sit?"

"The only place I know is the A&W drive-in. Do you want to eat something?"

"Not really. I shoulda..."

"Come on then. Go right when you go out of the parking lot. We don't have to go far."

She led him to a wooded stretch of road nearby, and down a short dirt road ending at a small river."

"It's a big parking spot," she said. "Just turn off the motor. The cops probably stop by a few times a night. Not me. I never did that here or anywhere else. Just like we all know Fritz the Cat, we all know this spot."

Dieterich turned off the engine and the headlights. They were both completely blinded by the sudden darkness. Elise had been sitting close to the window and leaning forward to see the road. Dieterich heard her settle back in her seat and quietly slide herself next to him, barely touching, but touching enough they were both aware of it. He was planning a way to begin but she spoke first, simply asking if he had done anything interesting while she was away. He understood her question as a recognition that they had so far only been talking about her vacation. This exact moment had been the start of all the many scenarios he had spun whenever his mind was unoccupied for the past week. Very few of the scenarios had progressed well and he had not devised a path forward from here, yet here it was and he could not hit reset if it all blew up.

"Elise..." *Damn! I almost said "Cathy!" There would have been no way to recover from that blunder!* He took a breath to begin again. The drama of his pause, he realized, might even help with the coming confessional.

"Yes, what. Is something wrong?"

"No, maybe." *Forgive my opening dishonesty,* he thought, adding to his hesitation. *The true answer is yes, something is wrong.* "I have a story to tell you and it is hard to tell so I'll just start at the end and then you won't be jumping ahead to see where it's going. While you were away, my plans changed and I will not be going back to school in the fall. I'll probably be going into the Army."

"What the hell! The Army? You mean right away? What, I mean what..."

"Give me a minute so I can give you the start of the story. The start could be when I met you at the picnic lunch by the pool. We didn't talk a whole lot, but I really liked you. And I did something I never did before – I asked you to go out with me even though I hardly knew you. I don't know why I did. I liked you and thought it was time to grow up and see if this very attractive girl would let me get to know her better..."

"Are you going to say I'm making you join the goddam Army?"

"No, there's not a negative word about you in this story or a negative thought about you in my whole mind. What changed was finding out I could not get into a decent college in the fall. That means I won't have a deferment, and nothing is likely to keep me out of the draft but the luck of my lottery number. My odds aren't good for that. So I could wait to get called within a few months or I could go to Canada, or hide underground or just go to jail..."

"Wait, I don't get it. Why..."

"Yes, I know. I have not gotten to the beginning yet. The Fourth of July was so terrific. I was kinda blown away by you. You were so interesting and smart and all. We talked and then we went home and you went away and I never told you everything there is to know. I was not hiding it, I think I wasn't. It's just not the first thing you tell a girl no matter how fantastic she is. The rest of the story makes sense when you know I was kicked out of school. They said it was grades and that's completely true, but they also say, I think it's true, it was not from being incapable, just from being lazy and irresponsible... I was never drunk, didn't do drugs, didn't chase girls. The big thing - I also didn't care much about my classes. I don't have a good explanation. I don't know what your dad was told, maybe nothing, maybe everything..."

"Did you get into campus politics... protests, stuff like that?"

"No. We didn't have much of that. Now that I think about it, I wish I had thought more about it."

"Well, I gotta admit, that was a big story... a surprise... and I think you told it really nice. Don't worry about telling me late. We never got married yet. There's gotta be lotsa things we don't know about each other. You want to give me any more details?"

"No. I don't have the details. I can't explain the past and don't know much about the future."

"You weren't scared to tell me? I mean it makes sense you didn't bring it up on our first date."

"No, I wasn't scared to tell you. I had to tell you. That's not brave. I did not want it to be true but there it is."

"Should I drop you now? Go home and say the movie was OK but we probably won't do it again?"

"If I thought you should go straight home now and never see me again, if I thought I was so bad for you, I would not have come tonight. I have some self-respect, think I can be a good human being. I keep asking myself if I learned my lesson and I don't know the answer. I was looking forward to a good year in school, in some school. Didn't mind getting out of Lehigh anyway. Getting kicked out was fair. Getting drafted seems unfair. I hear life ain't fair. I've had a lot of breaks. I was thinking you were one of the best, really. It's confusing to figure what I want from you, with you. My luck ran out. It shouldn't mean everything's gone."

"I'm not gone. We still have a few minutes before I need to be home. I got something for you first."

"It would be great if you could tell me something disastrous to make you my peer."

"No, I'll be in Ann Arbor next year. That's all set. But are you thinking when you get out of the Army you'll go to college and do something that lets you spend time with nature?"

Dieterich told her the admissions officers had said he would have no difficulty getting back into school after military service, that his failure at Lehigh would be attributed to his youth and his youth would be gone or nearly so. Then he gushed about his journal and how he was enjoying writing in it. He had developed an idea about being a high school biology teacher with projects on the side to get kids to appreciate nature more. And he would work in a state or national park in the summer as an interpretive ranger while enjoying learning ever more about the land and life in the relatively wild lands.

While he described this vision of life after military experience, Elise envisioned what she might be doing at his side and he at hers. She would not be his hiking partner and she was not excited by teaching high school, but she liked the idea of teaching at a college where she could set young minds toward enriching their lives and their roles in society through literature. It might even turn out that she liked writing fiction and would have support for that as a professor. This was a vision she had not formed before, her collegiate goals had remained vague.   Dieterich was inspiring her with his dreams although they were far off in time.

"Did you ever find something to read for when you're in your room after dinner?"

"I read *Sand County Almanac*. Pretty good. Wish I wrote something like it. It's why I started writing in a journal. Nothing much in it so far, but I write different things. Not smart things. I figure someday I might be a better writer or I might take a few thoughts from the journal and put them into something. Now I'm reading *Walden*. Did you know it has the subtitle: *Life in the Woods*? I like that. It's all based on Thoreau's journals."

"Do you read fiction?"

"No, not really. I didn't take a lit class last year. I like fiction, I guess. Probably I mostly read classic stuff so far. I can see how you, I mean you, Elise, not the generic 'you', read current things and know the world better for it. It's great to be smart and all, but all the people writing out there have each one of them their own experiences to help the reader see another piece of the world or see the same piece in a different way. If I hang out with someone as smart as you, I might get some guidance on reading more broadly. I could happily stick in my pattern, nature writing, and get less and less from reading every year.

"I don't read much modern lit but I'm thinking of majoring in American lit, especially moderns. I wouldn't want to be a professor with a PhD. My idea is to teach high school kids how to enjoy reading so it becomes a lifelong thing for 'em. And you just said why, not for empty entertainment, but for much more you can get from it."

"Gee, wish I had you when I took lit in high school."

"I read something this week that made me think about you. Not in a good way, but maybe you can recover from it. I was reading a short story from a Southern writer of a generation ago. You see, I've noticed you keep calling me 'smart'. She explains what that sometimes means. I can't quote her exactly but it was about when Southerners say someone is smart, they mean intellectual in a condescending way, smart being what you are when you can't be anything else, and it is better, at least, than being nothing."[11]

"And you imagine I think your greatest attribute is the shallow one of intellectualism?"

"Well, not exactly, more like..."

"You know I am not a Southerner in any way and not in my views on women. In my naïve lexicon, 'smart'

---

[11] She very nearly quoted Elizabeth Spencer exactly from her short story "First Dark," *New Yorker*, June 20, 1959.

is among the highest attributes in a friend, along with kind or serious. I have never made a list - I do not shop for friends or women. I know the common faint praise for a girl: she has a good personality. What one likes in a friend is mainly personality but comments on a girl are supposed to begin with sexual attributes. I don't know, do girls start comments on boys that way?"

"Please don't be offended, I only meant..."

"I'm not offended at all. Only, I'm worried you may think I'm only lukewarm on you. If I seem so it is only my lukewarm self-esteem showing through."

"Sorry, forget it."

"As you request, I will forget it in a moment. First, I'll mention the girl I took to the prom. The first thing anyone said about her was she's smart. What they meant was she got the best grades and knew the subject the best. She got 800s on her SATs and went to MIT. It was the first class that admitted women. She was not my girlfriend, just my prom date. We knew each other from church and school but I may have never spoken to her before arranging to pick her up for the prom. We were paired by friends of her's. If I had not gone with her I would not have gone and would not have minded missing it. Having gone, it was not much of an event."

"I didn't go to the prom."

"I shouldn't have. I was no rebel but not pleased with being that conventional. Still, Nancy wanted to go, to be part of it. Her friends were there. I was less significant than her corsage."

"I have a little book for you, just a paperback with a few short stories."

"I'm glad you are not casting me aside, Dear. It's been a hard few minutes here without the least of bad intentions."

He was thinking she might be sticking around with him for the evening so she could give him the book she had planned for after the movie. The book was *Nick Adams Stories in the North Woods*. Nick Adams was a representation of the author, Ernest Hemingway. The first stories were about a boy in the woods, fishing and hunting alone or with his father. The extraordinary part was that the stories are set in Michigan. Nick Adams does not have a girlfriend in the stories. Elise was writing herself in. She was not sure she belonged anywhere else.

17

Friday, July 25 Friday was busy at work until lunchtime. Wes decided the job of setting up the new space was close enough to being finished that Dieterich could work through lunch and then leave early, say two o'clock, if he wanted to. On Monday and Tuesday he would work in Grand Rapids so his time driving there on Sunday night would count for taking Friday afternoon off. Rusty said that seemed fair but he took his normal lunch, eating at his workbench and watching Dieterich without comment.

Dieterich was excited about taking another trip on his own. He did not mind doing the busy work of the past week but he preferred the respect implied by operating independently with the company's reputation in his care. He felt the pressure of taking on a job that might have any number of complications. And he wondered if he was, in fact, enjoying the pressure.

As soon as he got in his car, he consulted Freddy's map for someplace to hike near Grand Rapids. He found a promising park called Yankee Springs Recreational Area with a network of trails around the Devil's Soup Bowl and a beach on Gun Lake. The devil had gotten around America a lot and left behind innumerable relics that became hiking destinations. Dieterich had seen his footprint in three states, his soup bowl in two so far, his berry bucket, his notch, his teapot, his dome and he had heard of his canyon, his cave, his rocks, his cliff, his profile, his shadow, his tower, and his bowling alley. He knew of two Devil's Washbasins in New Hampshire. The Soup Bowl was enough foundation for a weekend plan so he started the engine, switched over to what he should do with his unexpected bonus of free time in the city.

AMBITION

I can go to that bookstore and get something for Elise. Absolutely! Why didn't I think of this before? When and if I see her again, that would be perfect, assuming I can find something that fits her as well as she did for me... If I don't find something that good, she won't care what it is. She'll like it. I can write a note inside... There is nothing I can get for Cathy. I'll do the driving tomorrow and buy her lunch. A present would be square. A box of chocolates or what? It's the wrong kind of date for anything like that.

He suddenly realized he had money. He was going into the Army or holding down a job for a year so there was no need to save for college, not the pittance he was earning over the summer. His summer earnings were only symbolic, an effort to show appreciation for what his parents paid for his tuition and board. After two years in the Army, if it came to that, he would have some savings and he would have GI Bill support.

Finally, a good thing! I don't have to be my usual cheap self with Elise or Cathy. I should get Elise a hardback book. Don't want her gift to look small. Damn, I'm thinking clearly now! Give me a calculus exam! I'll buy a shirt to wear tomorrow. No reason I have to wear one of my office shirts... Izod, three buttons, something like that. If I wear a t-shirt under it, I'll look a little bulkier. I'll ask at the bookstore where's a department store.

Saturday, July 26

Saturday morning was foggy from the rain on Friday, but the orange sun was bright enough to be seen through the fog. The rain had passed. The day would be clear, probably humid, probably hot, a good day for swimming in a lake.

Dieterich was nervous. Firstly, he was nervous about Elise. She had been so good about his being a drop-out. She did not seem to mind that he had not told her before. At least he had spit it out, the essence of it, without stammering like a child. They had a good kiss, friendly, not grasping for too much, before he drove her home. And then he gave her a chaste peck on the cheek at the door. *And now I'm about to pick up Cathy. Weird.* Elise felt like a better match than he ever expected from a girl, a bold impression to have on the basis of only two dates.

Cathy was not a back-up in case Elise decided she and he were finished. He wanted Cathy to want him. She was spectacular. It would build his ego immensely to be her boyfriend. He was not there yet, not her boyfriend. His lips on her face and his hands on her body were more than he had ever hoped to experience this summer and everything he had heard a woman could do without stepping across the line into the kind of sex that created dangerous expectations. Cathy knew what they were doing, he was sure. She drew the boundaries and she drew him toward them. He did not mind that she had been there before. It seemed inevitable in such a creature. Yet he was nervous to be learning her pleasures while Elise was... Oh yes, and there was the insecurity of his physique standing next to hers. That was reduced by having the new shirt. He could wear it while angling for an embrace with minimal fabric between them, if that fit within her boundaries. Later he could take off his shirt and run in the water quickly without being seen too clearly.

When Dieterich went downstairs to get milk for his cereal, Roland was cooking bacon and eggs for himself and Sam.

"Morning Deeter. You know you got a letter over here?"

There was a box for the roomers' mail but Dieterich had never checked it. The letter was from his mother and had just come in yesterday.

"Where you been this week? Upstate somewhere?" Sam had not seen Dieterich at first and his mouth was full of toast so he waved while waiting for Dieterich to answer Roland."

"No, man. Just working in fair Ferndale. Next week up in Grand Rapids, though."

"You want some bacon?"

"Thanks. I got my cereal. I don't do much breakfast."

"What you got on for the weekend?" asked Sam.

Dieterich looked around to be sure the Tylers were not nearby to hear anything. He preferred they did not know he was meeting a girl. They might have a conversation with Wes. He had not before considered himself a topic for gossip, innocent though it would have been. He did not need to feed the potential gossip, but he liked the idea of telling these two he had a girl in his plan.

"Wash some clothes, then take a girl up the lake for the day." He put his cereal and bowl and spoon on the kitchen table.

"Yeah, what lake?" asked Sam while Roland held his full attention on the sizzling frying pan.

"Lexington Beach."

"Where's that?"

"Up north a ways from here, south end of Lake Huron. She knows the place." Dieterich sat down and poured some milk into his bowl.

"Well damn, good for you."

"Yeah. Should be good," Dieterich added as he lifted a spoonful of Cheerios. "You doing anything?"

"Not one goddam thing," answered Roland quickly. "What do ya say, Sam, we go out to Lexington Beach?"

"Is that bacon getting close to done?" Sam asked.

At five past eleven, Dieterich parked on the street in front of Cathy's house. He looked to the front door, sensing she was about to come running outside, but he saw no movement. He stood tall and walked briskly up her short driveway and then across the lawn on stepping-stones to the concrete pad in front of her door. It was a single-story house with wooden siding and two windows on each side of the door. There was no doorbell or screen door. He rapped firmly twice with the door knocker. He did not want to make a weak sound and wonder if he had been heard. A tall woman with bleached hair and tight clothes opened the door. She looked at him without saying anything. Dieterich hesitated for just a brief moment as he took her in. She wore very short shorts, revealing lovely legs. He could not remember Cathy's last name if he ever knew it.

"Hi. I'm Deeter. Came to see Cathy."

"Hello. They're out back. You can go through here."

The woman stepped aside and waved down a hallway toward the living room and a sliding door to the shady patio in back.

"Right. Thanks." Dieterich could not think of anything more to say. He wondered who "they" meant.

Cathy was lying on a chaise longue next to a girl sitting in a webbed-plastic lawn chair. Cathy wore old bell-bottom jeans and a loose t-shirt. The other girl wore shorts and a flowered blouse. They each had a tall glass with ice cubes and something wet. The woman, probably Cathy's mother, followed Dieterich outside.

"Hey Cathy. Looks like you're fighting the heat already." He wanted to add "nice patio" but everything was so humble in scale, it might have sounded sarcastic.

Cathy jumped up, glass in hand and rushed over to Dieterich and greeted him with a kiss on the cheek. This is Margo. She lives just a block over. We were in school together but she's at Central Michigan now."

"Hello, Margo."

"And my mother, of course."

Dieterich turned around, surprised to see how near her mother was standing. He smiled in a way he thought was warm. "Yes, we've met."

"I'd get you some lemonade but we ought to go right away over to Margo's. She's in a rush. See if you can figure out what's wrong with her car. It shouldn't take long. She just needs some advice." Cathy was staring intently into his eyes. He nodded slightly to signal he understood what was going on even though he did not understand and his nod could hardly be seen as a signal.

"Okay," Dieterich replied. "Over to Margo's right away." Then he turned to Cathy's mother. "We can talk a bit when we get back, right?"

"Yes, when you get back and you'll be back soon. I'll be out here, I think. I'll get you a drink then."

On the walk over to Margo's, Cathy explained they were just going over there to get away from her mother to have a private conversation. Margo walked close to Dieterich and explained it was really so she could check out this guy her girlfriend had met. She pushed him into Cathy and laughed. "Better be nice to me 'cause I've got lots of influence over Cathy."

After the three of them went around the corner, taking them out of sight of Cathy's house, Cathy jumped in front of Dieterich, threw her arms around him and kissed him quickly on the lips. Margo ran ahead. They embraced for a few more seconds, not enough to be a public spectacle. His hands ran up and down her back, stopping for the briefest time at the strap of her bra.

"Mom's havin' a bad day. When that happens, it's bad for me too. When she drinks it's not lemonade but she's not a drunk. She gets depressed and things aren't too good for her these days. So she thinks I shouldn't be going to the lake. It's not you. It's not really me. She trusts me. She has to, anyway. She says you're a stranger but what the hell is that supposed to mean? I know you. I decide who I want to see. Goddamit, I'm nineteen. She doesn't want me to grow up and leave her, you know, but that's gotta happen. Not today. She's jealous. Nobody wants to take her to the lake."

"Including me," said Dieterich and he immediately regretted saying that aloud. "But we could take her if you wanted."

Cathy laughed. "If she goes, I stay. No, I never thought of that. She's just crazy sometimes. Not silly, I mean actually crazy. Maybe manic-depressive or something like that. Who knows? It's serious and she can get real mean if I fight her... Here, this is Margo's. Nobody's home but her."

The front door was open and they went in. Cathy guided him to the kitchen table. Margo asked if they wanted something to drink. Cathy answered they would not stay long, just enough to explain the situation. Margo went out the back door.

"It all came up this morning. Sometimes it's like that. She knew I going away for the day and then suddenly it was like some kind of crime."

"So we're not going today, right?"

"I need you to..."

"Look, if that's best, and only you know what's best, if we need to drop this idea, we will. Of course, I won't like it but I won't be mad. Sometimes things don't work out. We'll do something else some other day. We're still going to the concert, right? And I've got lots to tell you. Some big news. Too much to explain right now with your mother waiting for us. We'll have another day. As long as you want to."

"That's right, Honey. We'll get together again quick. I'll see you after Romero's on Monday and then the..."

"Not Monday. I'm in Grand Rapids Monday and Tuesday. I'll see you Wednesday."

"And then the concert won't be far off. This panic she went into probably won't come back for a few weeks at least. Besides, if we don't go out today, she might feel like she's in control and going on a regular date is just being normal... Wait here a sec. I need to go in the other room."

Dieterich looked into the back yard where Margo was rocking slowly on a swing. She was facing away from her house.

Cathy called from the room next to the kitchen. Dieterich went to her. It was a small room with two chairs facing a television.

"You didn't say how I look without my waitress outfit." Cathy came close and put her head on his chest.

"I can't find words to say how fine you look no matter what you wear. It is especially fine to see you in the daylight. I never did that before. And I love the casual clothes. So cool with the jeans and the cute cut."

They had their arms around each other. She pulled his shirt up and slid her hands inside, rubbing his back. Her t-shirt was already loose. He stroked her back from inside her shirt and realized she had taken off her bra. He felt her breasts one at a time, touching the nipples and hardly breathing.   Her eyes were shut and she moaned as if she were feeling the dream he was having. It was a stolen moment, not the time to experience any more than that. He put his hands on her hips and she pressed into him.

"Thank you, Deeter for taking me to the beach today and for putting up with all my business. You go on outside and tell Margo we're leaving. I'll fix myself up and be right out."

Dieterich tucked in his shirt as he went through the kitchen and out to the back yard.

"Margo, guess we won't have time for drinks. Listen, you seem like a damn good friend and I won't give you any cause to fight me."

"Cathy deserves the best."

"I have to agree and I'm sure that's not me so we'll have to figure that out somehow. For today, it's enough that I figured out your car, which I did not see in front of your house and you don't have a garage. Anyway, I think you had a loose connection to the battery. Off and on connection. Sometimes it caught and sometimes it rattled looser. It was simple to tighten up."

Dieterich had a short conversation with Cathy's mother, enough to make him suspect alcohol was playing a large role in her present behavior. Cathy tried to help her mother say something relevant, to focus on whatever was in the first part of the sentence. Then her mother got angry with Cathy, told her to bug off and reached out to hold Dieterich's hand. He shook her hand like a greeting and stepped back, smiled privately to Cathy as a way to communicate he saw the problem and did not hold it against Cathy but he knew he was not actually communicating with either of them. He reached out to hold Cathy's hand. When she did not give it to him, he stepped closer and took it gently.

"Nice to meet you, ma'am," he said with his head turned back and with enough volume to be clear over whatever Cathy's mother was trying to say.

Before he could continue and to draw Cathy out to his car, Cathy offered her free hand to her mother, linking the three of them.

"Deeter was just telling me he heard on the radio coming over here about a storm coming in from Lake Huron. It's not a big one but it's going to be rainy all afternoon at Lexington Beach. So maybe he can go into the office now and get some work done and the whole day won't be wasted."

"Tha's too bad. You didn't tell me where he wors, works," Cathy's mother slurred. Her response was immediate and quick, her eyes were sharp. He did not think he was seeing a drunken woman, but something else he could not explain.

"He can't go into all that now. He's got to get going. He's got an office in the city. Not fancy. Paperwork..."

He left about noon and drove alone to another park: Gun Lake Beach.

His first impression of Yankee Springs Recreation Area was all good, better than Sleepy Hollow and Gun Lake was better than any swimming lake park he knew in Connecticut, or, when he thought about it, better than any freshwater swimming he had seen anywhere, except, when he thought about it, not better than the pools where he had swum below wilderness waterfalls in Colorado, not nearly so fine as those. He wished, of course, he had Cathy in her bathing suit on a towel on the grass beside him, so they could warm themselves in the sun and then run into the lake, swim away from the shore and embrace. He did not imagine in detail how that might have been.

His mind was full of what had happened already today. He lay on his towel, writing in his journal. His shirt lay beside him. He was sunning himself to get some color in his body and felt no insecurity in exposing himself to view, Cathy being miles and miles away. His new shirt had fortified his confidence when they had been together.

His thoughts turned to Elise, not to the question of his betrayal - that had been argued away for now. He wondered if holding her breasts would be as exquisite, and how much of his frisson came from Cathy's offering herself and enjoying his pleasure. Then, with Elise in mind, he wondered how insecure he felt with her about his physique, which he immediately answered: it was not an issue at all. This surprising conclusion was worth a thoughtful journal entry. He suspected her withered leg would make her more accepting of his physical flaws. It may have contributed to her kind response to learning he had been kicked out of Lehigh. Or was he being ugly for thinking she could only match with a defective partner? It did not feel right to put that in her personality. She was a beauty, no "but" could alter that. And she was self-confident, personable, and, frankly, sexy. His journal entry on the subject reached no conclusion but it was sufficient to let him end his daydreaming about the two girls.

He stopped writing. It would feel good to swim, to swim hard and come back to the blanket with rubbery arms and out of breath. Then he could soak up some more sun before hiking one of the trails to the Devil's Soup Bowl. He sat with the journal in front of him and looked along the beach.

Two groups of girls in two-piece suits were noisily cavorting. Maybe some of them had seen him writing and thought he was an intellectual which he recently learned could be a negative compared to, say, beautiful musculature, but it was better than nothing. Maybe they would speak to him if he put on his shirt and walked past them on his way to the hot dog stand. "Buy me an ice cream, Professor?" Nothing they could say or do would make an impression lasting beyond a greeting and a smile. He had no room for, or wish for, any additional feminine attention, a condition he had not experienced before this summer.

A pair of hippies walked along the sandy shore. They wore sneakers, bell-bottomed jeans and tie-dye tee-shirts, but they did not appear to be imitating the style, just living it. The guy had long hair tied into a ponytail. The woman had frizzy blond hair, not coiffed or bleached. They were not posing for the beach crowd, merely walking by. Dieterich had not reflected on the beach crowd apart from checking out the girls. Until those two appeared, it could have been a scene from ten years earlier, including his own appearance. Cathy had looked like the hippies on the only occasion when he saw her out of uniform. Would she have worn a bikini or worn shorts and tee-shirt for swimming? Despite what he had told himself, he thought now he liked the cool version of Cathy that he had never considered before. He wanted long hair and bell bottoms. She could have short hair and dye it purple. He could have the bell bottoms if he joined the Navy but the long hair would have to wait.

He wanted to swim; it was in his plan; it was in the original plan with Cathy albeit at a different beach. Some part of some plan ought to be followed. His wallet was locked in the car but he still had to secure his car keys. Leaving them in his jeans pocket, packed in his Michigan State totebag lying on the beach, was probably OK but he needed to be more careful than that. He put the key in the pocket of his shorts/bathing suit and promised himself he would not tip his pocket while swimming. The water was cold when he stepped into it but he walked forward steadily, putting on a show for any girl who might be watching. When the water was deep enough to make walking almost impossible, he leapt up and forward for a few steps and then dove in, almost scraping his face on the bottom before rising smoothly into a crawl stroke. If one of those girls had been watching, they might think him athletic. He went a long way, "long" as measured by his energy reserves. Then he rolled onto his back and breathed heavily while looking back to the shore to see how far away it was. It could not be called far although he was farther out than anyone else. He rested on his back and kicked to get himself slowly moving back to the shore. He'd had his spurt of exercise. He was young and felt his strength recovering. He took a few lazy strokes on his side and then felt in his pocket for the car key which was, as it must be, still there.

On the beach, he bared his pale flesh to the sun. It felt good except for the damp in his shorts which began to itch and kept him from feeling drowsy.

He rolled onto his side and propped his head on his hand. He was facing a clutch of giggling girls which he did not mind seeing but he was embarrassed to be facing them, so he rolled onto his other side and rested his head on an outstretched arm.

Someday soon, I'll lie on the beach with my head on her belly and when I turn to speak to her, my face will brush against her breast and she will like my being there. When we swim, we will go out farther than everyone else and wrap our legs around each other and press together while we kiss.

Suddenly he remembered his mother's letter. It was in his bag. He sat up to read it while he imagined the girls on the beach might notice him and believe it came from his college girlfriend, who is somewhere else for the summer, and is hoping he does not find a summer romance. His mother offers only sympathy, not advice. She knows he has heard her advice already although it came through his father's lips.

"It is not so bad as you feel right now," she wrote. "Young men have setbacks. You have all the fine qualities a man needs. There will be a delay and, God willing, it does not take you into Vietnam, but you will be fine. It is not a big war and it is ending soon. Maybe Nixon will finish the troop reductions before you even finish training. It seems likely. It will be good to have you home in a few weeks. Then we will keep our fingers crossed about the draft." She put an untitled, original poem in her envelope.

```
His heartbeat, my firstborn, my motherhood
Brought ecstasy I could not have foreseen.

Together we played and learned his childhood,
'Til life demanded the role of enforcing.

Awed, I watched as he grew toward manhood,
Astonished by his call to soldier.

Proud his reply could not have been bolder.
Now worry weights my every heartbeat

That the price of service be not fatal to
   him,
That the need of nation be not false to him.
```

Gosh, Mom, I mean, Mother, you've formed a poem that may fit someday soon. I'm not there yet. Whatever I do, whatever I become, I know it will matter to you and I promise to remember that better. I wish I had learned from you how to appreciate poetry enough to dig up something inspiring from time to time. I'll have to write back. Better than a phone call to your way of thinking.

He paraded past the lively girls in skimpy clothes on his way to the snack bar. No one spoke to him and he made no eye contact so he did not start up an affair with a third Michigan beauty. He thought he would get an ice cream, but the hot dogs looked appetizing. He had not eaten one in several years. They were standard fare at picnics in his junior high years and when he went camping. He got one with mustard and one with relish. He ate his lunch happily as he walked out to the trail.

It would be an easy hike among a maze of wide, smooth, dirt paths traversing level ground. Overhead was a pleasant green canopy, not high as an epic poem would make it, scaled instead to the modest realism of lower Michigan. None of the trees was large although many were gnarled, and many had fallen without attaining the thickness common in the beech/maple/oak lands of New England. Still, he had not come in search of unprecedented natural glory. He had found solitude and fresh air on a path to the devil. He wondered why the devil had left his mark here. In Colorado, his mark was always on an unusual rocky outcrop or eroded remnant. The Yankee Springs Park was soft and safe and gentle. He looked for something extraordinary around the next turn. Paths connected without any logic. All seemed equivalent although there was no way to become lost as every intersection had signs pointing one way toward the Soup Bowl and one back to the parking lot.

Finally a sign indicated he had reached the Soup Bowl. Looking around for something remarkable, he saw an odd gully worn into a steep slope but he rejected that as the Devil's mark since the erosion was not big enough to be given a name. The Devil might take it as an insult.

Eventually he realized the Soup Bowl was the round ridge a hundred yards across on which the gully had formed on his side. It was an odd formation, not obvious from any single point of view for an impressive photograph or an interesting sketch. He could not guess at the geology that formed it. His best guess was a meteor crater too small to be famous. His second-best guess was the Devil ate soup here once.

He got back to his car as the sun was setting. It would be a long drive back to Rochester Hills where he could spend the rest of the evening with his journal, trying to record a very dramatic day. Except he could not find his car key.

The key was missing and dusk was approaching. He checked his pockets and everything in his bag. It was still missing. He suspected Wes would have a spare key since it was a company car, but he did not want anyone to know of his folly. He jogged over to the snack bar to see if anyone had turned in a key but he could tell when he was still a long way off that the shutters had already been closed on the shack. He knocked on the door and no one answered. It was late but not dark, so he began to jog while looking for a glint of metal on the route he had walked to the Soup Bowl. Within fifteen minutes he was no longer sure he was still on one of the trails he had taken before and he decided it was better to be back at the car before he was lost in the dark. When he reached the parking lot, he tried to retrace his route backwards from the way he had come the first time, and that was soon impossible. It was not only getting dark, it was hard to recognize the path while going in the opposite direction. Soon all the other cars were gone. He decided to spend the night in the Rambler and call the police for advice on Sunday morning. There had to be a legal way to get it started although it would likely require telling Wes. At least he wanted to go to Wes with a plan. It would be a boring evening until he got sleepy.

At 7:30, a man tapped on the car window.

"You gotta get out of here right now. The park's closed."

Dieterich got out of the car. "I know it closes at night and I'm really sorry to be here. I lost the key on the trail somewhere. I'll have to get it replaced tomorrow. It's a company car; I might get a spare key in the morning from my boss."

"Alright. You do that. But right now, you gotta leave."

Dieterich could not argue about the rule. It was reasonable, but he would not admit that calling Wes was actually his next option. He suggested he could hitchhike back to Detroit to get the key, but not at night. ...If only he could deal with it in the daylight. The park employee was unsympathetic and said he would have the police give him a cell for the night which he did not mean as a courtesy.

"Go to a motel or something, just not here."

Dieterich was frustrated by his situation and his inability to see a good ending. He needed the car before work on Monday. He tried another approach. With his voice sounding higher than it ought to sound and speaking faster than his brain could absorb the words he was forming, he told the park employee how he had worked in Estes Park, Colorado, for the summer and faced problems with the tourists as problems to be solved. He gave some examples. He spoke of the civic value of parks to inspire people with the beauty of nature, of the mission park employees have to share their resources, to be creative, to be sympathetic, at least. He agreed to leave and not trouble the police, but he expressed his disappointment as politely as he could. He did not give up easily. The employee let him rant. Dieterich almost stopped listening to himself and formulated a simple plan of walking away and then returning to sleep in the woods. In that scenario, his problem was not getting through the night. It was getting to work on Monday morning.

18

Monday, July 28 Monday morning after getting the replacement key for the Rambler and driving home, Dieterich left for Grand Rapids without having any breakfast. He would be meeting the managers of two plants at a pancake house on the edge of the city. They would both brief him on what repairs and maintenance was needed in their plants and he would only get a signature at the second plant. He liked the friendly arrangement to meet for pancakes and to trust one another so he could simply check out as he was leaving.

The sky was clear, the morning air cool and dry. He appreciated anew the perfectly straight, four-lane highways of Michigan, the global capital of automobile worship. Traffic was not initially heavy going north because he was leaving Detroit suburbs more than approaching Grand Rapids, easy driving, safe at 80, a chance to push a little more than before, see what this squarest of cars could do. The speedometer touched 90 and went no higher no matter how hard he pushed on the accelerator.

He was approaching a car in the left lane going ten miles per hour over the speed limit and therefore twenty miles per hour slower than Dieterich. He tapped the brake well before there was any danger of hitting it from behind; wide, straight roads on a clear day hide no traffic. But the car hid from him the sight of a row of barrels between the lanes, probably for some construction project that had not started for the day since traffic was allowed in both lanes. He braked a little harder and clipped the second barrel. He saw it leap into the air and fly across the right lane and out of sight down a slope beyond the road. He saw it only out of his peripheral vision because he stayed focused on not hitting any more barrels or the car in front of him whose brakes lights had come on solid. His car slowed to fifty. Time was flowing like molasses. He had time to decide no car had been hit by his barrel and no car had been close behind him. Maybe no one had noticed. The barrel collision had not felt too hard. It was certainly not filled with sand. And it may not have dented the car if it had only contacted the bumper. After the incident, he kept at least a car length behind the car in front of him for every ten miles per hour of speed.

The restaurant was only two exits farther. No one followed him down the ramp to complain. In the parking lot he looked for a dent on the right-front fender and saw nothing. He had better luck than he deserved, assuming Wes did not get a court summons for a hit-and-run by the company car.

He looked around the restaurant and saw no one likely to be a plant manager. And no one who seemed to be looking for him. He was ten minutes early and waited by the door since there were plenty of tables available. And fifteen minutes later two men, dressed like older versions of himself, came in and walked straight to him to shake hands.

"Sorry to be a little late. Hope you weren't too hungry," said one of them while they looked over their menus."

"My watch isn't precise enough for me to say you were late at all."

"Some guy out there was running later than us. Passed us going ninety at least. And driving an AMC Rambler! Can you believe it? Must have put some jacked up engine in there so no one knows what he can do."

They talked a while longer about the guy in the dusty, old, blue Rambler American sedan. Dieterich thought they might have recognized him or seen the car in the parking lot but their talk appeared to be simply the car culture exerting itself. After breakfast, he went to the men's room to be sure they left the lot before he went to his car and then he was careful not to park near either of the factories.

This thing is just like busting out of school – a chance to change something that damn sure needs changing. A hit-and-run charge possibly going to Wes wasn't the worst of it. That barrel could have killed somebody, some people. For sure I would've pulled over if it hit someone. I'm sure it didn't. Not on the highway anyhow. Why was I speeding all summer? Feeling cocky about meeting a couple beautiful girls? That doesn't make me Adonis. Doesn't even mean I'll ever have a woman so fine. Don't even know yet if I'm going to get away with it. But I know I won't be speeding any more. Not ever. Really. What a fool!

At the first factory, the secretary who sat near the door replied to him by name before he had time to introduce himself. He felt a pulse of pride to be known before he even arrived. She called someone named Sampson from the phone on her desk, only dialing three digits, announcing Mr. Kahler was there. She did not invite Dieterich to take a seat while waiting, which was appropriate because Sampson arrived in the lobby within thirty seconds of the call. Dieterich introduced himself although Sampson obviously knew who he was. He gave only his first name since he was going to be calling Sampson by his first name, assuming "Sampson" was his first name. They walked briskly onto the factory floor where Sampson explained the company had eight hardness testers.

Standing beside the first of these, Dieterich could not see to the end of the industrial space. The ceiling was thirty or forty feet high, with a large crane rolling silently from his left toward his right along a rail above them while the rail itself was moving slowly away from him along a pair of heavier rails. Dieterich watched while the crane maneuvered across the room toward some destination hidden behind the tall stamping machines and less recognizable heavy metallic equipment. He spotted a man leading the way, but he was not controlling the crane. His job seemed to be to ensure no one was standing directly under it. Before the crane disappeared entirely, Dieterich spotted the hoist carrying a coil of sheet metal close to the ceiling. Sampson waited while Dieterich watched and then pointed to the crane operator on a catwalk. The controls were in his hands and were linked to the crane with a bright yellow wire.

"Sorry," Dieterich said to Sampson. "There's just so much going on here at the same time. It's beautiful to see, hard to understand."

Sampson nodded affirmatively. While Dieterich was marveling at the beehive of activity around him, Sampson was patiently and meticulously rolling up his sleeves, folding more than rolling the ends. He did not rush Dieterich and explained he had worked there for several years so nothing looked strange about the operations to him, but he knew grasping the whole was complex beyond the comprehension of ordinary men. Sampson said he felt like a bacterium looking around at the human body from inside. Then he cast his attention toward the ceiling where some movement had caught his eye. Suddenly he turned sharply to listen to a muffled, throbbing sound from somewhere out of sight, the throb picking up its pace and swelling in volume like an orchestra. It stopped suddenly, leaving Sampson and Dieterich to wonder in each own's way if the sound portended trouble but no one was reacting, so they had to admit it had only worried them for a moment because they had ignored their own responsibilities and tuned in to the ever-present mysteries of someone else's responsibilities. Those anonymous strangers, each with his own specialized equipment and focused knowledge, molded and twisted and cut and bent metal and plastic into precise configurations that were pounded and screwed and riveted and bolted and glued and soldered into ever larger assemblies, none of which formed a product with any capability Dieterich could intuit. Sampson looked at the factory through Dieterich's fresh eyes.

"The strangest part of all: this is a successful thing they are doing. I am paid well every two weeks, and my superiors are pleased with my work and the work of my equally uncomprehending peers. Everyone knows what to do and does it very well. Does one thing, not a very difficult thing, not a boring thing (people tend to move to a new station every year or two)... Every person, every tool."

"Exactly like me," Dieterich replied, who knew his tiny function well and was not challenged or jaded by doing it without knowing how it contributed to whatever any particular factory was producing. He busied himself taking out his tools and placing them neatly on one of his clean rags. Sampson started to walk off.

"Sampson, where is the next hardness tester I should do?"

"If I showed you, you'd get lost trying to find it again. I don't know what you do inside that cowling but I have seen it done a hundred times. I know what it looks like when you're ready to move on and I'll be back for you. What do you think, 25 minutes if all goes well?"

"I figure I'm faster than most but I'm more careful too so, yeah, see you in 25 minutes."

The first part of the job was testing the current performance of the machine: was it accurate within allowed limits and (Rusty had departed from the manual with this test) did it feel right. Dieterich paid close attention to this initial check and then it was time to remove the cover and disassemble the upper mechanism. He could listen to his own thoughts at this stage.

Dad would not have cared for Sampson's odd phrase back there, his 'uncomprehending peers'. Dad has not worked on the factory floor since before I was born but he still sees himself as having come from them. He gave them respect as a matter of principle although he would not wish me to be one of them, not after this summer. On the other hand, he would have liked to hear me say 'this is beautiful'. I know he hoped exposing me to major American industry would get me out of my dreaminess over rare animals and pretty trees. It is from his blind respect for me that he imagines I will shift my values if I just get away from the naive entertainments of youth, too much encouraged by my mother's impractical, artistic temperament. 'Those who can, do. Those who can't, teach or sing or play baseball for a few years.' Once I see what 'doing' means, he imagines I will put tent and mess kit and boots in the attic to become a 'doer', then embrace my destiny in some branch of business. He thinks the dead branches in the forest need to be collected and burned, and the branches so shaded they die, need to be cut off. He thinks the harmful insects, somehow defined, need to be held in check and paths need to be raked. More than this he thinks the wilds need to be used to benefit the economy although he is sufficiently open minded to accept that a wide variety of tastes and talents contribute to the economy.

Dieterich did not time how long the first machine was taking. Sampson must have been watching from a distance because he turned up suddenly as Dieterich was about to latch his toolbox. As they walked together to the next hardness tester, Dieterich wondered what responsibilities were assigned to Sampson. He decided it was nothing that required rolled up sleeves. In the few minutes of their interaction, Sampson had projected competence at whatever he did. He fit well in this meticulous factory, a cut above the other places Dieterich had seen. NASA came to mind. *They must have the highest industrial standards.*

The third machine surprised Dieterich before he reached it. He had never seen one painted in bright colors. All the ones he had seen were a deep black that had been sprayed on and then cured somehow to yield a textured finish that did not show fingerprints and looked very "professional." When he looked more closely, he saw the bright colors had been sprayed on thinly letting the texture show through.

"How do you like it?" Sampson asked.

"Very nicely done!" Dieterich answered.

"It's art."

"I see that."

"We don't know who does it. At least I don't know. It turns up once a month, about that. Never know where. It's in all departments. The guys love it. They offer a reward to get something painted in their department, but the mystery painter never takes 'em. The boss doesn't like it. He thinks something will get damaged or maybe the warranty on a hardness tester will be invalidated. Something like that. He's keeps things strict."

"I see he does. This was a careful job. No paint on anything but the cover."

The sixth hardness tester was a bigger surprise.

"How do you like this one?" Sampson asked.

Dieterich looked closely, searching for the plate with a serial number on it. He thought it might be an old model but the plate had the name of a different manufacturer.

"Can you certify this one?"

"I think you know I can't, but I can check how good it's doing. Just give me a minute to do some tests." During the tests, using metal disks of known hardness, Dieterich tried to feel the quality of function. Was it silent, smooth and steady?

"It's reading too soft on the softer materials. That suggests the sensing bit has a chip but not too near the tip. I can see the chip, can show it to you right now with my loupe. That would be simple to fix by putting in a new diamond bit. That's the most expensive part, not because it's diamond exactly, more because it's precisely shaped. That is, it should be, but this one's not. Maybe something else is wrong too. I doubt it. The chip explains the readings. I can't fix it. I don't know if one of our bits would fit but, even if it did, I couldn't sell it to you."

"I figured you couldn't. Thanks for looking it over. What you said makes sense... Let's call it 1:00 and I'll walk you to the door. You're going over to the Century Street plant after lunch, right?"

19

<table>
<tr><td>Wednesday, July 30</td><td>Wednesday morning, Dieterich's first thought was of Elise. Still lying in his bed in Richmond</td></tr>
</table>

Hills, he wanted to tell her about the Devil's Soup Bowl. He had some interesting thoughts when he was there up until the moment he touched his empty pocket. He wanted some of those thoughts for his journal. *Why*, he wondered, *do I think it would it be better to tell her about the place before I write my notes? Doesn't make sense. But then if I go through it with her, I could write something more complete when I get to the journal. So far, everything is part sentences, lists, data... I may never start to write a real journal and if I decide to try, I may not even remember what the things I put in there were supposed to mean. Gotta do some real writing someday. I've got as much time for it now as I'll ever get.*

Something felt wrong in his logic. He was hiding something from himself.

What am I missing? I make these resolutions, like the one about doing school assignments better next year, so here's a way to jumpstart that. Don't make excuses, and I know the excuses: not really a writer, nothing much to see in a few hours of flat woodland, I'll do it later when I have more notes to work from, too much going on with the job and everything. No, better one is: too distracted by having two girls all of a sudden and I want more of whichever one is nearest at the moment.

He sat up and looked at the alarm clock. He was awake early but he did not lie down again.

What the fuck am I doing sitting here? What was I thinking about? Oh yeah, I'm hiding something from myself. Good, it's good to know that. It's a bad habit I've got. Like a sociopath. When I know I should be in class and I'm not, I don't even worry about it. But now I'm awake and I know something's wrong in my mental logic. I was thinking how good it would be to tell Elise about the Devil's Soup Bowl, how it was supposed to help with the journal. No, of course not. The big story is not the soup bowl, it's the stupid adventure of the car keys. And I am using the excuse that it is not fit for a nature journal when what I know is going on is this: I'm not going to tell her any part of it. Not any more than I'll tell her what I did in the morning before I went up there. I squeaked by without having to tell her dad or Freddy, and I do not need to prove how close I came to screwing up. That story can go out to Cathy. Her dad's not involved with it and she knows the start of the day already. She's the only one who'll get it. I'll tell her that too.

And here's the good thing: I already told Elise about flunking out and I don't need to tell Cathy about that. I thought I was just waiting for the right moment when I was really just waiting for the right excuse to never tell her. Don't need an excuse. Just make a decision. And I need to call Elise. Wonder when I can call. Maybe before I drive to the office. Is that too early? It's been a couple days since our date and that went real good. I should call. Out to the phone booth right after breakfast. What does she do all day? I should know. Have to ask.

"Wow! Cool! You answered the phone. It's not too early is it? I gotta drive to the office pretty soon and I wanted to talk to you.

"Not too early."

"So what are you doing today?"

"I don't know. I'm on vacation, I guess. If it's supposed to get hot, I could call Miriam to come over for a swim. You have time to come over?"

It wouldn't be any fun to be there with her girlfriend around.

"I'm not on vacation. It's cooled off by the time I get back after work."

The call with Elise gave Dieterich some relief. He agreed to go to her house for dinner but not this day, better tomorrow. It would not do to miss Cathy without warning after being away four days. He realized he did not have Cathy's phone number and felt foolish for that. He felt worse than foolish for not even knowing her last name. She did not know his surname either.

Rusty greeted him with an unusually big smile.

"Welcome back Deeter! Didn't hear anything about Grand Rapids burning down so I guess things worked out good enough?"

"If you do hear about the thing in Grand Rapids, it wasn't my fault."

"Sure you didn't lose something up there?

"What?"

"I got a call from Bob Merlin at Timmons Metal Supply. You met him."

"Sure"

"Said there was a crosshead screwdriver next to the hardness tester after you left."

"He's right. Should I drive on up there this morning and get it?"

"It's not worth much."

"It's not ours anyway. It was on the bench when I got there. You're about to check my toolbox and you probably know every scratch on everything in there, so give the crosshead a close look and you'll recognize it."

"No, I'll believe you this time. He said you were really good with the guys. Said you knew the machine good too."

"I've been trained. They didn't have any interesting problems. There's some wear on the balance rod on a machine at Cog and Gear. I showed it to them. It's an old machine. I said we'd check with them about getting a new or refurbished one. I didn't explain that I don't do sales but I'm pretty sure they didn't want to be spending any more money on my say-so. Even being as good looking as I am, I come across as too young and inexperienced to buy something as fancy as one of our machines from me."

"You put that in your report?"

"Not about being good looking but I underlined the thing about calling them to discuss a replacement. The serial number's there. We have records showing its age?"

"Age: yes. Mileage: no... You'll be helping me this morning. Go out with Freddy in the afternoon. You know you're out to Saginaw tomorrow, right?"

"Lookin' forward to it."

Freddy had a cafe he liked for lunch. They stayed longer than usual for lunch because their first appointment was not until 1:30. Dieterich did a one-paragraph, oral version of the tale he would give Elise about the Devil's Soup Bowl, and he credited Freddy's map with easing his exploration of the state's natural areas. Freddy had never heard of the Devil's Soup Bowl but he promised to take Natasha there someday.

Dieterich asked about the work on Freddy's trailer, except he did not call it a trailer, it was a home. Freddy was excited to describe what they had done on the addition. It was going to be bigger than how he drew it up when Dieterich visited him. Freddy was getting some help on the construction from some friends and in return, he was going to help reroof their house on Saturday.

"You ever done roofing?" Dieterich asked.

"I'm not handy with construction, but he said I can help carry shingles and stuff like that."

"Can I help? I helped do a roof one summer in Florida. I liked it a lot. Something I can do, like a skill kinda. It's not hard but it can be a hot job in summer. You know how big the roof is? How steep? Is he putting on a new layer of shingles on top or taking off the old ones?"

"I don't know any of those. Didn't ask."

"You sure he's got enough help. Really, I'd like to do it."

"Yeah, I can ask."

"Please ask. It'd be good to work on another roof... see if I actually know how. I mean the only other skill I learned up 'til coming here was camping. I can do that pretty good. Now I can do maintenance on a hardness tester, too."

"Probably easier to find work roofing but I know you're just screwing with me. You won't be doing jobs like that. I bet you'll do more school after you graduate in engineering."

Freddy took out a cigarette pack. He tilted it toward Dieterich, offered him one. Freddy's offer was an automatic movement, one he always made with friends. Dieterich smiled with the pleasure of Freddy's acceptance despite having just revealed how large the gap he assumed lay between their prospects in life.

"Bet, you say? I'll take that bet."

"Why what's wrong with more education when you're smart enough to do it and got the financial support?"

"It's fair enough you think like that. I had more than my share of good luck along the way. Here's the thing, and you can pay off the bet right now... This is true. I got kicked out of Lehigh for bad grades. No, not quite accurate. It was for abysmal grades, well earned."

"What you do? Musta been something, well, I don't know what. Doesn't sound like you. Too much protesting?"

"That's not what wins me the bet. I was going to go to another school, one that would take me, which means one that's not too good, and I just heard from my folks no acceptable school will take me for the year after getting kicked out."

"So, you do something else for a year. Stay here and work for us."

"I wouldn't mind that. But that's not going to happen. I need to prepare for September sixteenth. Know what happens then?"

"What?"

"The lottery's what."

"You're playing a lottery?"

"No man, the draft lottery. Haven't you heard they're giving us all a number and the low ones get drafted first? Depends on my number. My board says I'll need a really high number, really good luck. That's because we've got a lot of guys in my region getting deferments. If I was from Alabama or Louisiana, say, the local board wouldn't have to draft so many to meet its quota. After September 16 I've got no way to stay out. I'll be due to go in the spring, so I'll just probably sign up in the fall and get it started. Then there's a few wasted years. Who knows what job I'll want after? Probably try college again. I can't see grad school. By then I'll be itching bad to do something, some job. Can't dance, can't sing either; nothing in the arts. Wish I had the skills, the personality like you to go into sales. Not roofer either, I guess. My tender upbringing did not prepare me to take on that much real work. Something else in the trades would be good, I think."

"No. You're not serious. Any of that really true?"

"All of it. I'm forming some other ideas about what to do after the Army but there's no need to make a decision right away."

"Gee, I'm sorry about all that."

"How come? It's no worse than lots of guys."

"Yeah, but you were on the way to being an executive somewhere, VP of something by the time you're my age."

"I never wanted to be a titan of industry or an engineer either."

"I thought you mighta been a protester against the war. That's what gets a lot of college kids in trouble."

"Woulda been a better reason than the actual one. I'm not pro-war, just not anti-war. I'll go in the goddam Army 'cause they're going to take me anyway so what else can I do?"

"Bummer."

"Radical bummer, yeah."

"So, Wes and Rusty and anybody know about all this? You said some of the choices came up recent."

"Nah. No reason to tell them about it."

"And not Elise either then."

"I told Elise."

"Yeah. You like her."

"Sure."

"You got a girl back home?"

"No other girl anywhere. It was just easy to talk with Elise. You know her much?"

"Never met her. Wes talked about her some."

"She didn't run off when I told her. Of course, we just had a couple dates. Still, like you said, I like her. Did you have any serious girlfriends before Natasha? "

"Nothing serious."

"How long was it before you knew it would be her?"

"I wanted it to be her right off. You don't know right off what <u>she</u>'s thinking, right? After a couple months, we weren't too shy anymore and I figured it could work out."

"Yeah? How long ago was that."

"Lemme think about it. I knew before Christmas that year when she was in the church passion play. Would have been 1966. 'Bout two and a half years ago."

"You do a formal proposal? Down on a knee or like that?"

"It wasn't like that. I never really proposed. We went along awhile and then just knew we were going to get married The ring was good. It proved we were, both of us, committed. We went together to pick out a ring. That was last summer. Things didn't change then except it felt different after that. We could make plans; had to make plans. We don't want a big ceremony. Both our folks, hers and mine, expect something. Nothing fancy like what my sister did. Maybe that's why we didn't get married too fast. Once everybody thinks of us as a couple we don't need to fuss over it so much, you know?"

"I like the way you did that."

Dieterich was thinking Freddy might be a better model than his father but he would never say that out loud. His dad was great, nothing to complain about him at all. Or about his mother. But he did not want to be like them. Couldn't visualize being like them, living how they live, working jobs like theirs, caring about the things that matter to them. He had not distanced himself from their ways but he was planning to. Might have to wait until he got out of the Army.

After work, while driving in a safe manner back to Rochester Hills, Dieterich focused his attention, for the first time since losing his key, on the unresolved questions from before the weekend: in the long run, what career he wanted enough to do what it required of him and, in the short run, what to do about two beautiful girls before one of them hears about the other one. In the very short run, he needed to decide what to tell Cathy when he walked her home at nine o'clock: that he wanted her company ever more (very hard to say that truthfully and clearly), that he loved her body (an incomplete statement but the most certain part of a complete statement) or that he might be going into the Army in the fall.

"Cathy, you're real! I was afraid you were a dream."

"Sit still, Deeter. People will think you're going to have a fit."

"Right. I'll try to save the fit for later if you'll let me walk you home."

"Might not be all I let you do after being away so long. Don't place an order. I'll think of something for the cook. 9:00, right?"

Dieterich remembered he would have to mention he would not have dinner at Romero's on Thursday, and then he put that thought out of his mind to concentrate on the woman he would soon be walking through the dark streets to her home..

They met around the corner from prying eyes of the Romero's Restaurant staff although Dieterich saw no reason for hiding. He had met her mother and it was no one's business if he walked her home. Unless, he speculated, they knew some significant thing from her history, like an old boyfriend who might be jealous, or a scandalous affair, or an ongoing engagement with a guy away for the summer.

She was running as she came around the corner...

"Deeter, Deeter, pumpkin eater! Had a wife and couldn't keep her!"

"I think it goes 'Deeter, Deeter, dumpling eater, had a wife and never beat her'."

"That can't be right 'cause Peter put her in a pumpkin shell and kept her very well. There's no place to put a wife in a dumpling.

"'Pumpkin shell'! That's right. I would never have remembered that."

"Oh, I know my poetry."

"I see that!"

"What have you been doing for three days since my mother and I ruined your weekend?"

"<u>You</u> did not ruin my weekend. It would have been way better if we went to the lake together, but it was pretty wondrous to see you out of uniform. I liked it a lot."

"So, I'm sorry my mother ruined your weekend."

"No, the worst of it wasn't her fault either. It was my own."

"What'd you do so bad?"

He thought he ought to ask how her mother was doing, not that there could be a good answer to that, but to show his concern for her family situation. His query would have sounded hollow in the words that came to mind for it so he gave up on courtesy and answered her question.

"I lost my car key."

"Sorry about that. How is that worse than skipping going swimming with me?"

She shoved him playfully. He rocked back as if he had been hit by a truck.

"How was it worse? All right, I'll tell you how. First of all, I was in a near coma when I lost my day with you and I drove unconsciously to a park up by Grand Rapids. I knew about it because I was thinking of seeing something natural if I had some time on Monday or Tuesday. And it turned out to be a pretty good park. I went swimming a little and that was not too good with you back in Rochester Hills..."

"Wait a minute! You're saying you drove all the way up to Grand Rapids on Saturday to go swimming alone?"

"Yep. And then I went for a hike in the park. It was pretty good, nothing to tell you about, really, but nice, quiet woodlands. I wandered around until it was almost dark and got back to the car before I realized I'd lost the car key."

"Bummer! How'd you get back?"

"It was bad enough that I lost the key but it got worse 'cause I didn't handle it right. I probably should have called my boss right away. Told him he had a clumsy employee who needed help on a weekend. He probably had a spare key. It's a company car. That would have been embarrassing, obviously, so I figured I got all day Sunday to figure things out. But there was nothing to figure out and the more I thought about it, the later it got. So I decided to spend the night in the car and hitchhike back here in the morning... See if the boss was home and had a key. Maybe on Monday I could get a bus or even a taxi... I'd pay whatever it cost. He'd probably find someone to drive me up there. Have to postpone the work I was supposed to do on Monday. Lose a day's pay, obviously."

"So that's what you did?"

"No, I didn't do the best thing or the second-best thing. A park ranger came by the car and told me to leave. 'Park's closed.' I was not in a compliant mood so I argued. As nicely as I could, but persistent. Told him I worked in a National Park (like that outranked him) and how we tried to help people with problems. I'm not a great con man but I did manage to attract his sympathy. I was a man who could have been him. The shoe might have been on the other foot; my error, losing the damn key, was so innocent. Or maybe I simply wore him down.

He offered to let me use his phone to call around for a room. Then I think he saw how that wasn't much help and said I could have dinner with him and his family, a wife and kids. When I still didn't tell him how he was saving my clumsy bacon, he said he would drive me to a motel."

"Whoa, you really got to that dude!"

"It says more about him than my power of persuasion. All I did was remind him he's a public servant with an opportunity to serve. I'm not really used to being in need. I think I might have panicked in a very subdued way. I told him he was offering more help than I had hoped for and how back in my National Park job I never offered so much but I would have loved to have had a chance to."

"So did you ever actually work in a National Park?"

"Oh yeah. Last summer I was in Rocky Mountain National Park in Colorado. What a summer! But I wasn't a ranger. I worked in a concession shop inside the park. Still, I got to see the park a whole lot. So I wasn't making up lies but I exaggerated, if that's any different from lying. We had thousands of tourists with problems, I guess, but they didn't come to me for help. I wouldn't have been as generous as he became once he thought about it. I would if it was someone a friend sent to me, something like that. Or if you had shown up needing something.

"I felt bad about the dinner and all so I talked him into going back to my original stupid, dead end strategy. He agreed to let me sleep in the car and to use his office phone in the morning after eight o'clock. I called the local police. My car key did not interest the cop on the phone but there didn't seem to be anything else for him to do so he agreed to come out to the park and jimmy the door lock. He thought there might be a code in the glove compartment that a dealer could use to make a key. It took him two hours to show up and ten minutes to jimmy the lock. He never asked to see my ID.

"I went back to the park office and worked the yellow pages for the nearest AMC dealership. Kalamazoo, got to be in the top names for cities in America. More important, the dealer said he could make me a key, even on Sunday, which is a good day for car shoppers.

"The ranger sent me off with a map of the state including the route to Kalamazoo: west on route 42 and south on highway 131.

"I got lucky right away hitching a ride going west. I had figured west was going to be the harder leg to hitch since it's a relatively minor road. I've hitched a few times before, always getting a ride eventually but sometimes it took as much as an hour. Don't suppose you ever did it?"

"Not good for girls on their own. I never had any place I had to be like what you're talking about."

"I was feeling good when that big ol' rusty Buick stopped for me. A couple old enough to be my grandparents were yakking away. I told them I was feeling good because things were working out for me after a really tough Saturday afternoon. I didn't tell 'em how Saturday morning had some really good and some not so good. They said Sunday was always the best of days. They were headed north on 131 so they wished me godspeed on my journey.

"A middle-aged man in a station wagon picked me up after thirty minutes along 131. I'd walked until I came to a good place to pull over and stood thirty yards north of it. The man introduced himself and asked me for my story, like he regularly picked up hitchhikers for the company. I made it brief and asked the man (he'd said his name was 'Martin') what he did for a living. I didn't want to say too much 'cause I didn't trust him much."

"Why not? He do something funny?"

"No, we had a good conversation. Probably I didn't trust my good luck would hold up for long."

"You believe in luck now?"

"Not consciously I don't. It feels real sometimes. Anyway, Martin was on his way to the dentist in Kalamazoo. When he dropped me at the car dealership (he had insisted on driving all the way there), he said he'd be back in two hours if I wanted a ride back to my car.

"At this moment, I felt the presence of God, that is, I felt like something extremely capable was taking unreasonably good care of me. But if I were to believe that, I would also have to believe God had allowed me into that circumstance, God or the Devil. God I might believe in, I used to believe in. Yes, I know he is famously mysterious, but he is incomprehensibly complicated, so I doubt his existence heartily. The reality of the Devil, on the other hand, I have never accepted for a moment, not at any age. Funny, I suppose, since the world has so much that fits his personality. I believe in God the most when I am in places little affected by humans.

"Lately I've noticed I've been protected throughout my life by forces far beyond my understanding, or else I have been on a 19-year run of good luck. Not that everything has been perfect. I can name thousands, millions, of things that could have been better. No, only thousands. Born in America to upper middle-class White parents who love their children; smart enough; healthy. Could have been smarter. Should have been better looking; that would have been nice. The Devil left a few marks. And then suddenly, like nothing I ever experienced before, this goddam fantastic girl accepts me as if I deserved her company! It's hard to figure."

"What if I'm a gift of the Devil?"

"Then I'm on the Devil's side. And maybe you are too. God got tired of my taking in all that good luck without offering any thanks in return. It was before I met you when he cut me off the gravy train.

"Martin came back to give me a ride. Damn nice guy. The car key worked, I drove two hours back to Rochester Hills Sunday night. Got up early on Monday and drove two hours up to Grand Rapids. Probably drove too fast but I was fired up, like I was on drugs. I guess that's what it would feel like. Did my job for two days. Came back and you are the only person to know or ever know this story of floating between good luck and bad, between a tired God with waning concern for me and a creative Devil who seems to find me increasingly amusing."

"Your boss never heard you lost the key?"

"The subject never came up. Did my work in Grand Rapids. Never got back to the park. Next time I go swimming it'll be with you. I saved Lexington Beach for us. Think you can get away for that?"

She threw her arms around him, pressing her body against him as if demanding more attention although he was already entirely focused on her. She whispered not because her words should not be overheard, but because her lips were next to his ear.

"I took off Saturday last weekend and I can't do it twice in a row. We've got the concert next week. Oh, you know that's gonna be good, Honey."

20

"Instead of thinking what men did to the mountains, [John Muir] kept his mind on what the mountains did to the men..."[12]

Thursday, July 31

Elise answered the door before he knocked. She was wearing a peasant blouse in a solid color, with a gathered neckline that revealed her throat and could be slid over a shoulder or both shoulders. It was a blouse Dieterich had never seen on anyone else, but he thought it was something Cher might wear. Her jeans were tight and hid the difference between her legs when she stood up straight. She guided him to the kitchen to get a soda and a bowl of pretzels. Her mother was preparing dinner. Elise offered to set the table, but her mother insisted they go down to the rec room in the basement. She would call them when her father got home and dinner was ready.

The rec room was down a steep flight of wooden steps without risers between them. A short pile rug covered the floor wall-to-wall. A television perched on a foldable stand made of gold-colored aluminum tubing next to the radio and hi fi cabinet, a full entertainment center. Elise had a box with two rows of 45s on the radio side of the cabinet. She had arranged them in order from her least favorite to her most favorite although she explained her preferences tended to shift over time and everything she had was worth hearing. Dieterich thought it was excessively controlling of her to prepare the evening song-by-song although it would be less

---

[12] Wallace Stegner in "The Rediscovery of America: 1946," essay reprinted in *The Sound of Mountain Water*, 1980

controlling if she did not insist on discussing each song as it came on. Her phonograph could play a stack of 15 so they would not have to put on a new record every two minutes.

"You want to sort through and take out a few to play?"

"Sure. Do I put a marker where I took out a record?"

"Oh no!" Now she laughed. "The order doesn't matter. I could probably remember where they were but so what? ...You said you don't play records at home but you like music."

"Yep, cool. Is this all rock?"

"Hard to say. Mostly I would call it pop music. Motown's not rock, is it? Soul? I've got the *Hair* album. Most of the *Revolver* album on 45s. Some of *Sergeant Pepper*. Fun stuff. No jazz if that's what you're asking. That's not on 45s. Oh yeah, and don't judge me by some of the stuff that's for junior high kids. I started buying songs when I was twelve."

"Ooh, you got any doo-wop? *Leader of the Pack*? *Do Wah Diddy Diddy*? Four Seasons?"

"It's a bunch of stuff but not everything that's good or funky or groovin'. Can you dig it?"

"Yeah. Say, what's that called? Do you have it too?"

"What? No wait! You mean 'canyoudigit, canyoudigit, canyoudigit canyoudigit'! It's called *Grazing in the Grass*. I don't have it but that's a good one."

For the next hour, Dieterich was the DJ and they lounged in sloppy, stuffed chairs and talked on matters they would not mind being overheard by her parents and his boss. Sometimes they told each other what they liked about a particular song or group. Sometimes they stopped just to listen. Sometimes a topic carried through a few songs. Dieterich was hardly thinking, as surprised by his own spontaneity as by what he was hearing. Elise was from a background anyone would describe as similar to his yet her experience differed from his in every detail. She grew up in places similar to his, around people and institutions familiar to him, in the same years as him but she was a beautiful, smart, confident and handicapped girl and he was a fairly smart, but otherwise unremarkable, boy which made for all the difference.

Dinner was comfortable. Wanda did most of the talking, asking Dieterich about the office, quietly teasing her husband as if he had never explained to her what he did all day: Do you fellas make these Wilson Instruments or get them already assembled from a factory? and Where do you get spare parts for them?   Once Dieterich realized her game, he changed his answers to versions of: I'm not sure, they don't tell me everything and You should ask Wes about that. After a couple more questions she saw that Dieterich was not serious either and everyone laughed.

Then Wanda switched over to questions she actually wanted answered which led to: How long will you be working before you need to leave? Taking some time for vacation before school?

It was a sensitive question that Dieterich should have thought about since learning he was not going back to school this fall. It seemed stupid of him to have no answer. He did not want to stutter or hesitate or lie or tell the truth.

"I haven't given notice to my employer yet. I kinda had in mind finishing at the end of August. I'm not looking for a vacation, in fact I never thought of it. I'm reaching a serious age; be twenty in October. Dunno.

Wes, how much notice should I give once I know what I'd like to do?"

"We'll need to find and hire and train a guy to fill in after you. With all the work you're doing, we might need to hire two guys. Guess you ought to let me know at least three months before your last day."

Elise stepped in to distract her parents from insisting on an answer. "I'm going to freshman orientation starting right after Labor Day. As long as he stays around 'til then... I won't care anymore when he quits the company."

"Ooh, that's cruel!" from Dieterich. "We won't get through all those records before that."

No more hard questions were asked. Dieterich tried to sound less frivolous by asking what Wes knew of the state parks in Michigan. He stayed for dessert, and they offered him a digestive: whiskey or a coffee, which he would not take because either would be so far from his lifestyle it would have felt like acting and, despite having some secrets, he did not want to pretend to what he was not.

Elise walked him out to his car and stood there with him in view of the living room windows for twenty minutes. She suggested he could pick her up on Friday night before dinner, then eat someplace cheap. She'd check on the movie schedules. He said Saturday would fit better if the roofing job with Freddy was done on time. She said Sunday was no good, how about Monday, and Monday was agreed upon. They exchanged chaste kisses and promised each other much more for Monday.

AMBITION

July 31, 1969
Rochester Hills, Michigan
sitting on my bed

Had dinner with Wes, Wanda and ELISE,
thereby missing CATHY. I feel I have to
explain whenever I miss dinner at
Romero's. These two are crowding too
close together although they are both
entirely innocent of pushing for attention.
Indeed, I love having either of them
near... not both. I try to isolate one from
the other, to be with one at a time and
never to compare them. My mind is hard
to control to that resolution.

This journal is not for reveries over
finding a girlfriend like I always thought
I would but never seemed to be nearing.
Or about how to deal with two girlfriends,
both better than I ever expected to have,
not even for a few weeks.

These people in Michigan whom I have
known only briefly seem more important
than anyone I knew outside the family
before coming here. I had such good
friends in high school, camping buddies,
guys in the band, a couple from church
fellowship (no girls). Why were they, every
one, irrelevant to me after graduation?

Were they not good friends? I thought they were. I got along fine with a lot of guys at Lehigh and know I will never attempt to contact any of them and they will not contact me. I don't even mind it is that way but I am surprised life is like this. Real friends must be more than having a good time together but I would think it begins with that and then develops into a certain loyalty. Maybe they are wondering the same as me, waiting for me to call them although I do not know the phone number or address for anyone outside the family. Actually, I only know my own phone number and address back home, no one else's.

I don't do any of the things I did with my friends in high school. Were they valuable to me only as entertainment? Is it like that for them? For everyone? Or mainly for people in my stage of life? Did we talk about important things? About personal things? No, even with my best friends, Jeff, Chris, Mike, Doug, Billy, personal problems and triumphs were not discussed. I did not think of them as taboo, just none of my business. They seemed to think the same of mine and I would not have wanted to talk about my problems or even to admit I had significant problems.

Suddenly, I realize my professors, all of whom I respected for their knowledge and accomplishment and power, no longer matter in the least to me. I do not dream of joining their ranks though a few months ago I might have thought that was an admirable but unrealistically high ambition. And the humble position Freddy holds, with its attached career path, is looking beautiful to me except for the embarrassment of revealing this appreciation to my parents. They would not accept that I am as irrelevant as I believe everyone to be, that is, everyone who is not connected to me by family ties renewable on major holidays, or who is not currently entertaining me.

I will ask Freddy if he keeps in touch with the friends he made early in life. How else would he find new friends without moving to a new city or joining a fraternal organization or taking a job with more co-workers? And why would he want any new friends if the ones he developed as a boy are still his friends? I have lost the first generation of friends and failed to start on a new generation at college as I expected to do. I doubt I will keep in touch with Freddy or Wes or Rusty after the summer. Cathy?? Elise?? Life needs a way to tie to a woman like either of them though changes in location, work ambitions, declining health, failure. That tie refers to both wanting to and insisting on partnering though all those things. Damn that sounds like the corniest wedding vow. I will not declare this in a ceremony but it is what I desperately wish and have for the first time glimpsed as possible.

Or can I become or should I become a modern version of Henry Thoreau, John Muir, Aldo Leopold, or Edwin Teale? I have stumbled here into a good question for this journal! (If I formulate a coherent draft of an answer, I can discuss it with ~~Cathy~~ Elise. She would like that and she could discuss it well enough that I might revise my answer. Or with Cathy.)

Sitting here on my rented bed, wondering about an evening just past both commonplace among people with my background and yet unique in my experience, I cannot envision Thoreau as my model. Frankly, and all entries in this journal strive to be frank, I probably do not know enough about him to know how to follow his example. I suspect he was more philosophical than I care to be.

To be a Muir would be excellent, but impractical for he lived in a time when wilderness was more available. Today, I would have to go to the Amazon basin or the Hindu Kush to get as far from civilization as he did and I do not appreciate wilderness for its challenge to personal survival.

Following the footsteps of Aldo Leopold is comprehensible. I can appreciate the wilds and more than that, the almost wild, the locally wild, more than the vast unknown wilderness of adventure. That's mostly what's left in the U.S. anyway, especially in the East but I don't need to stay in the East, or even in the U.S. Except I am terrible about learning languages. I would not want to be a tourist, a week or two here and there with a guide or an outfitter. Aldo was more than merely content with modest places. The best thing about Aldo is not that I can go where he went in the manner he went there, it is that he did something with his appreciation and his growing understanding of ecology. I have no inclination to join the peace activists, though they are probably right, but a conservationist, more or less like Aldo, is a perfect fit for me. I could function at whatever level my brain and my energies allow and end up with considerable self-respect out of it. And if I find a good fit in a career, I might not become irrelevant as fast as the people I have known so far seem to become. I am not likely to leave an appreciable legacy if I do not aspire to one, to a specific, feasible one.

21

Saturday, August 2

Dieterich was nearly as excited by the chance to spend a day roofing for Freddy's friend as he would have been to go on a date with one of his two girlfriends but that was partly because those two girls were tearing him apart. Neither knew there was a woman tugging in an opposing direction, and still he could not dismiss the image to accompany the stretch he felt in his chest as his right and left sides pulled away as far his skin and sinew would allow. On the roof, he would be free from his uncontrollable, incomprehensible personal desires. That freedom for a day would be worth the sunburn, sweat, scraped knuckles and exhaustion he associated with the task.

As planned, he arrived early at the job site. He left time in case he had trouble finding it, but he also left time to be sure he was present when the roles were doled out. He wanted to be on the roof, measuring, cutting shingles and nailing them in, not cleaning up the mess on the ground below and doing the mule work of hauling the bundles up the ladder. He was pleased to see the house under the roof was a small, cheap one with two sloping planes, flat enough to stand on, broken only by a small cover over the front entry. A homeowner who needed to hold down costs would appreciate free labor and forgive any minor weaknesses Dieterich might expose in himself.

Two guys arrived in a blue Dodge Dart convertible with one fender showing white primer from a repair. The driver walked quickly toward Dieterich while his passenger went to the trunk to unload some tools.

Dieterich put his hand out first and asked, "1964?"

The driver took his hand and held it while he looked wistfully back at his undoubtedly beloved car.

"Close, 1963. Needs new shocks, tires too. Still runs real good though."

"I don't know cars much. Recognize the Dart. Got its eyes far apart like it's wide awake."

"Yeah, I can see that." He let go of Dieterich's hand. They exchanged names. The driver called himself "Dinty" and his buddy "Hammy."

"So Deeter, Freddy says you already know how to do this."

"Did he? Sounds like an exaggeration. Willing to help. Doesn't look too difficult anyway. You gonna leave the old shingles on or rip 'em off?"

"I don't know. It'll cost me some to haul off the old ones so I'd like to keep 'em on. What do you think?"

"My opinion's not worth a whole lot but I'll give you one after I get a look up close. Need to see if both sides have the same wear too. Is there a ladder coming?"

The ladder was in the back yard, the tools in the trunk of the Dodge and the shingles came in a delivery truck from the hardware store before Deeter had time to get up the ladder for a look. The truck driver helped the three, wannabe roofers pile the shingles near the house. Dieterich wondered if the right quantity had been delivered but knew it was not his place to ask.

Dinty propped the extension ladder against the house. He did not damage a gutter by leaning on it because the house had no gutters. Dieterich went under the ladder, stood it up straight, and pulled the rope to raise the upper ladder about five rungs. His brief exposure to roofing taught him the ladder needs to stick well above the roof to give a handhold when you walk onto the roof. It was a bad sign that Dinty did not know this and a damn good sign that he did not argue about it. As Dieterich raised it, he said "Just a little higher'll be good."

Dinty and Hammy met Dieterich on the roof. Dieterich did most of the talking. He mainly wanted to be sure the roof did not already have two layers of shingles. He thought three layers was too many. He commented on how very few of the shingles were torn and suggested Dinty's hope to avoid removing the old ones was validated. Then he described the process of starting at the bottom with a whole row, putting three nails in each shingle along the top.

"Then we snap out a chalk line for the top of the next course, and over and over."

"Chalk? We got any chalk Hammy?"

Dieterich was uncomfortable being in charge. He had only done this on a few houses and there might be other ways to do it. But these fellows did not even know what a chalk line was so he might have to run things.

"You asking if you have a piece of chalk or chalk powder for a chalk line? You know, a cord coated in chalk that you stretch out and snap to leave a temporary line?" They looked skeptical. "All right. No problem. Well just measure the next shingle from the previous one. We'll cut a couple ticks on a scrap piece at exact distance so we don't need to use the tape measure every time. Didn't Freddy say he was coming today?"

"Yeah, he did," Hammy said with certainty, the first words he had spoken.

"Let's get back down to earth. I'll look at the tools and see if we got enough to keep everyone busy." He was now playing the role of Rusty as project supervisor.

Freddy drove onto the lawn. "You finish it yet?" he asked as he got out of the car carrying a tray of coffee cups and a bag of breakfast sandwiches from Big Boy.

"Whew," Dieterich gasped and wiped his brow facetiously. "I'm ready for a break! Whatta you got in the bag?"

Dinty and Hammy both took a coffee and plunked themselves down on the front steps to light a cigarette before taking a sip. Meanwhile, Natasha emerged from the car with a folded card table and a picnic basket. Freddy helped her set up the table. She spread a plastic tablecloth over it and laid out the Big Boy sandwiches, sugar for the coffee, napkins, a jug of ice water, cups and other paraphernalia.

Dinty called over to Freddy. "Your boy knows his shit all right. He's in charge now."

"I know just enough to be dangerous." It was something his dad said to be funny. It might have been funny the first time. Dieterich did not critique his father's humor, expecting it to be out-of-date at best. It sounded terrible coming out of his own mouth. No one seemed to mind. At least it could be interpreted as a modest thing to have said. It was intended as a denial of responsibility. "Dinty, you notice how this whole affair got a whole lot better when Natasha came out of that car?"

Eventually, they developed roles. Dinty and Hammy carried the bundles up the ladder and stacked them near the roof peak. This was the hardest work of the day and would have to be done later on the opposite slope as well. Dieterich started nailing in the first course of shingles, hoping to figure out how to do it best before the others started nailing. Freddy took on the skilled role of cutting the shingles at the end of a course and fitting them along the seam where the main roof met the small roof above the entry. Dieterich did not explain how to make the seam; he did not know any more than Freddy or the others. Freddy could figure it out although Dieterich planned to look in on him just to be sure it looked watertight.

Natasha went up on the roof to watch the operation and wanted to do something up there. Dieterich thought she could have done some nailing but she was wearing shorts and it would have scratched her knees to be squatting on the gravelly shingles. "Next time we do a roof, you get a hammer," Dieterich suggested. She might have a chance to work on the roof of the addition to their house on the lake but Dieterich would be gone. Dinty and Hammy might be helping then.

Natasha had lunch ready at one o'clock, not too fancy, very middle America: chicken salad, ice water, buttered biscuits, pickles, apple pie. It was hard to go back up the ladder after eating. They calculated it was possible to finish today and it was possible to come back on Sunday to finish. Dieterich was tired but he did not want to use up his other day off. He was debating whether to say he was unavailable on Sunday or to try to push the group to get back to work and try when Dinty spoke up. "We've got five hours of daylight left. Get us as far as you can today, and me and Hammy can finish what's left. All right? So now lift your asses off the grasses, and put your backs into it."

Grazing in the grass, it's a gas, thought Dieterich. "I can dig it, you can dig it, he can dig it, she can dig it, we can dig it. Sock it to me!" he sang aloud as fast as he could and it sounded pretty good.

22

Sunday, August 3 On Sunday, Dieterich woke more tired than usual. He felt the aches in his shoulders and his right arm, the one that swung the hammer. He had played a game with himself to drive the short, big-headed, galvanized shingle nails in two strokes, one to set the nail and one to drive it. He also felt the sunburn on his neck and arms. He had taken a long-sleeved shirt, one of his work shirts, to ward off the sun, but the sun had not really shown bright all day through the haze, so he left it in the car - should have bought some tanning lotion. His medicine kit currently had only insect repellent and some band-aids. Yet, he was not feeling sorry for himself, not at all. He was high with the pleasure of doing a job as well as he could, done it all the way. And he had helped out his friend Freddy whom he wanted to please. He had earned a day for solitude. For Sunday, he had no commitments. Solitude was the plan, solitude in a natural place.

He had already consulted Freddy's map, ignoring the places marked as state recreation areas or even mere state parks. He chose Shiawassee National Wildlife Refuge, almost 10,000 acres, largely wetlands, for migratory waterfowl. It was not too far up Route 75, towards Saginaw.

He had already accepted that he would never see Kirkland's warbler in the jack pines and doubted he would ever see the tens of thousands of geese passing through the refuge as they would in October. So much the better for his goal of solitude. No one would be there just to see flat, marshy acreage; no one but himself. He was prepared to walk knee-deep as needed to get around. His sneakers would survive. His journal was half filled, meaning it was still half empty, leaving room for sketches. He double-checked his bag to be sure he had at least two pencils. He would get a hat with a wide brim to protect his neck when he stopped at 7-11 for coffee and donut, lunch sandwiches and whatever snacks caught his eye.

August 3, 1969
Shiawassee Reserve, Michigan
Overcast morning

On my first break, I did a sketch. I am used to writing and know I will write something but trying to sketch requires more effort. I won't give up just because the first hundred are terrible and don't seem to be getting any better.

The parking lot at the refuge HQ was empty and I haven't seen anyone on the trail either. Right away I was tempted to wish I had my binoculars since I saw some songbirds and some distant waterfowl, but I am now feeling they would have pushed my attention toward the twittering and the flashes of movement instead of exploring the wide-angle vista the wetlands allow. And speaking of wide angle, I brought no camera to Michigan this summer. My pictures from Colorado were largely to prove where I had been and what I saw. If I had realized I was doing that, I would have stopped. If I had admitted to myself I was doing that, I would have been embarrassed and stopped. It was done with artistic pretentions.

Why have I decided to sketch? I do not know exactly, just like I was not fully aware of why I took photos last summer whenever I went out of the shop, like that was my job. If I could sketch, I would feel closer to my heroes, the naturalists and explorers of old who predated photography. Yes, that feels right for my first guess. It is not an artistic pretention. That would have to follow drawing something better than I did in fifth grade. (As a reminder for a day when I am old and rediscover this journal, my first, I mention fifth grade because I was so excited by an assignment from the art teacher that each of us should draw with crayon someone in the classroom. I had never thought of drawing someone, an actual person as opposed to a generic person. I had never thought of drawing an actual house although I had drawn many generic houses, most of which were the same, the way a house looks, I thought, without looking at a house. My drawing of Charleen had two eyes, two ears, one nose, one mouth, long brown hair and a neck. You could tell it was a girl, not the way a girl should look, not like Charleen, but a girl. I have never tried to draw a person since that day. I wonder if I can cast any blame on the art teacher for teaching me only how bad I was at it.)

AMBITION

Almost noon

I climbed a tree to see farther. This
reserve has no hills to command a view.
A sketch was made while up the tree
because it is hard enough to draw from
life that I will avoid drawing from
memory, even if the memory is only a
minute or two old. I could see 25,278
Canada geese from the tree, geese that
will arrive here in about six weeks,
feeding for their long migration
southward. They must be making a
terrible racket, honking with excitement,
and whooshing with the air when more
than 50,000 at a time change locations.
When I see even one individual fly up and
circle back and continue feeding, I feel
an ancient jealousy at the ability to lift
off the ground upon a whim.

I've seen flocks of goldfinches and blue
jays and herring gulls that fly up at some
disturbance I did not cause and then
settle back where they were, more or less,
after flying in a flowing arc over my
head. The geese will do that once they
get here, but do it in a thousand times the
volume of space and sound. I expect the
flocks at Shiawassee are just like the ones

Aldo Leopold knew as a boy. Why do I doubt so strongly that my son, should he ever exist, will not have the chance see the spectacle? If I have a son, I pray he will want to see what nature remains.

1:30, lunch break
Promise kept — I did not shy away from the flooded trail when it went where I wanted to go. My sneakers will never be white again. The mud-gray stain will remind me of a day skirting a reedy marsh on one of the Federal refuges that ensure migratory waterfowl continue for the present generation to experience.

The trail is dry here and I have a fine old log for a bench. Few trees are big enough

and sturdy enough to serve as my
furniture. The mosquitoes may not trouble
October's geese but they are available for
the chickadees and whatever other avians
have quick wings and a small precision
bill.

I am lost right now. I don't want to
retrace my steps exactly, proud as I was
of tramping through deep mud. I doubt I
could anyway. The trails would look like
spaghetti on a map and are seldom
marked with their destinations. The sun is
refusing to help guide me, so far from
visible behind clouds that are starting to
spit on me and everything else here.

It is good to be off the map. I never had
a map of the trails but I saw one back at
the parking lot and had imagined I could
guess where I was. I've got something to
guide me. All morning the clouds have
come from the southwest; I noted them
doing it. I started out northerly from the
parking lot and then bounced to the
southwest when I reached the park
boundary. I'll work east, if I can
estimate where that is, southeast is cut off
by the marches. In Michigan, one can go

in any cardinal direction and fully expect
to hit a road within an hour.

    3:30
    A parking lot, not the one with my
    car
On the good, I am not lost any more. On
the bad side, I can be at the car in fifteen
minutes and will leave a little earlier
than necessary rather than starting on a
new trail. On the good, I am pretty tired
after finding only one place to sit and
rest all day. On the bad or maybe the
good, it has been raining solidly for an
hour and I am chilly. I hate to overly
appreciate comfort on my day away. I
can walk in the rain but the sketching has
ceased.

My day of solitude has not been what I
expected except that it has been
thoroughly enjoyed. I will remember it
fondly. How fine to be young enough to
act so freely and irresponsibly without
danger to self or harm to anyone.

On his drive back Dieterich was planning his
evening, whether to go someplace for dinner or just eat
the snacks he bought at 7-Eleven, whether to read in bed
for as long as he could pay attention to a book, or to go to

sleep early. Or should he go knock on Cathy's door? It was an easy choice to consider seeing Cathy because showing up out of the blue at the Elias household would have been shocking.

How different, he noticed, it would be to end a day like this by going home and finding a wife to tell about his adventure and to be told about hers. *A wife? Can't say I've ever imagined that so specifically. She, I don't know who, is a long way off.*

23

Monday, August 4 | Monday fit a new pattern. Dieterich worked with Rusty in the shop all morning and took some appointments around Detroit in the afternoon. Tuesday and Wednesday were likely to be similar. Freddy stopped by to say hello and thank Dieterich for helping on Saturday. He said they might be going out of town together on Thursday which sounded good to Dieterich.

That night, Dieterich had his date with Elise. Just like last time, Dieterich insisted on stepping inside the house before driving off with her. He only saw Wanda but that was enough to fulfill the ritual courtesy.

Dieterich started the car but did not drive away immediately. He looked at Elise sitting beside him; she looking back at her house. Her short skirt did not hide her weak leg. He did not want to make her leg an issue in his mind but he was surprised to notice it was exposed and still she looked really sexy. She noticed the delay and turned toward him.

"What? Is the car all right."

"Wow, is it ever nice to see you! Just give me a moment more and then I'll be able to look at the road. Your folks don't mind letting you out of the house looking so fine?"

"Corny."

"Sounds corny to me too. Had to be said though. Where to now? You know someplace simple like you said before?"

"Let's act our age and go to Big Boy; eat hamburgers and fries and drink cokes. We can have popcorn for dessert at the theater."

"Gotta love a date this cheap. But you know I've never been to a Big Boy and yet I had breakfast from there over the weekend." He told her about doing the roof. He admitted to being sore and tired on Sunday but mentioned that he would have been fine if he were doing physical work regularly and how that was an appealing thought.

They sat at a plastic table in Big Boy. Dieterich had a milkshake with his dinner. He told her about having a milkshake every day when he stayed with his grandparents in Florida. They stopped at Burger King to get him one because they thought he needed to gain weight. Dieterich agreed he was too skinny but he did not think consuming more calories was going to improve him. It would be better to spend the days roofing. But he liked milkshakes.

Elise had brought the movie listings from the newspaper.

"You want me to read you all the ones playing within driving distance?" she asked.

"I probably don't know most of 'em. What do you think's good?"

"No, you gotta give me your opinion first. Then I'll decide where we go."

"All right. That sounds democratic. But let's skip the westerns. I think John Wayne has another one now that he can hardly ride a horse anymore. And you can skip anything based on Broadway. Or a musical of any kind."

"Not even *Hair*."

"Right, not even *Hair*. Any movies left?" *I hate the music. Seems like it's pretending to be cool. Astrology? Get naked on stage to get attention for the play! Do they copy that in the movie and not get an X-rating? The movie's got to be worse.*

"How about *Midnight Cowboy*?"

"Isn't that a western? We saw one already." *Butch Cassidy was OK but we shouldn't make it our thing.*

"It's about New York City. Seedy side, contemporary. Kinda artsy, I think. X-rated."

"Maybe not that one. I don't mind an X-rating. Of course I've never seen one, but still..." *I wonder if an x-rated movie is good to see with a girl or if it's just embarrassing for them to sit there wondering what the other one is thinking.*

"You don't like the X? Probably don't want *Bob & Carol & Ted & Alice* then. The four of them end up in one bed. That's in the poster. Not sure it' even at the theaters yet anyway. *Downhill Racer*?"

"That's skiing, right? Makes me think of fancy clothes and expensive gear. The resorts in Colorado were so crowded and artificial. I love the mountains, but skiers aren't my people. Could be a good movie if the skiers are satirized."

"Don't think that would be the point in this one." *Goodbye, Columbus!* could be your people. A bold Radcliffe club girl gets a working-class boyfriend. Sounds like rich, Northeast city style versus not-much style. She's got a brother who's having trouble figuring whom to be after college."

She knows college people are not my people. Maybe she thinks she's college and I'm the outsider in the film. "Different people but the upscale setting and questionable future like *The Graduate*?"

"*The Graduate* would be good but it's not playing around here... I've got two more, both of 'em steeped in the counterculture. *Alice's Restaurant...* it stars Arlo Guthrie. You know the song? I think the movie's a comedy. With him in it, probably true to the culture."

"The song's a comedy, but it's too short for a movie. Wonder what else is in it. Maybe the song is just the start or maybe it's just the end. I'd guess it would be better as an ending." *Probably good for Cathy to see, hippies and all.*

"*Easy Rider.* Three guys out to see America the poster says. On motorcycles. In the South. I think the South is not ready for them. They go to communes and do drugs. Some problems with the culture and the counterculture."

"Sounds like my people. Sounds like Micky, one of the free people I met camping in Sleepy Hollow."

In the movie theater, Dieterich was in constant contact with Elise, aware of her, pleased to be with her, and yet not focused on her. The movie commanded attention. Afterwards they went to the place she knew for parking. He could not tell what sexual contact she wanted from him. They had analyzed the film during the drive. When he turned off the engine, he suddenly realized where the climax of the film was. She was already moving close beside him, putting her head on his shoulder, grasping his arm with both of her hands.

Dieterich was still thinking about the film. "You know when Peter Fonda said 'We blew it?' That was the key. The movie was not saying the rednecks in the South that killed the lawyer guy George were the whole problem. It would have been easy for a movie to do that. Like the song *Alice's Restaurant* just ridicules straight people and leaves out that Arlo was littering, not consistent with the counterculture as I see it. We're supposed to be sensitive to the environment, aren't we? Anyway, Peter Fonda and Billy are obviously unethical, being drug dealers. That's not what got them, though. It was their arrogance, their disrespect for the mainstream. They got along with the farmer and the hippies but they had to, you know, separate themselves from the people around them. They should have been smarter... Stop me, Elise, I can't write a review for the New York Times. I did see something in that film, more than I can explain."

"I love seeing you struggling with it. That's what a good film does to you. Or literature of any sort, I guess. If you are open to it."

"I wish I had you to help me think about the books we read in lit class."

"Yeah? What did you read?"

"Not going to review that now. There're better topics for the precious moments with you."

"We still have some time left."

"Left for the evening, yes, a little. In the summer, not enough."

"How long will you be here?"

"I'll stay 'til September 16, the lottery. Then I'll make a plan. Could stay until boot camp in the spring; could stay until classes start someplace for me next fall; could stay here in this job for a year. Most likely, I leave when you go to Ann Arbor."

"Would you stay here longer if I could see you?"

"What was I saying? I speak a fantasy, a fiction, foolishness. If I know anything it is that you should go to school, focus on it, and be good it at."

He wanted to say more and did not know what or how to say it. She only allowed him a second's hesitation before she threw her arms around his neck and kissed him more passionately than ever before. He pulled her across his chest, cradled her in his left arm, crowded by the steering wheel. He caressed her face and her hair and her ear with his right hand. Using one hand, she undid the buttons on his shirt without separating her lips from his, then slid her hand inside his shirt and around him as far as she could reach. He slowly slid his right hand down to stroke and press her breasts. The kiss ended.

"You can take it off. Let me sit up so you can reach it in back."

24

<table><tr><td>Wednesday, August 6</td></tr></table>

On the night of the concert with Cathy, Dieterich went to Romero's for dinner knowing Cathy had the night off. He thought it might detract from the intrusive attention given to their relationship by the restaurant staff. He could give the impression he was there for the food not the waitress. He dressed in his usual dinner clothes, tie and sport coat. Afterwards he went back to his room and changed into his jeans.

He rang the doorbell at Cathy's house exactly at the promised hour and minute. She did not answer immediately and he was about to knock when the door opened. His emergent fear that it was the wrong night or the wrong time or that she had changed her mind ceased the instant he saw her face. She was, above all, radiant with happiness and, secondly, more beautiful than he had ever seen her, more beautiful than anyone he had ever seen up close, more beautiful than anyone he had ever seen in life or pictures, more beautiful than Elise. He knew his own face was not beautiful but it would radiate his version of ecstasy at being in this moment. His gaze stuck firmly on her face although he took in everything: her sheer blouse with long sleeves, well worn, hip-hugger jeans, and leather-strap sandals. She let him stare at her for two or three seconds and then whispered, "C'mon, Honey. Let's go."

"OK," he stammered softly, almost silently since he had forgotten to breath out to form his words. "What's your mother's name? I'll just say 'good night' to her."

"We don't need to do that."

"You're right, we don't. But just let me say a word of respect."

"Lorraine. I've never called her that."

"My mother's 'Elizabeth', 'Lizzie' to some. I never called her either one."

Dieterich stepped inside the house and looked back toward Cathy. She pointed toward the kitchen. She did not accompany him down the hallway.

"Hello, Lorraine. We're going now. It'll be a good concert."

Lorraine looked up at him from the table where she was drinking from a tall glass with ice. A few crackers formed a pile in front of her. She tilted her head and broke into a broad smile, as if it had taken a moment to recognize who had spoken to her.

"OK, Dear. You kids have real good time."

He noticed she had not addressed him by name.

"Was she happy to see you?" Cathy asked as they walked out to the car.

"She was smiling. Happy enough, I think. Not as happy as me."

Dieterich opened the car door for Cathy. By the time he had gone around to his side and opened the door, Cathy was wriggling crazily.

"Cathy! What's the matter?"

"Nothing, Honey. I'm just takin' off my bra"

"Cool." Dieterich replied without emphasis. As they were passing Romero's, he mentioned he had dinner there a half hour earlier. She nodded silently but he missed that movement since his eyes were on the road. He asked what she did call her mother.

"Mom."

"I used to call my mother 'Mommy' and my dad 'Daddy' until one day I decided it was babyish. I switched to 'Dad' and 'Mom'. The first time I tried it out, it felt strange but I liked it. I had grown up a step by seeing the step and taking it on my own initiative. My dad never said anything but my mother said, almost angry, like it was an insult: don't call me that! I was not going back to 'mommy' so she said I should call her 'Mother' which she spoke with gentleness in contrast to the way she pronounced 'Mahhhm'."

"And she never told you why?"

"Nope. Just being weird."

"They're all freaks."

"Right. Every one of 'em but you and me."

During the drive, they talked about his hike on the weekend and about how she was trying to change her schedule at both her jobs to leave time for school in September. He did not say anything at all about his plan for September. Whenever it would have been appropriate to mention it, he asked her a question instead.

Their excitement built up again when they entered the huge parking lot for the arena. It was not full but there were thousands of vehicles, forcing them to park many rows away from the doors. It took nearly thirty minutes more to get to their seats. They were not close to the stage which bothered Cathy until Dieterich reminded her, despite this being his first popular music concert, that the speakers near the stage were likely deafening.

"And I bet they don't start until a half hour after the scheduled time," Cathy suggested.

"This'll be good. I kinda like Simon and Garfunkel. I don't do hard rock or the bubble gum stuff... They're a little folk. That's all right sometimes." Dieterich was being honest in his reserve, but he might have said the same thing if they were his favorite group because he was not sure how much Cathy liked them and how much she just wanted to go to a big concert.

"Oh. you're so generous!" She mocked. "They're better than that! Don't you like *A Hazy Shade of Winter*?

Poetic. Not like Dylan but poetic in their own way. There's no pop music sound. 'Take it or leave it', they're saying. Not some big production the suits designed. You know, Motown is like that – a package."

"I take your point but I like Motown anyway."

"Good. Got to like Motown. It's commercial. Simon and Garfunkel are too. They make plenty I guess. Just look around the arena!"

"I liked *Sounds of Silence*. That was poetic, too. Maybe it all is but sometimes I notice it more. *At the Zoo*, you know it? ...Less poetic but pretty clear. Saying something."

"I've heard it. Didn't think much about it."

"I don't know all the words. It goes through the animals and says what's wrong with their personalities, monkeys, elephants, birds and stuff, and, obviously, it has nothing to do with actual animal personalities."

"Did you see *The Graduate*?"

"No. I don't go to the movies much." *Is that a lie? It feels like one. It is literally true but it is more true that I just went to the movies and I chose not to see The Graduate because I was worried about the sex in it getting in the way with the girl I went with.*

"Me neither. We gotta go together! It'll be the other half of our Simon and Garfunkel phase."

"Good idea. Let's pick a day soon. Finish this phase and then we can start a new one."

"What else did they do? I can't remember right now."

"*America*. I like that one. It sounds like them musically. They seem angry."

"Two young lovers out to see America. You shouldn't say 'they seem angry'. It's all Paul Simon."

"Is it? I thought Garfunkel was the leader."

"You're way off. All Paul Simon. How could you not know that?"

"I cannot explain why I do not know many, many things. I was probably prejudiced by Garfunkel's being tall and gentle looking."

"Hey, is something wrong? What's with all the lighters?"

"The animals are getting restless."

The concert began with "Bookends Theme," accompanied only by acoustic guitar. It was a modest opening, peaceful, thoughtful, perfect for Dieterich and Cathy, privately snuggling in the 93rd row.

> **Time it was**
> **And what a time it was**
> **It was a time of innocence**
> **A time of confidences...**

For the next two hours, the musicians fed their well-prepared thoughts and emotions into the vast audience whose every particle absorbed these messages in his or her individual context. There were few love songs in the show, but seats 93 AGG and 93 AGH found reason in every song to touch and press each other as if the law required it.

The concert ended with *Old Friends*,

Can you imagine us years from today?
Sharing a park bench quietly,
How terribly strange to be seventy.

This song stuck in Dieterich's mind as they drifted out to the car. He could not imagine, as Paul Simon had asked him to imagine, sitting on a park bench with this woman so near and intimate. She burned too brightly to last until seventy, to hold him in her affections. He could not keep up with her. She was no overachiever, just a flame consuming him. His talents would run out. At best, he could hope to be a solid partner, doing his part, including loving his wife entirely and eternally. He wanted to be beside his wife in fifty years. Cathy will want excitement over and over, far beyond his ability. She can dance. She can party. She's done three kinds of drugs already or she will soon. This concert was among her people, embracing the moment. He was too square in his core personality. It was an effort to say "cool" without showing embarrassment. And this mismatch, for all its depth, is not a problem because it will not live past another four or five weeks. Cathy will be at college and some guy with a good heart (she will recognize that) and a lot of fun and likely damn good looking, too, will win the game and take her where Dieterich could not. When some part of his brain outside conscious control placed Elise on the bench beside him, he felt comforted. He stopped the thought. It was not fair to think it in the company of Cathy. He had the innate skill to put a worry aside upon command.

Once they navigated out of the crowd and onto Route 75 toward Rochester Hills, Cathy unfolded the idea she had kept in her pocket for the last few weeks.

"You remember, Honey, when I told you about that concert in New York? Woodstock? It's upstate, not the City."

"I remember. You still thinking about it?"

"It's going to be the biggest ever! Really, they've got the best bands. I can't remember them all but I know them all. I have a flier at home. I shoulda brought it. Three days in some fields in the country. It'll be all young people who dig the music: hippies, peaceniks, communes, poets, freaks, whatever you got."

"Three days? Where do people stay in the country?"

"I don't know. Camp out. You know how to do that. Maybe they have some big tents for people. ...August 15. Nine days away."

"Is that a weekend?"

"No. It's during the week. You gotta do this. This is our time, our breakaway from all the animals in the zoo. Around folks being real. Peace. Sharing. Music. Poetry. If we meet some kids from one of the communes, I want to hear about their life."

"I don't know about getting out of work for a week, counting getting to New York and back. I'd lose the job. I need the money." He lied about the money because he thought she might accept that excuse.

"You're being responsible. I like that. It's a big part of you. But you know sometimes, Honey, sometimes you need to let it go."

Is this where I disprove her charge of my being overly responsible? I can do that in a few sentences. Is this where I lose her, even before she is stolen away by a better man than me, one she hasn't even met yet?

"What're you thinking, Honey? You need to talk to the people at work?" Cathy wanted an answer. She knew the time was getting short.

"What I'm thinking is a big blur. First of all, I am thinking this woman in front of me is so surprising to be asking me, letting me, be with her. You are a dream I never had the courage to dream."

"You shouldn't think like that. I'm just a girl in a dumpy town. You're the tall, smart guy with class and a future."

"I grant you your town's not too exciting but you're not just a girl. Look how you've got the spice to get out of town to join the real people, meet them, be them. Cathy, you know, you scare me. Listen to me a minute because, as you know, I have been around a little more than you. I find myself wanting you and knowing I will never have you. You will go to college and boys with better brains and bodies and futures than me will be dazzling you. When you recognize your worth, you'll be glad you didn't go too far with that guy from this summer."

"Deeter, my sweetie, you don't know! I've seen boys before. I know some of them want me. I never met one like you."

"You will, and I love you enough to want you to find your choice from among them."

"Fuck, Deeter, we don't have to get married. There's no one else going to take me to Woodstock! We don't even have to go to some goddam rock festival. You sound like you're finished with me. What'd I do?"

Cathy was crying now, wiping away each tear as it came from her ducts, as if she could hide them from Dieterich. He gave her his handkerchief which only made her sadder because it was a gentlemanly gesture that she had never seen outside a movie.

She collapsed into him with her arms held close so he could embrace her completely. He rubbed her back while she pressed into him.

"I'm sorry," Cathy sobbed. "I shouldn't have pressured you. I was thinking you might want to go like I did. We can stay here until you need to go back to school. Then we can see what we want. There's plenty we can do now."

Dieterich had said what he needed to say. He was afraid to say more. He kissed her on the top of her head, holding his lips to her, knowing she could not feel the warmth in them to match the personal texture he was sensing in her hair. He tasted her head, smelled her perfume, felt the firmness of her torso and wondered that she could be an actual person, so perfectly smooth, so soft to his fingertips, so firm to his hands, so tantalizingly sculpted, so receptive, so welcoming to his touches.

25

Later

Cathy quit working at Romero's by the end of August and began freshman orientation on September 8, the Monday after Labor Day. That gave her a week working only one job, but she took extra hours at the supermarket. She was afraid she had driven Dieterich away with her dream of Woodstock although the news about the Woodstock event was so exciting she realized she had been right to have had the dream. She turned it in for the dream of college which was not exciting at all. She had never liked being a student and did not expect to start liking it. She was ready to commit to it because she saw it was essential to winning Dieterich. She was sure he loved her well enough now but saw that he wanted to share things with her, things you learn in college, not just things you figure out on your own. The boys at her school would be, she assumed, like the boys she knew in high school, not like Dieterich. She could not say how they were different, but she knew no one had affected her like the shy fellow who wore a tie and jacket to his lonely dinners at Romero's. She guessed he was just more serious, more responsible, more self-confident. She always felt secure with him.

Dieterich went north for the Labor Day weekend. He eyed Caberfae Peaks during his planning because it was advertised as one of the oldest skiing areas in the United States. He called up the resort to hear about the mountains but the person on the phone was unable to convince him there were any real mountains available. So he went to the Upper Peninsula, clearly the only place in Michigan where he belonged. Most of it was preserved parklands of various State and Federal designations. His tent was his plastic tarp from a hardware store. Finding a spot to camp was easy in all that land. He only built a fire when he was camping legally. His journal was halfway through its second volume. His sketches were filling a separate, blank book. He was not troubled that the sketches were not getting better, not in the sense of representing reality more accurately. They were not becoming more artistic either, but he was pleased that they were focusing him on sights he had formerly ignored: textures of bark and stone, eddies in a stream, fallen twigs and leaves, crumbling mushrooms, patterns of shadow, his stocking feet as viewed while he lay on his bedroll. Later he hoped to figure out how to represent the sights that moved before he had time to even take out his pencil: a chipmunk digging up an acorn, waves made by a passing breeze over a pond, the flame from his cooking fire, a deer turning to leap away, a duck lifting off the water. For three days no worries about the future, no regrets from the past diverted him from the casual exploration of his immediate surroundings.

On Tuesday he cleaned himself in the rest room of a gas station and drove to Saginaw for a relaxing day of hardness tester repair. He focused on his work but in the evening in his motel room, he realized his subconscious had been processing his time on the Upper Peninsula, so he wrote with unprecedented ease and nearly filled the second half of his second journal. As with his sketches, he saw no improvement in the merit of his words, but he was very pleased to be producing them. He had always hated writing assignments in school. Somehow, away from any class assignment, he was enjoying the preservation of his experience and his thoughts. The words meant something to him, and he sensed they would mean more to him when he read them again years from now. Some parts of the journal could be read to Cathy or to Elise... As this thought was forming, he caught his breath as if he had ducked underwater. Everything was so complicated again.

On Wednesday, he worked in Grand Rapids. He bought a spiral notebook of lined paper, the sort he used for taking notes in school. He planned to transfer whatever he put into this notebook into a proper journal as soon as he got to a proper bookstore.

On Thursday, he worked at the home office in Ferndale. Wes asked to lunch with him. They went to a café where Wes ordered a sandwich and Dieterich a hamburger. Wes asked about the Upper Peninsula and showed real interest in what Dieterich had seen and done.

"Someday, Wanda and I will take a vacation up there. We've lived in this state for fifteen years now and I don't think we can call ourselves Michiganders without seeing the UP."

"It'll be worth doing, but you need to give it more than three days, like I did. It's a big place."

The waitress brought their lunches. Then Wes said the reason he asked Dieterich to lunch was to talk about how long Dieterich might be staying. Dieterich apologized for not being clear about that and offered to leave as soon as Wes hired a replacement. Wes said the company could be flexible and Dieterich should not worry about his replacement. This flexibility sounded like deference to his father's position.

"I could stay until Christmas, I think. I'm not sure what I'll be doing next. I'm taking the lottery on the 16th."

"The lottery? What do you mean?"

"The draft lottery. You know about it?"

Wes had heard about it but not paid much attention. He was confused about its relevance since Dieterich had a deferment from school.

"I guess you're getting a number then. That's this month, is it?"

"Right. September 16. Next Tuesday. First one ever."

Wes could not find something to say. He wanted to ask, to shout, so what's this got to do with your plans. Dieterich sensed Wes' confusion in his hesitation but more so in the expression on his face until Wes looked down at his sandwich. At least it proved Elise had not explained it to her father.

"OK, I'll explain the situation in two parts. Firstly..." Dieterich stopped for a moment to feel the drama he was providing. "The way it works, if you get a good number, a low number, you can offer yourself for the draft even if you could have a deferment and if you don't get drafted within a year, you'll never be drafted. So you could wait to see your number and then decide whether to put yourself out there."

"Oh," Wes looked relieved to see why Dieterich said he would offer himself for the draft. But then he felt it still did not make sense.

"Now wait. That's not my case. The second part is my case. I won't have a deferment next year. Long story there. I simply face the draft with whatever number I get. What's a low number? Depends on the Board, on where you registered. And on the year, of course. For my Board next year, probably need to get above 250 to be safe. Remember there's 366 numbers. Probably could feel pretty safe with 225."

Wes heard the part about his having no deferment and he heard the part about Dieterich not wanting to explain why.

"So you have no choice but to hope for a high number next Tuesday."

"There are other choices. I thought about them, thought seriously because this is a serious matter. I did not come close to trying any of 'em. You know, fake a medical, go to Canada, go to jail, go underground; join the clergy. Could sign up for three years in the Air Force or Navy to stay out of Vietnam. Could be drafted and stay out of Vietnam anyway."

"I didn't know. Not a good time to be nineteen."

"And male."

"Right, and male."

"So, you see, Tuesday I can plan better. If my number is low, I would go in the spring. Go in the Army, I mean. When I leave here is still an open question in that scenario."

Dieterich decided the purpose given for the lunch had been fulfilled although he suspected Wes had also wanted to ask about Elise and himself. He continued. "I guess Elise has a plan for the next four years, at least. Have you heard how she is doing with freshman orientation?"

"Just one phone call. She seemed happy and secure. Being a year older than the other freshmen may have been good for her. She asked me to give you the phone number on her floor at the dorm. Here, I wrote it down for you."

"Thanks, I'll give her a call tonight after work. I was going to ask you for the number...."

"I was wondering..."

"Wait, first let me say a little to reduce your wondering. Elise already knows all about my draft status and why it is like that. Another thing, we don't have any plans for each other beyond next Tuesday. I don't mean we won't keep in touch. I don't know. We agreed to see what happens for her at Michigan and how the draft works out. Gosh, she's a great young woman. I know that. And she's been better to me than I deserve. No, don't object to that. I'm not being polite. You are the father, not my boss for the moment. I have thought this through a lot. If I become a better man, I may gain the feeling I deserve her someday. We're both at moments of transition."

"Thank you for speaking up..."

"I'm sure you know she's got good sense. Don't worry about her and don't worry I could do her any harm."

"Yes, well, of course we trust both of you... and, well..."

"Rusty will be on my case all afternoon if I don't get back soon. Thanks so much for the phone number..."

Rusty made no comment on the long lunch Dieterich had with the boss. He hardly thought about it since the lunch was none of his business. In Rusty's eyes, Dieterich was different from himself in every way: younger, better educated, better connected. He could see Dieterich might be Wes' boss someday and probably would rise above that. Rusty did not resent what he saw as Dieterich's prospects. Some folks were born higher up. Not their fault. Some folks cheated and bullied their way up but Dieterich was not one of those. Didn't need to be.

From the gas station phone booth in Rochester Hills after work -

"Hellowhoyoucallin'?"

"Is Elise Elias there?"

"Who? Whoyouwan'?"

"Elise Elias?"

"Oh, I don't know."

"Is this Rene Rogers Dormitory? Third floor?"

"Rene Rogers, yeah. Who you callin'?

"Elias, I mean Elise Elias."

"Hang on. I'll ask around."

Dieterich thought of saying, "the girl with a withered leg," but he would not do it. She came to the phone soon.

“Hello. This is Elise.”

“And I am so glad to hear your voice. Tell me how it has been this week.”

“BABY! It’s you. My Baby.”

“Yes, it is your baby. Your dad gave me your number at lunch today. How’s Michigan? Any problems?”

They talked for twenty minutes about her first days. She’d had no problems, met some nice girls in the dorm, hadn’t met any guys. The dorm mother wanted to move her to the first floor but Elise said she could handle the stairs although she admitted to Dieterich she let her pride get in the way of good judgement. He did not say much about the Upper Peninsula because he wanted more details on her but he promised to send her some passages from his journal.

Suddenly her tone changed. “All right, all right! I see you. Give me another couple minutes wouldja? My mother’s in the hospital!”

“What? She is? What happened?”

“No, I just had to get that girl to go away. Sorry you had to hear that. See what a bitch I am? That’s just for when I’m talking to you. But seriously, I need another couple minutes with you. I’ve been thinking. What about this... You do what you have to do with Uncle Fucking Sam and then go back to school heading for teaching biology or ecology or something in high school or junior college, no higher than a small local college. You take kids out on field trips, spend the summer as a park ranger, build up a museum at the school. I’ll be teaching literature at the school and writing short stories and novels out of school. I’ll probably be finished at college ahead of you so I can help financially getting us started.”

“You’ve put some detail into this dream, girl.”

"Yeah, it's not the whole idea, of course. Nice to have an idea though, isn't it?"

"I want to read your short stories and your novels."

"Here she's coming back. Can you call me at this time tomorrow?"

"I'll call."

Elise started speaking loudly mixed in with sobbing sounds "Call me if she gains consciousness, will you? I'll get a bus back home. And tell her I love her even if she's still unresponsive. She may hear something." And in a low voice, "I gotta go. Love you."

"And I love you."

Tuesday, September 16 On Tuesday, Dieterich was back in his room in Rochester Hills by six o'clock. He sat on his bed and tried to write something in his journal but did not manage to get a full sentence written by 6:45. That is when he went out to his car and turned on the radio. The lottery announcement began at seven o'clock. The first tantalizing half hour of the broadcast consisted of explanations about the historic nature of the event and the process for selecting the numbers. It then started to read off the number for each date, beginning with January 1, which received the excellent number 241. By January 15, Dieterich could see how slowly the broadcast was going. His date in late October was a long way off. He worried the car battery would run down, so he started the car and drove along the streets of his current small town, past Romero's and then turned right to go past Cathy's house. After that he drove aimlessly, assuming he could not get lost on the grid of straight streets, guided by the lingering glow of the sun in the west. However, it was nearly dark as the October numbers were slowly determined and read to the radio audience. He drove by Romero's two days before his birthday and pulled to the side of the road so he could focus on the next words. He had been born on the 28th and always thought it would have been luckier to be born three days later, on Halloween, his favorite day of the year except for Christmas. His actual birthday, October 28 drew the number 79. He did not hear what number was given to October 31st although the radio continued to speak.

"Hello Mother. I hope I am not calling too late. I don't think you go to bed quite this early."

"Deeter! Thank you for calling. No, of course it is good to hear from you. Did you get any word about your draft number? Is that why you are calling?"

"That is exactly why I am calling. The numbers were announced on the radio. Mine is..."

"Wait! Let me get your father on the phone too."

Dieterich heard the telephone being placed on the table and heard his mother calling to his father, followed by footsteps, and his mother picking up the phone again.

"OK, he'll be on the other line in a..."

"Hello, Deeter. Glad you called. What did you hear?"

"Hi, Dad. My number is 79. That's pretty low. I am very likely to be drafted. The Board, you remember, said they expected to fill their quota for the year, for 1970, before the summer." He was surprised neither of his parents had interrupted him yet. He smiled to think they had been surprised, that they might have assumed he would not be chosen for this. "It means they would send out all the notices by then and some guys would still be actually joining up until the end of the year. They can only guess about it. Depends on who passes the physical or gets a new deferment or enlists; stuff like that."

"Why do you think 79 is low enough to be drafted?" his mother asked in a weak voice. It was a question likely addressed to Dieterich but his father answered in a gentle, firm voice.

"Lizzie, we talked to people at the draft board, and they said they would be calling up everyone with a number below 250 or thereabouts for a physical. With a 79, he will be called. He can choose when he goes or he can wait for the call."

"What if they find something in the physical that keeps him out?"

"We talked about this. He said he did not want to make up some medical excuse, right Deeter? But it could happen. They could find a heart murmur or something. Almost no chance of that. He's basically healthy. Just what they're looking for. His number came up Lizzie. That's where we are."

"I don't know what to say, Deeter," his mother said flatly, as if reading to herself. Normally she was assertive. This night she was at sea.

"That's because there is not really anything more to say about it, Mother. Or we could say it would have been better if I had gotten decent grades at Lehigh. Too late for that now."

"So what do you think is best going forward? You want to wait for the draft board or get started? Could be the war will end by next summer," his father asked.

"I'm getting off the phone now," his mother said. "I will support whatever you decide, Deeter."

"OK, Mother. Dad, I'd like to talk to the Board again and to some advisory groups on the draft. Make sure everyone who might know agrees the draft will be proceeding past my number. Then get it started. I'll give my notice to Wes after that further check. Probably be back with you this month."

"That sounds like the right steps. If you sign up, we can look at OCS or another service to get you farther from Vietnam."

"I've already looked but we can look again."

"Tell me about how you liked the job this summer. Think you're looking differently at a career in business like your Old Man?"

"Just like you expected, I got into a lot of factories and learned a lot about what it's like to work in them. I don't mean like the way I worked, in-and-out, short-term and all. I saw the guys who work there permanently. I saw their output. And yes, I could better appreciate it's a respectable way of life. The people I saw were proud of what they do. They were honest with their efforts. The guys in Wes' group are rock solid citizens. It was pretty different from anyone I knew before."

"So you think you'll be more excited about getting into engineering or management when you're back at Lehigh?"

"I think I'll be a better student for the experience of busting out and knowing I deserved it and seeing how much it screwed up things."

"What can I do to help?"

"I'll let you know if I can think of anything. The near future looks pretty clear. I'll phone when I figure out when I'm going home. I don't want to leave Wes short-handed although he said I shouldn't worry about that."

September 16, 2024
Rochester Hills, Michigan

Note: The draft lottery was held today. A random number between 1 and 366 was assigned to me, 79, so summer is over. Dad asks if I learned the lessons he thinks I came here to learn. Here is what I already knew and confirmed over the summer:

- I do not want a career that takes up all my energy.
- I do not want to be rich by American standards - no big house, no fancy car, no boat larger than a canoe, no substantial power over fellow citizens.
- Engineering is not for me. The math I could do but I don't like it and I don't want my job to depend on doing it right.
- My parents are not hip but they could not love me more than they do.

- Exposure to natural lands fuels my soul.

  Here is what I learned this summer:

- Never lose the car keys.
- Drive safely.
- Without any more college, I could earn a respectable living in the working class without glory or misery, have good friends, marry a wonderful woman.
- Do not be tempted by mere financial benefit to go into sales.
- I should set my goals higher than living in a trailer by a lake and/or living in a state built like a Cartesian plane.
- An intelligent, completely beautiful woman can love me in the short run.

AMBITION

U.S. Army
Fort Dix NJ

November 4, 1969

Dear Elise,

I did not recognize myself in the mirror after they shaved my head on the first day here. While I was never much to look at (no need to try politely protesting – I can't hear you from here), but I was used to my appearance and my current look is, frankly, ugly. Everyone who was on my bus got a haircut at the same time. I doubt it takes a full minute to do one guy. Then we went into a bathroom with about twenty sinks on one wall. It was not obvious to me which of the heads in the mirror was mine. I moved my hand a little to be sure I was about to stare at the right face.

I am glad you will never see me this way. I'll grow out my hair when my time is up before I take off my hat in your presence. For now, in this environment, appearance means nothing. Every one of us is ugly to our former selves. To our present selves, no one is ugly. We are all merely the same, head to toe. "We" does not include the drill sergeant. He is different, of course, different from us but fitting closely into the cartoon world. He differs by wearing a starched uniform and a Smoky-the-bear hat; just as bald and ugly.

I feel like the same person that got on the bus in Hartford. I'm sure you're the beautiful, bright, blossoming women I met six months ago, but nothing else is the same as it was. I am living in a cartoon with ridiculous characters, bizarre rules of behavior, and senseless hardships. And none of that matters. It is stupid hour by hour and void of pleasure but not hard to endure. I am effectively jailed for two years, not for crimes I committed, my sins were not crimes, but for the crimes of my country. Whether or not I go to Vietnam, the draft was due to Vietnam. My punishment is not the wasted time taken from my ebbing youth, it is that I have taken on the prospect of committing very real crimes to actual human beings. This obvious statement is so unbelievable that we in this barracks do not accept the facts we know are true. Some guys say a little about the danger of being harmed, but that is nothing.   At   our   age,   we   all   feel invulnerable.

What, some would ask, about the crimes of whoever is on the other side of this war? I understand little about who is more wrong but it is the crimes of my country that got me this far along the path toward Vietnam.   Should I have known more?   I skipped the teach-in we had at Lehigh. We had no protest marches. I have always read past the international news and most of the national news as well. Hey, I'm not eligible to vote yet!   I played almost no role in getting America to this situation.

This is an inhumanly simple way to live. During our training period, we make no decisions. We are told what to wear and how to wear it, where to stand and how to stand, where to eat and what to eat. We already had class in how to brush our teeth and how to inflect our voices to exert authority.   We   come   from   various backgrounds (few as fortunate as mine) so our vocabulary narrows into the Army argot. It has been embraced, even sought out, so avidly, I sense that a large portion of these fellows are desperate to belong to something.   Not many were on track to achieve their dreams before coming here. I thought the draft would have made this group representative of America but I had not thought that through very well. Deferments do not merely defer when one is drafted. They tend to defer getting drafted at all, or so it seems from here. My view of the world is very small, so do not believe what I say applies to anything larger than the 150 guys I train with and a handful of drill sergeants pulling our strings.

I'm sorry to be so selfish in this letter and speak only of what I am doing. I wish I could talk to you about your first term. Hear about adjusting to the place, starting your classes and all that. I'm guessing you will be home at Christmas time. I will try to call you there.

Remembering our agreement on how to sign off on letters, I remain simply,

Deeter

AMBITION

U.S. Army
Fort Dix NJ

November 4, 1969

Dear Mother and Dad,

The bus ride from Hartford was comfortable. I slept most of the way which was good because we stayed up until midnight to get ourselves organized with new clothes and bunks and chow.

Although I have never done this before, basic training seems familiar. I have seen it in movies and read about it in books. The reality is less than the dramatizations. Of course, I have only been here a week but it is already becoming routine. Within an hour, we looked like we were in the Army. And no one knows anyone else so we are equally strangers which makes it easy to be friendly. Maybe starting basic in November is less than ideal, but the only hardship is in the wastes of time: the hour waiting for a ride to the shooting range, the lectures designed to teach us something we should already know or could learn in ten minutes, the two years of whatever I end up doing in the service of America.

Sure, I remember your sound advice to make the most of it and your understanding that the way to make something of it was OCS. A week here has only confirmed your insight. As an enlisted man I will do nothing to make myself a better college student or prove myself a more desirable employee unless I manage to mature significantly in two years. I did not doubt you were right in your advice but my logic that two years is better than three or more remains valid.[13] Remember, from my perspective, three years is the time from being a sophomore in high school to being in Ft. Dix.

I do respect the drill sergeants. They are very well trained in whatever they are doing with us and behave in the most precise way possible. Even their ludicrous profanity when acting as if we need to be forced to obey every command is programmed in advance.

We were all ordered to write home this evening. There is not much to say yet but I'll write more when I have something

---

[13] Draftees must serve two years. Going through OCS and becoming an officer would extend the enlistment to at least three years.

more to say. The odd details of this camp are not interesting, unless being taught how to brush our teeth counts. As intrusive as the Army is, no one here reads our letters, but they did say very clearly we should reassure our parents that we are quite fine and have nothing to complain about large enough for you to mention it to your Congressman. It sounds as if we can get an audience with our CO[14], whom I have not seen yet, by saying we are sending a complaint to someone in Congress.

What are you doing for Thanksgiving this year? If you gather some of the family at the Vineyard house, tell me who you are having and I'll send each a short greeting. The address on this envelope will work through basic and probably not get forwarded very quickly after I leave here.

I'll write more and better next week.

Deeter

---

[14] Commanding Officer

AMBITION

U.S. Army
Fort Dix NJ

December 4, 1969

Dear Freddy,

I hope I did not put too much extra work on you by leaving suddenly. All you guys were good about letting me go but I suspect it put the biggest additional load on you. Like I explained, I wanted to get the military time done as soon as possible and get back into a normal life, only do it better than I was doing before. And now that I'm a cog in the green machine, I think that was the right move. I don't know yet where I will be assigned after training. I filled in the request form for Alaska because I figure hardly anyone will ask for that and so I might get it.

The hardest thing here was adjusting to the haircut. The drill sergeants scream and swear but they've got a tough job pulling this unruly and little educated bunch into a disciplined unit. Tell Rusty he would be good at it and should think about signing up if the industrial instrument business doesn't work out for him.

Say hello to Natasha for me and give her my apologies for not making it to the wedding. You two gave me a vision of where I'd like to be someday, in love and living on a lake.

You can't use this address to write to me so don't write. I'll move to another base soon and take some more training although I don't know yet what kind. Then I'll get a long-term assignment and do something to repay this investment you taxpayers put into me. I'll let you know where I am going.

Regards,
Deeter

AMBITION

APO: LZ English
173rd Abn Bgd (Sep)
Company C
Vietnam

May 2, 1970

Dear Elise,

During a routine training exercise yesterday we waded through a swampy area. I really enjoyed it, seeing the exotic plants and insects here. I know I should not pay attention to them because the point of the training is to be alert to Charlie[15] but we were in a safe place anyway. I fell in the water, which I did not mind on a hot day but later I realized my wallet had been soaked and a poem my mother wrote me was ground to pulp. Did I ever show you the poem? I don't think so. She sent it right after we realized I would not have a deferment for this year. I can't remember all of it. She knew lots of poetry by heart but I did not inherent that ability (I have tried). I do recall the last lines:

---

[15] Charlie is GI-speak for the Viet Cong.

That the price of service be not fatal
to him,
That the need of country be not
false to him.

She wasn't a soldier's mother when she
sent it but she was already feeling like
one. I'll write to her to send me a new
copy of it. Maybe you are among the
many trying to be strong and yet feeling
fear. She needs to worry as I am her son
and she feels responsible for me even
from half a world away. You should not
be worrying about me. Almost half my
tour is over already. Invest your strength
is being a better student than I was.

I was on guard duty last night and
started thinking about the moon landing.
Remember how I did not even know it was
coming up but my landlord in Rochester
Hills talked me into watching on TV? I
was like everybody else, impressed as hell
at how competent NASA was to do
something so different from anything
done before, and do it perfectly. I think
I learned a false lesson that night.
Before that night, I, in my naiveté, had

little opinion about the government. After that night, I believed the government had tremendous expertise in its agencies, so much that I could not criticize it. It is like my professors who knew so much more than me within their own subject matter, I could not argue with them. I came here because I figured Uncle Sam knew so much about the situation, I could not argue about it. All the resisters had moral arguments or unproven claims that I could not sort out. It was too convenient to say the war that wants to draft me is wrong although other wars have been necessary. Now I have a different view but you should not listen to me and start criticizing your professors. – No, wait, that's wrong. Criticize them when they're wrong. Sure, they'll solve the calculus equation right every time, but they are open to critique on other things. Like, why should America be fighting this war? No one has the perfect answer to that. Some things have no perfect answer like there is in calculus. I am sure Uncle Sam is not motivated to report the whole truth about the war or about anything with political implications. Citizens have a duty to argue on big things like wars until

they are convinced. Wish I had been old
enough to vote when the draft called on
me. Maybe I would have felt the
responsibility to be part of the decision.

I got to get
some sleep. I
didn't answer
anything in your
most recent letter
because I already
answered the last
letter I received
from you. Please
write me more.

Deeter

AMBITION

Rene Rogers Dormitory
University of Michigan
Ann Arbor MI 48100

June 7, 1970

Dear Mr. and Mrs. Kahler,

    I am the daughter of Wes Elias, Facility Manager at Wilson Instrument, Ferndale, Michigan, where Deeter worked last summer. I don't know if he mentioned me to you. We have been writing since he left Michigan. In case I was not mentioned, I hasten to assure you that Deeter and I are not committed to anything, not engaged or officially going steady. We are good friends although I would be pleased to build that into a stronger bond when he is back in control of his future and I am finished with my BA, at least, here at the University of Michigan.

    Since he went to Vietnam, the mail has been slow. We write regularly, about once a week, but our letters do not arrive regularly. I have not heard from him for three weeks now and I wanted to be sure he is all right. I can understand he may not feel like writing to me like clockwork or the mail handling has been delayed more than usual. He does not seem to worry about his safety but I am sure there is stress in just being there.

I don't really know what it is he does there. He is not secretive but he prefers to talk about my courses and I follow his lead on this. Still, being 11B ~~worries~~ scares me.[16]

Please don't tell him I was impatient to hear from him. He does not need to feel any pressure from me. I am not so lonely I need his letters. It is fine if he simply does not feel like writing. It's just that he always has felt like writing so I would like to be sure he is not sick or something.

You have a great son in Deeter. He spoke of you both often and how you framed his values, if not his actions. I am fortunate that we spent time together and I look forward to much more time with him later.

Yours truly,
Elise Elias

---

[16] 11B is the military occupational designation for small arms infantry.

AMBITION

June 10, 1970
224 Porter Hill Road
Greenwich, Conn.

Dear Elise,

Thank you very much for writing. Deeter did speak of you before he went to boot camp. It was the first time we heard him be in love and we appreciate what you brought to his life. We wanted to get back to you earlier, but he never mentioned your last name.

Deeter was injured by a land mine on May 14. He survived for four days but was sedated too much to send us any message during that time. The Army called us on the day after his injury. An officer and a chaplain came to our door on the day after he passed away. His commanding officer sent a telegram with personal regards. He described Deeter as an excellent soldier, skilled and generous to those less skilled in the unit, which we felt showed he really did know Deeter. He also said Deeter deserved better than he got, which we knew and did not care to hear from him.

We received a box of his personal items yesterday, the same day your letter arrived. In the letter he filed with the Army when he went to Vietnam "in the event of," he asked us to send you the journals he wrote in the Army and the several journals he left in his room here at our home. He hoped you would write books someday but not use his journals or his story. He says that would tie him to you forever and he wanted you to remember him as "just a summer romance." The letter requests that his funeral be attended only by family. He says that is because "they will not forget him and Elise should." His words, not ours.

There are two journals in the box we received and four written last summer, all of which we are sending to you today via parcel post.

I hope you do not mind if we call Wes at home tonight. I assume he can give us your phone number. Our home number appears below.

With the deepest regrets a parent can feel and with sympathy for you in loss of your friend,

Earnest Kahler   *Elizabeth Kahler*

Telephone: (203) 749-3390

---

[i] *The 20th Century*, JG Press, Inc., Lorraine Glennon, ed., p. 369.
[ii] Paul Lynch. Prophet Song, Atlantic Monthly Press, New York, 2023, p. 25.